NO JOB FOR GENTLEMEN

Tim Martion

NO JOB FOR GENTLEMEN

Copyright © 2021 Tim Martion
All rights reserved.
ISBN: 9798495320222

For Lena, my inspiration for everything and without whom nothing is possible

All the names, characters, businesses, places, events and incidents in this book are either the product of the author's imagination or used in a fictitious manner. Any resemblance to actual persons, living or dead, or actual events is purely coincidental.

NO JOB FOR GENTLEMEN

PROLOGUE

Jack Hudson felt the deep, visceral throb of the V12 engine ripple through the tips of his fingers, traverse his arms then nestle satisfactorily somewhere in his groin. He stroked the leather of the Aston Martin's compact steering wheel in what he hoped was a suitably suggestive fashion – the lack of a gear knob and its associated imagery was the only downside to the paddle-shift automatic transmission. He flicked at one of the paddles to change down and simultaneously gave the accelerator a brief kick, feeling the car surge forward. Glancing to his left, he grinned as he saw Emma Collingwood's curvaceous body pressed more firmly back into her seat by the resultant force. It was definitely time for him to combine his renowned magnetism with the allure of the car and to enjoy the consequences.

"What do you think?" he asked.

"Of the current situation at Riverjack Crypto?"

"Must you bring work up at a time like this? Of the car, of course."

Emma looked briefly at Jack and then scrutinised the interior in a bit more detail. It was certainly striking: beautifully designed with the controls exuding a combination of technology, luxury and power while the seat seemed to be perfectly contoured for her comfort.

Jack broke into her thoughts. "You know, this car is a brilliant performer on the open road; a grand touring car that can be comfortable when needed and tenacious when the asphalt gets complicated. The steering, braking and cornering all happen without effort or alarm…"

"What are you talking about?" Emma interrupted. "Are you trying to impress me by quoting the brochure?"

"An online review, actually," said Jack, laughing. "I thought it was total bullshit too, but I wondered if it would have the right effect on you."

"You think I'm that superficial? Thanks a million."

"Hardly likely to do that after today's meeting." He turned to look at her. "I don't think I have ever had a new CFO get to grips with the challenges in a business as quickly as you. Ten days in and you are busting my balls on cashflow and revenue projections. I can see why Peter recommended you. I can't keep up. I'm a technologist, not a bloody accountant."

His eyes focused on the provocative swell of her breasts; at least, he was sure that was how Ian Fleming would have described it, had he been Bond. Fleming was clearly a misogynist whose hero would have drunk himself dead before the age thirty if he had really maintained the alcohol consumption credited to him, but he could describe a woman more erotically with a couple of sentences than any author Jack had read. He absent-mindedly flicked at the paddle again and continued to admire Emma.

"Will you watch the bloody road?" she screamed at him, breaking through his trance.

"Jesus." He was brought back to reality by the sight of a large cow grazing on the narrow nearside verge, its ample rear quarters stretching into their onrushing path. It swished its tail, completely oblivious to its near miss with fate.

He gripped the wheel hard and yawed the car to the right. His right foot lifted off the accelerator and forced the brake pedal to the floor.

The car slewed round the cow which looked up from the serious business of selecting the next patch of grass to chew. It was clearly used to speeding cars as it had no reaction except to expel a large pat from its backside.

"That's what it thinks of your driving" scoffed Emma. "Frankly, I agree with it. You clearly scared the shit out of it and pretty much did the same to me. Will you just concentrate and refocus your mind on the task in hand?".

"That is the problem with the Cotswolds: far too rural. In any case," Jack added. "I was merely paying you compliments regarding your business acumen."

"The current circumstances hardly require deep forensic accounting skills. Our cash burn is out of control; our revenues appear to be extremely sketchy…"

"I wouldn't say 'extremely'" interjected Jack. "We have just adopted, shall we say, an aggressive approach to revenue recognition."

"So aggressive that the auditors have resigned, I noticed."

"Well, that is why we hired you; to get things back on track."

The country lane they had been driving along meandered into a bend and which brought them to a junction. Jack brought the car to a halt and peered through the growing dusk at the signpost in front of them. He switched the headlights on and started to consider options.

"So, Jack, a question," said Emma.

"Fire away."

"This car: it is clearly brand new. When did you buy it?"

"Nothing gets past you. This afternoon."

"And how did you buy it?"

"Well, I went into the Aston Martin dealership in Cowley and told them that I wanted to purchase the DBS that was on display. The unpleasantly fat salesman spent forty-five minutes trying to convince me that I should purchase the car that I had told him I was actually there to buy. I then had to sign some papers and…"

"No. You know that is not what I mean. How did you pay for it? You can't exactly put an Aston Martin on the company credit card."

"Well, actually, at my last company, our first customer wanted to pay for the software we sold them exactly like that. Two hundred thousand dollars on their corporate Visa without flinching. But the credit card company refused it because they said they couldn't cover the insurance." Jack paused and looked at her. "Bourton-on-the-water or Moreton-in-Marsh? There is a great gastro-pub I know in Bourton."

"Neither," Emma insisted, "Until you tell me how exactly you have paid for this car. And I am asking you in my official capacity as CFO of Riverjack Crypto." She glared at him. "I mean it, Jack. How the bloody hell are we driving around in a very expensive sports car in the middle of the Gloucestershire countryside? Tell me you didn't steal it."

"I didn't steal it and calm down," Jack said. "It is all under control."

"I recall that is what you told me on my first day. Subsequent events have not exactly proven you a reliable judge. The question remains: how did you pay for it?"

"It's a company car."

"Jesus, Jack." Emma leant forward and thumped the top of the fascia. "What do you mean, company car? Don't tell me you've put it on Riverjack Crypto's books."

"Founder and CEO's privilege."

"Like fuck it is. How much does one of these cost? It must be, Christ, I don't know, at least two hundred grand. And we don't have two hundred grand in the bank. "

Jack turned to her and smiled. She looked at him and could not believe that his charm was succeeding in overcoming the condescending glint in his eye. This must be how he had won his legendary reputation at fundraising, persuading hard-nosed venture capitalists to invest in the businesses he had founded based on his charisma and an enticing PowerPoint presentation. What was particularly impressive about his track-record was his ability to raise money from the American market; something that was notoriously difficult for a British entrepreneur. It was not surprising that he had secured money from a US firm, Aardvark Venture Capital, for his latest business, Riverjack Crypto, a new cryptocurrency powered by blockchain technology which provided an international payments platform designed to disrupt the core business and lucrative revenue source of all the multi-national banks. Aardvark also had a strong presence in London; he liked the British link, but their deep pockets had sealed the deal.

"No," he said. "You are quite wrong."

"Well, that is something," Emma said.

"More like two hundred and seventy-five thousand. Mind you, that is with the full specification including alloy wheels and special metallic paint."

"For fuck's sake, Jack" Emma yelled. "The company doesn't have the cash. And what do you mean, anyway? You have to pay extra for the paintwork at that price? Jesus!"

She paused, looked away from him and took a very deep breath. Suddenly his intoxicating magical spell was broken and she was entirely in command of herself.

"Right. Here's what we are going to do. We are going to drive back to Oxford right now. You are going to park this car at the office and sleep in it tonight to make sure it is not stolen. Tomorrow, you are going to the dealership and you are going to make them take it back."

"You can't just return a car like that," Jack objected. "It loses twenty percent of its value just by being driven out of the showroom."

"That is just bloody great," said Emma. "A company asset that I haven't even had the chance to register yet and it is now worth eighty percent of the cash we haven't got, before the money has even left our bloody bank account. Anyway, once you have taken it back – and don't interrupt me – we are going to call Peter at Aardvark and explain the situation to him. If we are lucky, we will get emergency bridge funding from him. The price of that will probably be your job, Jack, but frankly, even you can understand you can't carry on as CEO behaving like this."

After her tirade, she looked at him quizzically. The tone she had used had had the appropriate effect on directors who were far more experienced, recalcitrant and prejudiced than Jack. It was her most intimidating broadside which could usually force a sexist dinosaur to quiver with fear across the boardroom table. Jack just seemed to take it in his stride; in fact, he seemed to be smirking.

"What would you do if I told you that Peter had approved the money?" said Jack.

"There is no point in even starting to discuss that, because Peter would not approve the expenditure this side of the next millennium. Forget it, Jack! As I said, you are going to take this car back to Oxford right now and..."

Jack just continued to look at her and smiled. She felt herself once more becoming distracted from the main point at hand. With an effort she continued to berate him.

"Jack, there is no way Peter would allow you to spend the company's money on this sodding car. Not with the technical problems we are having;

the failure to meet both sales and delivery targets; or the cashflow issues I reported to him," she said, surprised at the slightly desperate note in her voice.

"I asked you a question," Jack said. "What would you do if I could prove that Peter approved it?"

"Nothing, because it isn't true," she retorted immediately.

"My side of the bet is dinner at the gastro-pub I mentioned – on me. I can tell you that is worth quite something as it has two Michelin stars. And so you have to offer something in return – much more than nothing," he shot back, still smiling. "After all; there's no risk because, as you say, it can't be true."

It was his confidence; the devilish allure of his smile; the blue-grey twinkle of his eyes – she could not really understand what made her say it; but she just blurted it out.

"If you can prove it, I will give you the best bloody blowjob of your life."

"Now? In the car?" he clarified.

"Sure. Wherever you like. It's not true so let's just head to Bourton-on-the-Water and burn a hole in your credit card. Afterwards back to the office and my original plan."

He did not make any effort to set off. He just sat there, looked at her and smirked in satisfaction.

"Get going, then" she added, forcibly. "It's getting dark and I want to see more of this beautiful Cotswold landscape before dinner."

She could not believe what she had said to him. Maybe she had subconsciously wanted to show him that she was not just the straight-laced finance "evil queen of numbers" she had been told was her new nickname. It might not be immediately apparent but she was at heart a party girl – at least that is what she told herself on a regular basis as her career kept her late nights in the office and out of the nightclubs with her ever-decreasing circle of friends. Perhaps she actually wanted him to prove their investors had approved the expense, because then she would have to... She shook her head as if to rid herself of that idea. He laughed as if he could read her increasingly confused thoughts.

"Let me tell you, you are going to be far too occupied on the drive to Bourton to look out of the window. I will buy you dinner after, though. Least I can do."

She looked at him, concern growing in her mind. There was no way Peter would have approved it. Gordon would not have let him, after all. Jack reached for his mobile phone, which had been charging on the USB jack in the centre console. He tapped in his code and brought up email.

"Here you have it," he read out loud. "Email from Peter Williamson to Jack Hudson, CEO Riverjack Crypto. Sent today at 9.53am. 'Jack, following the extremely positive conversation you and I had yesterday about the latest product status; customer feedback and the impact Emma has already had on the business in such a short time' – you see, I really do speak highly of you – 'I am pleased to confirm in today's partners' meeting, I was able to gain consensus for Aardvark to support Riverjack Crypto with a bridge loan to the next major funding round. The investment will carry the same terms and be at the same valuation as our current money; we will advance one million pounds to Riverjack Crypto as this facility. The money will be used as general working capital but is subject to immediate repayment by Riverjack Crypto if the new product schedule changes materially (more than two weeks' further slippage on committed dates). I am organising Tom to draw up the paperwork and you can expect the money in the company's bank account today.'"

Jack put his mobile back into the recess. He flicked at the gear-change paddle and the car moved forward. Emma grabbed at his phone; the email was still there on the screen, almost leering at her.

"Bourton it is," he said. "I am looking forward to dinner. But not as much as I am to what is going to happen before we eat. Think of it as an amuse-bouche." He laughed, observing her feverish review of the email. He was pretty certain there was no way she would back out; he was relying on both his charm and also the hint he had detected of her desire to break out of her self-imposed behavioural straitjacket. Again he felt a throb in his groin, but this time, it was not just caused by the engine.

"I can't believe it," she said. "But of course, this is not an approval for the car; just the bridging loan we need before the investment round, giving us the buffer to stop suppliers' putting us on credit hold and fulfilling the basic need to make payroll."

Jack smoothly accelerated the Aston and said: "I am CEO. I am therefore in charge of all executive and operational matters in the business; most particularly how we manage our working capital. The cash that Aardvark have just committed is to be used for working capital – you just read it. I decided that I needed a sports car to reflect my image as successful CEO – it really helps, you know, to pull into a prospective customer's carpark with confidence. Therefore, you get dinner and I get the best blow-job of my life."

He reached down to his side and unclipped his seatbelt.

"I am going to need to loosen things up a little to get the most out of this," he said, smiling . "And so are you," he added almost as an afterthought, reaching over to unclip her seatbelt as well.

"Spending the company's cash on this car was bloody stupid," she said. "There are a thousand and one better ways to deploy resources than on some 'boy's toy' for your pleasure."

"And my pleasure is what we both need to be absolutely focused on right now. Our bet had nothing to do with the wisdom or otherwise of what I did; it was whether Peter had approved it; and he did," he concluded definitively.

"There is no way Peter would have approved it, if he had known this is what you were going to do with the money," said Emma, in a tone of rising panic. Jack ignored this and just smoothed the car around a tight bend; the effect on Emma seemed even more pronounced now that neither of them was wearing a seatbelt.

"Now don't tell me you are going to renege on our deal," said Jack. "When we first met, you told me that you valued integrity above everything else."

She hesitated and did not move for a moment. Then, on impulse, on absolutely mad impulse, as she thought, she said decisively: "The best bloody blow-job of your life is what I said you would get and so you will; you are going to need to hold onto the wheel tight for this."

Confidence was flowing through her as she suddenly found that she was massively turned on by the sheer inappropriateness of the situation and how brazen she felt. She banished any thoughts of what anyone – parent, friend, Board member, sibling, herself even – might say and leant forward.

Jack could not quite believe that events were turning out so well. When he had called her from the car as he drove into the Oxford Science Park, where Riverjack Crypto's offices were located, he had asked her to come down to reception. She had repeatedly said that she was busy reviewing the draft budget for the next fiscal year but he had insisted that he needed to see her. Emma had been astounded to see the Aston outside; and even more bewildered to see Jack step out of the driver's seat and beckon her over. It had been amazing enough that she had actually agreed to get into the car.

"I think more coherently when I drive," he had said. "And we need to talk about a number of key strategic elements about the business."

That had been enough to persuade her to get in; seemingly against her better judgement. He had driven out onto the ring road and headed for the Cotswolds, remaining silent while waiting for her to prompt him to speak. She, however, had remained steadfastly taciturn, which had surprised him. He had thought she could be intimidated into making small talk by the uncomfortable silence and wanted to get the psychological upper hand. At this moment, however, events had absolutely moved in the way he intended – and much faster too: he would had expected cocktails, dinner and at least a bottle of wine before he would have been in a position to make an indecent proposal. It seemed now that she was not at all threatened but entirely in control. He was rather surprised but enjoyed the new sensation. Not, however, as much as he enjoyed the sensation of Emma's getting onto her knees on her seat, leaning over the central console and swiftly undoing the buttons at the top of his trousers and pulling down his flies. He could feel himself growing hard as she pulled his trousers down several inches. She sensed that he was not fully focused on the road as he sighed.

"You just concentrate on your job and I will concentrate on mine," she breathed, reaching inside his trousers and adjusting his underpants so that his erection sprang out to meet her. She was relieved to see that he was not endowed with porn-star proportions. It was surprising given his overwhelming confidence; perhaps there was more depth to him than his boyish bravado. After all, she mused, he was a very successful entrepreneur and had already exited two businesses he had founded, earning himself a lot of money (which no doubt he had spent). She gently stroked his length with her fingernails, causing him to jerk up slightly. She giggled and flicked her tongue onto his now fully hardened member. Her hand drew his foreskin down and she lowered her lips down to the top of his glans. She sucked briefly and felt a tremor flow right through him.

"Holy shit, Emma, that feels incredible," he gasped.

She pulled back and said without looking up "That is just the beginning. Get ready for the experience of your life, Jack. It would be better if this console wasn't in the way, but I guess it is called a console because that's what girls do to their men when they're leaning over it." She glanced up when he didn't respond; at that moment, the engine suddenly howled in protest as Jack had inadvertently hit the wrong paddle and changed down which immediately alerted her.

"Open your sodding eyes," she yelled at him. "Are you mad? You will bloody well kill us both. I catch you one more time with your eyes not locked firmly on the road and this deal is all off, you hear?"

He managed to croak out: "My eyes are glued on the road. Don't stop". Indeed, it was quite dark now and driving did require a degree of concentration even though the powerful headlights were lighting up the narrow lane. They had evidently come into a forest as the hedgerows had been replaced by tall, solid beech trees. The lights flickered on the trunks as the Aston went past, gripping the road admirably and more or less driving itself. This was probably just as well as he felt the warmth of Emma's mouth once more wrap around him, this time sinking him deep into her throat while caressing him with her tongue.

Emma was right. This was absolutely promising to be the best blow-job he had ever had; the entire erotic experience was emphasised by the way her hair was lightly brushing across him as she toyed with and teased him.

In the most recent budget, in a bid to show that the age of austerity was over, the UK Government had announced a massive increase in road infrastructure investment, even allowing for the arcane accounting in the public sector where the same budget allocation is announced and re-announced multiple times for political impact. More than £28 billion was to be spent to make the motorway network fit for purpose. In addition some £425 million pounds was designated, after pressure from motoring and insurance lobbies, to addressing the pressing problem of potholes. After years of road surface decay, the number of accidents and damage caused by those of all sizes was on the increase; in fact, reported incidents were doubling year on year and the repair-bill picked up by insurance companies was now well in excess of £1 million pounds a month and increasing exponentially. The lobbyists on behalf of the august Asphalt Industry Alliance said that this was grossly underfunding the problem and that actually some £8 billion pounds would be needed to address the problem across the entire country. Unfortunately, when it came to the country lanes of the Cotswolds, they were absolutely right. As the Aston surged forward, it is doubtful whether Jack would have seen the pothole in the middle of the road in an undistracted state in bright daylight. As it was, unheeding of Emma's warning and unable to keep his eyes open as he felt his climax building, he uttered what would have been prophetic words had he had any religious belief.

"Jesus Christ, I'm coming," he moaned.

The Aston proved less proficient at handling complex asphalt than promised. Its front offside wheel buckled as it sank into a deep pothole. This had the unfortunate consequence of knocking Emma suddenly off her stroke. It had the more unfortunate consequence that Jack was violently thrust upwards out of his seat. As a result Emma found herself deep-throating him far more aggressively than she would have chosen; at the same time her muscle spasm reaction to her head's banging with extreme force against the steering-wheel was to clamp her teeth around Jack's erection as her unconscious head lolled forward.

"Fuck!" he screamed. His foot shot forward in an automatic reaction to the sensation of having his manhood chomped by well-maintained molars. Emma's bright smile clearly had a downside. The agony was too much for Jack to control where his foot landed; the powerful brakes remained unused as the accelerator was pressed to the floor with all of his weight. Still screaming expletives, he tried feverishly to pull Emma off him, which only exacerbated the jaw-clenching pain as her teeth dragged over his still rigid penis; meanwhile the Aston jumped forward like a cheetah, pushing both Jack and Emma back into the seat as the torque of the engine surged.

Jack's last thought as the Aston collided with an extremely large beech tree was that with his penis feeling like it had been literally dismembered, perhaps this was a blessing in disguise – there were fates worse than death. The force of the impact rendered the airbags useless and Emma and Jack flew through the windscreen, still locked together in a grotesque and ultimately terminal embrace.

A few minutes later, two squirrels, who had been terrified by the sound of the crash, came back down from their refuge to explore the very tasty supply of nuts that had conveniently been knocked out of the tree they had been climbing. What had seemed like an earthquake to them had stopped and the huge, fire-breathing monster that had smashed into the tree was silent. They came down and cautiously climbed onto what remained of the Aston's bonnet. One of them buried through clothes and picked up a large nut that had nestled in Jack's scrotum. Its sharp claws seized the nut and skin together; regrettably Jack felt nothing and neither did Emma as the squirrel's partner scrabbled at the still alluring swell of her breasts to retrieve its own supper.

CHAPTER ONE

The Tube train lurched around the turn and shuddered to a halt. Lisa lost her balance despite the press of the Monday morning crowd and found her nose unceremoniously thrust into the armpit of the man standing next to her. She clutched for something to hold onto and her hand gripped onto what she hoped would be a handle hanging from the rail but which turned out to be his ear. As she extricated herself, she looked up.

"Sorry," she mouthed. "I lost my footing."

Something similar had had happened the previous Friday on her first such journey and the man in question had been extremely rude. He had smelled as if he had not washed for weeks and had leered at her in a way she had not liked at all. She had tried to move away from him but had had nowhere to go with the people crammed into the carriage and had had to endure his lurid comments for two stops. As this was only her second day commuting to her new job, she was extremely nervous. This time, however, her fellow passenger smiled at her kindly. She saw him appraising her and wondered what he was thinking.

"You can bury your face in my armpit any day of the week," he said. "Is this your regular commute?"

She nodded and the train moved off in a series of jerks that only London Tube trains have mastered – no other metro system in the world, not even New York's, can rival the Tube for sheer, overcrowded discomfort. Lisa lurched towards him again. He managed to hold her up this time, gently but firmly grasping her arm.

"Well, mine too," he added. "We must do this again. Shall we say this time tomorrow?"

Lisa nodded nervously. The train pulled into Green Park station.

"This is where I get off. I look forward to our next meeting."

Lisa did not know what to say to this as the man turned and stepped off the train on the platform, moving purposefully down towards the exit. He had been good-looking and had a lovely smile, Lisa thought. He clearly worked out; she could see that in the way he wore his suit – elegant and tailored – and his grip had felt strong. Suddenly she came out of her reverie: Green Park was her stop as well. She tried to squeeze past an old man who was muttering to himself but the warning beeps sounded and the doors closed. She stood transfixed for a moment, open-mouthed and wondering what to do. She was already late for work and this would exacerbate the problem. The train lurched off again and she collided with the old man who turned round and snarled at her. As she gasped and backed away; her heel sank into something soft.

"Watch where you are bloody going, love," said the man whose foot she had just skewered. "Dozy bitch."

She whimpered and turned away just as the train pulled into Piccadilly Circus. This time she did succeed in descending onto the platform but not before she had been sworn at by a woman reading a book, whose arm she had jolted with her handbag as she struggled to get past. She wondered whether it would be quicker to walk back to the office but, not trusting her sense of direction, she decided to cross over to the other platform and head back to Green Park.

Lisa did not know London well at all. In fact, she had only been there once before, when her parents had taken her on a weekend visit for her twelfth birthday. She had grown up in the outskirts of Loughborough in the Midlands and the largest town she had ever seen was Nottingham so she had been excited if extremely anxious about the trip. It had not been a success. First, the coach in which they had been traveling had broken down on the M1 motorway and they had had to wait four hours for a spare coach to pick them up. Then, with the traffic at its usual standstill heading south into London on a Friday, Lisa had found the stop-start motion of the coach too much for her and had promptly been sick. She had spent the rest of the journey either in the tiny, extremely unsanitary bathroom or enduring the looks of the other passengers who clearly hadn't appreciate the aroma of vomit wafting around the unventilated, confined space.

When they arrived at Victoria coach station in central London, they discovered there was a strike on most of the Underground: there had been a mass walk-out by workers in protest at the sacking of one of their number. This was allegedly an act of wanton bullying by management; actually the driver had been caught on CCTV mooning at his female supervisor when she had politely asked him to return to work when he was 25 minutes late back from his allotted coffee break time, which meant that the line he worked on had basically been at a standstill. His subsequent dismissal for gross misconduct had been portrayed by the union as a heinous example of capitalist exploitation of the working class; most of the Underground staff had thought that he got what he deserved but decided that they could do with the extra couple of days off.

Lisa's parents were not familiar with London either, so that finding the right bus to get them to their modest hotel in Earl's Court had been absolutely beyond them. The information desk had had a sign on it saying "Closed for the day due to strike action" – so, they eventually decided to take a taxi. Of course the taxi driver had immediately recognised that they were not local and taken them on a forty minute circuitous route rather than the much shorter time it should have taken, charging them at least triple what they should have paid.

The hotel Lisa's father had booked had turned out to be a shabby looking place; the neon sign advertising "The International Palace Hotel" blinked intermittently in fluorescent pink, with several of its letters broken. Lisa's father had checked in and discovered that the hotel was overbooked so the three of them would be sharing a single room; they had been given a spare mattress which did not fit in the space between the wall and the bed so they had to fold it to make it fit. Lisa slept there while her parents crammed themselves into the single bed.

The next day, they had resolved to make a success of the trip despite the setbacks set out to see the sights of London of which they had heard so much. Unfortunately, it had been a fine English summer's day, which meant that it had been constantly pouring with rain. The Underground was still not working – this time it was not only the wildcat strike but the planned maintenance closing pretty much all the lines in central London. Refusing to be fleeced by a cab driver again, Lisa's father decided that despite the weather, they would walk to the London Eye, the massive Ferris wheel newly installed by the river Thames. Further bad luck ensued when they eventually arrived on the South Bank, somewhat wet and disheveled, as they discovered that it too had broken down; the only blessing being that they were not among the crowds of Japanese tourists who were stuck in it at the top for several hours. Several workmen were standing around while one of their number prodded uncertainly at the mechanics of the main drive. In the end it was the London Fire Brigade who both rescued the passengers trapped in the lower capsules and managed to use an emergency winch to rotate the wheel enough to bring everyone to ground. This was not before one of their fire engines had reversed over an inquisitive Chihuahua which had escaped from its owner's grasp and run up to investigate the rear wheels. All that had been left of the poor animal was its lead. The father of the distraught child whose dog it was had a blazing row with the watch manager on duty, threatening to sue for millions. However, both he and his offspring were suitably mollified by an offer to ride in the fire engine while the crew stood around working out how they could use union regulations regarding trauma on duty to their advantage.

That evening they ate in an over-priced Italian restaurant near their hotel where Lisa's father had made some very uncomplimentary remarks about the food, foreigners and the general state of immigration in the country. He read The Daily Mail and had very clear views on such matters, views which were not open to argument. He swore that he and his family would never come back to London and, having struggled back to the coach station on foot, dragging their luggage, and completed the return trip home (armed this time with two plastic bags for Lisa's convenience), he was true to his word.

Lisa had not been the most academically gifted of students but she had scraped through her A-levels and managed to obtain a place at university to study Geography, making her first person in her family to go on to tertiary education. Her mother told her regularly how very proud she was but her father just muttered regular comments throughout the three years of her degree about the uselessness of academic education compared to practical vocational training. Lisa's academic prowess had not been obvious but she had at least managed to obtain a degree, much to her tutors' considerable surprise if not to hers.

She had been uncertain what to do with her life, so her cousin Samantha had suggested at a family wedding that she could come to London and get a job as a PA or Receptionist. Lisa had not liked Samantha when they had been children. Samantha was two years older; she was cleverer and much more confident. She did not have Lisa's natural prettiness but her assertive nature completely intimidated Lisa. However, before the wedding they had not seen each other for a few years and Samantha now seemed determined to take her under her wing.

"If you have no idea what you are going to do, you must come to London," she said.

"Oh I don't think I could," Lisa stammered. "It's far too big and dangerous. You hear all those stories about moped thefts and knife crime. It sounds, like, well, New York or something."

"Nonsense," countered Samantha. "You just have to be a bit careful about where you go; and certainly don't walk along swinging your handbag. But there is so much opportunity. And so many men just looking for someone as pretty as you."

"But I don't even know what I want to do."

"That is so easily settled. There are dozens of Private Equity and Venture Capital firms that are just desperate for bright young things to join their team."

"Where would I stay?" Lisa wailed, in a quavering voice that meant she was about to give in. She did not know what Private Equity or Venture Capital firms did but did not have the temerity to ask.

"There's a spare room in the flat I rent," said Samantha. "Nothing more to be said. I will email you the address and you can come down the week after next."

With that, Samantha had turned away to fetch herself another glass of champagne and to inveigle her way into conversation with an extremely good-looking although unidentified wedding guest. She was disappointed after thirty minutes of highly entertaining, flirtatious conversation with him that, on her suggestion they meet later, he responded with an apologetic smile, saying that he was gay.

Lisa had left the wedding feeling miserable. She had probably outstayed her welcome at home; even her mother had started making subtle comments about her finding her own way in the world while her father had been even more direct than usual. He had told her she had until the end of the month to find a job and move out. Her mother had tried to pacify him and reassure her daughter that he did not mean to be as draconian as he implied, but Lisa was more than aware that she was lucky to be given at least a couple of weeks to sort her life out. So, on the one hand, there was nothing to be miserable about because Samantha's offer had been a lifeline. On the other, it meant going back to face London once again. Just the thought of the journey down made Lisa feel queasy.

However, that night left her in no doubt that it was time to move out. Her father had been watching a TV interview with Sadiq Khan, the Mayor of London, in which he addressed the latest outburst from Donald Trump about London being a haven for terrorists. Lisa's father had not held back on his opinion that the Mayor himself was a bloody terrorist who should go back to where he was from. Lisa had timorously expressed her opinion that Khan was as British as her father, to which he had exploded in ferocious anger and told her that if she ever came home with "one of those", he would disown her forever.

In fact, in her Fresher's Week at university, Lisa had met and fallen in love with a PhD student from Pakistan. She had willingly lost her virginity to him and had become besotted. She had wondered as their relationship developed how she would introduce him to her parents but that scenario never came to pass. He had been called back to Pakistan by his father for an arranged marriage to his second cousin and being a dutiful son, he had obeyed. Lisa gave him a tearful send-off from the railway station; he was rather less upset because he had already determined that Lisa's ability to stimulate inside the bedroom far exceeded the excitement of being with her outside it. Their conversation had not exactly been vibrant with intellectual debate. Besides, he had seen pictures of his bride to be and they were definitely promising;

even more promising was that fact that she was the daughter of the owner of a string of sweat-shop textiles factories and therefore extremely wealthy. The substantial dowry that awaited him was more than adequate compensation for breaking Lisa's heart.

Lisa finally determined that at least living with Samantha for a while would be preferable to remaining up home. She announced the next day that she was leaving.

"But darling," said her mother. "You really don't have to listen to your father."

"Yes, she bloody does," contradicted her father. "Good for you. Finally setting off to make something of yourself. Well, good luck."

"But where will you stay?" asked her mother.

"Samantha has said I can stay in her flat. It's all arranged. Apparently, it's really close to the Tube and her flatmate is never there so she says it will be no problem at all."

"Samantha?" asked her father. "You mean your cousin. Good God! I'm surprised she's not doing time by now. Or at least shacked up with some sugar daddy. If half the stories about her are true, it's enough to make your hair stand up on end. Just make sure you are on the bloody pill before you go cavorting around London with her, my girl. They say she's going to need a Y-shaped coffin when she checks out."

"Graham! Stop it!" said her mother. "That's no way to talk about my sister's daughter. I heard she has a respectable job with a fashion magazine."

"There's no such thing as a respectable job in fashion." Lisa's father, who was the manager of the main DIY store in Loughborough, had very clear views on these things. "To make it up the ladder you have to sleep with the boss or resign yourself to writing the Agony Aunt column every month."

"Not in these #metoo days, Dad," responded Lisa. "Besides, she says I will easily get a job in like, Venture Capital or something. I don't know what it is but it sounds exciting."

"Bankers? They are the worst of the lot. Cocaine-fuelled sex orgies day and night, so I've been told. Well, in all events, at least you are moving out and that's the main thing."

"I will worry so much about you, Lisa," said her mother. "I can't think where all the years have gone. It seems like only yesterday that my little girl walked out of that door to go to your first day at primary school. And now look at you: a graduate heading to make her fortune in London."

Her mother looked at her, crossed the room and gave her a hug.

"What time are you leaving?"

"I have the coach to catch in two hours."

"Coach?" interjected her father. "Take some bloody travel pills, for God's sake. I won't forget the last time we took you on a coach in a hurry."

"Yes, Dad," said Lisa.

She turned to her mother to hug her again but her mother had already got over her unusual display of affection towards Lisa and had stepped into the hall.

"I have my hair at eleven," she said. "So I won't see you again before you go. I am sure you will be fine. Ring us when you can," she added somewhat absent-mindedly.

With that Lisa watched her disappear down the hall and heard the front door open and close. She turned back to her father but he had already settled himself behind his newspaper. When she came down with her suitcase an hour later, she went into see him but he was snoring in his favourite armchair; so she ignored him, got in the taxi she had ordered which by some miracle had actually not only shown up but was also more or less on time, and made it to the bus station. She had to change onto the London coach at Nottingham but did so surprisingly without incident.

As the journey progressed, she felt less and less confident. At least she was not travel sick but her mood was not helped by a group of already drunk Leicester City football fans on the way to the late afternoon game at Chelsea who sang loudly and out of tune the entire journey, only stopping to cheer gleefully as Lisa got up to use the loo – thankfully considerably more sanitary than her previous experience – and then to break into a different song as she stepped out. She could not make out the words but it sounded like "Do you take the underpass?". She was confused but decided not to ask for any further clarification and shrank back into her seat.

Lisa finally arrived in London and this time the Underground had been working normally, or at least as normal as it ever can manage, and eventually made it out to Turnham Green station in the west of the city. She turned the wrong way out of the station and found herself walking across Chiswick Common in the gathering dusk. She did not like the way two young men, sitting on a bench across from her path, wolf-whistled at her as she walked along. She liked it even less when she saw one older man furtively usher a younger man into the public convenience, both of them looking around as the former took out his wallet and gave his companion a twenty pound note. She rapidly turned back to the station and was relieved finally to make it to the address Samantha had given her, a nondescript low apartment block.

As she walked up the short steps to ring the bell for number three so Samantha could buzz her in, the front door of the block opened and a young girl of about twelve walked out. She nonchalantly held the door open for Lisa and then let it go to close on her as she dragged her suitcase over the doorstep. The girl laughed maliciously as the door caught on Lisa's foot causing her to yelp with pain. Still struggling with her suitcase, she turned up the single flight of stairs to find number three on the second floor. Out of breath, she paused for a moment and then pressed the doorbell. She heard chimes inside the apartment but other than that, there was just silence. She waited a minute and then pressed it again; once more it definitely rang but solicited no response. Finally, she thought she heard a sound but it wasn't clear so she fished her mobile out of her handbag and started to look for Samantha's number to call. However, just then she heard a male voice shout.

"Well, OK, I will bloody go then, but you can see I am in no state to answer the door. What if it is a nun collecting for the local convent?"

Lisa recognised Samantha's voice giggling in reply: "Well, I'm not sodding well going starkers. Hurry up and see who it is and then come back here pronto."

The male voice broke out into lascivious laughter; Lisa heard footsteps and the door opened. A man of about thirty stood there, naked except for a towel wrapped around his waist. His obvious erection was protruding like a proverbial tentpole, startling Lisa, who dropped her phone. She bent down to pick it up and found herself level with the bulge. She blushed and stood up quickly. She saw that he was smiling.

"Don't get up on my account," he chuckled.

"Who is it, Steve?" Samantha's voice came ringing clearly from inside the apartment.

"I have no idea," he replied over his shoulder. "We haven't had a chance to be introduced yet. She's been too busy on her knees with her hands full."

"My name is Lisa Brown. I'm Samantha's cousin," said Lisa, standing up and flushed with embarrassment. "She should be expecting me," she added, doubt creeping into her voice. "At least, she said she would be in at this time and I thought I just heard her."

"Oh you're Lisa," said the man who was evidently Steve. "Sam mentioned you. Good to meet you. Come on in. Let me help you with your suitcase."

"Should you? I mean, won't your towel... er...?" stammered Lisa.

Steve stepped out of the door with one hand holding his towel, his protrusion still visible but less menacingly than before as the protracted scene at the door started to dampen his ardour. Samantha came into sight, wrapping a pink silk dressing gown around her.

"Hello, darling," she crooned, leaning forward to give Lisa a peck on the cheek. "Glad you could make it. Steve and I were just..."

Lisa blushed once more, this time a deeper red than before. Steve laughed out loud again.

"Coitus bloody interruptus," he snorted. "Looks like I am not going to get laid until later. Come on in and I will open some wine."

Lisa smiled sheepishly and followed Samantha into the main living room. Steve picked up her suitcase with one hand, brought it inside the apartment and closed the door behind him.

Samantha went through the living room and opened a door on the far side.

"You are in here, darling," she said, going into the bedroom. It was a small but comfortable-looking room with an en suite bathroom. "Will this do?"

"Yes," said Lisa sheepishly. Steve came in with her suitcase, still wearing just his towel. As he bent down to put the suitcase on the bed, it had snagged on the door handle and left him standing completely naked. Lisa gasped; Steve just laughed and grabbed the towel.

"Put some bloody clothes on, Steve" Samantha, "And let's get that drink." She had turned to Lisa and asked, "How was your journey down?"

Before Lisa could respond, she went on, "It is so exciting to have you here. There's so much to discuss. We need to work out your future. I can see such big things for you."

Still smirking, Steve went back out to the living room and crossed over to another room, going through the open door.

"Sorry about that," said Samantha, "Steve is quite an exhibitionist but you could see for yourself why I put up with his behaviour."

"Oh yes," replied Lisa, "He's clearly very... I mean," she faltered and turned bright red again.

"Hung like a donkey, darling, is the expression you are looking for. And he certainly knows what he is doing with it as well."

"How long have you known him?"

"A couple of weeks, actually. He came to a fashion evening the magazine was organising with his girlfriend. I should say now his ex-girlfriend."

Lisa stared at Samantha, open-mouthed and stunned.

"Don't look so shocked, Lisa. All's fair in love and war. I saw him across the cocktail reception; he was looking unbelievably handsome but bored at the same time. I went across to him and introduced myself. He and his girlfriend had just had a row about something and she had left early. But he couldn't go with her because his firm was one of the main sponsors. We got on fabulously well; I usually get on well with a man when I want to. Unless they're gay", she added, evidently thinking back to the family wedding. "He had no chance."

"So did he take you on a date?"

"I wouldn't exactly call it a date," Samantha stifled a laugh, "But let's just say after that night, she was definitely his ex-girlfriend."

At that point Steve called out from the living room, "Are you two girls going to come in and enjoy a glass or stand there gossiping all evening?"

"Are you decent?" called out Samantha.

"Always," he retorted. "In fact better than decent, I would say."

"Arrogant bastard," said Samantha, laughing. "Come on through, Lisa."

They had spent the first part of the evening drinking wine and talking about Lisa's job prospects. At least, Steve and Samantha discussed Lisa's future while Lisa herself sat there in something of a whirlwind trying to keep up with the conversation. It turned out that Steve worked for an investment advisory firm, helping start-up companies in the technology industry raise investment capital. It sounded incredibly complex to Lisa and she really did not understand much of what Steve talked about. Also, as he opened a second bottle of wine, she found herself getting drunk and the room started to swirl about her. They ordered an Indian takeaway from Uber Eats and continued to chat. Samantha told Steve that she was relying on him to find Lisa a job; Steve then said that actually he had a friend who had been looking for an Executive Assistant for some time now but had really struggled to find the right person.

"Well, that sounds perfect," said Samantha. "Who is it?"

"Peter Williamson at Aardvark Capital. He's a lovely guy. He told me the other day that he could scarcely get any candidates to interview, let alone appoint someone. He was offering more money to try to attract someone and had thought that a career in private equity would appeal to far more people, especially graduates. But it seems that they are either joining the major consulting firms and banks or are wanting to make the world a better place and volunteering for Greenpeace."

"It sounds ideal. Lisa, what do you think?"

"Er, yes, I guess. I've, like, no idea what private equity is but Peter sounds nice."

"Don't worry," said Samantha. "You'll figure it out."

"Can you type?" Steve.

"Yes," said Lisa. "That's one of the things I can do."

"And what was your degree?"

"Geography."

"Excellent. You will have no problem finding your way about." He laughed, although not unkindly.

"Great," declared Samantha. "Steve will make the introduction and I reckon the job is in the bag. Now then, Lisa. Tomorrow, we will go shopping so you have a suitable outfit for the interview. But for now, Steve, get some more wine and we will really make a night of it."

"I am not sure I can drink any more," protested Lisa.

"Nonsense. I want to hear all about your time at uni and we have so much family gossip to catch up on."

They talked late into the night; at least, Steve and Samantha did as Lisa listened and tried to keep up through the increasing fog in her mind. At some point, Steve and Samantha seemed more interested in each other than keeping the chatter going and finally let Lisa go to bed. She staggered into her bedroom.

"I hope you are a heavy sleeper," giggled Samantha. "We don't want to keep you awake."

"Just keep your door shut," laughed Steve. "Samantha sounds like a wildcat when she gets excited."

Lisa was too drunk and too tired even to blush. She woke the next day with the worst hangover of her life. Samantha and Steve, however, seemed to be none the worse for wear. Samantha mercilessly took Lisa to Kensington High Street and picked out a couple of outfits that she said would be guaranteed to get any warm-blooded male to give Lisa a job. Lisa tried to protest feebly that she could not afford the clothes but was overruled by Samantha who warned her that this was just the start.

Steve turned out to be true to his word and Lisa had an interview with Peter Williamson at the Aardvark offices. She got lost twice on the Tube but for once had left more than enough time and so spent a nervous forty-five minutes in a nearby Starbucks waiting for her appointment. As well as Peter, she also met someone called Theresa who she found highly intimidating. However, Peter had been indeed very kind and when she was flustered by his questions allowed her time to compose herself and actually prompted her through her answers. Theresa on the other hand made her quail and shrink in her chair; she looked over her half-moon spectacles and fired questions at her with what seemed to Lisa like machine-gun rapidity. Theresa eventually finished, showed Lisa back to reception and asked her to wait.

Peter had asked her if she had any idea what a venture capital firm did. She shook her head and looked down.

"Not to worry," Peter had said. "Few people really understand our business before they get involved. Basically, we raise money from institutional investors to create a fund for investment into technology companies. We take an equity stake in those companies and get closely involved with their management team to help them run the business successfully and grow it. We charge a management fee on the funds we raise which pays the monthly bills and report back to our investors on a regular basis on the progress of the companies in our portfolio. Eventually we hope to generate returns on the capital through exits, either trade sales or very occasionally, through IPOs."

Lisa looked at him and hoped that her complete absence of comprehension was not showing in her expression.

It probably had, because he added, "Yes. As I say, it is rather complicated but you will get the hang of it eventually. The good news is that you won't have to understand what we do straightaway. I really need you just to manage my diary and help with setting up meetings and other basic administrative tasks." He paused and continued with a smile, "We won't ask you to run your own investments quite just yet."

Lisa was not sure at all how to take this and thought it through in an agitated fashion as she sat waiting in reception.

Meanwhile, Theresa was with Peter in his office, arguing about Lisa.

"Honestly, Peter. She can hardly string two words together. I cannot believe she actually went to university. They must hand out degrees just for writing your name on the exam paper these days."

"She's not that bad, Theresa. You are just too intimidating. I remember you scared me when we first met."

"And I still can," she remarked primly. "All I can say is that I wouldn't trust that girl to find her way to the kitchen, even with a degree in geography."

"Look. All she has to do is to answer the telephone and book the occasional trip. I do most things myself; I just need some help. The modern graduate must be equipped to manage those basic tasks, after all. It's not that hard."

"Well, it's up to you. But aside from being without doubt very pretty, I think she will be a disaster. Don't say I didn't warn you. She's hardly one to inspire confidence in our firm. I dread to think what she might be capable of saying on the telephone. I mean, she hardly seemed to understand anything I said to her. But if you must hire her, go for it. On your head be it."

"Brilliant," said a relieved Peter. "I will go and tell her the good news."

So much to Lisa's surprise and delight, Peter came into reception, took her back into his office, and offered her the job immediately. Everything he said just seemed to pass Lisa by but she took in enough to know that the salary he was offering was more than she had ever dreamed of making. She left with a promise to be back at nine a.m. the following Friday to start work.

"It will be good to get you in for your first day when the office is not quite so busy," explained Peter. "Besides, I'd like you to get going as quickly as possible, if that is ok with you."

Lisa had just nodded, still nonplussed that she had secured a job so quickly. When she told Samantha later what had happened that evening back in the flat, however, she was less than impressed.

"Darling, you didn't take his first offer? Forty thousand pounds a year? You could have held out for fifty, easily."

"Oh," said Lisa, disappointed at her cousin's reaction. "But I thought that was so much money."

"Well, it's a start, I suppose," conceded Samantha. "What did he say your promotion prospects were?"

"We didn't really talk about it, actually. I mean, like, it all went by in such a rush. I was so surprised and relieved to get the job particularly after my meeting with Theresa. She was so scary I could hardly say a word. I was just amazed when Peter came in and told me I was hired."

Samantha yawned deeply and chuckled, "Sorry, darling. I am so tired. Steve and I didn't get much sleep last night, if you know what I mean. I guess it is a good result; you have a job after all and that's great. But I can tell we are going to have to teach you the London way if you are going to get on."

She reached behind her to a bookcase, tapping her fingers as she searched for what she wanted and then pulled a book down. She threw it over to Lisa.

"This is going to help you get ahead. It's a rough world out there and you need to be prepared."

Lisa had looked doubtfully at the book and read out loud in a hesitant voice, *Nice Girls Don't Get The Corner Office: 101 Unconscious Mistakes Women Make That Sabotage Their Careers* by Lois P. Frankel."

She paused and thought for a moment. She opened the book and started to read; then the full significance of the book's title hit her.

"There are a hundred and one things you mustn't do?" she moaned." How can you keep track of so many things at once? I am sure I am doing most of them already without realising it."

"That's the point: they are unconscious mistakes! It's just advice to make sure that you are not too compliant and accommodating. You've seen how I speak to Steve. You have to be confident and make sure the world knows it."

"I am sure I wouldn't know where to start; and I couldn't speak to a boyfriend of mine as directly as you do to Steve. I'd be too embarrassed."

"You just take the book and see how you get on with it."

So Lisa had started to read the book that night but it had made her terribly worried about how she should behave when she got to the office on her first day. As it turned out, despite the unsavoury character she met on her commute, the day seemingly passed her by in a blur. Lisa had never worked in an office before and, as this was her first job apart from working in her father's DIY store during vacations, she had no real idea what to expect. Peter welcomed her and then said he had a lunch appointment and asked Theresa to take charge of her, which she duly did. The human resources, payroll and health insurance forms Lisa had to fill in were bewildering and seemed to take forever to complete. Theresa took her for lunch and eventually brought her back to see Peter, who started to explain what he would need her to concentrate on in the short term.

"It's pretty fast-paced around here," he said. "I'm going to treat you as if you have been here for a year and know everything. I know you will make mistakes but that is fine. We will figure it out. You OK with that?"

Lisa did not know what to say in reply and so just nodded. She rather hoped that he meant it when he said it would be fine to make mistakes because she wondered how many conscious or unconscious ones she had already made just in the first few hours of her career. She certainly did not feel very confident and, as Peter went on, the whole experience just seemed more and more daunting.

"There are very few people here today," said Peter. "Gordon Fairbanks – that's our senior partner; Henry Farrell-Wedge – he's another partner; Edwin Snape – he's our junior investment director; they are all out at a corporate golf day. My official title is investment director which basically means I do all the work and get shouted at by Gordon and Henry."

He smiled at this point. Lisa looked at him, horror on her face.

"I'm only joking. They don't shout; at least," he paused. "Not all the time. Tom, our in-house lawyer is away dealing with a rather difficult matter at the offices of one of our portfolio companies. So you just have Theresa Mitre, who you have met already, of course. She is our Finance Director and looks after all the administrative side of the business. Then there is Gordon's and Henry's Executive Assistant, Mary, who is working from home today because she knew no one would be in. You'll be actually working for me but also helping out Edwin from time to time."

Even this level of detail was enough to confuse Lisa but she nodded and tried to remember not to show the apprehension she was feeling.

Peter turned to her and said, "Actually, Lisa, this will be a pretty quiet first day. I have to leave the office early myself. Why don't you just log in and check your email account is working then familiarise yourself with the setup and then we can really get going on Monday. I tend to be in early but be here by nine and that will be fine. OK?"

Lisa gaped at him slightly wide-eyed and open-mouthed but managed to articulate some sort of acknowledgement. This seemed to be sufficient as Peter turned away out of the door with a "Right, then, see you next week; have a great weekend" as he left.

Lisa sat down at her desk and listened; the office was entirely quiet. There was indeed seemingly no one around at all. She turned on her PC and studied the piece of paper Theresa had given her with her network user name and password. She changed her password when prompted (making sure to write it down so she would not forget it) and spent the rest of the afternoon getting the printer in her office to work – it did so with surprisingly little difficulty – and googling terms such as Aardvark (why her new firm was named after "a nocturnal badger-sized burrowing mammal of Africa, with long ears, a tubular snout, and a long extensible tongue, feeding on ants and termites" was beyond her) and Finance Director to try to understand what Theresa did. Although the detailed description of the Finance Director role left her with more questions than answers, she felt as though she had at least achieved something during her first day. She wondered at what time Peter had meant it would be alright for her to leave, worrying that she would be in trouble if she left too soon. As the clock ticked towards 5.30pm, she thought that this would probably be fine and stood up, gathered her handbag and headed for the door. She spent several minutes looking for the light switch but without success and so, shrugging slightly, she closed the office door behind her. The office was still completely quiet and so she made her way downstairs to the front entrance without seeing anyone. She said goodnight to the building receptionist who looked up, startled to be spoken to, and headed out to the Underground station.

The following Monday, after her misadventure on the Tube, she rushed breathlessly up from Green Park station along Dover Street to the office. She was so flustered that she first went into the wrong building entrance and was stopped by a fierce concierge who informed her in no uncertain terms that she was in the wrong place. She ran back outside and went next door; she said good morning to the same receptionist who looked at her skeptically.

"All visitors to sign in, please," the receptionist said.

"But I'm not a visitor. I work for Aardvark. I started on Friday and saw you. Don't you remember me?"

"No, I don't," said the receptionist frostily. "I can't be expected to remember everyone. Have you got a badge?"

"No," said Lisa. "They didn't give me anything like that. And I am in a real hurry so please can I just go up?"

"Whether you work here or not, you have to sign in if you don't have your badge on you," insisted the receptionist in a remorseless tone. "It's for health and safety. No exceptions, whatever the circumstances."

Lisa hesitated for a moment then turned back to the reception desk and filled in the visitor's book.

"You haven't said which company you are from," said the receptionist critically. "You must fill in all the information."

"But I am from Aardvark," wailed Lisa. "And I am terribly late now. It's only my second day and I don't want to get into trouble. I can't put 'Company: Aardvark', 'Visiting: Aardvark'. That would be silly."

"Well, you can't leave it blank."

Lisa complied reluctantly and fretted as the receptionist seemed to take an age to check her entry. Then she rushed to press the lift button and waited for what seemed another interminable length of time before resolving to take the stairs instead. She heard the lift arrive just as she got to the first, small landing but carried on, hurrying up the second flight. She was now extremely hot and bothered and the immaculate appearance Samantha had approved that morning had become somewhat disheveled. It was several minutes after nine as she rushed down the office corridor, through the small reception area and, ignoring the "Who are you?" she heard barked from one of the other offices, dashed into her own outer room and through into Peter's office. He was sitting at his desk, talking to a man who was just rifling through a pile of papers.

Lisa started to gasp an apology for being late and then yelped once more, making both Peter and the man look up at her for the first time. The stranger was the man from the Tube.

CHAPTER TWO

Lisa stared in disbelief at the man, who looked at her and smiled. He turned to Peter.

"You mentioned you had a new assistant called Lisa," he laughed. "We've met already although I think she has not quite come to terms with the challenge of the London commute. I told you about the very pretty girl who looked terrified when she buried herself in my armpit on the Tube and nearly yanked my ear off trying to stay on her feet."

"Sorry about that," said Lisa, struggling to find her composure. The morning, it seemed, had already resulted in her committing at least five more of Lois Frankl's cardinal sins. She blushed again and did not know what else to say.

"Don't worry," said the man. "It will eventually heal so I don't look like Mickey Mouse."

Peter said, "Lisa, this is Tom Farrow. As I mentioned, he's our lawyer here at Aardvark. Tom, Lisa Brown, as you rightly surmised, my new EA. She is just getting to know the lie of the land."

He turned back to Lisa and asked, "How did things go on Friday afternoon?"

Lisa paused for a moment, still embarrassed about her first meeting with Tom and the fact that she had been so flustered she had clearly missed her stop in front of her new colleague. The fact that he was so good-looking and was clearly very amused at the situation was doing nothing to help her stay calm.

"It was, like, ok," she said, faltering over her words and looking sheepish. "I managed to log onto the network and made the printer work so I feel like I accomplished something."

"A great start," said Peter.

"Better than me," interjected Tom. "You remember when I joined last year, Peter, I couldn't log on for three days. Theresa thought I was a complete idiot until it turned out my name was misspelt on the system."

He turned encouragingly to Lisa and added, "So well done. I will know who to come to when I need IT support."

Lisa blushed again and wondered what to say next. She blurted out, "I couldn't find the light switch, though. Also I looked up what an aardvark is. Why is the firm named after an animal like that? I mean, it doesn't seem to have much to do with investing."

Peter smiled indulgently, "No, nothing at all, actually. And given that an aardvark is a cute-looking, furry thing, it is not quite the image we want. We are called Aardvark because our founder decided that among other things, a critical component of success for attracting investment and entrepreneurs would be to be first in the directory of VC firms in both San Francisco and London. He was right, too. It's amazing how many companies say they came to us because we were the first tech VC on the list."

"Nothing to do with our competence as investors," said Tom. "Clearly if we were called Zebra we wouldn't get a single company looking at us."

"By the time they got there, they'd either have given up trying to raise money because they were so hopeless or would have secured it and wouldn't need us," added Peter.

They both sat back and laughed; they high-fived each other and Tom said something to Peter under his breath which Lisa did not catch completely but sounded as if he was being rude about someone.

Peter chuckled again and said, "For God's sake, don't tell him that, he'll go ballistic."

Tom smiled and said that he knew when to keep his mouth shut.

Peter turned back to Lisa who was still standing there, looking between the two of them and struggling to work out if they were serious or not.

Peter said, "Look, Lisa, Tom and I are just discussing something pretty grave, actually, that has happened in one of our portfolio companies. Go and settle yourself in and would you mind fetching the two of us a coffee. I take mine white without. What will you have, Tom?" he asked.

"Could you manage a cappuccino?"

Lisa hesitated for a moment and then said, "Yes, of course, won't be a moment." She turned around and went through the door, closing it behind her.

Tom turned to Peter and said, "I can see why you hired her, Pete, old chap. Bloody gorgeous. Not perhaps the sharpest tool in the box but who cares? She will definitely brighten up the place. Don't tell her the lights are on automatic sensors, though. You could have hours of fun with that. Has she met Gordon yet? That's going to be interesting. And as for Henry, we had better keep an eye on him or we will be facing a sexual harassment lawsuit within a week." He thought for a moment and then added with a smile, "And I will prosecute for her."

"I bet," said Peter, a warning note in his voice. "As long as that is all you do for her, Tom. I know you well enough and the last thing I need is for you to get sacked because you groped the secretary."

"Now, Peter," retorted Tom, "I object to the very insinuation that I could be capable of such a thing. At least, capable of such a thing if it wasn't consensual. You know, there's nothing wrong with asking the question; you just have to make sure the answer is going to be yes before you do. Otherwise you get yourself into one heap of trouble."

"And we have enough bloody trouble already with Riverjack Crypto," interjected Peter. "Tragic for Jack and Emma and a massive problem for us. So tell me, what does the initial police report say?"

"You will not believe this," said Tom. "Actually, I couldn't at first. When we learned that the accident had happened, you know I contacted the Oxfordshire police to ask them for details. Initially, they didn't want to share anything with me but when I told them that I was on the Board of Riverjack Crypto and that the two dead people were the CEO and CFO respectively, they became a bit more amenable. I was put through to the case officer. He was just finishing his initial report. He offered to read it to me but, at a certain point, when he came to the part about the cause of the accident, he just started laughing and totally lost it. It took him an age to calm down and get a grip. I will admit that at first I was really cross; and then he explained what had happened."

"And that was?" asked Peter, bemused.

"It seems that as they were driving along, Emma was giving Jack a blowjob."

"What?" exclaimed Peter. "No fucking way. She's the archetypal ice queen; or she was. Not a chance in Hell she would be doing that to Jack. She'd only known him a fortnight. I know he could sell sand to Arabs but I just don't believe it."

"You better had," contradicted Tom. "Completely true. They reckon the car must have hit a pothole and somehow as a result she sunk her teeth into his dick. It is not completely clear but they think he must have hit the accelerator by mistake in a sort of reflex action and careered into the nearest tree. Rather unfortunate, really. Not exactly the happy ending he was expecting."

"How the hell did the police figure all that out?"

"Well, according to the report, there were tell-tale skid marks across the country lane they were going down leading back to a pothole, and they were found with their respective necks broken having flown through the windscreen and, get this, she still her had teeth sunk into his manhood when they were found," explained Tom, starting to laugh.

"Jesus H. Christ, You mean she still was blowing him as rigor mortis was setting in. I can't believe it."

"Now you see why the policeman lost it. He said in thirty years he had never come across anything like it," said Tom. By this stage he was laughing so much that tears came to his eyes. He gulped, tried to control himself, and failed.

Peter looked at him and did his best to keep a straight face.

"What a tragedy," he said, and paused and went on. "Mind you, rigor mortis means Jack died hard. He would definitely appreciate that on his gravestone."

Tom looked at him and started to howl with laughter. Peter stayed calm for a brief second and then he burst out in uncontrollable laughter as well.

"For fuck's sake," he babbled. "I can't believe it. The CFO is blowing the CEO and they waltz off to the pearly gates together." He started to choke with laughter.

"And her wearing a pearl necklace to go with her angel wings", spluttered Tom, gasping for breath. He leant forward in his chair and started to slap the desk in hysterics. Peter leant back in his chair and roared uncontrollably.

At that moment, Gordon Fairbald stormed into the room and shouted, "Will you two stop howling like a couple of demented fucking hyenas. I was trying to talk to Theresa about the latest portfolio performance report and you two sound as if you've lost your fucking minds. What the hell is going on?"

Gordon's arrival had the sobering impact of a bucket of water thrown over the pair.

Peter stammered in response, "Sorry, about that, Gordon. We were just talking about the unfortunate demise of Jack and Emma over at Riverjack Crypto. How are you, anyway? How was the golf?"

"Never mind about the damned golf. The trouble at Riverjack Crypto just increased tenfold. A sad story but it is going to be sadder for us if we don't sort that company out. Even with the chaos going on there I would have expected you to treat the recently deceased with a bit more respect."

"Sorry, Gordon," said Peter again, looking at Tom for support; however, he just remained silent, refusing to catch Peter's eye. "Tom was just acquainting me with the rather unusual circumstances surrounding their untimely demise. They crashed in Jack's car, you know. And the crash itself was caused by, er, well, how shall I put it?"

He looked at Tom and saw that Tom was about to start laughing again, so he quickly looked away. Fortunately, Gordon spared him any further embarrassment.

"I haven't time to get into details now but I want a full update later on. And find out where Jack got the Aston from. It better not have been from that capital we just advanced him or there will be hell to pay."

"No, of course it won't be," said Peter, suddenly alarmed. He had worked with Jack for just under over year and knew had been capable of anything. He was hoping Tom would add something to diffuse the situation but he was wisely busying himself with some papers from his briefcase.

"And while we are on the subject of full updates, who on earth is that girl I just saw running into your office like a whirling dervish? I called out to her but she ignored me."

"Oh, you must mean Lisa. She's my new EA, supporting me and Edwin. Today is only her second day and she was late so in a rush."

"Not her fault," said Tom, feeling as though he should come to her defence. "We ran into each other on the Tube. She was somewhat distracted as we pulled into Green Park and by the time she realised it was her stop, she couldn't make it out of the doors in time. You know how crowded the underground gets during peak hours."

"Not really," replied Gordon. "I haven't taken public transport for years. I drive myself in. Much more civilised."

He paused and went on, "Anyway, as I was saying, Riverjack Crypto is heading for a total clusterfuck and I want to know what you are going to do about it. Losing Jack is bad news; losing Emma is a total disaster. We put her in to sort things out. As I said, I want to know…"

At that point he was interrupted by a loud bang and a scream which seemed to have come from the kitchen.

"What the hell was that?" exclaimed Gordon.

"It sounded like Lisa," said Peter.

"I think she's lost a fight with the coffee machine," added Tom. "I'd better go and check." He got up and hurried out.

"You'd better go too, Peter," said Gordon. "I have better things to do than to clean up after your EA. I will see you later. We are not done talking about Riverjack Crypto; not by a long chalk."

"Sure, Gordon," replied Peter. "Tom and I are all over the Riverjack Crypto issues. I'll give you a full briefing when all the facts are known. Just a blip, I'm sure."

Gordon scoffed at this and Peter thought that whatever was happening in the kitchen would be a welcome distraction. He got up and scurried out of the door.

When Lisa had left Peter's office, she had gone back to her desk for a moment, put her handbag down and wondered what to do. She now regretted committing to making Tom a cappuccino and considered going out to the Starbucks she had found while waiting for her interview. However, she resolved that Lois would treat that as defeatist and set out to find the kitchen.

Her first endeavour was not successful. She managed to navigate her way back to the corridor without any trouble but opened a door to find it was a storeroom with stationery stacked on shelves, a broom, mop and bucket carelessly placed in a corner and a photocopier pushed against the wall. She detoured via the washroom which turned out to be unisex; it did boast a shower cubicle but seemingly no lock on the door, which left her feeling a little perturbed. But she finally made it into the kitchen. She went in and found that, although small, it was clean and seemed to be quite well-equipped with a fridge built into the wall, a stainless steel sink and on the side, a microwave and a coffee machine. Lisa's heart sank; the coffee machine looked incredibly complicated to operate, just like the one in the nearby Starbucks. It sat silent and menacing, a single red light blinking at her as if it was eyeing her up and being distinctly unimpressed with what it saw.

Lisa approached the machine nervously and looked more closely. On top of the machine there was a transparent container with coffee beans in it; at least that was a start. There seemed to be a plethora of switches and lights which were utterly confusing but in the middle of the machine there was something which at least looked like a coffee granules container. It had a round cup with a silver handle at the end and reminded Lisa of the sort of thing she had seen coffee shop baristas manipulate with such dexterity; there was also a small pipe leading from it back into the machine.

She reached up and opened a cupboard; inside she found a collection of various mugs; she took one which had "Don't fucking talk to me until I've had coffee" printed on the side and placed it tentatively under the pipe on the small tray which protruded underneath the granules container. She looked back at the machine. There seemed to be a number of coffee choices – Espresso, Americano, Latte and, thankfully, a button that said "Cappuccino". She pressed it hopefully. For a moment nothing happened, then she heard a grinding noise and the machine started to hum; a green light came on below the "Cappuccino" button which made her feel more confident. The machine continued to whirr, however, without producing anything and started to make strange, deep noises which made Lisa uneasy. The only thing she was sure of at this stage was that there was no coffee coming out.

She looked around helplessly, thinking that, as she was trying to make a cappuccino, she had better add some milk. She opened the fridge and was relieved to see three pints of milk stacked neatly in the door. As she took one, the machine started to vibrate in an alarming way. The green light had been replaced by a flashing red one. She noticed there was a flap on top of the machine next to the bean container; she opened it and peered in. It seemed to Lisa to be the right sort of place to pour liquid – a bit like the tray where you put detergent into a washing-machine, she thought – and so, opening the milk, she tipped the entire pint in. There was a moment when the gurgling coming from the depths of the machine sounded promising. However, an instant later there was a loud bang; the silver-handled container flew off the machine spreading coffee granules over the worktop, onto the floor and over

Lisa's blouse. At the same time a large jet of hot milk squirted out of a hitherto unseen tube at the front of the machine and hit Lisa firmly in the face, causing her to scream. She staggered back and the milk continued to fly out of the pipe at high pressure.

"Help!" she tried to shout but her cry was drowned out by another jet of milk, this time hitting her squarely in the mouth. She weakly cried out for help again and reached for a cloth on the side of the sink. She tried to staunch the jet of milk with the cloth but the pressure was too much. As she lunged for the machine, she felt her foot give way on the tiles which, now covered in milk, had the characteristics of an ice rink. She fell down onto her back, her legs akimbo, her skirt riding up. She struggled like a crab on its back, kicking her legs desperately in an effort to stand up but to no avail as milk continued to arc from the machine.

At this point, Tom came in. He took one look at Lisa and then could not prevent himself from taking another as he was afforded a rather delectable view of her panties – black lace from Victoria's Secret, no doubt, he thought with a smile. He calmly stepped forward, turned the coffee machine off at the wall and offered Lisa a hand to get up. Lisa had been too preoccupied with struggling on the floor to notice Tom's illicit admiration of her underwear and gratefully grasped his hand.

"What the bloody hell have you been doing?" Tom asked with a smile. "It looks like a cow just went on the rampage in here."

"I don't know," wailed Lisa. "I was trying to make coffee and the machine just went berserk." She looked down at her blouse, covered in milk. "What am I going to do?" she said as an afterthought, looking miserable.

Tom suppressed the temptation to suggest that she enter a wet t-shirt competition. He felt that would probably be unduly inappropriate. The thin, lace bra she was wearing would definitely not have been much of an impediment to first prize. He also thought about offering her his shirt to wear but realised that, as he did not have a spare one, he probably should not spend the rest of the day walking around the office bare-chested.

At that moment Peter walked in accompanied by Mary, Gordon's and Henry's assistant.

"Oh, you poor wee thing," said Mary, who was in her mid-fifties; her children long since had left home but whose maternal instinct was still strong. She had a strong Scottish accent which Lisa struggled to understand. "I heard the commotion and thought I would come along to see if I could help."

"Mary," said Peter. "That is very kind of you. This is Lisa, my new assistant. It's only her second day; I think taking on the coffee machine was a bit ambitious so early in her career at Aardvark."

"I'm sorry," said Lisa, gulping back a sob. "I was trying to make a cappuccino."

"With no water in the machine and the milk poured into the coffee grinder, by the looks of it" said Tom, peering at the machine. "You certainly managed to get it to do things I've never seen a coffee machine do."

"Be quiet, Tom," interjected Mary. "Lisa, a pleasure to meet you, my dear. Come with me; I will get you sorted out right away. In the meantime Tom and Peter can make themselves useful and clean up this mess. About time they did some actual work around here."

"Now look here," Peter started to say. But Mary was not interested; she put an arm around Lisa and guided her out of the door. Peter and Tom looked at each other and shrugged.

"I will leave you to it," said Tom. "You know I need to start drafting the emergency Board resolution for Riverjack Crypto. We have to do a Board call this morning to appoint an interim CEO. Do you want to do it or shall I?"

"It looks like I have to be janitor here first," said Peter. "But I guess it had better be me. Put me down for it; I will take over and go over to Oxford and try to work out what the hell has or hasn't been happening there."

"Right you are," said Tom and added as he went out of the door, "Good luck clearing this place up."

"Thanks a million," muttered Peter to himself. He went out of the door and down to the stationery cupboard to fetch the bucket and mop. "A degree from one of the best universities in the world; sailed through the chartered accountancy exams with top marks; headhunted into venture capital; and here I am, cleaning up milk in the bloody kitchen. Not exactly what I dreamed of growing up to do. Still, no good crying over it, I suppose."

He grinned to himself and then resignedly put some water in the bucket and started mopping up the mess.

CHAPTER THREE

Peter had in fact grown up dreaming of being a professional cricketer. He had undoubtedly had real talent and found himself aged just thirteen playing for his school first team. On his debut he had succeeded in making a very composed half-century against considerable odds: his own teammates, four or five years older and resentful that they had a junior flea, as they called him, in their side, encouraged the opposition fast bowlers to do as much damage to him as they could. Peter displayed considerable tenacity and resilience and actually won the respect of both sides for his innings.

As the season progressed he still found himself the butt of many jokes and on several occasions was made to wait alone in the minibus after away matches while the team stopped at the pub en route back to their school. The team coach had been a former professional player who had a rather liberal view on schoolboy drinking, believing that, as he and his fellow professionals had spent pretty much every night after playing in the pub, his own charges should learn to do the same. However, the success that Peter enjoyed on the pitch meant that the humour was by and large good-natured.

His ability on the sporting field also meant that he was held in high regard by his peers and the older boys at his Public School, so he was largely unaffected by the usual bullying and generally odious behaviour of the Sixth Form boys towards the junior pupils; as a result he enjoyed his boarding school and managed for the most part to avoid any of the kinds of nefarious activities so often associated with those institutions. He was confident and popular by the time he left and clever enough to obtain a place at Oxford University to read PPE – Politics, Philosophy and Economics. "The degree of politicians, business leaders and the secret service," his father would proudly announce to his friends at the golf club, who smiled resentfully whenever he regaled them in the bar after a round with Peter's latest academic or cricketing success.

He had found that his cricketing prowess was good enough to get him into the Oxford University team during his first summer term. Although the standard had slipped over the years, tradition still had it that the university team played the professional county sides, usually at The Parks in Oxford, a picturesque ground at which the professional players all enjoyed playing because the opposition was not the highest standard and nights out in Oxford were always entertaining. There was perhaps less chance of persuading young, impressionable female students to come back to their hotel rooms than there had been for past generations but there was always the possibility to discuss while playing during the day and it remained a tradition the next day in the dressing room to recount exploits and tales of conquest from the previous night; whether made up or real, they were always suitably exaggerated.

Peter found that the standard of cricket was challenging but not insurmountable and he did well overall. It was rather unfortunate that for three straight years, injury or illness prevented him from playing in the annual match against Cambridge University at Lord's, the home of cricket in London, and thus formally being recognised as a "Blue", but he found he could match the professional bowlers and quite often received grudging acknowledgement of his talent. They would start against him not trying very hard and, by the time they started to exert effort, realising he was not the usual student pushover, he had usually grown in confidence and scored well.

However, Peter took a careful look at the life of a professional cricketer and realised that although he probably could make his living playing cricket, he would be the archetypal "journeyman pro". He realised the domestic professional game would be his limit and he would not be good enough to make it to the international level. That was where the real money was to be made and where cricketers could enjoy rock star lifestyles and income levels as well as mixing with the rich and famous as equals. Peter knew to his chagrin that this would be beyond him and, as he decided that earning money was an important motivation for his future career, he became determined to knuckle down and work towards his degree rather than spending his last summer term just playing cricket, drinking beer and chasing girls.

He did have a series of love affairs which, with the intensity of student life at Oxford, had seemed to last for months or years but mostly ran for a few short weeks before the excitement faded, at least for Peter. This essential aversion to commitment beyond the initial exhilaration of a new relationship came from an unfortunate and seemingly life-shaping experience in his first year. He had fallen for a girl named Katherine who was studying experimental psychology – a degree subject which, as far as Peter could work out broadly involved observing the behaviour of rats from which largely erroneous conclusions about the human psyche would then be drawn. He had been completely in love and, as it turned out, oblivious to the fact that he was in fact the one being experimented on.

For almost the entire summer term in his first year, they had walked together for hours along the River Cherwell, talking the usual philosophical nonsense and indulging in the intellectual masturbation that is the domain of the clever student. She had come to watch Peter play cricket (something which he found incredibly exciting, as it was a sign of her commitment to the relationship, he thought) and they had made passionate love in their respective college rooms and once, most memorably, in a punt tied up under a willow tree at dusk. Peter had not been able to imagine how his existence could be more perfect. Their conversations aroused his intellectual curiosity, so he excelled in his academic work; her apparent deep interest in him and willingness to expand their sexual repertoire augmented his physical capacity so that the combination of testosterone and adrenaline that flowed into his bloodstream meant he had had never played better cricket.

It had therefore been rather a shame, when he unexpectedly called round to her room one late afternoon to find her in bed with her best friend. It had not been so much that she had been unfaithful – in truth, he had only been mildly ashamed to admit to himself that the thought of his girlfriend engaging in lesbian sex was illicitly exciting. The problem had come when she explained later that it was an experiment to see how she herself felt about the activity; how her friend would react both to the suggestion and to the act itself; and finally how Peter would react when she told him. She did not regard it as being unfaithful to Peter; as she put it, it was just research for her degree, albeit very enjoyable research which she admitted she would not be averse to repeating. Peter gradually realised during the course of this conversation, held in the same bar of The Eagle and Child pub where many years before C.S. Lewis and Tolkien had read extracts from the Narnia Chronicles and The Lord of the Rings to each other, that he could not continue in the relationship.

He knew his awkward conversation with Katherine hardly merited comparison in terms of literary merit, but nevertheless it seemed as historically momentous, as he felt his world collapsing in the ruins of her frankness. He was still completely besotted with the girl but he understood as he kissed her goodbye – a brief, desultory, calamitous peck on the cheek – that although she was undoubtedly fond of him, maybe indeed loved him in her own way, she would not hesitate to sleep with his own best friend (or friends) just to see what reaction he would have. He walked out of the pub alone and, for the first time in his life, with tears in his eyes. He went back to his room and listened miserably to "Honesty" by Billy Joel on repeat play for hours, lying on his bed, unable to sleep or take his mind off her body, early evenings in moored punts and philosophical postulations.

The next morning, at breakfast in the College dining hall, he told three of his friends what had happened. They had expected him to join them on a pub crawl the previous night and had speculated as to where he had got to when he failed to put in an appearance. Through their respective hangovers they tried to treat the painful subject of Peter's break-up with Katherine with respect but singularly failed to do so. They just burst out laughing at several lewd jokes about being caught in flagrante delicto and whether he had stopped to take pictures; by the end of breakfast, Peter was laughing with them and, while still regretful at the end of the relationship, resolved to move on.

In his final year, the question of future career raised itself. His father, who had also been up at Oxford, as he put it, had rather hoped that his academic tutor might suggest that "he meet some people in London I know" in the manner of George Smiley of the British Secret Service.

"I don't think MI5 recruits that way these days, Dad," said Peter. "They have a Facebook page and encourage you to do the Civil Service exams. And it is hardly the life of James Bond, you know. More reading countless, boring reports about the economies of former Soviet Bloc countries."

"There's always GCHQ," said his father hopefully. "You know, they are always looking for the brightest stars."

"I don't see myself as the next Alan Turing. And I don't want to live in Cheltenham trying to listen into Donald Trump's conversations. Besides, they pay terribly and you can never tell anyone what you actually do for a living."

Peter interviewed with the usual investment banks and major management consulting firms but found himself uninspired by what they had to offer. Against all his previous prejudices, it was ironically the prospect of working for one of the global accountancy firms which he found interesting. Although he was going to have to study hard to take his professional accounting exams, it seemed that life would be pretty much a continuation of his university days and he was excited by the promised exposure to a variety of businesses across different industries. Someone he had played cricket with had joined the firm the previous year. He told Peter that the culture was great – "a lot of really good evenings when you are away on client site" sounded very entertaining – even if the hours were long. Moreover, he mentioned something that was really music to Peter's ears and that he would not forget: "If you can qualify and then continue working for three or four years, the venture capital firms are really going to want you, particularly if you have exposure to the tech industry. For God's sake, don't go into manufacturing as that is just counting boxes and banking is all about detailed regulations; high tech is really the most dynamic industry nowadays. And as I say, that's the best route into private equity and venture capital and that is where the real money is."

Peter duly moved to London and shared a flat in Maida Vale with two other friends who were also starting their careers in the City. He followed the advice of his cricket-playing friend and managed to get himself assigned to the Technology practice of the large multi-national firm he had joined. Having succeeded in his exams and qualified without any problems over the course of three years, he spent another five years in fast progression up the ranks. An executive search company had called him out of the blue to discuss the position of Investment Director of Aardvark and he had decided that the time was right to pivot and chase the real wealth that his erstwhile friend had promised. He successfully interviewed with Gordon and Henry Farrell-Wedge and then met and duly been intimidated by Theresa. He also did a call with Mitch McPherson, the head of the firm based in San Francisco, which gave him some insight into the business in the US – where the focus was also on investing in early stage technology companies and where the firm apparently had a stellar reputation.

The combination of his obvious intelligence, track record and extensive experience in the technology industry meant that they made him an attractive offer to join the firm. He was not yet a full equity partner but was given a small percentage of any profits made by their current investment fund. Now, after several years at Aardvark he had built a reputation as an insightful, collaborative investor; other VC firms would have welcomed the chance to invest alongside him but actually found the partners of Aardvark in London quite overbearing and difficult to work with. Peter himself had wondered about leaving from time to time but he enjoyed his job and very much liked the exposure it gave him to the US market. He had occasionally thought about moving to Silicon Valley, where the combination of available capital, investment opportunity and his British accent would probably lead to sure success. Riverjack Crypto was the first investment that Peter had led from start to finish and on more than one occasion, Gordon, Henry and Mitch had intimated that a successful outcome (or "exit", the technical term for an equity stake by a venture capital firm that is sold) would mean a full partnership in the firm; by contrast, a failure would probably mean an exit of a different kind for Peter.

As required by company law, they had held a rapid, emergency Riverjack Crypto Board meeting and Peter had been officially nominated as interim Chief Executive. As he drove down to Oxford that afternoon, he thought about how Jack Hudson had first come to pitch him the idea of a new type of company that would revolutionise the way businesses made payments to each other, eliminating a major revenue stream for the traditional banks. Jack had been extremely convincing as he explained that Riverjack Crypto was a new type of payment platform which took advantage of the latest advances in blockchain technology to launch the new cryptocurrency – the eponymous Riverjack Crypto – with the idea that it could integrate with existing payments' systems while providing a secure, fast and cheap way to bypass the fees charged by financial institutions, and thus allowing businesses to connect directly to their suppliers and customers online, and to manage international transfers and multi-currency challenges seamlessly using an equivalent of Bitcoin. The idea of subscribing to the service rather than paying by transaction seemed to Peter to be incredibly compelling. Jack had brushed aside any disparaging comments about the company or currency name and articulated his vision with total confidence. Jack himself was one of those rare successful entrepreneurs based in London who preferred to raise money from UK-based firms. With two companies founded and sold behind him, he was also someone who was highly sought after by the entire investment community in London. Peter had eventually won the deal by offering not only attractive terms to Jack but also selling him on the advantage of working with Aardvark because they combined British culture with strong, natural ties to the US.

Every investment in a VC firm has to be approved formally by the investment committee: in Aardvark's case, for UK investments this was Gordon, Henry and Mitch. A majority vote was all that was required and the debate had been heated. Mitch had really liked the innovation; Henry liked the idea of backing a new company founded by someone of Jack's stellar reputation; Gordon had not understood anything about the business and had found Peter's presentation of the investment thesis to the three of them hard to follow. He decided in the end to back it while raising severe objections because he was astute enough to be able to read which way Henry and Mitch were going to vote. He had done this on the gamble that, if the investment was a success, he would be able to say that he had been in favour all along. Equally, if it collapsed in a heap – and Gordon had heard some rumours about Jack's reputation as a Chief Executive that made him think that, however brilliant his idea, it just might fail – then he would be able to legitimately claim that he had been against the idea from the outset.

Peter had been excited to report to Jack that the investment had been approved and Aardvark had invested an initial five million pounds to own just under twenty percent of the company. By American standards this amount had been paltry and it was not usual for the main VC investor to take less than a controlling stake in the company. At that point Mitch had questioned whether it meant that they should not back Riverjack Crypto at all because, the company seemingly lacked ambition if this was the amount they were seeking; equally the terms of the deal from their point of view were not particularly attractive. Gordon had continued to object to the company on the grounds that the name was "as bloody stupid as that Jack Hudson himself" although Henry had pointed out that this was de rigueur for every new internet start-up particularly in the cryptocurrency world and won the day with his argument that taking on the investment in the face of steep competition meant that their reputation would grow in the market.

Peter had found Jack challenging to deal with: as CEO, his reports to the Board were late and lacking detail; financial information (the lifeblood of any investment by a venture capital firm) was difficult to obtain; hiring seemed haphazard and unrelated to any budget constraints. Equally, Jack seldom returned Peter's calls and, even worse, the state of product development was not at all clear. When he did manage to get hold of him, Jack gave regular, optimistic views as to how well things were progressing but the requests to see a demonstration of the actual technology were adroitly sidestepped.

At the most recent Board meeting it had become clear that Riverjack Crypto was in need of further capital, and quickly. Peter had had a difficult afternoon where he had had to present the latest update to Gordon, Henry and Mitch, asking the investment committee to approve additional funding. He had asked for a further two million pounds and was glad to receive approval for half of that. The fact that he had been instrumental in persuading Emma Collingwood to take over as Chief Financial Officer to bring the haemorrhaging of cash under control and get a grip of the company's administration was a crucial element in getting the further money agreed, as was a promise to organise a formal product demonstration to the three partners as well as initiating a further full round of funding where an additional venture capital investor would be sought.

Peter did regret the fact that Jack was dead as he had liked him and definitely admired his approach to life: it seemed that he died as he lived, very much on the edge. But he was even more sorry to learn of Emma's demise. She had been the CFO of a technology company where he had been in charge of the audit for a couple of years. They had established a good relationship and he had complete respect for the authoritative, precise, detailed way she had managed the financial matters of the business. It had not been a surprise to Peter that, when the business had successfully been sold to a larger competitor, Emma had decided to form her own consulting firm to act as interim CFO to venture-backed companies. He had been lucky, he felt, to find that she was available when he called her about helping Riverjack Crypto.

He wondered vaguely when the funeral would be and whether he should attend or just send flowers; he was concerned that in some shape or form her relatives would blame him for her death. The one thing he could not believe was the idea that she had actually been fellating Jack (he smiled despite himself at his use of the proper term) at the time. It seemed totally out of character; Jack could hardly have forced himself on her while driving so it must have been a totally willing act. Perhaps it was Jack's legendary sales skills that had closed the final and perhaps the finest deal of his life.

Peter had had a couple of calls with Emma about the business in the brief time she had worked there and her verdict on Jack had not been promising:

there was a plethora of ideas and extreme creativity; an unwavering belief in his ability to be successful; and an undoubtedly talented team which had been attracted by Jack's previous track record of making all his managers very wealthy. However there was precious little sign of a working prototype of the product. Two early adopter customers had been identified and contracts had been signed but they were starting to get cold feet as the promised product delivery dates were repeatedly postponed with less and less conviction that the next deadline would be met.

These relatively random thoughts passed through his mind as he turned off the M40 and headed towards the business park on the outskirts of Oxford. He wondered what he would find at the office and what the prospects of the business would be now.

In the meantime, Ewan Starman, the Riverjack Crypto Sales Director, was engaging in a little prospecting of his own with Abigail, the receptionist. He had been with Riverjack Crypto for about six months and had spent pretty much all of that time trying to persuade Abigail to go to bed with him. She was tempted for sure but had resisted so far because, as she pointed out, it could only get them both into trouble. More to the point, she had a boyfriend and however attractive she found Ewan, she was not really sure she wanted to trade. Ewan, however, felt that this was unnecessarily conservative behaviour on her part. The unfortunate events with the car crash had inspired him to continue his personal sales campaign, particularly as work at Riverjack Crypto had virtually ceased in the absence of the two senior executives.

Ewan wandered down the stairs to reception holding two cups of coffee. Jack had insisted on installing a proper cappuccino machine in the kitchen and Ewan had to admit that, having mastered its workings with significantly more adroitness than Lisa, the coffee it produced was pretty good. There was no coffee shop on the business park where their offices were located and as a result this self-sufficiency was very necessary. He walked through the door to reception and saw Abigail sitting behind the front desk, looking extremely bored and browsing on her iPhone.

"Morning, Abigail," Ewan said, in a breezy tone. "Lovely afternoon."

"Oh, it's you," replied Abigail, seemingly without interest. "I suppose it is."

"Now then," said Ewan, walking over to reception and placing one of the two coffees he was holding in front of her. "I have brought you a Ewan-special cappuccino as a present. No one makes coffee like I do."

"Thanks," she said absent-mindedly and took a sip. He was right; it was rather good.

"So, what's up, Abigail? I know everyone's a bit miserable but let's face it, life must go on. After all, it's what Jack would have wanted."

"Actually, I think he would have wanted the tree not to have been there," she replied sardonically.

"True, that," replied Ewan. "And for Emma to finish what she had started." He laughed loudly.

"I can't believe she was doing that. I mean, I hardly knew her but she didn't really seem to be the sort who would behave like that," said Abigail.

"Our Jack could be very persuasive; you know, you should see him in front of customers. He was absolutely brilliant. He could convince anyone to do anything, given the chance. I am not surprised his charm worked on Emma. Take Jack, add an Aston, and she was bound to fall for whatever he said," said Ewan with a mischievous grin.

"Where did the car come from anyway?" asked Abigail.

"No idea. There's a rumour going around that he spent the company's money on it but as our head of Finance is playing a duet with him on the golden harp, no one seems to know what is going on. I guess at some point Peter from Aardvark will show up. Until then," he paused, took a sip of coffee, and looked at Abigail straight in the eyes, "Will you let me buy you dinner tonight?".

"Ewan, I've told you. I don't think it's a good idea. And besides, what about Gary?"

"Gary? Really, you are wasting your time with him when you could have me."

Abigail looked at him appraisingly. He was definitely more attractive than Gary and, as befitted his profession, certainly knew how to sell himself. Ewan read the silence as an opportunity to move in for the kill.

"Besides, you really don't ever look excited when you mention his name. I mean, you hardly make it sound like he lights your fire. I bet the sex is uninspiring to say the least."

"Ewan!" exclaimed Abigail, going red. "That's none of your business; whatever it's like."

Ewan laughed, "So I am right?"

"No, I mean," she stammered and paused. She thought back to the date she and Gary had been on the previous Saturday. They had been to see a movie that he had chosen and which she had endured. He had put his arm around her in the cinema (back row seats as if they were bloody teenagers, she thought) and surreptitiously fondled her breast; she had not objected to this but equally had not found it particularly exciting. He was clumsy and just seemed to have no rhythm. Afterwards he had driven her back to her parents' house, where she still lived. As they were away, she had invited him in, without any real enthusiasm but because she had figured she might as well. They had slept together a couple of times before but it had not been earth-moving, to say the least; perhaps it was worth another go.

However, this time, with Gary lying on top of her grunting and grinding away in a manner designed to ensure that she would never reach orgasm even if he continued indefinitely, she really felt absolutely underwhelmed by the whole experience. Her mind started to wander and she found herself wondering whether her plans to move into her own rented flat with a girlfriend would have to be put on hold in the light of events at Riverjack Crypto. The rent was going to be a stretch even on her receptionist's salary, and impossible if the business now folded. That would be annoying as it was becoming increasingly difficult to live with Mum and Dad and she really felt it was time she stretched her wings. It would be a pity if they lost the flat they had been looking at in East Oxford. It would be really convenient for the office and was perfect for two girls to share.

With a jolt she realised that Gary's breathing was becoming heavier and his pace increasing; she dragged herself back to the business in hand and did a passable enough imitation of Meg Ryan's "When Harry met Sally" performance to fool him. As he got up to put his clothes back on, she wondered if he would have noticed if she hadn't bothered to make any effort at all. He seemed pleased with himself and pretty self-absorbed. Typical bloody man!

He told her how amazing she had been and clearly expected reciprocal praise which she gave him in a distracted fashion if only to avoid prolonging his departure. He misinterpreted what seemed to him her slightly confused air as being the aftermath of incredible sex and headed back home feeling suitably proud of himself. Abigail took a brief shower and discovered to her surprise as she got into bed that she was feeling extremely horny. She thought about doing something about it herself but then surprised herself once again by falling asleep before she had even begun to fantasise. What had surprised her even more was that she had subsequently dreamt of being seduced by Ewan; it was this thought she was trying to put out of her mind as Ewan leaned over the reception desk, his eyes twinkling.

"That good, huh? I bet he doesn't even make you come."

"If you carry on like this, I will tell HR."

"They're too busy trying to figure out what happens next around here," said Ewan. "But he doesn't, does he?"

"Well, what's it to you?"

"A girl like you deserves to enjoy herself. Particularly now there's nothing to do around here. I mean, we are not going to get any visitors. I should know; we are struggling to get customers to talk to us, let alone actually come here." He paused and looked at her. "And if anyone is actually going to come here, then I think it should be you."

She giggled despite herself. "What do you expect me to do? Let you have me right here?"

"No, I can do much better than that. This is all about you. You just sit there and let me take care of things."

Ewan put his coffee down on the reception desk and walked round to where Abigail was sitting. He looked at her with a smile as he pushed her chair slightly back on its casters, knelt down and crawled backwards on his knees into the alcove beneath the reception desk, then looked up at her. She looked at him in astonishment.

"What the hell do you think you are doing? Get out of there. Someone will see us, I mean, you," she said.

"I told you, no one's around. Now, I want you to think about Bill Clinton and Monica Lewinsky, only in reverse. Just think of me as your intern. I'm here just for you to enjoy yourself." He pulled her chair forward and leaned in.

"Ewan, for the last time," said Abigail, more forcibly, "You can't do this here. OK, I will have dinner with you, but you need to stop this now."

Ewan ignored her protests and leant forward, gently kissing the inside of her thigh just above the hem of her skirt. She felt the warmth of his lips on her skin and couldn't suppress a slight moan as his tongue flicked at her. She felt his lips move up her leg and despite herself, she started to wriggle.

Ewan smiled and tried to ease her skirt up gently. After a moment's hesitation, then Abigail lifted herself up slightly to allow him to push it back, leaving her underwear exposed.

"You naughty girl, Abigail," he said with a sly grin, looking up at her and then kissing the top of her panties, making her involuntarily open her legs with an almost imperceptible movement – although Ewan noticed it and smiled even more broadly. "Do you always wear a G-string to work? Were you expecting me?"

Abigail's response was to grab Ewan by the hair and push his nose down into her crotch. "If you are going to do this, get on with it and shut the fuck up."

She could feel his mouth against the thin strip of material, which was pushed into her as she opened up for him. He breathed in her scent and was pleased to find how wet she was as he reached up to pull the delicate triangle aside and probed her with his tongue.

Abigail gasped, twisting his hair harder and pushing him deeper inside her.

"Fuck, yes" she muttered, as she leant back in her chair. Just as she closed her eyes, she caught a glimpse of a blue car pulling up into one of the visitors' parking spaces. She tried to speak but the words were caught in her mouth as Ewan's tongue found her clitoris and she squealed with pleasure. She slid slightly down the chair with her eyes closed, ignoring everything except the feel of his tongue and heat of his breath on her. She lifted her hips up and pressed herself harder at Ewan while squeezing her thighs together so that he could not raise his head – not that he showed any inclination to stop his ministrations. She could feel an incredible orgasm starting to build inside her.

"Abigail, how are you?" she heard a voice ask. For a moment, she imagined it must be Ewan.

"Incredible," she gasped, "Just don't fucking stop".

"Stop? Stop what?" asked the voice in a surprised tone.

She opened her eyes and gave a little scream. Peter Smithson was standing in front of reception, looking perplexed.

"What do you want me to stop?" he asked again.

She could feel Ewan freeze. She surreptitiously pulled her chair closer to the reception desk so that there was no risk of Peter's seeing anything untoward and clenched her thighs together even harder. Ewan made a muffled noise in protest but she immediately slapped his head to make him be quiet.

"Oh, er, hello Peter," she said, desperately trying to pull herself upright and running her hands through her hair, hoping it did not look too dishevelled. "Sorry about that," she added. "I think I must have dozed off for a moment. To tell the truth, I haven't slept at all since I heard about poor Jack and Emma. I was just so tired that I dropped off. Really sorry. It won't happen again. I think I must have cried out in my dream." She lifted her hands from her hair and put them on the desk in front of her.

"That must have been an interesting dream," said Peter, with a sympathetic smile. "But don't worry, I totally understand. I think it has come to a great shock to all of us."

For the past few seconds, Ewan hadn't moved. But now Abigail gradually felt his head tilt; a second later she felt his tongue starting to explore inside her once more. She did not dare take her hands away to slap his head again to make him stop. She could feel Ewan's hands grasping her thighs and try to push them apart. She made a token effort to resist but she was as weak-willed as he was insistent. She tried desperately not to think about what was happening to her and said, "What brings you here? I mean, obviously, I know why, but, er... what can I do to help?". The last word came out as a yelp as Ewan's tongue had delved once more inside her. This time it was accompanied by two fingers which simultaneously started to stimulate her.

"I actually came here to see Ewan, mainly", said Peter. "Do you know where he is?"

"Um," said Abigail in a high pitch as Ewan's attention made her twitch in her seat. "No. I haven't seen him. He's... er... probably up, I mean, upstairs, I should think." She tailed off as another spasm of pleasure shot through her. "Why don't you go on up?".

But to her horror, Peter seemed inclined to linger and talk. She could feel the pressure building inside her. Whatever Ewan was doing, she had never felt anything like it. All thoughts of Gary, Peter, Riverjack Crypto and anything else were rapidly being overwhelmed by the impending arrival of what was promising to be the most powerful orgasm of her life.

"You know, I am really touched by the how the tragic news about Jack and Emma has affected you, Abigail. That speaks volumes for you. How is the mood in the office overall?" he asked in a solicitous tone.

"Aaargh!", was the only answer as Ewan's tongue found her clitoris once more.

"Sorry," said Peter. "What a stupid question. Of course everyone is upset and I understand exactly what you mean. It must have had quite an impact on the team."

"I'll say," panted Abigail.

"I can tell you are distraught, Abigail. I won't trouble you further. I'll just go up and see if I can figure out where Ewan has got to. You can come too, when you're ready."

"Definitely," she gasped in reply. "Very soon."

Peter smiled and turned away. He paused and turned back, pointing at the coffee cups. "You really should tidy these up, however. They give the wrong impression to visitors."

"Yes," she yelled. Peter looked at her, shocked. "I mean, yes, I will" she corrected herself in a calmer tone, managing momentarily to control herself. Peter smiled again and turned and went past reception to the door upstairs to the main office. As he went through, he heard Abigail shout out, "Oh God, I'm coming now." He turned, smiled reassuringly once more and put his thumb up. He turned and went upstairs. As the door closed behind him, he heard her exclaim loudly in what he took to be a sob.

"The accident really has hit her hard," he said to himself. "I'd better keep an eye on her to make sure she is OK. She was acting a bit strangely. You never know how this sort of thing is going to affect people; I guess we all react very differently."

Behind him Ewan was standing up, emerging from underneath the reception desk.

"He's gone?" he asked.

Abigail nodded and looked down to adjust her G-string back into place and smooth down her skirt. Ewan's face was as glowing as hers felt and his hair was ruffled. He had a self-satisfied look on his face.

"You fucking madman," she exclaimed. "Why the hell did you carry on when Peter came?"

"Because I thought it was only fair for you to come first. I was nearly right. Besides, I could hardly get up while he was there. What would I have said? 'Hello, Peter. Excuse me while I just finish off down here and then I will be right with you?'."

Abigail giggled. "Oh my God, I have never come like that," she admitted.

"So you did enjoy yourself! I told you to leave everything to me. Still on for dinner tonight?"

She nodded and then stared at him: "…But you can't go up now. Peter's going to ask where you have been. "

"Right," Ewan said. "Good point. I tell you what, I will nip outside, wait ten minutes, then I will go up, telling Peter I have just come back from visiting a prospective customer. I will tell him it was that bank that Jack and I visited last week."

"Ok," said Abigail. "But you had better splash water in your face first. You look like you've just, well, you know. And you can't walk around with that on your face." She reached over a plucked a short, blonde hair from his upper lip. "I tell you what though. You can bring me a cappuccino any time you like."

Ewan laughed and headed for the bathroom. He came out a few moments later, waved to her and walked out of the main entrance.

CHAPTER FOUR

That evening, Susannah Bierson had just got home to her apartment in Presidio Heights in San Francisco when her cellphone rang. It had been a long day to start the week and for once, the amazing view her apartment offered of the Golden Gate Bridge and the Bay failed to inspire her. She was tired and, as her cat Ginger came from his regular perch on the windowsill to greet her, it occurred to her what a complete cliché it was that a professional, successful, career-oriented single woman in her early thirties should have a cat as her only companion. She had acquired Ginger on impulse from a stray cats' charity earlier that year having read *Wallbanger* by Alice Clayton. The story had resonated with her and she had decided that a cat would complement her lifestyle just as it seemed to do for the book's heroine. Ginger was the one colour that he did not have on his fur so she enjoyed calling him that to confuse her friends. He was a total mongrel, Susannah decided, although not sure that the canine adjective could be ascribed to cats.

However, beyond Ginger, the problem, she admitted, was that, unlike Caroline, the novel's main character, she did not have a devilishly handsome, interesting, wealthy neighbour to fall in love with. Certainly the occupant of the apartment opposite had made no attempt to befriend her and there was absolutely no chemistry between them – she rather suspected that the chemistry in his life was focused on dealing various types of drugs so she judiciously avoided him and the disparate characters who quietly visited him at all hours. Her Prince Charming had not arrived in her life and she rather felt that her last fling, a couple of months or so previously, had been a mistake, albeit a surprisingly exciting one to have made.

She walked over to the window, glanced at the 'phone and answered the call.

"Mitch, how are you?" she said without enthusiasm, just glad that it was her boss and not her mother. She did have the stereotypical relationship with her mother, whom she loved but who insisted on giving her unsolicited advice, particularly about the need for Susannah to marry one of the supposed long succession of suitors and thus to provide grandchildren.

"All good, Susie, but we need to talk," said the booming voice on the other end of the line.

She winced. She had worked for Mitch McPherson for three years now. When they had first met, he had called her Susie and her attempts to get him to use her full name had fallen on deaf ears. She considered "Susie" an abomination.

"OK, fire away" she replied, trying to summon up the energy to sound engaged. She had a reputation for being a workaholic but even she was surpassed by Mitch's apparently indefatigable appetite for long hours. His intensity was both an inspiration and absolutely exhausting. There was no doubt that she felt privileged to work for someone who was acknowledged as one of the leading venture capitalists in the Bay Area; his reputation was only just below the more famous partners at Benchmark Capital or Andreessen Horowitz. However, in spite of everything she had learned from him, and the way that working for Aardvark put her at the forefront of the Silicon Valley investment community and meant her reputation was growing rapidly, she sometimes needed a break.

"Have I caught you at a bad time?" Mitch asked. He always asked this question but was never interested in the answer. Good or bad he would invariably plough on, regardless.

"No, all good. What's up?"

"Because I need to talk to you about what's going on at one of our UK investments – Riverjack Crypto."

Susannah thought for a second as she tried to recall the details. The success of Aardvark meant that they had several different active investment funds and multiple companies in their portfolio. Her role as Operating Partner meant that she had to stay abreast of developments in pretty much every company they had invested in as well as engaging at a detailed level with the management team of those she was supporting at any given time.

"Ah yes," she said, recalling the details. "They're the new payments platform company, right? Using cryptocurrency. Founded by Jack Hudson in the UK. Looks an interesting play, although I am not convinced by the name. Too many risky puns if it goes wrong. But that aside, it's pretty disruptive for an industry stuck in the dark ages. I like it."

"Well, here's the thing," said Mitch. "They've managed to disrupt themselves good and proper. Jack wrapped his Aston around a tree with his CFO as a passenger."

"Oh no," exclaimed Susannah. "Are they badly hurt?"

"They instantly transformed themselves into angel investors." Mitch laughed out loud at his joke. Angel investors were wealthy private individuals who both contributed money to one of Aardvark's funds and also would invest directly themselves.

Susannah hesitated and wondered what the joke was; then she gave a sharp intake of breath as she realised what he meant.

"That's terrible, Mitch. What a shock. I never met Jack but I heard a lot about his reputation as an entrepreneur."

"He certainly had a reputation, Susie. I won't go into details; decorum prevents me. But I am sorry to say his sins found him out."

Susannah had never quite been able to reconcile Mitch's undoubtedly authentic religious faith with his hard-nosed business modus operandi and any reference to it made her uncomfortable. She was at something of a loss as to what to say.

"Sorry to hear that, Mitch," she eventually came up with. "But other than the sad story, I am not sure where I come in."

"Here's the thing, Susie. Riverjack Crypto was starting to emerge as a real basket-case. Product late; expenses out of control; no customers to speak of. Not a great story so far. Could be our Jawbone."

Jawbone was famous as one of the costliest VC-backed startup failures of all time. The company had raised something approaching a billion dollars in funding over many years and fell into liquidation as it failed to get traction with its wireless headsets and fitness trackers.

"We haven't put that much in, have we?" asked Susannah.

"Susie, I thought I taught you better than that! It's not just about the money; it's our reputation that we are investing every time we take on a new company. If Riverjack Crypto doesn't deliver, then Aardvark's judgement comes under scrutiny and every damn twenty-year-old entrepreneur will question whether we are the right firm to work with."

Susannah knew Mitch was right. Competition amongst VCs in the Bay Area was ferocious and the rival firms, although often partners in shared investments, would also not hesitate to trash each other's reputation if they felt it would give them an advantage in a bidding war for the latest hot company to seek money.

"Ok agreed, Mitch. But where do I come in?" She could guess the answer but asked anyway.

"I just talked to Gordon in the UK," said Mitch.

"You did?" questioned Susannah. "But it's, let's see", she added, looking at her watch "It must be about 4am there."

"That's what he said when I woke him at home. I told him it wasn't here and that we urgently needed to discuss Riverjack Crypto. I said I was sending you over to get to grips with what is going on there, and to ascertain whether we should take any emergency measures with the business. And actually, while you are there, do a full review of the portfolio. It's time we licked those Limeys into shape!"

"You told him you were sending me over?" asked Susannah in a voice she hoped did not sound too petulant.

"Absolutely! I need someone I can trust over there. You know I can't go myself with everything that we have on right now. And the timing is really good: Gordon told me that he is planning an offsite for his team to go through the portfolio performance and work out where the problems are."

"The timing is not good, Mitch," objected Susannah. "You know I have next week off. I really need the break."

"But you hadn't planned anything in particular, had you? Nothing you can't postpone?"

This was unfortunately true. She had admitted as much to him when she had asked for the leave a couple of weeks previously. She still wasn't sure what she wanted to do. Hawaii on her own was not appealing; she didn't feel as though she had the energy to do a longer haul trip to Europe, despite frequent invitations from her former Harvard classmates who now lived there and the fact that some of her favourite cities in the world were there. She had wondered about going to Yosemite and just losing herself in the wilderness for a few days. But the only decision she had made was that she needed a break from the relentless pace of the venture capital business in Silicon Valley.

"That's true, I know. But I really want to take myself away and recharge."

"Well, why don't you take a break once you've been to the UK. You can head over to Europe and visit Paris, Rome and all those other places you have always told me you like so much. Your trip to London can run for a week or so and then take as much time off as you need. Besides, you know Gordon already, so it will be easy for you to fit in, right? You met him at the investor conference in Vegas a couple of months ago, obviously, and I remember you hit it off pretty well. I know when I mentioned to him I wanted you to help out with the Riverjack Crypto recovery effort he was very keen to have you over."

"I see," said Susannah. She added somewhat pensively, "Yes. It will of course be good to see Gordon again."

Susannah knew when she could push back on Mitch and when his tone allowed for no disagreement.

"Ok Mitch, you win," she said. "Of course," she added, "I'd be glad to lean in and help sort any portfolio problem out. When would you like me to go over?"

"That's my girl," said Mitch. "I knew I could count on you. Get yourself on the next flight out of SFO. Gordon said he would take care of the hotel reservation if you just drop him an email with your flight details. And I will wait for your report with interest. Let me know if you need anything my end. Just help Gordon and his team figure out a rescue plan."

"Will do, Mitch."

"Thanks Susie, stay in touch."

And with that, he hung up leaving Susannah standing holding the phone, frustrated but knowing when she was cornered.

"Well, Ginger, my man", she said out loud to the cat who studiously ignored her, "I guess it's that long haul trip over to Europe after all, whether we like it or not."

She wondered whether, if she opened a bottle of wine, she would feel guilty and would hear her mother's voice in her ear warning her about the dangers of drinking alone.

"Yes," she countered. "But she's not dealing with an intransigent boss making her go on an unwanted trip to the London office, cancelling her vacation in the process. Nor is she dealing with Gordon," she added.

She ignored any further protest from her inner voice and went into the kitchen, reached into the wine fridge for a rather expensive bottle of Pinot Noir that had been recommended to her by Frank, the gay owner of the local bottle store. She appreciated spending time in his shop, browsing and adding a few bottles to her cellar, as she liked to call it. The cellar – her wine fridge – could comfortably accommodate thirty bottles, she joked to Frank. She enjoyed his anecdotes about the frustrations of being gay in a post-HIV San Francisco and she admired his expertise about wine and normally took his recommendations. Most of all she liked the attention of a man who took her at face value, was obviously not trying to get her into bed and welcomed both her custom and her friendship without any other agenda. She hated to admit it to herself but it was one of the few places where she felt completely relaxed and authentic. In her business dealings she did not suffer from impostor syndrome – she was confident enough in her own abilities, education and role at Aardvark to avoid that – but she did sometimes find the plethora of entrepreneurs and fellow VCs in the Valley who assumed that she did and tried to get the better of her rather debilitating.

She poured herself a glass and savoured the aroma of the wine, as Frank had taught her to do. She held it up to the light and looked at the colours swirl in front of her. She smiled at her own pretentiousness, took a swig and appreciated the calming effect of the wine ("with a hint of blackberries, truffles and chocolate", she said to herself, laughing inwardly). She tipped a handful of mixed nuts from an open bag on her sideboard into a small bowl and carried bowl and glass back into her living room. She placed both onto a small table and went back to the apartment's small entrance hall to fetch her laptop. Fortified by another mouthful of wine – Frank was right, it was very good indeed – and a mouthful of nuts, she started to browse flights. At least Aardvark had a sensible travel policy, she thought. They all regularly flew business class, while naturally insisting that their portfolio companies implemented a "cheapest coach fare only" travel policy.

"After all," as Mitch was fond of declaring, "when the management teams of our portfolio companies have become multi-millionaires on the back of our capital, they can fly in their own fucking private jets. Until then, a little hardship never did any early-stage company any harm."

Susannah smiled to herself again as she remembered Mitch's booming voice pointing this out the previous week to the CEO of one of the companies they had invested in, who had had the temerity to tell him that making everyone fly United Airlines economy class around the world meant that animals were typically transported in greater comfort.

So, United Airlines was absolutely out of the question. She had no desire to be arbitrarily thrown off the flight or generally insulted by the flight attendants who would clearly rather be anywhere than doing their particular job. However, the only availability for the next day was on one of United's two flights to London. So, she decided that she would not take Mitch at his absolute word and booked for the day after on British Airways. Besides, she, thought, I need the next day or so in the office to get through any number of action items before turning my attention to Riverjack Crypto and whatever the hell is going in the UK.

"I'd better let Gordon know my plans," she thought. And then she hesitated, thinking back once more to the Vegas conference. She definitely needed another glass of wine before she got in touch with him, so she got up and sauntered back to the kitchen to refill her glass. She wondered how she felt about seeing him again. She said to herself, "To hell with it; quit worrying, Susannah. Email him and then just play it by ear."

She sat back down, had another deep draft from her glass and opened up email. It was about twenty minutes later that she came back to the task in hand, having been distracted by several new messages in her inbox. She ignored a couple of further messages and started to type:

To: Gordon.Fairbald@aardvarkvc.com
From: Susannah.Bierson@aardvarkvc.com
Subject: London trip

Hi Gordon,
I hope all is well with you. I gather you spoke to Mitch about my coming over to work with you on the portfolio and Riverjack Crypto in particular.
I am going to get on the Wednesday night flight on BA so I land on Thursday about midday. Mitch said you could get your EA to take care of hotel reservations – can you get her to get me an early check-in somewhere close to the office? Allowing for immigration delays and getting into the center from Heathrow, I reckon I can be with you about 2.30pm once I've had the chance to freshen up.

Mitch also said something about an offsite you were organising to do a full portfolio review? If you can take care of all the logistics, I'd be glad to be part of that as well. I have an open return so let's say I will be in London for 10 days or so.
It will be good to see you again and meet the London team.
Susannah

She wondered whether she should add an "xx" at the end of the message but decided that would be both unprofessional and not necessarily reflective of how she felt about him; so she pressed "Send" and lay back in her chair, closing her eyes for a moment and letting her mind relax.

She awoke with a start and discovered she had been asleep for a couple of hours. It was close to eleven pm and she felt hungry. Ginger was curled up on her knees, and she stroked him absent-mindedly before realising that he had pushed her laptop onto the floor as he had jumped up to go to sleep on her.

"Damn you, Ging," she exclaimed. "You had better not have broken the goddamn thing." The cat yawned, stretched and stood up, still balanced on her.

She reached down with one hand and picked up the laptop while simultaneously brushing Ginger off her with a disdainful sweep of her hand. He landed without a sound on all fours, looked at her disapprovingly and strutted off towards his favourite windowsill, nose in the air.

Susannah looked down at her laptop and was relieved to see it seemed to have suffered no noticeable damage. She checked email again and saw that she had a reply from Gordon. A swift piece of mental arithmetic on time zones told her he was up early, at least for him. It must have been the call from Mitch after which he obviously had not gone back to sleep.

To: Susannah.Bierson@aardvarkvc.com
From: Gordon.Fairbald@aardvarkvc.com
Subject: Re: London trip

Hi Susannah
Great to hear from you!! Yes, Mitch called me – at 4am our time, can you believe? He wanted to talk through Riverjack Crypto and to get you to come over. I thought about Las Vegas and 101 inappropriate things went through my mind when he said that!!!
Your timing is good. It will be fantastic to get you involved in the offsite. We start on Sunday so you will have plenty of time to get over your jetlag and to see the sights – maybe I can show you some myself!!! We might even find time for some work LOL!

Mary will sort everything out. We will get you booked into the Whitehaven when you are here – boutique hotel, close to the office.
Shall we plan on dinner together Thursday night?
Really looking forward to seeing you again!!
G

She read the email through twice and looked up the Whitehaven Hotel on the internet. It was indeed close to the London office and looked like a luxury boutique hotel. She found herself excited about going back to London and decided she could deal with the potentially problematic bit about dinner with Gordon later on.

Susannah yawned and closed her laptop; any reply she sent to Gordon could wait until the morning. She had bought herself a valuable 24 hours or so to finish off a couple of key tasks she had to get done before flying out and she felt that it would probably be useful to brush up her detailed knowledge of the payments industry before figuring out what to do with Riverjack Crypto. As she fell asleep an hour or so later, her last thought was that, even by the standards of billion-dollar valued unicorn technology companies, it really was a very silly name.

CHAPTER FIVE '

Gordon lay awake next to his wife, Cressida, browsing his iPhone and smiling at the prospect of seeing Susannah again. He wondered how she would react at their next meeting; he felt a flutter in the pit of his stomach at the thought and smiled again. He looked at his wife, asleep next to him wearing an eye-mask and ear-plugs. Not exactly the most alluring image to wake up to, he thought regretfully. Cressida had taken to wearing a rather sexless onesie to sleep in. Once, whatever she had worn in bed would have been designed to separate him from whatever he was working on and lure him to her; now he rather felt that it was designed to act as a full-body chastity belt.

He looked at his iPhone again and re-read his reply to Susannah. It was hardly surprising that the thought of her made him excited. He looked at his paunch, which was pushing the bedclothes up; it was true that perhaps Cressida's protective overalls, as he liked to think of the onesie, had been caused at least in part by his own bodily decline. Financial and business success had come in complete inverse proportion to the attractiveness of his own physique. He did pay the monthly subscription to a gym close to the office (well, at least, Aardvark paid it for all employees) and they were members of the David Lloyd Centre sports club near Twickenham where they lived, but he could not remember the last time he had used either facility.

Still, his intellect was as powerful as ever and clearly his charm was not as out of shape as the rest of him. He thought back to Las Vegas and Susannah, smiled again and wondered where he would take her to dinner on Thursday night. At least he was free; Thursday was the night when Cressida had her Book Club. The downside of Thursdays and Cressida's absence was that on Fridays, she would come back either insisting that he read some bloody spiritual novel about the emancipation of women in Nigeria in the 1990s or, presumably fueled by her conversations with her friends about the total inadequacies of their husbands, she would berate him for his lack of intellectual curiosity, the amount of time he spent devoted to the office or his general failings as a human being. The one thing he had to admit was that, while Cressida may not have worked since she had had their children, she remained as attractive as she had been 25 years earlier when they had married. She was in amazing shape for a woman in her early fifties. When she said she played tennis three times a week and tried to swim daily, by the looks of her she was not lying.

"Probably shagging the professional at the Club," Gordon thought vindictively. "She certainly isn't shagging me."

He felt her stirring next to her and looked balefully and resentfully at her in equal measure.

"Bugger it," he thought, pulling the duvet aside and stepping out of bed. He trudged into the bathroom, shaved and plunged into the shower, still in a slightly depressed state of mind. He looked down and realised that although in his youth he had had a proprietorial pride in the size of his member, his belly had now expanded to the point that he could not even enjoy the view.

Nevertheless he pushed to the back of his mind any doubt that the dinners, long hours and copious amount of alcohol consumed over the years did not represent the necessary price for his career achievements. He thought back to Vegas again and declared to himself, "Not sure where these doubts are coming from, Big G. You still have it for sure!". Thus reassured he stepped out, toweled himself dry and went into his dressing room to get prepared for the day ahead. At least he and Cressida had not yet resorted to separate bedrooms; that really would spell the end, he thought, and the end means divorce, and divorce would mean a ruinously expensive settlement as well as problems with Mitch. He had seen how much it had cost Henry – and not just once, he added to himself.

"So that isn't bloody well happening, whatever else may be going on," he declared out loud.

He finished dressing – he still wore a suit and tie to the office even though Henry had recently been telling him that it made him look so out of touch with the internet crowd – and went downstairs to the kitchen. He was surprised to find Cressida sitting there, with her back to him, sipping a cup of tea.

She turned around as he came in.

"Good morning, darling," she said in a surprisingly friendly tone which put him immediately on his guard.

"Jesus Christ, what the hell is that on your face," he exclaimed.

"It is a mud pack from the Blue Lagoon in Iceland," Cressida said, primly.

"Well, it makes you look like something from the black lagoon for sure. It's far too bloody early in the morning to be faced with something like that."

"It has rejuvenating properties which feed and moisturise the skin. You remember what they told us when we were there last year. I decided to order a series of treatments online and they arrived yesterday. I think it will do wonders for my complexion."

"It's going to take more than some overpriced volcanic ash price to fix that," said Gordon, meanly. "What did you pay for it? Two hundred quid?"

"More like five hundred, darling."

"For fuck's sake, what a total waste of money." He was even more resentful when he thought back to the surprise weekend in Iceland; he had booked it to try to rekindle excitement in their life. As far as he could recall, the last time they had had sex was in the private room offered to those guests at the Blue Lagoon willing to pay for the VIP experience. Although that had definitely been pleasurable, the illicit nature of it adding to the excitement for both of them, as their relationship had deteriorated since then, he had come to resent Iceland for it.

"Just like that ridiculous gym subscription you never use," countered Cressida. "At least I am putting my wasted money to work."

Gordon could not think of anything pithy to say in response.

"And what was that call at 4am?" asked Cressida.

"I didn't think you could hear anything through those ear plugs of yours."

"More than you would think," she rejoined. "Was that Mitch getting his time zones wrong again? My father always used to say it was the one thing he couldn't really get the hang of."

"Oh, he knew what time it was, alright. He just didn't care. We've had, er, a spot of bother at one of our companies and he wanted to know what the status was. He's, um, sending over one of the team, Susannah Bierson, to help us sort it out. She lands on Thursday so I will be taking her out to dinner and probably, um, staying up in town as it will be too late to drive back, of course." Gordon casually mentioned the last point and busied himself in the fridge, fetching a glass of orange juice, so he did not have to look at his wife.

"Thursday? She will just have to have dinner on her own," interjected Cressida. "I think you have forgotten I have tickets for us to see *Dans La Brume* as part of the Twickenham French Film Festival."

"I am her host, Cressida. I have to look after her," replied Gordon. He did remember now that he had agreed some time previously to go with her, just to avoid an argument. "And you know I really hate pretentious French films."

"You said you would come with me weeks ago. There is a question and answer session with the writer, the director and the two stars plus a 'Moules Frites' supper afterwards. You will be there, Gordon Fairbald, and I am not taking anything other than a 'Oui, ma chérie' from you."

Gordon tried to keep the disappointment and angst out of his voice.

"I need to spend time with her. We have a crisis at one of our companies and she has come over to lead the rescue effort," he asserted. "Besides that, we have to talk about the offsite we are planning next week. I told you about it; it starts on Sunday and runs until Tuesday."

"Well, you can work with Susannah during the day like every other normal person. She will have had enough of you by the time the evening comes anyway. And besides, she will probably need to catch up with Mitch and her US colleagues," responded Cressida. She paused and then went on, "And what sort of crisis?"

"It is too complicated for me to go into the details now," he said aggressively. His evening with Susannah now looked a distant prospect. Still, he had the offsite to look forward to.

"I think you forget that I am still my father's daughter and complicated crises at companies are not exactly a closed book to me," said Cressida, demurely. She went on, "And about the offsite, I have told you, I am going to be there too."

"Cressida, for God's sake, we have discussed this any number of times. It is not appropriate for you to be there – no one else will have their partners or spouses there – and it is going to be unbelievably dull as I will be busy all day and night."

"Yes, Gordon, I know what you say, but I have told you, I am coming with you. It will be good for me to spend time with Henry again and I would like to meet the younger members of your team. Besides, I wouldn't like to think how you plan to stay busy day and night."

"What the hell do you mean by that?" exclaimed Gordon.

"Just put it this way, Gordon Fairbald, if I discover you've been misbehaving, I will slap you with divorce papers faster than you can ever imagine. And you know what Mitch will think of that."

"I cannot begin to think where your deluded imagination has got that idea from," said Gordon indignantly. "You know I only have eyes for you, my darling." He added after a pause with a forced laugh, "Well, I prefer it when you are not wearing mud all over your face."

"Then you could at least act as if that is true, Gordon," said Cressida, suddenly looking very sad. "You haven't come near to me in months and I don't know why."

"You know how tired we both get; and besides, you have hardly given me any encouragement," countered Gordon.

"Well, for a start, you could do something about looking like a beached whale when you get into bed. What happened to the svelte young finance executive I fell in love with?"

"That is just so utterly typical of you," shouted Gordon, getting up angrily. "You always resort to insults and telling me my inadequacies as a man, husband, lover and even damned venture capitalist."

"Well, I think I am pretty qualified to pronounce on all four."

"I haven't got time to discuss any of this now, anyway," he said. "I am already running late."

"Just remember, darling," she said in a dulcet tone that fooled neither of them, "You will be with me at cinema Thursday night and likewise I will be with you at the offsite. I don't think either of us would like to contemplate the consequences of the alternative."

Gordon looked at her with loathing and said nothing. She just smiled at him through her face mask and took a demure sip of tea. He turned and went out of the kitchen shaking with anger but also knowing that her threat of divorce was real. The consequences of that did not bear thinking about.

Gordon's temper was not improved by the traffic, which was diverted off the main road into central London because of yet another protest march against Brexit.

"Can't these useless bastards get a job instead?" he snarled to himself as he found himself crawling along the diversion route. Gordon himself had found that Brexit in investment circles was such a divisive subject that he had long since kept his views to himself and refused to say which way he had voted. The truth was he had actually forgotten to vote as on the day of the referendum he had found himself getting wonderfully drunk with an old schoolfriend and by the time he got home on the last train out of Waterloo and remembered he had not actually voted, the polls were closed. His only concern was that the impact of Brexit on London's venture capital business could only be negative. Although his worst fears were not yet coming to pass, the bloody French and Germans were doing everything they could to build up the Paris and Berlin investment scene and it did not bode well for the future of Aardvark. They were intending to raise another fund next year and the chances of getting European investors on board after the total fiasco of the Brexit political process were receding weekly. He drove to his usual carpark in a less than pleasant mood and walked over to the office, determined to take his anger on someone. Peter would be a perfect target given the clusterfuck at Riverjack Crypto.

He walked into his office and barked at Mary to find Peter at once. She came back unflustered at Gordon's temper. She was used to it and not easily intimidated and calmly told him that Lisa had said that Peter was spending time at the Riverjack Crypto offices and would not be back until Thursday. This put him in an even worse mood. which was not improved when Henry walked into his office with a self-satisfied look on his face.

"Morning, Gordon," he said airily. Then he looked at his colleague again. "Hell's teeth! You look like you are halfway through shitting a chilli. What's up with you?"

"Riverjack Crypto, that's what. Mitch called me in the middle of the night to shout at me about it. I told him that I had expressed my doubts in

Investment Committee but he just ranted about lack of discipline and poor oversight. He said he held me accountable and that I should have done a better job supervising young Peter who should never have been entrusted with so much responsibility."

Actually, Mitch's tone had mostly been pretty constructive and he had mentioned nothing about lack of discipline, but Gordon decided there would be more impact if he painted a different picture of the conversation.

"Indeed," said Henry, sympathetically, "We all know what Mitch can be like when he gets going."

"And to make matters worse he's sending over Susannah Bierson to review the Riverjack Crypto rescue plan and to go through the portfolio performance at the offsite. Just what we damn well need – not."

"Ah yes, Susannah. We've obviously spoken countless times but I've never met her. She looks stunning on her LinkedIn profile," mused Henry.

"For God's sake, Henry. Keep that sort of comment to yourself or you will end up with your arse sued so fast you won't know it from your elbow. You know what these Californian girls, I mean, women, are like. One word out of place and a reputation's ruined."

"I think my reputation is pretty much ruined already," replied Henry, totally unconcerned. "Nothing to worry about there."

"But after the last divorce settlement you'll end up in bloody debtors' prison if you find yourself paying out for sexual harassment."

"That's a fair point," said Henry, reflectively. "I will try to rein myself in."

"I look forward to the day," said Gordon. He looked at Henry again somewhat circumspectly. They had known each other for many years as colleagues and had both been promoted to partner at Aardvark at the same time. Henry's flair for investment opportunities was matched only by his ability to make unwise marriages and then pay huge sums to his ex-wives. He had nicknamed the last investment fund which had paid out to the Aardvark team "My Alimony Fund". Knowing him as he did, Gordon knew he was unlikely to learn from his mistakes; he fully expected the fourth Mrs Farrell-Wedge to come onto the scene sooner rather than later. Mitch regarded Henry as a hopeless sinner, but tolerated him because many of his investments had delivered returns that could only be described as "home runs" in the venture capital vernacular.

Gordon thought about the smile that Henry had had on his face when he came into his office.

"So, Henry, where were you last night? I am guessing by the look on your face, you had fun."

"The bar of the W, my friend. A new watering-hole I have discovered."

"The W? That chain has a reputation for only one thing. I remember a few years ago I read about a businesswoman staying at their hotel in Miami who was attacked by hookers who thought she was muscling in on their patch."

"Well, it certainly is a party hotel! I can tell you it also happens to have won the contract for the Emirates crew on their London layovers." Henry paused and went on, laughing, "And layover is the appropriate word. I met a charming air hostess from Brazil last night who was definitely up for the samba, if you know what I mean. One bottle of champagne later and, well, I won't go into details but let's just say we agreed to meet up again tonight before she flies out."

"You are totally incorrigible, Henry," said Gordon, not without envy in his voice. He wondered how Henry managed to have a succession of fabulously attractive women seemingly at his beck and call and be such a brilliantly intuitive investor. "Just for God's sake don't feel as though you have to marry the girl just because you have slept with her!"

"That," said Henry, "Is a remark beneath you, Gordon Fairbald. You know I need to have at least three dates before I propose. Besides, after Amelia I am not sure I can afford it."

Gordon recalled the events that had led up to Henry's latest divorce. There had been an Investment Awards ceremony at the Grosvenor Hotel and Aardvark had actually been nominated. Henry and Gordon had hosted a table for the team and it had been a riotous evening. The champagne had flowed and around midnight Henry had found himself in deep conversation with a partner (female, of course) at another venture capital firm. She had suggested that they carry on the party at a quiet cocktail bar around the corner and she and Henry had disappeared. He had come back the next day with reports that future collaboration between their two firms was guaranteed and that they had discussed a number of potential joint investments to pursue. Henry had found much to his pleasure that his companion had made all the running and performed, as he put it, what the newspapers would describe as a sex act on him at two am in a side street. It was perhaps not seemly for two executives to be behaving that way, he admitted, but it was late and they were both extremely drunk. Unfortunately for Henry, Amelia, his third wife, had already suspected he was not completely loyal to her, and had hired a private investigator to follow him.

"A downright, deceitful act showing no trust," he complained later to his divorce lawyer who, not unreasonably, pointed out that the photographs he had taken rather justified her suspicions.

"But can you tell that it's me from these?" queried Henry. "They are extremely dark."

"I think it is the H F-W embroidered on the pocket of your dinner jacket that gives it away," said his lawyer, showing Henry a blown-up version of one of the photos. "And there is no doubt what is going on, either. I think that the fact these were directly sent to me shows where Amelia's intentions lie. I will do my best to reach a settlement without ruining you."

"So, when does Susannah get in?" asked Henry, interrupting Gordon's reminiscences.

"Thursday at about midday," replied Gordon. "She's going to go directly to the hotel to freshen up – we've got her staying in the Whitehaven – and then she will come straight over here. I will introduce her to the team and we can review the plans for the offsite. I know she'll want to go through the status at Riverjack Crypto as well; that's the main focus for her coming over here."

"Jack's getting blown has certainly blown it down there," said Henry, laughing. "What a total clusterfuck."

"Funnily enough, that is exactly the word I used to describe it myself this morning," replied Gordon.

"It will be interesting to see if Peter can come up with any sort of credible rescue plan," said Henry. "I guess he knows what's riding on it."

"Sort this out or forget any chance of a partnership, you mean?"

"Mitch doesn't forgive or forget, even if we were inclined to."

"And frankly, I am not so inclined."

"I guessed as much," said Henry. "Rather unfortunate for young Peter. I like him, you know. Super-smart, hard-working, well-meaning. He deserves better. Excellent cricketer as well."

"He doesn't have your nose for a deal, though," said Gordon. "No way are we going to cut him the slack that you enjoy."

"Few get that sort of privilege," said Henry. "Anyway, I do think he is much better than that half-brain, Edwin. You know his latest suggestion: a micro-finance platform for illegal immigrants, would you credit it? He says the customer base in the UK and the rest of Europe is growing exponentially and they are all coming over here, looking for a better life. When I pointed out to him that the downside is that they are illegal and it is tough to make money from people with no money, he said that it was all about volume and that Brexit was just increasing the potential user base."

"Sounds like typical bloody Edwin." He paused and asked, "Anything else interesting in the pipeline? We could do with a distraction for Susannah at the offsite rather than just focusing on what is going wrong around here."

"Actually," said Henry. "I did have something I came across which has promise. Steve Miller from Westminster Capital Advisors has talked to me about it. I have got Edwin doing some preliminary research. Potentially really interesting: a sort of "Facebook for Pets" meets Tinder.

"A what?" spluttered Gordon, incredulous. "That sounds fucking ridiculous. Don't talk to me about another bloody social media start-up. The obsession people have with sharing every minute detail of their usually pathetic lives is beyond me."

"I tend to agree with you," said Henry. "But Facebook is extremely useful for staying in touch. How do you think my new Brazilian friend and I are planning our next assignation? Besides, any successful social media platform is a licence to print money. Online advertising growth carries on going through the roof."

"I know, I know," said Gordon. "But have you ever actually bought anything from an online advert, personalised or otherwise?"

"No," said Henry, "But we aren't the target market. It's the next generation, you know. Millennials buy anything and everything based on the latest trend. That's why Facebook revenues are skyrocketing quarter on quarter. It's the 21st century equivalent of 'Keeping up with the Joneses'."

"So what's this latest great idea?" asked Gordon. "Pet dating? The next billion dollar start-up, no doubt. What does it do? Owners get their pets an account, some algorithm pairs up likely owners and animals combos and the next things you know the owners are in bed with each other and the dogs are at it in the kennel?"

"Actually," said Henry, laughing, "You've got it in one."

"You have to be fucking kidding me, Henry! I was joking," exclaimed Gordon.

"And I am not, Gordon. I am actually deadly serious. We missed out on the major dating start-ups and the combination of sex and pets is perfect. People are willing to spend a lot of money on both, you know."

"True," said Gordon, reflecting on it. "I have a friend who spends more on his stupid Alsatian than on his mistress, and I know she is not cheap. But even in a growth market, I can't see it as something Mitch would approve of."

"Mitch will always be prepared to sacrifice principles if he can see he can make money from it. You know that. I have Edwin looking at the business model now. Frankly, I think we could be onto a winner. There are already players in the same space so the market exists. But I think the dating angle is a very nice one."

"You can't tell me it's a real business. It is a crazy idea."

"That's what you said about Skype, Gordon. And look what happened to them. Social media; pet ownership; dating – it's the perfect combination. You know, my intuition really says we are onto something."

Gordon stared at him.

"What's the bloody thing called?" he asked.

"Mixandmatchbypet.com. You know, I am right most of the time on these things. Trust me on this one, Gordon. Besides," Henry went on. "At the very least it is something to distract Susannah with at the offsite. Better to talk about the potential of Mixandmatchbypet than Riverjack Crypto's going down the drain."

"That is a very good point," said Gordon.

Henry smiled and left the office. He knew just how good he was as an investor but he did recognise his failings; it was not a lack of self-awareness but complete disregard for the consequences that was at the heart of his behaviour. In a perfect sequitur, he decided it was time he became better acquainted with Lisa. He nodded at Mary who judiciously ignored him as he sauntered past. She could not be flustered or impressed by anything Henry did and they both knew it. They had reached that conclusion years ago and therefore co-existed in mutually silent antipathy. Lisa, however, was definitely different sport, and he intended to enjoy himself.

He found Lisa in her office, staring at her computer and looking perplexed.

"Hello, Lisa," he said, in his most charming voice. She looked up nervously.

"Oh hi, er, Henry. Can I help you?"

"How have you enjoyed your first few days with Aardvark? Has Peter shown you the ropes?"

"The ropes? No, I don't think so. Where are they kept?"

"No," laughed Henry. "You know what I mean? Have you figured out how everything works?"

"Ah, I see," said Lisa. "Sorry! I didn't know what you were talking about. I am doing OK, thanks. Just trying to figure out the calendar system."

"Excellent," said Henry, leaning on Lisa's desk. "That's perfect because I wanted to talk to Peter about Riverjack Crypto and Edwin about Mixandmatchbypet. Do you know where they are?"

"Oh, I'm afraid they are both out. Peter's in Oxford at Riverjack Crypto and Edwin said he had to go out for a meeting. I was just checking his diary but I couldn't figure out where he was as someone just called for him as well."

Henry looked more closely at the screen she had been studying. All day was blocked and it said "Out of the Office – Offsite".

"I think you are looking at next week, Lisa", said Henry with a smile. "Although the offsite ends on Tuesday so I am not sure why Edwin has got Wednesday blocked off.

"Oh, that must be my mistake," mumbled Lisa. "I wasn't sure of the dates. Do you know what they are?"

"We start on Sunday in the pm then it finishes on Tuesday. You had better block all three days," said Henry.

Lisa tentatively opened up the diary entry and tried to change the dates; she felt intimidated by Henry being so close and struggled with the task. Henry leaned over, smiled at her again, and moved her hand gently off the mouse then clicked a couple of times. He looked at Edwin's diary entry which said "Coffee with Silvia from TAC ventures."

"I wonder what he is doing there," said Henry. "Anyway Lisa, can you let him know I want to see him when he gets back?"

"Yes, of course, Henry," said Lisa, relieved he didn't seem cross at her for her mistake with the calendar.

"By the way, I heard you had some problems with the coffee machine the other day. A bit unfortunate, that."

"Oh, I know. I didn't mean to. It just, you know, took me by surprise."

"I understand. These machines can be so very complicated. Perhaps I could give you a hand later if you need a lesson; a private lesson, you know. I have definitely mastered the art of the barista."

"Oh, yes, please," said Lisa, innocently. "That would be very kind. I'd really like to be able to make Peter a proper cappuccino. He's been such a good boss to me so far and that would be a lovely surprise."

Mary came in at that moment. She felt protective towards Lisa and knew better than to leave her at Henry's mercy for very long.

"Henry, I will show Lisa how to use the coffee machine, thanks very much," she said in a tone that allowed for no disagreement.

"Of course, Mary," said Henry, standing up. "I was just checking in with Lisa about Edwin and Peter but they are both out."

"Indeed? I guess they are doing their jobs," said Mary, acerbically. "And maybe you should let Lisa get on with hers."

"Absolutely. I was just helping her out, actually. Good deed for the day, you know."

"Well, I came in to remind you of your meeting. Your visitor is waiting for you," said Mary.

"Who is it?" Henry asked.

"Steve Miller, the advisor from Westminster Capital," said Mary. "Here's here to discuss Mixandmatchbypet. I've put him in the boardroom."

"Oh yes, of course. Tell him I will be right along, please, Mary" said Henry. "Nice to catch up, Lisa. Tell Edwin to join us as soon as he comes back. See you later." He walked out with a cheery wave.

"Lisa, my dear," said Mary. "Don't let Henry get under your skin or take any trouble from him."

"Trouble? He was just helping me, that's all. It was very kind of him," said Lisa.

"Well, you can have too much help from Henry; I'm just telling you, that's all. Anything you need, please ask me," said Mary with a frown.

"Of course," said Lisa. "Thanks very much."

Mary went out and Lisa turned back to her computer challenges, totally confused by what had just been going on.

Not long afterwards, Edwin came back into the office. He was relatively slight in stature, wore glasses which gave him a permanently bemused, owlish look, and never appeared at ease with himself. Unlike many of his contemporaries in the London technology investing market, he did not have a stellar academic background. He had a degree in Business and Accounting from a minor university and then, after a couple of years with a niche management consulting firm in Manchester, had managed to scrape through his MBA class at a relatively obscure Business School. He had applied to the major schools in the USA but had not even been asked for interview.

After rejection letters from London Business School, INSEAD, Warwick and Cranfield in the UK, he was getting desperate and had been both surprised and thrilled to be offered a place anywhere. The MBA he earned had not turned out to be the path to fame and fortune he had anticipated but at least it gave him some credibility as he decided to move into the world of venture capital. He felt he was extremely lucky four years earlier to be hired by Aardvark. Indeed, he was shrewd enough to realise that he probably had been taken on by Henry, who had been his primary interviewer, principally on the grounds that he was someone who could be ordered around with impunity.

Edwin ruefully reflected that Henry had been proven right. They both knew that Edwin's reputation didn't have the other London-based VC firms queuing up to poach him from Aardvark so he had to put up with Henry's and Gordon's overbearing criticism on a daily basis if he wanted to continue working in the industry. He had wondered about leaving to start his own firm but knew he would never be able to raise a fund; equally he was devoid of ideas in terms of starting a new technology company. He just marveled at the creativity entrepreneur after entrepreneur demonstrated in their pitches to secure investment capital. More often than not, he was unable to differentiate a potential golden goose from a total dog, as Henry would put it. However, apart from being a useful sidekick and punchbag, he did have the asset of being extremely diligent and hard-working. He did not really resent his situation and ultimately remained grateful for the opportunity.

As he walked in, Lisa looked up and said "Hello, Edwin. Henry's looking for you, I think."

"Ah OK, thanks Lisa. Another beating, I expect."

"I wouldn't think so, he's just been very kind to me," contested Lisa.

"I can't imagine why," said Edwin sardonically.

"I expect he just wants to make sure that I have settled in. He was particularly keen to help me with the coffee machine after the, er, unfortunate time I had."

"Of course. A private lesson?"

"He said so," replied Lisa.

"Naturally," said Edwin. He wondered why he could not muster the nerve to talk to the opposite sex with anything like the confidence needed to make him at least somewhat attractive to them. He knew that he would never win any girl over with looks alone. Given his job and the company he worked for, he should have been an alpha male, parading through the jungle with the lionesses following his every step, he thought, getting his animal habitats somewhat muddled. As it was, whenever he was out with friends he was always the shy one of the group, never saying a word and, more often than not, he left alone at the end of the evening as various couples, old and new, dispersed to continue getting to know each other better in more private surroundings. He even found himself unable to speak to Lisa with any real confidence. Perhaps he should go and see someone, a psychologist maybe or someone else who could help him.

He sighed and smiled at Lisa who looked back at him with her seemingly permanent worried expression. She wondered if she had made any more of Ms Frankel's 101 mistakes.

"Henry is in the boardroom, I think," said Lisa, uncertainly.

"Righto," said Edwin, and wandered off without enthusiasm.

Lisa watched him walk out of the office and turned back to her screen. She was trying to study the basics of Excel using a YouTube course Peter had recommended to her. It was, he had said, a very good way for her to invest her time.

"Using Excel is a key part of our work", he had explained the previous day, "And you really should get familiar with it. I don't expect you to be able to write macros or even build pivot tables, but you should be able to master the basics of a spreadsheet. I will need your help in the coming weeks on things where knowing the basics will be essential for sure."

So she had started to study but had not found it intuitive at all. It all seemed extremely complicated and she could not get the sample exercises to match the model answers presented at all. It was very confusing.

Edwin endured a torrid couple of hours with Henry where his experience, intelligence and investment acumen were belittled in equal measure. He had learned to switch off when Henry went into one of his long diatribes about the qualities necessary to be a really effective venture capitalist. However, once Edwin had taken him through his preliminary findings about the business model of Mixandmatchbypet.com, Henry was somewhat mollified.

"Well, Edwin," he commented. "You seem to have got that less arse over tit than you usually manage. Not a bad analysis, actually. We could do more on the overall market potential but the basics of the business model to support the planned growth seem pretty clear. What do you think, Steve?"

Steve had watched the proceedings with taciturn amusement. Now he sat up and pondered. "A couple of things to keep in mind, I think. I can ask Mixandmatchbypet what they have in terms of market data to help your investment case. Edwin, I will share whatever they can come up with."

Edwin nodded dutifully.

"But you know, Henry" he went on. "This deal is going to be particularly competitive. We are really confident of getting the money raised. It's going to be about valuation and value added by the selected investor."

"You always say that, Steve, about every deal you bring us," snorted Henry. "You know you like working with us because we move fast and we have the US connection – where else are you going to get that combination in London for them?"

Steve smiled and said nothing. Henry went on.

"And just to ensure the value add from Aardvark, I guarantee, if we win the deal, that Edwin," he paused and Edwin looked across at him, listening attentively. Perhaps this was going to be his big opportunity. He leaned forward, excited.

"That Edwin," continued Henry, "Will be kept as far away as possible from any interaction with the company going forward. That should guarantee there are no fuck-ups."

Steve and Henry laughed uproariously in a conspiratorial fashion. Edwin shrank back into his seat, looking deflated.

"Don't look so down-hearted, Edwin," said Henry. "We'll let you loose on an investment one day." He paused again. "After I've retired, of course."

He and Steve chuckled again.

"Right," said Steve, getting up. "Enough of this frivolity. It's a bit early but the sun is over the yardarm somewhere. Can I buy either of you a drink? And is Lisa around? She's flat-sharing with my girlfriend at the moment."

"Lisa?" said Henry somewhat incredulously.

"Yes. Absolutely. I was the one who recommended her to Peter. Didn't he tell you?"

"No. It's news to me," said Henry.

"Ah. I hope it's not a problem," said Steve. "How is she working out?"

"Well, she certainly has brightened up the place. Mary and Theresa are so bloody boringly efficient. Lisa on the other hand; I mean, did you hear about her encounter with the coffee machine?"

"No," said Steve. "What happened?"

Henry related the details of the incident, much to Steve's amusement; even Edwin, who had heard the story several times, still found it funny and laughed out loud, for once not sycophantically.

"That is bloody hilarious," said Steve. "Wait till I tell Sam. She will howl. Is Lisa in now? Let's invite her along for that drink."

"Yes, she's in her office," said Edwin.

"Excellent," said Steve. "Coming, Henry?"

Henry looked at his watch. He had to make it across to the W to meet his date. She was on the first flight out in the morning to Dubai, and had imposed a 10 pm curfew on him, so he did not want to delay any further.

"Actually," he said, "Unfortunately I have a prior commitment. But you go ahead with Edwin. He might learn something."

Edwin looked at him, wide-eyed and as always, hurt and dismayed.

"Sounds good," said Steve. "Come on, Edwin. Look sharp. Let's find Lisa and then retire to the Bunch of Grapes."

Steve and Edwin left Henry to his devices, and headed over to Lisa's office where they found her still engrossed in her Excel course.

"Hello, Lisa," said Steve. "I've come to escort you home, via the pub, of course."

Lisa looked up in astonishment.

"What on earth are you doing here? Have you really come to take me home? Was that Samantha's idea? Did she tell you about the trouble I was having on the Tube?" she said in a flurry.

"Not exactly," said Steve. "But you can tell me all about it over a drink with Edwin. Actually, you remember that I was the reason you work at Aardvark in the first place."

"Oh yes, of course," said Lisa, thoroughly embarrassed to have forgotten the connection.

"You'd totally forgotten, hadn't you?" said Steve.

"No, no," said Lisa, mortified. "I'm really grateful and, I, er, love it and it's, you know, going, like, er, really well, I mean," she spluttered to a miserable halt.

"Relax, no worries, Lisa, I'm teasing you," said Steve. "It's all good and it will look even better with a drink in our hands. Come on, both of you. It's on me. Edwin, pay attention, as you might just learn the secret of venture investing, at least after the third pint!"

Truth to tell the first part of their time in the pub was awkward. Edwin did not want to say anything that could be reported back to Henry as being either naïve or stupid; Lisa was shy and preoccupied with whatever unconscious mistake she might not know she was making. But after a couple of Bacardi and cokes and pints for her companions, she and Edwin relaxed so that the conversation flowed. Once more she did not understand any of the technical discussions but found that she liked Edwin very much, not least because he clearly had as little confidence as her, and Steve, of course, because he was extremely handsome, charming and attentive. In fact, he reminded her a lot of Tom in the office.

After three hours, Steve escorted a decisively drunk Lisa into an Uber and they headed home together. Edwin staggered off to the Tube muttering about having an early start and how he had to get to bed. She told him about what she thought about Tom.

"Tom is definitely a great guy," said Steve. "I really like him. He's single, too, you know. Just went through quite a traumatic break-up, I believe."

"Really?" asked Lisa, realising even with the multiple drinks working their way through her, that she probably was betraying too much enthusiasm in her voice.

"Absolutely. And he definitely needs a nice bit of skirt. Would that be you, then Lisa?" chuckled Steve with a grin.

"Oh no, no, I mean, he is very handsome but he's a colleague. I couldn't possibly, I mean, well," she faltered. "Could I?"

"No one's going to judge you, Lisa" said Steve, knowing that that would be exactly what everyone would do. He decided he should be kind to her. After all, she was Samantha's cousin and, as he was getting well and truly smitten with Sam, he did feel somewhat protective towards her. "But I would just take it slowly. Maybe give him some indications about how you feel and perhaps have a drink together one day. But not as many as you've had tonight," he added, as Lisa closed her eyes and her head lolled on his shoulder.

They made it back to the apartment and Steve rang the bell. Sam buzzed them in and Steve found that he was basically carrying Lisa upstairs. He paused outside the door and waited for Sam to open it, which she did, wearing some extremely alluring bra and panties under a leopard-skin patterned silk dressing-gown.

"What have you done to Lisa?" asked Samantha. "Have you let her get out of control?"

"Relax," said Steve. "She enjoyed herself. I will just put her to bed and then come and deal with you."

"I take that as a promise, not a threat," said Samantha, and flashed him her underwear. "And I have a treat for you. That present I bought for you arrived today. Wrapped in brown paper, you know."

"Aha. That is very good news," smiled Steve, licking his lips. "I downloaded the app today in anticipation."

Samantha giggled as Steve brushed past her, still carrying Lisa. He took her into her bedroom and laid her gently on her bed, wondering whether he should undress her. The thought excited him for a moment but he disqualified it as inappropriate for any number of reasons, so he just pulled the duvet over her and crept out. He heard Samantha shout out from the bedroom, "Hurry up! I'm ready for you to play with". He walked quickly across to the bedroom door and pulled out his iPhone; opening up the app in question as he walked in; he pressed a button and heard a delighted squeal.

CHAPTER SIX

The next day, Gordon was buried in a couple of spreadsheets of his own, looking at share structures for another potential investment he had been working on. However, his mind was not on his work and continually turned towards San Francisco, Susannah's impending arrival and his thwarted plans. He glanced frequently at his watch, thinking about what time it was in San Francisco and what time Susannah would be leaving for the airport. Not for a while, he thought. With the eight hours time difference it would be after midnight in the UK before her plane took off. What time was it over there? "About 7am," he mused out loud. "She will just be getting up". He sent her a brief email to wish her a safe flight then dragged himself back reluctantly back to his work.

Susannah herself was not having a particularly easy time of it. The previous day had been highly productive, although Mitch had been slightly surprised when she came into the office, as he had expected her to be en route to London already. She explained she had agreed with Gordon that she would get over for Thursday and he seemed satisfied enough with that. Nevertheless, she had been able to clear most of her immediate "To Do" list so was grateful for the extra day. She was also much more confident in her knowledge of the Riverjack Crypto target market having spent a constructive hour talking to her contact about how global payments were evolving and the relevant market opportunity for a cryptocurrency play.

However, that morning Mitch had texted to ask her to represent him at a breakfast meeting early at Menlo Park (where many of the main private equity and venture capital firms in the Bay Area have their offices) with a potential investor in the new fund Aardvark was raising; he had double-booked himself, he wrote, and as she had not yet left for London, he needed her to cover for him. She had planned to pack in the morning so the message caused her something of a panic as she rushed to get ready for the meeting with no time left to think about dealing with clothes for her trip. Then she had to head down to see another of their portfolio companies which was based beyond San Jose, more than fifty miles south of San Francisco, for another emergency meeting that seemingly could not be postponed. It was a significant drive from there back up to the city at any time of day and having pushed that meeting back by a couple of hours to accommodate the investor breakfast, she calculated that she would be probably be very tight for time.

Her flight was at 4.30pm and because she found herself already running late, she realised she was going to be cutting it very fine indeed. In the end, the journey on Highway 101 back up to San Francisco went at slightly faster than its usual snail's pace but the traffic still meant she only arrived back in the city at about 2.30pm. She rushed to pull clothes together and threw them without much thought into her suitcase. She ordered an Uber and knew she was in trouble as it was already after 3pm.

As the Uber arrived, she threw her suitcase into the back and said breathlessly to the driver, "Can you get over to the airport as quickly as possible? I have my flight to London in less than ninety minutes and I can't afford to miss it."

"Certainly, pretty lady," replied the driver, the description somewhat surprising Susannah. "I am from Bangkok and I know how to drive fast. The traffic never stopped me there and it won't stop me here." The car surged forward and the driver barely slowed down for the Stop sign at the end of Susannah's road, tyres screaming in protest as he gunned the car around the corner and set course for the airport. She grabbed for her seatbelt and fastened it, just in time, as the driver had to brake hard to avoid a bus that seemed to be on the wrong side of the road until Susannah realised it was actually their car that had veered too far over to the other side.

Susannah was a seasoned traveler and usually took no notice of taxi rides, typically passing the time doing email on her mobile or attending a conference call en route to the hotel or airport in whichever city she found herself in. However, even she had to admit that she had never experienced a journey like this one, particularly in the US. She rather suspected that her driver was high on something that would incur a death sentence in Thailand as he was driving faster than was at all safe; at least, it felt that way. Making the flight suddenly did not seem to be worth the risk.

The car itself was a Renault or Citroen, she thought. It was very spacious inside with a high roof and a lot of glass. The problem was it was not designed for this rally-type driving as its road-holding ability was not up to the task. As a result the manoeuvres caused Susannah, her suitcase and nearly the contents of her stomach to lurch from one side to the other with more twists and turns than the worst ride the Disney Imagineers had ever come up with. The driver roared up the ramp onto the freeway leading south out of the city towards the airport, cutting across one car and then weaving through the extremely narrow space between two trucks. He seemed totally oblivious to any angry sounds of horns he left in his wake and, even when Susannah urged him to slow down just a little, all he said in response was "You won't miss flight because of me, pretty lady."

Susannah felt that it was probably best just to stay quiet, hang on and pray that they made it in one piece. She attributed the fact that they did to a combination of the blessing of the Gods and the driver's evidently real experience in Bangkok traffic. As they careered towards the international terminal departures level, he asked, "Which airline?"

"Anywhere here is fine," said Susannah, who decided not to push her luck having survived thus far.

This statement prompted the driver to stand on the brakes and slide into a vacant space by an entrance to the terminal. "You see, pretty lady, on time for flight."

He looked at her hopefully. She glanced at her watch and realised that despite their record-breaking run, it was less than an hour to departure. She figured that check-in must be closing but also thought that an offering to the same Gods who had acted to protect her so far might just do the trick so she handed the driver a twenty dollar extra tip with the words, "Indeed. I hope you make it back to the city alive."

"No problem," called the driver after her as she got out, dragging her suitcase behind her.

"Maybe, maybe not," muttered Susannah.

She focused on the immediate problem of making her flight. The British Airways check-in desks were of course at the far end of the terminal from where she had abandoned her Uber and, as she got there, the last BA representative was hanging up a sign which read "Check-in for BA012 to London now closed".

She ran up breathlessly and said, and in her most polite, desperate voice, said, "Please, please tell me I am not too late to get the flight to London."

"I am afraid you are, madam," came the reply from the man in a suitably British accent, who did not look at her and busied himself with some imaginary task behind the check-in counter.

"But I have to catch the flight. I am traveling business class; that must make a difference," begged Susannah.

"Business class was over-sold, madam, and is full," came the stern reply.

"I have to get to London," said Susannah, urgently. "And I have a confirmed business class ticket." She looked at his name badge. "Please, Michael. Is there nothing you can do?"

The man looked at her, sighed and said, "Please show me your ticket and passport."

"Oh, thank you," said Susannah, handing them over.

He looked at her documents, tapped on the computer keyboard in front of him in that inexplicable way all airline check-in personnel do and stared at the screen with a perplexed look on his face. He was silent for a few moments and then asked, "Do you have any bags to check in?"

"Just one," said Susannah and simultaneously put it on up on the scale as if to reinforce the fact that she would make her flight. As she did so she noticed that it was much lighter than usual and wondered what she had forgotten. "Never mind," she thought. "I will buy whatever I need in London. I just hope I can get there."

The clerk seemed to take an age to process her check-in; he made a call and spoke inaudibly into the telephone. He turned to Susannah,

"Good news and bad, madam," he said. "The good is I can get you to London this evening and your bag as well. The bad is I only have a coach seat left. It is at least an aisle seat but it is the last row. Would you like it?"

"But what about my confirmed business class ticket?"

The man laughed at her. "In the airline business, nothing is confirmed until you have a boarding pass in your hand, madam, and even then we reserve the right to change our mind at your inconvenience. I am afraid we were already overbooked in Club World so, when you didn't show, you won the prize of being the first passenger to be bumped off the flight. Coach at the back is all that I have to offer. I need to know," he looked at his watch and paused, "In the next ten seconds."

"Premium Economy at least?" said Susannah hopefully.

"Five seconds."

"Ok you win. Give me the seat. But my bag had better make it to London."

"Of course, madam", said Michael. He asked the standard security questions, tapped a couple more keys on his computer and attached her luggage label to her suitcase. He pressed a button and the conveyor took the suitcase away into the bowels of the airport.

"I hope there's nothing in there you value," he said, looking at her seriously, "because the chances of your ever seeing that bag again are as high as the Cubs winning the World Series."

"But you said…," she started.

The clerk interrupted her, "My little joke, madam. I could tell you wouldn't be a baseball fan. The Cubs won the World Series two years ago. Your bag will be in London and will probably have a ride that is a lot more comfortable than yours. I wouldn't make my dog fly economy on British Airways. Good luck!" Susannah had no idea what to say to this. He smiled and reached down for something under his desk. He handed her two vouchers.

"You will need these," he said. "The first one gets you through fast track security; the second one access to our lounge as a guest – we can at least give you that perk of your now defunct business class ticket. Not that you will have time to use it, as the flight's boarding shortly. I would hurry if I were you." With that, he turned away and disappeared through a door set in the wall behind the check-in desks.

Susannah gathered her belongings and literally ran for security. Fast track actually proved for once to be true to its name and she made it through without any problems. As she got to the lounge and showed her pass, the hostess at the front desk told her the flight was on the final call, and she had to go immediately to the gate.

"I need a drink before I go," said Susannah. "It's been one hell of a day so far and I am stuck right at the back of the bus."

The hostess looked at her unusually flustered appearance and said, "Go on, you do look as though you could do with a glass of champagne. I will tell you a secret: they always call 'final call' when there is actually about ten minutes to go. The gate is just next door. You've got about two minutes before they start threatening to take your bag off the plane but you can grab yourself something."

Susannah rushed into the empty lounge. There were two staff at the bar dressed in British Airways uniform and surreptitiously drinking champagne. They started guiltily when Susannah came in.

She marched over the to the bar and said, "Give me that!"

Without standing on ceremony she grabbed the bottle from one of the men, who looked completely startled, and poured herself a drink into the nearest glass she could find which happened to be a beer tankard. She downed it in one; poured herself another and did the same thing. A final serving followed.

"Thanks," she said, as both men just stared at her, totally flummoxed. "You know, it tastes just as good out of a beer glass. I don't have time to tell you how much I needed that. Have one on me." She smiled at them sweetly, handed the bottle back to one of the men, turned and hurried back to the gate. When she got there she was not surprised to find that she was the last to board; she was, however, surprised to find the check-in clerk waiting for her.

"Hello again," she said, brightened up by the champagne.

"Do you make a habit of being late for everything, madam?" he asked, sardonically.

Susannah ignored him. "I don't suppose a Business Class seat freed up in the interim?" she asked hopefully.

The clerk laughed again. "We are so oversold on this flight that we were wondering if we could put seatbelts into the toilets and use them. Consider yourself lucky. Boarding pass and passport, please."

"You guys make United look customer-centric, you know that" retorted Susannah as she handed her documents over, her mood suddenly switching to anger due in equal measure to frustration and alcohol.

The clerk checked them meticulously, apparently just for show, scanned the boarding pass and then handed them back to Susannah.

"To fly to serve, madam. Have a nice flight."

With a grunt, Susannah headed down the gangway to board. She looked longingly at the sign for Business Class passengers pointing to the upper deck of the A380 aircraft but steeled herself and headed to the Economy section on the lower deck. Immediately after she boarded an authoritarian voice said over the tannoy, "That's boarding FINALLY complete. Cabin Crew, secure doors and cross check", and she heard the door close behind her.

The air hostess looked at her scathingly and said "Welcome aboard, madam" in a very British accent which, despite the circumstances, made Susannah smile. "Your seat is to the left, far end of the aircraft. Please hurry up. As you just heard, you are the last passenger on board and we are about to push back."

Susannah nodded and headed down the aisle, enduring a number of hard stares and tuts as she walked past. She smiled to herself at the restraint of the British; if she had risked causing a delay to a United flight she would have been roundly and directly abused instead. She got to the end and found that at least she did have the aisle seat as promised. Next to her was a young girl who was clearly traveling with her boyfriend, as they were engaged in a passionate embrace. He was leaning over the girl, mouths intertwined as they moaned; his elbow was resting on the armrest of Susannah's seat, encroaching into her space. Susannah looked at the two of them and then opened several of the overhead lockers to place her laptop bag there. The lockers were completely full. As she was standing there, wondering what to do, a booming British voice came over the tannoy once more. "Ladies and Gentlemen, please take your seats as quickly as possible as we are ready to leave and any delay in our departure from the gate may make us lose our take-off slot."

Susannah realised she was the only person standing in the entire cabin. A stewardess came up to her and said aggressively, "You are delaying the flight, Miss. You need to sit down, now."

Susannah resignedly forced her bag under the seat in front of her then sat down with a prim "Excuse me" as she firmly pushed the elbow away. The young man extracted his tongue from his girlfriend's mouth and said in a strong London accent, "Alright, alright. Keep your 'air on".

He sat back into his seat and his girlfriend said to Susannah, "Just 'aving a bit of fun. I know you Americans don't understand that." The two of them looked at each other and giggled.

Susannah sighed without saying anything and then reached down for her Bose headphones. There was not very much legroom but at least she could block out everything around her for the next eleven hours. A further announcement was made but she could not hear anything except a muffled announcement – the noise cancellation was working beautifully. She closed her eyes and then almost immediately opened them again as she was tapped on the shoulder by the same air hostess who had told her to sit down.

"Excuse me, Miss. Please remove your personal headphones for the safety briefing."

Susannah looked at her and decided that compliance was her only option – she really did not want to be manhandled off the flight and arrested for being a "difficult passenger". She reluctantly turned her attention to the safety video. She knew that airlines were always trying harder to get passengers to pay attention to the pre-flight briefing and it looked as if British Airways had decided to brighten up the otherwise dull routine with a whole load of comedians and actors. She found that she only recognised Michael Caine in the whole thing and that most of the humour rather passed her by. Finally it was done and she reached for her headphones again. Just as she was doing so, she heard the suave, urbane, and reassuring voice of the captain coming over the tannoy.

"Good evening, Ladies and Gentlemen, Boys and Girls, my name is Captain Fairbald and I am delighted to welcome you on board British Airways flight 12 to London."

Despite herself, Susannah sat up at the mention of his name. It seemed quite a coincidence and, as the pilot continued his standard spiel, her mind drifted to Gordon and their meeting in Las Vegas earlier that year.

Mitch had decided that Aardvark should have a significant presence at the investor conference taking place there. He, other partners and staff from the San Francisco office, including Susannah, had flown there en masse and Gordon had joined them. Gordon was not pleased at being dragged over from London at relatively short notice and was not hiding his displeasure.

He said to Susannah on their first night as they met downstairs in Le Central bar at the Paris hotel before dinner, "I bloody hate Vegas. Every time I come here I remember why I say I will never come back here again. It's the worst of America: so vulgar, gauche and fake. It's all glitz without the glamour; even the casino workers look totally bored. As for the shows, you wouldn't catch me dead going to watch bloody 'Donnie and Marie' croon 'Puppy Love'."

Susannah actually agreed with him for the most part but found his manner so overbearing and pompous that she felt as though she had to defend Vegas and indeed her country.

"Actually, the quality of spectacle here rivals anything on the planet, you know. And yes, the focus is on making money but it is designed to create fantastic memories for everyone who comes here. For some, it's about recreating scenes from 'The Hangover'. For others, it is about just entering a fantasy land for a few days where they can forget about real life for a while."

"And lose everything they have and throw themselves out of their hotel window," scoffed Gordon. "I mean, look at those girls over there. They look so fake: false eyelashes; false smiles; false tits. Everything is so overblown here. I mean, some people go to the Venetian then come back and think they've visited Venice."

"True," admitted Susannah. "But you have to admit it is the only place on the planet where you can dine al fresco indoors. The recreation of the canal and St Mark's Square is quite something."

"Not if you have seen the real thing," snorted Gordon. "I expect none of the people staying there have ever set foot in Europe. And take this bloody Paris Hotel. Mitch wants us to dine in the imitation Jules Verne restaurant up the fake Eiffel Tower. I mean, it's not exactly like the actual place. Not that you'd know, I expect," he added, disparagingly.

"Actually, Gordon, I've spent a lot of time in Europe and have indeed dined in the real Le Jules Verne and been to St Mark's Square," Susannah retorted. "I think it is because I have seen the actual places that I can appreciate the imitations here. They are trying to create an experience for their guests and I think they do it pretty well."

She turned away from him and took a long pull at her drink. She turned back and saw Gordon looking at her with surprise and a very different level of interest. No doubt, she thought, he had expected her to be someone who had thrived on her looks alone. He probably thought that her undergraduate degree (in Business Psychology) had been a complete non-subject and that she had talked her way into Harvard to do her MBA by luck and looks rather than academic prowess. She had evidently surprised him by being able to hold her own. Well, now he would know there was more to her than he assumed and that she wasn't one of those Americans who thought going to Tijuana and Hawaii made them well travelled. A clean kill, she decided, and had another slurp of her martini. She rather spoiled the effect of her victory by dropping the olive down her blouse. "Damn," she said to herself. "I hope the arrogant SOB hasn't noticed." She looked up and saw Gordon smiling in a supercilious way which meant that he clearly had and was enjoying her embarrassment.

At that point Mitch arrived and they went up to the restaurant for dinner. Susannah had been there once before and remembered that the quality of food did actually get close to its French equivalent – just as well because, at those prices, if the dining experience was not perfect, the social trolls would have it all over Facebook, Instagram, TripAdvisor and anywhere else they could think of and the French Maitre D' would get it in the neck from customers who knew how to complain. Her memory of her last visit was tainted, as her boyfriend at the time, who she had vaguely wondered about marrying, had told her that the Vegas trip he had hoped to bring them together was in fact making him decide that they were not right for each other; that he was not ready to commit; that he wanted a girl who was less self-assured and more dependent on him; and that finally even though he was not ready to settle down, he would welcome an open relationship as he liked Susannah a lot. Laughably, he had suggested that they still go back to the hotel together and reset their relationship on his terms. She had politely declined the offer, left him to settle the bill, rapidly returned to their room to pack and flown out that night.

That experience had certainly put her on her guard, principally against herself; she had recognised that she had a habit of treating every date as her Prince Charming and actually still rather hoped that one day she would be swept off her feet, even while knowing that fairytales never materialised in real life. This was her first time back in Vegas since then. It was also some time since she had slept with anyone and far from being happy with her spinster lifestyle with Ginger, she was clear that self-induced orgasms were not nearly as much fun as those attained in company.

Mitch was on good form. He was excited about a couple of their portfolio companies that had recently received enormous offers to be acquired and he thought that the investor conference they were attending had real promise in terms of building their international network. He ordered an eye-wateringly expensive bottle of Mouton Rothschild and then another, complimenting the sommelier on the recommendation. It seemed to Susannah that the three of them relaxed into each other's company over the course of the evening. She even started to appreciate Gordon's British sense of humour and was certainly enjoying his accent. He was clearly a successful, experienced investor and he seemed to be treating her with less condescension now.

Over coffee Mitch set out his expectations for the conference.

"Here's what I want you and Susie to focus on," he said to Gordon, who noticed that she flinched every time that Mitch said her name that way: "Build out the international connections beyond London. We need to start sourcing deals, particularly out of Singapore and Mumbai. Work closely together on this over the next couple of days. I am going to focus on the New York set. We'll catch up each night during the conference and see how we are getting on."

The conference itself proved to be a great success. Aardvark already enjoyed a good reputation in Silicon Valley and Susannah and Gordon were able to create excellent connections with investors, advisors and bankers from the Far East. This was a new market for them but, in the last two or three years, the Singapore government had really supported the technology start-up community there, with many initiatives to encourage entrepreneurs. India, too, was starting to boast a thriving early stage ecosystem although, in typical fashion, it involved far greater chaos and much less organisation than their Singaporean rivals. The connections they made promised to lead to a significant uptick in their deal flow and even Gordon ended up being pleased that he had made the effort to come over.

After the gala dinner on the last night, Mitch had declared himself thoroughly satisfied with the conference. One of the other Aardvark attendees had suggested that they all go to a show and had got tickets for the extremely risqué 'Zumanity' Cirque du Soleil show in the New York New York hotel. By this time Gordon had relented in his views on Vegas entertainment; more surprisingly he and Susannah had actually found themselves liking each other and enjoying each other's company over the previous couple of days. The show was advertised as an erotic, graphic and a revolutionary sexual experience, and it did not disappoint. She observed with a sardonic smile that Gordon found himself having to cross his legs on several occasions, turning away from Susannah to hide his growing erection. She was not ashamed to enjoy it as well, unembarrassed as she laughed, gasped and applauded with as much enthusiasm as any of the drunk Bachelorette party attendees. The outrageously priced bottle of champagne Gordon had ordered only added to the occasion and party atmosphere.

Afterwards as other Aardvark staff headed off to different parts of Vegas, Gordon suggested a nightcap in the Rhum Bar of the Mirage Hotel, where they were staying. He also proposed walking back as the evening was extremely pleasant; he confessed that for the first time in his life he was enjoying the absurd over-the-top brilliance of the famous Las Vegas strip. They walked past the Bellagio and Caesar's Palace and discussed the different movies that had been set in Las Vegas. They agreed that their favourite had been *Ocean's Eleven;* that the two sequels had been almost as good; that *"The Hangover"* had had its moments but the sequels were relatively dull repeats; that *What Happens in Vegas* was a mindless RomCom even though it had made them laugh and that *"Leaving Las Vegas"* was just depressing even if it was moving.

They turned into the Mirage hotel, walked past the volcano that erupted spectacularly for every couple getting married there and into the Rhum Bar. There is no day or night in Las Vegas so even after midnight, the bar was absolutely alive with people's laughing, joking, eyeing each other up, speculating on what could happen, and of course drinking.

Gordon fought his way to the bar, bought two Moscow Mules and saw that Susannah had managed to find a table.

"How did you do that?" he asked. "I'm impressed. It looked like there was no way to find anywhere to sit."

"Years of experience in American college student bars," she replied. "You look for the couple who, er, how shall I put it, seem like they both agree they need to go somewhere more private pretty much immediately and just hover. I am fairly good at reading the signs and those two" – she pointed at a young couple who were walking hurriedly into the hotel, arm in arm – "were just too obvious. She was evidently on heat and he was clearly barely able to hide his erection – you know, Gordon, crossing your legs doesn't really hide the bulge."

She laughed out loud and sat down. He stared at her and for the first time in as long as he could remember, blushed. He could not believe that he found himself stammering.

"Well, er, I mean, you know, it was, er, very hot and, well, those girls were doing extremely erotic things."

"No worries," said Susannah. "Believe me I had the same reaction. When they got that woman from the audience up on stage, well, I was just glad it wasn't me."

"Too bloody right," said Gordon, relaxing and grinning and sitting down.

They both had a sip of their drinks and then Gordon asked, "So, this isn't your first trip to Vegas, obviously. But if I may be so bold, I noticed you were less than comfortable when we had dinner with Mitch in Jules Verne the other night. Bad memories?"

Susannah stared at him. Had he really been that perceptive? That was impressive and, again, it led her to think differently about him. That pompous English exterior certainly belied the man underneath, she thought to herself. She added as an afterthought, "Christ, I must be drunk. I am starting to think like I'm in a Jane Austen novel. And if I am Elizabeth Bennet, who are you, Gordon? Mr Darcy or Mr Wickham?"

She told him her story about the former boyfriend.

He listened intently and said, "What a stupid bastard. He could have had you and he blew it."

Susannah smiled and said, "I'm not sure I am that much of a catch. Career woman; cat; girlfriends who will pull any man I date apart."

"And extremely defensive about taking compliments, I notice," said Gordon.

Susannah for once turned her eyes away sheepishly; he really was a perceptive bastard!

Their conversation flowed and Gordon went to fetch another round of drinks. He came back and Susannah saw him surreptitiously observing her as he waited at the bar. She could read the signs and knew she had to make a decision: she was pretty sure that at a certain point, probably sooner rather than later, he was going to make an indecent proposal – after all, she had more than enough experience to tell what was going on in his mind – and she had to decide whether she would accept if he did or whether she would take herself out of the firing line and save them both the embarrassment of facing each other in the morning after she had refused him. As he turned back towards her, drinks in hand, she made a decision. Rather than getting up and declaring she was tired so would not have that drink after all, she smoothed her skirt down and smiled at him. She wondered whether he could read what she had been thinking in the last few minutes as he smiled back.

"Are you an inveterate people-watcher?" he asked as he sat down next to her,

"I admit I am," she said, laughing. "I find you can learn so much about human nature just by watching interactions in a bar – particularly at 1 in the morning. Hopes, aspirations, stratagems, intentions, relationships good and bad; they are all here right in front of your eyes. It becomes a habit but then I reckon it has served me pretty well in boardrooms as well."

Gordon took a sip of his drink. After a moment she guessed that he had decided the best way forward was not to think anything through too deeply and just to let it flow.

"You see over there," continued Susannah, enjoying the chemistry between them and pointing to a couple who were sitting at the bar, saying nothing to each other and both studying their phones intently. "Those two are either so comfortable with each other that even in the world's most exciting city they can play on social media without any issue, or so bored with each other that this place is having no impact and they will be," she paused and looked closely at their hands to see if they were wearing rings, "contacting divorce lawyers when they get home."

"Which do you think it is?"

At that point the man said something; the woman laughed out loud and the man brushed her hand with his and put his arm around her waist while simultaneously pocketing his phone and asking for the bill.

"I'd say that Vegas magic is working its charm," said Susannah.

"Now over there," she continued, pointing to a group of men at a table at the far side of the bar, "Are three friends who have come to Vegas to try to recreate "The Hangover' and it hasn't quite worked out as they liked. They are drinking, laughing, pretending to have a good time but they are all wondering where all the girls are and how they can get laid – each is probably trying to assess what stories the others would tell about him back home if they were to pick up a hooker."

"A dilemma, indeed," said Gordon.

They both fell silent a moment and simultaneously picked up their glasses, drank and put them down again in perfect synchronisation. They looked at each other and laughed.

"And what," said Gordon, "If you were sitting over there, watching, what would you say about us?"

"Now that," said Susannah, "Is a very leading question. I think I would clearly see two colleagues who had just finished attending a conference having a final drink before leaving in the morning."

"I see," said Gordon. "Nothing more?"

"Would you want it to be more?" said Susannah, looking at him, quizzically.

"That depends," said Gordon.

"On what?" replied Susannah with an amused tone. "I think you should always do what you want, Gordon."

"Well, right now, I want someone to be standing by us, watching us, waiting for the person she is with to fetch drinks and realising that our seats will be free in a moment as we are about to leave.

Together," he added, after a pause.

Susannah looked at him, took a large pull of her drink and said, "That almost sounds like an inappropriate proposal you are making, Gordon."

She looked at him, eyes sparkling with mirth, interrogating him.

Gordon looked back, his own eyes twinkling. "That almost sounds like an inappropriate answer, Susannah" he said.

She laughed, finished her drink, put the glass back onto the table and got up. Gordon followed suit and they stood there a moment, looking at each other.

"Just as long what happens in Vegas stays in Vegas and does not make it onto Facebook, Instagram or the front page of the San Francisco Chronicle," she said.

Without another word, he took her hand and led her back into the hotel. They walked quickly through the casino to the large bank of elevators at the back. They stood there, still hand in hand, without saying anything, and stepped into an elevator.

"Your place or mine?" giggled Susannah.

"I have a suite on the top floor," said Gordon.

"Just as long as there are no piles of dirty underwear lying around," said Susannah with another giggle.

The elevator doors closed and they were alone. Without another word Gordon stepped forward, took Susannah into his arms and kissed her.

He was tender and assertive at the same time; an incredibly enticing combination, she thought, as she felt his tongue flick at hers. She pressed herself against him and sighed very softly.

"Dirty underwear is all carefully hidden, I promise," Gordon breathed in her ear.

"That's good," she whispered as she felt him nibble her ear.

The elevator reached its destination floor and they pulled apart briefly. Gordon ran his hand lightly over her neck and down the small of her back as she stepped out. He followed her, took her hand again and led her to the door of his suite.

He pressed the cardkey against the lock; the door did not open and the light on the lock blinked red. He did it again and still nothing happened.

"You have to be bloody kidding me," said Gordon. He reached into his jacket pocket, pulled out his wallet and his spare key. He tried again but to no avail.

Susannah watched him with silent mirth in her eyes,

"Here, let me try," she said. "It's all in the wrist, you know. I would have thought you would have had the knack."

She flicked at the lock, it turned green and the door opened. She turned back to Gordon and handed him the key.

"You see," she said. "It's all about technique."

"I'll show you technique," he said, and pulled her into his room.

The suite itself was spacious with thick shag pile carpet, a broad leather sofa at one end of the main room facing a large television set and chairs arranged around a glass table in the middle. The curtains were open and, broad, full length windows looked out over the Las Vegas strip, stretching in its neon glory away from them.

Susannah separated from Gordon, ran to the window and stared out.

"That is absolutely beautiful," she said. "What a fabulous view."

Gordon stepped up behind her, and put one hand on her pert, athletic buttocks and the other around her, cupping her breast.

"I can only agree," he breathed and kissed her neck

"I see," she jokingly admonished him and turned to face him again, kissing him.

He pulled her tight to him and manoeuvred her onto the sofa. They sank intertwined into the soft leather upholstery.

Gordon reached for a remote control and pressed a button. The lights that had come on automatically when they had entered the room dimmed, casting strange shadows on the walls.

"That was very clever," said Susannah. "How did you manage to do that?"

"I will show you just how clever I can be," said Gordon softly.

He eased her out of the jacket that she was wearing and started to unbutton her blouse.

"I suppose I will let you get to first base on our first date," said Susannah.

"Oh, I was rather expecting to hit a six," replied Gordon.

"A what?" asked Susannah.

"Ah, a cricket term, you know" he said, as he finished the last button, pushed her blouse back and leant forward to kiss her breasts. "It means hitting a home run, roughly speaking."

"I never understood that game," she said as she felt his tongue on her warm skin and rested her head back on the soft upholstery. "It really lasts five days and then it ends in a tie?"

"Far too subtle for you Americans," said Gordon, reaching behind her to unclip her bra. She barely felt his hands on her and there was no pressure as her straps fell away and he pulled it away from her. His hands brushed her nipples which were rock hard with desire.

"You got past first base pretty fast, Mr," said Susannah. "How did you learn to take a bra off like that? Most men fumble, wrestle, yank your boobs this way and that and kill the moment before they start."

Gordon kissed her skin and started to work his way down her smooth stomach.

"A friend and I at university bought a mannequin and every type of bra imaginable," he whispered by means of explanation, pausing to kiss her skin every few words. "We practiced for hours with the different fastenings until we could deal with every kind in the dark. We kept it quiet so that no one knew what we were doing. Buying the underwear was the tricky bit. We did it when we were London, so no one saw us but we still got some very strange looks from the shop assistants. But it was more than worth it; over the years it's a party trick that has come in handy."

"I bet," said Susannah. "With fingers as delicate as that I bet you get to second and third base no problem at all."

Gordon just smiled and undid the zipper on the side of her skirt. She lifted up her hips uncomplainingly and wriggled out of it, letting it fall to the floor. Gordon lent over, stroked the inside of her thighs and kissed her just on her panties. She sighed and enjoyed his touch and the feel of him on her skin.

He stood up and reached for her hand. She stood before him, semi-naked in the translucent light and kissed him again. She started to unbutton his shirt and it fell to the floor. Frankly his corpulent stomach was not his most attractive aspect. He sensed her hesitation and pulled her hand towards the bedroom.

"I may be a little large but I promise I am as light as a feather," he said.

She smiled although she wondered if he could keep this promise. She did not want to get flattened under his weight but was so turned on that she was prepared to go along with him. She looked down at his trousers and could see a large bulge.

"It looks as if other parts of you are in proportion," she laughed, and stroked him through the material.

"I've never had any complaints. Come, I will show you."

He pulled her towards the bedroom and, as they stepped in, brushed a light switch so that a couple of gentle spotlights illuminated the ceiling.

"Another party trick, I see," she said, suddenly nervous and wondering just how much she was going to regret this in the morning.

"I am full of them," said Gordon.

He lay her gently on the bed, pulled her knickers down over her ankles and discarded them. She looked at him, slightly embarrassed by her nakedness but still glowing with desire.

He stared down at her, appraising just how unbelievably sexy she looked, lying waiting for him, her legs slightly apart and her nipples still hard. He pulled his socks off first, a relief as seeing him only in his socks could certainly have killed the mood. He undid his belt, unbuttoned his trousers and let them fall down, stepping out of them. His erection was pushing his underpants away from his body; he stretched the elastic and tugged them off. She looked at him and was impressed as he approached the bed. He hadn't been lying – he really was in proportion. She reached for him and stroked his hardness, enjoying his size.

"Of course it matters," she thought to herself.

Gordon lay down beside her, leant over and kissed her again. She stroked his back and side and he slowly nibbled his way down her neck and curled his tongue around her nipple, before licking the valley between her breasts. She had always been worried that her breasts were too small and was self-conscious about them. However, Gordon did not seem to be objecting in any way. She enjoyed his touch but she had discovered long ago in her first High School fumbles that unlike her girlfriends, as they swapped giggling stories in the bathroom about the inept clumsiness of the various boys they were dating, that her breasts were not constitute her major erogenous zone. However, she was never comfortable asking her partners to do what she wanted so she allowed the traditional moves to take place. She still invariably enjoyed herself in bed; she just wished she could eliminate her untypical coyness to provide some guidance to her lover of the moment. She normally needed to know someone pretty well before she could be comfortable enough letting him into that part of her mind.

Gordon slowly breathed his way down her stomach and she felt his fingers play at the top of her mons, stroking her small strip of pubic hair. She had discovered the "billet de métro" style in Paris – it was indeed the size of a metro ticket – and she had maintained it ever since, much to the amusement of the Thai girl whom she saw regularly in her local waxing parlour. She sighed and felt her legs open for him. His touch was delicate and light and although the sensation of his stomach pressing against her could not be described as pleasant, it was not as much of a turn-off as she had feared.

She felt his finger explore her outer labia as he kissed her again. Suddenly she felt an onset of lust and pulled him towards her. He climbed on top of her and she felt his erection against her.

"Gordon," she whispered. "Use a condom." She actually hated the feel of the rubber but, as she had been temporarily retired from the dating scene, she had come off the pill, feeling as though she should give her body a break. She really did not want to get pregnant – that would definitely be a career impediment.

"I fire blanks," he said.

She stared at him, hard. "Don't lie to me. I know you have children."

"Yes, but I had the snip."

"The what?"

"A vasectomy. We call it the snip."

He leaned forward and kissed her. She wanted to pull him into her but hesitated once more.

"You promise? I mean, I reckon we are both unlikely to have AIDS or STDs, but I really will slice your balls off if I get pregnant."

"Clean as a whistle, I promise," he said. "If you do, it's not mine. I was basically gelded nearly ten years ago, so really no issue on that score."

She looked at him with a penetrating stare. She had never gone for the 'I'll pull out before I come' line and usually insisted on protection in the early stages of a relationship, but she could see in his eyes that he was not lying and scratched her nails lightly down his back.

"Come on then, Mr Fairbald. Do it for King and country."

"Queen," he corrected, as he entered her. "Our esteemed monarch is still very much on the throne."

"And that's where you are going to put me if you carry on like that," she laughed.

Gordon had been right. Whatever his bulk he felt incredibly light. He kissed her as he slowly pushed himself deeper inside her and she found herself quivering; his size was definitely having an effect on her and she felt a deep, rich, hot desire form at the base of her spine. She met his thrusts with passionate energy and drove her hips up to meet him. She heard him gasp in unexpected pleasure; Susannah was indeed a girl who enjoyed herself and was not one to hold back. As he drove into her again, however, she felt him start to be overcome by a fervour that she feared he could not control. She was not ready to let him loose yet and wanted to slow him down so she could catch up.

"Let me climb on top of you," she said. She did not want to offend him by implying he was squashing her; he was actually incredibly gentle and was evidently taking most of his weight on his elbows. "That's what a gentleman does." She remembered a girlfriend telling her this in college after she had complained about being flattened by her boyfriend of the time. He had thought that grinding her hard into the bed was erotic; for her it had just been a sign that she needed to strengthen her stomach muscles if she was not going to find herself vomiting over the side of the bed – a passion killer, for sure.

"I want to feel you inside me that way," she added to ensure that there were no hurt feelings.

Gordon assented without objection and he shuffled into the middle of the bed. She climbed on top of him and guided him once more inside her. She leant down and kissed him. He brushed her hair aside with one hand and while the other traced patterns down her back, just brushing the top of her buttocks. As she thrust herself forward and felt his touch, she moaned. He responded by continuing to stroke the small of her back as his fingers lightly stroked the cleft between her buttocks. Immediately she responded with another deeper, more powerful moan and his fingers stretched deeper towards her rosebud, as Victorian erotica would describe it.

"Oh God, yes, play with my butt," she shouted, inhibitions suddenly lost, passion aroused and Victorian decorum forgotten.

Gordon was seemingly only too glad to oblige. Susannah could feel his own passion matching hers as she rose to a crescendo. Her orgasm was building inexorably to a climax. She felt Gordon's finger push inside her tight muscle; she squeezed him hard, shouted unintelligibly and came hard around him. She felt him simultaneously explode and for a moment, it was both pitch black and an explosion of fireworks in her mind. She opened her eyes as he took his hand away and collapsed on top of him.

"Holy shit, Gordon. That was incredible. How did you do that?" she groaned.

"I guess we both like that," he said with a self-satisfied smile. "You are amazing, Susie."

"Don't call me that, now," she said, looking at him fiercely.

"I thought I saw you flinch when Mitch said it. I like it. What's wrong with it?"

"It's what my asshole older brother used to call me to be condescending. Call me Susannah or we are going to fall out big time."

"I certainly wouldn't want that," replied Gordon, feigning meekness. "At least, I wouldn't have wanted to fall out of you just now," he added and laughed out loud.

Susannah reached for a pillow and hit him over the head.

"No chance of that; the size you are," she said.

"I'm glad you enjoyed yourself. I aim to please," he replied.

"You sure do, Mr Fairbald", she gasped and collapsed again beside him on the bed. Her toe tickled his leg. He reached for her and kissed her. She looked at him deeply, smiled at him, and kissed him back, more slowly this time, opening her mouth and letting her tongue play with his. He reached down and stroked her very shapely bottom.

Just at that moment, they heard a mobile phone ring. Gordon recognised his ringtone. He sat up with a jerk.

"Who the hell is that?" he exclaimed.

"Leave it," ordered Susannah. "Whoever it is should know you are in Las Vegas and this is hardly an appropriate time to ring."

The phone stopped for about fifteen seconds and then started again.

"Fuck," said Gordon. "There is only one person who would call so persistently."

"Not your…" hesitated Susannah.

"I'm afraid so," said Gordon. "I'd better answer it."

Susannah rolled over and realised the implications of what they had just done. At the same time, she doubted very much whether this was the first time Gordon had transgressed his marital vows so her initial twinge of guilt dissipated.

Meanwhile Gordon had answered the 'phone. She could only hear one side of the conversation.

"I was in the bathroom when you rang…Yes, I had got up to pee No, I am not drunk; it is nearly two am here so why are you ringing at this time…? Well, what the hell do you want me to do about it from here? Just call a plumber and it will get fixed…It doesn't matter how expensive it will be. Did you really expect me to be able to do anything from here, for Christ's sake? Well, of course I am going to get shirty with you. It's bloody stupid to have called… Yes, tomorrow evening my time so I land the day after, early morning…Yes, see you then."

Gordon turned back to the bed to see Susannah lying there, looking at him and clearly not knowing whether to laugh or feel totally ashamed.

"She would take it upon herself to call me at this time to tell me that the loo is blocked and she needs a plumber," he said, rolling back onto the bed next to Susannah and placing his hand once more on her posterior.

"What on earth she thought I could do about it, God only knows," he added. "Still," he carried on brightly, "just as well she didn't ring thirty seconds earlier. Bloody hell, Susannah. I can't remember the last time I came like that."

She looked at him, bright-eyed, flushed and immediately shy about how she had behaved.

"You are definitely forward for an Englishman," she said, smiling sheepishly at him.

"But you evidently enjoyed yourself," said Gordon.

"Too right," she replied. "Boy, I needed that."

"You needed that!" he exclaimed. "You are not the only one."

They looked at each other and both instinctively laughed. He patted her behind.

"At your service any time, ma'am," he said, still laughing.

"I will bear that in mind," she replied.

She got up, looked around for her underwear and started to get dressed.

"Don't feel you need to leave on my account?" said Gordon in a disappointed voice. "Come back to bed," he added, indicating the side of the bed she had just vacated.

"You can have too much of a good thing," she replied with a smile, adjusting her skirt and blouse which she had fetched from the other room.

"Now," she went on, "Rules of engagement."

"Oh, oh," said Gordon. "Now it gets serious."

"I think we can both agree that this was, er…" she tried to find the right words.

"A lot of fun?" asked Gordon.

Susannah paused and thought.

"Yes, for sure," she said. "But, as we said, not something we broadcast to anyone else, right?"

"I think we safely say it is going to stay between ourselves. After all, why would I want to let anyone know the way to get you going?"

"You know what I mean," said Susannah in a serious tone. She paused and went on in a lighter voice "And even if I am surprised an English gentleman would behave that way, I sure as hell know he would never tell anyone!"

"Absolutely not," said Gordon, in mock horror. "The merest thought could never even begin to cross my mind, as your orders are clear. And I always do as I am told. You gave me an order and, of course, as I say, I followed it unquestioningly. Quite successfully, I rather think."

"Quite successfully, you rather think," she said in an imitation British accent. "I can't believe you really speak that way. It is so hot!"

"And I can't believe that your imitation British accent is as bad as Dick van Dyke in *Mary Poppins*".

"Anyway," said Susannah. "Strictly between ourselves, of course?"

"Of course," said Gordon. He got up from the bed and followed her as Susannah walked out of the bedroom.

"Always a pleasure, Miss Bierson," he said. He leaned over and gave her a kiss on the cheek. She leant in and gave him a hug.

"Indubitably, Mr Fairbald," she replied and turned towards the door. "And if we don't see each other tomorrow, safe travels and I guess we'll talk on Mitch's next staff call." She smiled once more and went out into the corridor – doing the walk of shame for her first time since College.

She felt a tap on her shoulder again and opened her eyes. She was amazed to realise that her reverie had taken so long that they were already twenty minutes into the flight and the seatbelt signs were turned off. She had been completely unaware of take-off and hoped that in her day-dreaming she had not started to moan. She turned towards the girl who had tapped her on the shoulder.

"Excuse me," she said. "I need to use the loo."

"Of course," said Susannah. She got up and let the girl, who looked back at her boyfriend with a giggle, go past her, then sat back down in her seat and wondered how long it would be before they served drinks. She could see two stewardesses slowly pushing a trolley, serving passengers with an incredible lack of haste; it was a long flight after all, she thought, but still, it seemed to be miles away.

"Excuse me, love," said a voice. She looked up and saw the man standing up. "I need to pee as well and you're in the way."

"Charming," said Susannah. She got up and let the man go past. He looked back at her and winked. She stared back impassively, completely unimpressed.

"Wonderful," she said to herself. "Such pleasant travel companions."

She sat back down again and started to flick through the movies on offer. There seemed to be nothing but romantic comedies and she didn't think she could face some form of Hollywood sugar as boy meets girl and somehow get through any number of legitimate obstacles to live happily ever after. She had always wanted to write the sequel to any one of those films, dealing with the reality of life two years into the relationship. How many of those couples would actually survive, she wondered.

Certainly, for most of them, the relationship would hardly go beyond the sickly sweet romantic kiss as the boy catches the girl on the plane (forget the niceties of actually needing a ticket, passport and boarding pass to get through security and get on the flight) before she leaves for Paris and tells her that he loves her, that sleeping with her best friend was the biggest mistake of his life and they can get the puppy that she has always wanted to the applause of the other passengers and cabin crew (without any of the officious, "Excuse me, sir, you are delaying the flight"). They would get home, she thought, and the girl would realise she should have gone to Paris after all as she could never again trust the bastard not to bed whichever other girl came his way (or who he met at a conference in Las Vegas, she thought with a self-deprecating smile).

She settled on *Terminator*. She liked the idea of the passing the time with some mindless violence. But before she settled down she needed go to the bathroom herself – with the drinks trolley still an eternity away, she got up and headed to the washrooms.

There were five separate bathrooms at the back of the plane. The first one was occupied. It occurred to her that her two traveling companions had been gone a while and she suddenly was pretty sure she knew why. She knew that look in the girl's eyes –it was exactly the one she had seen in the girl from the couple whose seats she and Gordon had occupied in the Rhum Bar. She thought for a second and checked the other four washrooms – they were indeed all unoccupied with the tell-tale green sign on the lock. She went back to the first bathroom and listened closely. At first she heard nothing but then her ears tuned in and there was a gasp, a grunt and some general heaving against the door. Susannah glanced over her shoulder and saw that the drinks trolley was at last getting closer to the last row. Suddenly the frustration of being rammed at the back of the plane with two inconsiderate assholes got the better of her.

"Revenge is a dish best eaten cold, my friends. You were messing with the wrong chick! I think it is time you learn the benefit of politeness," she muttered.

On her frequent travels Susannah had learned the trick of how to open a plane's washroom from the outside. The small, metal "Lavatory" sign on each door is actually a flap; raise it and you can slide the bolt back and open the door. It is not widely publicised, for obvious reasons, but it does allow the crew to gain access in an emergency.

Just as the drinks trolley reached the back of the plane, Susannah lifted up the flap on the door where her two travel companions were clearly involved in joining the mile high club, pulled the bolt back and pushed the door open. She immediately ducked into the bathroom next door as there was a high pitched scream and shout from inside.

"The bloody door's open," the girl screamed.

"Christ," shouted the man.

A stewardess came back to see the commotion. The sight of the man's naked buttocks facing her was decidedly unattractive while the girl, who was spread-eagled sitting on the sink, had a look of horror on her face as she looked into the eyes of the stewardess.

"Get the captain, Lucy, right away," said the stewardess. "We've got some mile-highers here."

"Oi," shouted the man, pulling back and turning around. "Fuck off and leave us alone."

"Jesus, pull your trousers up. I don't want to see you like that," said the stewardess.

The man looked down as his erection protruded in front of him.

"Ha! Best you've ever seen, I bet," he mocked.

"Shut the fucking door, Darren," screamed the girl, who was scrabbling to retrieve her knickers.

He looked at her and realised that this was the best course of action. He pulled the door closed and the sound of sobbing came from inside together with vociferous commands from the man to "shut your bleedin' gob".

At that point the urbane voice of the captain intervened.

"Now then sir, madam. I am going to open the door. Are you dressed?" he said.

By this stage a small crowd had gathered to observe the scene. Susannah opened the door of her bathroom and came out.

"What's going on?" she asked the stewardess in all innocence.

The couple themselves emerged from their own washroom. The girl was crying and shriveling with embarrassment in front of everyone. The man maintained his bravado and was arguing with the captain that they had done no harm, that it was just a bit of fun and that they should just be left alone.

"I am afraid it is a lot more serious than that, sir," said the captain. "Please sit down. I will be reporting this and it will be a police matter… for gross indecency, I should think. If either of you moves from your seats for the remainder of the flight or utters a word, I will have you restrained. Do you understand?"

The man started to protest but his girlfriend grabbed him and said, "It's bad enough now, Darren, for Gawd's sake. Sit down and leave it out."

He finally seemed to register the seriousness of the situation and sat down, chuntering beneath his breath, but not so loud that anyone could hear.

Suzanne said to the stewardess, "Excuse me, I can't be expected to sit next to this couple. Not after what has just happened."

"But we have no other seats available, madam. I am very sorry but you will have to," said her favourite stewardess in a tone of deeply self-satisfied intransigence.

The captain overheard the conversation and turned to Susannah. "Madam. I am so sorry you had to be involved in this. Please gather your things and come with me."

The stewardess looked extremely surprised but said nothing. Susannah did as she was requested and followed the captain back up the aisle.

They moved through the entire Economy section, through the Premium Economy section and into First Class. Ahead Susannah could see the steps leading up to the cockpit. Another man in uniform was coming out of the cockpit door.

"All OK, Jim?" he asked.

"Yes. No problem. Just another mile-high couple. They got unlucky as the door opened on them so they were caught in the act. Let's see how they behave before we call the police – after all, we know the paperwork we will have to do if they get arrested, not to mention dealing with the bloody press."

He turned to Susannah. "We always keep a spare First Class seat for crew rest on these long-haul flights. But actually we have two extra pilots on board on this flight for training, so we don't strictly need it. Therefore you can have it with our compliments and apologies."

He called over to the steward in charge of the First Class cabin.

"Graham, please look after Ms…er," he turned to Susannah.

"Bierson, Susannah Bierson" she said.

"Ms Bierson," he said. "Treat her as well as we can."

"Certainly, captain," said the steward. "Madam, please follow me."

In something of a daze, Susannah followed him over to the large seat located in its own secluded area at the front of the cabin.

"Champagne, madam?"

"That would do very nicely, thank you," said Susannah, and sank back into the comfortable upholstery.

"Karma," she said to herself. "Total karma. The asshole should have known he was fucking with the wrong girl and so it turned out."

The rest of the flight passed in a blur of champagne, caviar, lobster (clearly defrosted rather than fresh but Susannah was not going to complain) and petits fours. Eventually, she settled back into the extremely comfortable First Class bed (which the steward had made up for her) and slept until she was woken gently by the same steward with a cup of coffee and the message that they were twenty minutes from landing.

Her mood slightly deteriorated as they had the usual delay at Heathrow waiting for their stand to become free. There was a lengthy queue at immigration and she had forgotten to ask for a fast track pass. Despite her protestations, she had not been allowed to bypass the long wait with just an Economy boarding pass. Susannah had never arrived Heathrow and experienced the bags delivered in anything like a reasonable time; this time there was apparently a problem with the plane's cargo door, which it took British Airways an age to resolve. The passengers on the flight were starting to get extremely restless, particularly in the absence of any information but eventually, to loud cheers, the carousel started up and the bags arrived. Susannah's bag was of course almost the last to appear. She had almost given up hope when she finally saw it emerge from behind the rubber flaps and crawl round to where she was standing.

She went through customs without a problem, then thought about her best option to get into central London, eventually settling on the Heathrow Express. For once everything was running smoothly although she did wince at the price of a single ticket and declined the special offer to upgrade to First Class for 'only another twenty pounds.' The frequency of the trains meant that she had no problem sitting down and made it into Paddington railway station in the west of the city without any mishap. Then she took a black taxi from the stand above the station. She had forgotten how talkative the average London cabbie is and she found herself having to give her opinion on Brexit and Donald Trump, and agreeing by means of the occasional "Right" and "Yeah" and "Uh-huh" with his monologue about why football (soccer, he meant of course) was so much better than American football.

They eventually made it relatively unscathed to the Whitehaven Hotel. She was looking forward to taking a shower before walking over to the office. The hotel was situated in a mews just off St James's Street; Susannah admired the cobbled path up to the front entrance and the old-fashioned wooden façade. It reminded her of her favourite parts of old San Francisco, although she guessed that the building had been constructed considerably before any part of her home city. She pushed open the heavy door and walked over to reception. There was no one in sight, so she put her suitcase down and waited. After a couple of minutes she said "Hello" in a hopeful voice then again in a louder one. She was just wondering whether the hotel reception had shut down for the afternoon and what she should do about it when a man came out from a door at the back. He looked remarkably like the British Airways check-in clerk. Susannah studied him further; he really was his doppelganger.

"Sorry to keep you, madam," he said. "How can I help you?"

"Er, do you have a brother called Michael who works for British Airways at San Francisco airport?"

He looked at her with a bemused expression.

"No, madam. I have never been to America and as far as I know, neither has any member of my family."

"Oh," said Susannah, looking flummoxed. "Sorry; I know that sounds totally random. It's just that the person who checked me in at SFO looked just like you."

"Really, madam? Quite a coincidence indeed."

How did the British manage to convey such disdain so politely? It was a trick that Susannah could not master although she was proud to have overcome her genetic programming so that she could recognise irony – at least when clothed in a heavy wrapping of sarcasm.

"Anyway," said Susannah, "I'm here to check in."

"Certainly, madam. Welcome to the Whitehaven Hotel. May I have your last name, please?"

They completed the formalities and he handed over her room key. She was intrigued to note that it was an actual key rather than the usual electronic card.

"Your room is on the second floor, madam. You will find the lift just around the corner. Do you need any help with your luggage?"

"Lift?" queried Susannah, hesitated and then went on, "Oh yes, of course, elevator."

The receptionist smiled at her, his supercilious contempt reverberating loudly in the silence.

Susannah ignored him and added, "And no, I can manage my bags, thanks."

"Very good, madam. May I wish you a very pleasant stay at the Whitehaven Hotel?"

"Thank you," said Susannah and headed in the direction indicated.

The lift gave the impression that it had been built at the same time as the original building. It wheezed and whirred its way down when Susannah pressed the call button. When it eventually arrived a light went on above the door, which had a handle to open it rather than being automatic. She was faced with a folding brass gate across the entrance which she wrestled wide with some difficulty before dragging her suitcase into the confined space. She pressed the button for the second floor and nothing happened. She tried again and still the lift did not move. She wondered if the combined weight of her and her suitcase was too much for it to cope with but dismissed that as she noticed the sign stating that it could accommodate a maximum of six people, unlikely though that sounded. She pondered the problem and then realised that she needed to pull the gate to. She reached for it and pulled it closed but managed to nip one of her fingers in the process, causing her to yelp and swear softly. However, it seemed to satisfy the contraption as it set off on its seemingly interminable climb to the second floor.

When it eventually croaked to a halt, Susannah fought with the gate again, this time being careful to avoid the folding mechanism that was clearly designed to trap the softer parts of the body and lurched out with her suitcase. She wondered if the stairs would have been a better option. Shrugging her shoulders and feeling a strange sense of accomplishment at having made it thus far, she headed down the corridor towards her room, which was the last on the left. She was surprised to find the door open. She was even more surprised to hear a very British accent just at the moment shout out "Fred, for the love of Nigel Christ, shut the fucking water off; the bloody toilet's flooding."

"Right you are, Bill", came a distant reply, seemingly from the floor below.

"Shit," said the first voice.

Susannah walked into her room and peered round the bathroom door. Her first impression was that it would not have been out of place in a museum, with heavy brass pipes, large white taps on the bath, a wooden seat on the loo and the cistern wall-mounted above with a rusted chain hanging down. Water did indeed appear to be cascading out from the bowl onto the floor. The man, who was evidently Bill, was desperately trying to mop it up with the guest towels, but was losing the fight as far as Susannah could tell.

"Excuse me," she said. "This is my room. I'd like to unpack and take a shower. Are you going to be long?"

"No idea, darlin'," came the response. "Bit busy now as you can see. If I were you I'd tell his lordship downstairs on reception to get you another room. If that bloody idiot Fred doesn't turn the water off soon we all going to be swimmin' in here. Fred," he yelled again, "What the hell are you doin', son? Turn the soddin' water off now."

At that point there was at least some relief as the cascade stopped, although there was still the occasional slop over the side of the bowl, which was completely full.

"Well, that's something at least," said Bill.

He went on, "You said shower, darlin'? No shower in here, even when it ain't a swimming pool. Bath only."

"Well, isn't that just dandy," she said, in her best southern American accent.

"Like I said, I'd ask his nibs downstairs to find you another room. This bathroom is going to be out of order for a while," said Bill, looking down at his soaked overalls.

"Fred," he yelled again, "Bring some more bloody towels up here, will you? On the double, son, before the water starts going through the floor."

A considerable volume of water did seem to be seeping through a gap in the lino under the sink and disappearing at a rapid rate.

"Jesus," said Bill, trying to staunch the flow with already sodden towels.

Susannah surveyed the scene and decided that she had better go back downstairs and sort out a different room. However, she knew she could not face tackling the esoteric lift again with her suitcase.

"I am going to leave my bags here while I see if I can change rooms," she said.

All she got in reply was a grunt as he was on his hands and knees trying to wring towels out into the bath.

She grabbed her laptop bag and backed out of the room. She nearly collided with a boy who was also dressed in overalls; he looked still a teenager and was carrying a pile of towels.

"Oh, sorry," he gasped. "I'm in a rush as we have a flood going on in number eleven."

"Yes, I know," said Susannah. "That's my room."

"Bad luck," said the boy, and pushed past her, hurrying into the room.

Susannah heard Bill ejaculate "About bloody time," and continued on her way. She eventually found the staircase. She was confused at first, forgetting that the first floor was not the ground floor on this side of the Pond and losing her way in another corridor of bedrooms but she did eventually make it downstairs. She went back to reception but found it just as empty as before. She repeated the routine, calling out in ever louder and more frequent cycles.

Eventually the same receptionist appeared.

"How can I help you, madam?" he asked in his urbane, slightly nasal voice.

"My room upstairs," said Susannah.

"Indeed, madam. Is there a problem?"

"You could say that," said Susannah. "The bathroom is flooded. There's one of your men up there shouting inanely and there is no shower."

"None of our rooms has a shower, madam. It is part of the charm of the hotel."

"Well, I don't find it charming at all," contested Susannah, embracing the ugly American role that the receptionist had clearly assigned to her in his own mind.

"And I don't expect to be paying whatever it is to find the room flooded when I have just stepped off a twelve-hour flight and need to freshen up before a number of key meetings," she added, raising her voice and finding herself banging her fist on the reception counter.

The receptionist looked at her and looked at her fist. He seemed totally unperturbed.

"I am sorry to hear of your difficulties, madam," he said.

"I don't need your apology, buster! I need you to get me another room and now. And if you don't have showers in your bathrooms because you think it quaint and traditional, you might advertise the fact on your website."

"I can assure you, madam, that the website is quite specific about the amenities in every room," he said in a calm, suave voice which only served to madden Susannah.

"It didn't say anything about flooded bathrooms either," she yelled aggressively. "I suppose that is another charming feature?"

"It is a risk that we run by preserving as much of the original plumbing as possible, madam. But I can assure you that our maintenance staff will rectify the problem as quickly as possible."

"I don't share your confidence," she retorted. "And frankly neither does Bill or whatever his name is, judging by what he was saying upstairs. All I want now," she went on, "is a room where the john doesn't flood and the plumbing doesn't look like it dates back to when the Founding Fathers were still English."

The receptionist looked at her with frosty disdain; but his tone remained impeccably polite.

"I am sorry to say we are completely sold out, madam. Number eleven – your room – is the only one available. We are always sold out, madam. It is because of the English charm of the hotel."

"So what do you suggest I do?"

He smiled in a way that made Susannah want to smack him.

"Well, madam," he replied. "As I see it, you have two options: you can wait until Bill has resolved the problem in your bathroom. He's been with us for many years and there is no one who knows our plumbing like Bill."

"Good for Bill," interjected Susannah with heavy sarcasm.

"Indeed, madam," said the receptionist.

"And my second option?" asked Susannah.

"To go to your various meetings and come back later; by that time, we should have your room back to normal," he said.

"Whatever normal means for you guys," said Susannah. But she was realising she may have met her match.

"Indeed, madam," he said without a trace of emotion in his voice.

"Are you sure you don't have a brother who works for British Airways in San Francisco?" asked Susannah once more, by this time totally exasperated.

"Absolutely sure, madam," he replied. "As I told you…"

"Yes, I know," interrupted Susannah. "None of your family has ever been to the States. Our gain, your loss, buddy," she added in as vitriolic a tone as she could manage. "You missed a third option," she went on.

"Indeed, madam?"

"I could just move to another hotel."

"That undoubtedly is your prerogative, madam. Of course, under our cancellation policy, you would still be required to pay for your stay here in full, but naturally, if you prefer to switch hotels, that is absolutely your choice."

"Supposing I said I wanted to see the manager and right now," said Susannah, fearing defeat but still refusing to back down.

"Of course, madam. One moment, please."

The receptionist turned and went through a door into an office behind him. Susannah stood there, composing her thoughts and thinking about the tirade she was about to unleash on whomever was the unfortunate individual who had to supervise the stiff-arsed Brit she had just been dealing with.

The receptionist came back out of the office.

"Don't tell me he's not available," said Susannah, looking at him with fire in her eyes.

"I am the manager, madam. How can I help you?"

Susannah looked at him incredulously.

"You have got to be fucking kidding me," she yelled. "Do you think this is some sort of joke?"

"I never joke about my work, madam. I was actually just calling Bill to check on the status of your room," he added, before Susannah could say another word. "It does look as if your three choices remain as it is going to take some time before the room is actually ready for occupancy. I do apologise for the inconvenience."

She gave him a murderous look, which he returned without blinking, with a hint of triumph in his eyes.

"Fine," she said. "I give up. I will be back about six pm; just make sure it is ready by then or, well… there will be trouble."

"Indeed, madam" said the receptionist or manager, with a raised eyebrow which reminded Susannah of Roger Moore at his best.

"Just making sure you know you've been warned," muttered Susannah, and turned to leave.

"Have a good afternoon, madam," he said, "And thank you for choosing The Whitehaven."

Twenty different retorts went through her mind at once but she decided immediately haughty silence was the best option, so she left without a word.

The receptionist went back into his office and sat down at his computer. He brought up Gmail and typed:

> *Hi Mike, how is the US treating you? I trust you are making progress in your one man mission to civilise them. I have to tell you I have just been doing my bit for the cause, entertaining myself with one of our American guests called Susannah Bierson. Typical California dumb blonde who just had no idea how to handle the situation. Her room was flooded when she got here – not planned, I promise you – so I had a blast. She said she met someone who looked just like me checking her in at SFO. It must have been you. Do you remember her? I hope you had as much fun as I did. I know over there they call it 'yanking your chain'; well, let me tell you, her chain is well and truly yanked. All the best, older but clearly not wiser brother. Rog.*

CHAPTER SEVEN

Meanwhile, the London-based team of Aardvark had gathered in the boardroom of their office. Gordon had called them together to discuss the final logistics of the upcoming offsite and also to prepare for Susannah's visit. There was always a general nervousness whenever a senior member of the firm came over from head office and Gordon had decided to play on this to reinforce his authority. He was concerned that, with Henry's investment track-record and the situation at Riverjack Crypto, he could somehow find himself undermined. Of course no one else knew about his "special relationship" with Susannah, so that definitely gave him an edge. He had smiled to himself as he sat in his office, working out the final agenda for the offsite and thinking about her. He had got lucky in Las Vegas when Mitch told him the story of Susannah's previous experience in the Jules Verne restaurant with her loser boyfriend. That had definitely aided his cause during that evening and given the impression that he was a sensitive, observant soul. But equally, she had enjoyed herself as much as he had and so he did not really feel that there had been any real harm in the mild deception.

He glanced at his watch. Nearly 2.30pm. Time to get the meeting underway and to banish thoughts of Susannah from his mind or he would be sitting there with his legs crossed again.

Everyone else was in the room when he entered. He noticed Henry was absorbed on his mobile phone, unconcerned by anyone else around him. Theresa was flicking through papers which were covered in numbers and charts. Mary sat next to the new girl – what was her name? Lisa, that was it. She was decidedly attractive but looked incredibly nervous. Mary had obviously taken her under her wing as she was talking to her quietly and smiling. Edwin was also sitting there, blinking like a guppy fish and looking about as sharp. Meanwhile Tom and Peter were sitting together conferring closely, both with slightly worried looks on their faces. Riverjack Crypto would, of course, be dominating their thoughts.

He wondered how Peter had got on in Oxford. He only spoken to him briefly after Monday's call to appoint him as acting CEO. Peter had shared the details of the accident on that conference call so Gordon understood now why he and Tom had been laughing so loudly. He had decided to remain suitably serious as befitted the senior non-executive director of a company who had just lost their two Board executives but had privately been howling with laughter as well. He had also been suitably impressed by Jack's ability to persuade anyone to do anything – he knew Emma quite well and presumed that it was pretty much out of character. They were both big losses in their different ways – he really could not see a way back for the company, if he was honest. And, judging by the expression on Peter's face, the last two days had not gone well.

Time to take control.

"Afternoon, everyone," said Gordon, sitting down and shuffling a couple of papers in front of him. Mumbled greetings and nods came from around the table.

"Now then," he went on. "We have a lot to get through today. Susannah Bierson landed in the UK a couple of hours ago, so I expect her to come over from her hotel at some point. Let's get one thing straight: she's here to assess how much we can be trusted to perform and I for one am not going to countenance her going back to Mitch with anything other than a stellar report. So I expect everyone to remain totally focused during her visit. We have got to show her that we are the same calibre as our American colleagues – indeed, that we are better! Do I make myself clear?"

Gordon looked about the room. He was pleased with the authoritative tone he had set and wanted to observe the impact he had had. Edwin was nodding enthusiastically, of course, and Peter and Tom were paying dutiful attention. Theresa nodded curtly; Henry had not looked up from his bloody phone and Mary just stared at him without any emotion. Lisa still looked terrified.

"We will get to where we are with Riverjack Crypto in a minute. Susannah is going to want to go through every detail of that business. When she comes I want everyone to review the draft report from Peter and Tom while I will spend time with her one on one."

There was a pause and Gordon wondered if he had imagined a faint snort coming from Henry at this last remark. He was going to have to be careful, for sure.

"And before Susannah gets here, let's talk about the logistics of the offsite," he went on. "It must go like clockwork. Mary, I am depending on you to keep us all on track when we are at the hotel. You know, meetings starting and ending on time; coffee served really hot at breaks; dinner of the right quality to impress our guest. You've done it often for us so you know what you need to do."

Mary looked at him impassively and said, "Gordon, we have discussed this a number of times. It is my thirtieth wedding anniversary this weekend and I will not be at the offsite."

Gordon looked at her in shock. He now recalled that she had said something to that effect when he had first suggested the dates. She had told him she would not be available but he had not really listened to her and just assumed that she would rearrange whatever personal commitment she had for the good of the firm.

"But you must be there," he insisted. "We need you. Can't you just postpone your wedding anniversary?"

"Postpone? The date is the date," she said, still staring coldly at him.

"You know what I mean. Postpone your trip. I know Lucas will understand. After all, you've been married thirty years so a week or so either way doesn't matter, does it?" he said.

Mary looked at him with icy coolness. She said very quietly, "I think you mean Luke."

"Bugger", thought Gordon to himself. He added out loud, "Yes, of course, Luke. What I meant of course."

There was a pause before he continued in what he hoped was a mollifying tone, "Congratulations to both of you. Thirty years! You get less for murder."

He laughed in a somewhat forced manner. Edwin followed suit. Henry just looked at Gordon and the corners of his mouth twitched as if to say, "You really have fucked that up, haven't you?". Theresa just looked at him and slowly shook her head.

"So, you will postpone it then?" said Gordon.

"No, Gordon," said Mary. "We will not. Luke has booked a surprise trip. We leave tomorrow morning.

"But where are you going? It can't be far. Surely postponing wouldn't be that hard," insisted Gordon.

"I don't know where we are going," said Mary in an intransigent tone. "That's why it is a surprise. What I do know is that I will be leaving. On at least two occasions I told you that the dates of the offsite would have to be changed if you wanted me there. You didn't change the dates, so you evidently don't want me there. Besides," she went on, turning to Lisa. "Lisa will do a grand job, won't you, my dear?"

Lisa looked at her open-mouthed and quailed, "You mean, you won't be there and I have to organise everything?"

Gordon looked at this as a lifeline.

"There you are, Mary," he said. "You can't leave Lisa to cope with us on her own," he urged.

The look of horror on Lisa's face was increasing by the second.

"Please, Mary, say you will be there. You must be there. Please!"

"Unfortunately, it is what it is," Mary said, more gently. "I am not going and that is final."

She turned to Lisa and patted her arm in a comforting manner.

"You will be fine, my dear. And I know Edwin will help you in every way possible," she said.

Henry looked up from his phone.

"So, Lisa is going to be in charge supported by Edwin? Suddenly the offsite prospects are looking up. The possibilities are mind-boggling. Excellent!" he said and turned back to his phone.

Edwin looked decidedly uneasy with the sudden responsibility.

Mary went on, "And let me be very clear about one thing. If I hear that anyone has been anything other than totally supportive of Lisa, they will answer to me."

She looked very pointedly at Henry who simply pretended that he had heard nothing and carried on with his nose buried in his phone.

"I am sure that we will all chip in," said Gordon, who knew he had somehow lost control in the last couple of minutes. "So, Lisa, it looks like it is all on you."

Lisa looked as if she would shrivel up and collapse there and then. Tom decided it was time to play the chivalrous role.

"Hear, hear, Gordon" he chimed in. "I for one know Lisa will do a great job. She is more than capable and after all, we are all adults and don't need constant supervision."

Henry looked up and scoffed again. Tom gave him a dark look and turned to Lisa who smiled weakly at him in thanks. He gave her the thumbs up sign and looked at her reassuringly.

"So that's that, then, I suppose," said Gordon in a resigned tone. "But now we should turn our attention to the matter of the moment: Riverjack Crypto. Peter, what is the current situation and what the hell are we going to do about it?"

"Well," began Peter. "I have as you know taken on the role of interim CEO and I was down in the office in Oxford for the last couple of days to get a full picture of the business, the team and where we stand."

"And? What have you found?"

Peter was just about to answer when the door opened and Susannah came in. She had walked up from the hotel and found the office without a problem. Gordon leapt up as she came in – a little too hastily.

"Susannah, how are you?" he said and gave her the customary peck on both cheeks. "Welcome to the UK. How was your trip?"

At least that looked natural enough, she thought.

"Well, I won't go into details but let's just say, pretty eventful so far."

"That sounds intriguing," said Gordon. "I look forward to hearing all about it later. But let me introduce you to the team."

He went around the room and introduced everyone in turn. Susannah shook hands with each of them and exchanged pleasantries. When it came to Peter they did have a brief conversation about Riverjack Crypto but Gordon interrupted them, saying that there would be time to discuss that later on. Henry was the last to greet her and held onto her outstretched hand just a fraction too long for comfort. She had heard of Henry's reputation from Mitch and, although she shared a warm, Californian smile with all of them, when it came to Henry she appraised him critically and found her antennae telling her to be exceedingly wary.

She sat down and was about to open proceedings when Gordon pre-empted her.

"Right," he said. "Now that introductions are done, I think we should go ahead as follows: I will take Susannah in my office and go through the detailed plan for the next few days with her. I want the rest of you to work through the Riverjack Crypto action plan so that we are fully ready for the offsite. Are you OK with that, Susannah?" he turned to her with a questioning smile.

Susannah wondered if she should actually insist on staying to hear the Riverjack Crypto rescue plan. After all, that was the primary reason she was there. And she was not sure she wanted to be alone with Gordon quite so soon. She was going to have to lay down some ground rules for her visit and the offsite in particular and he was probably not going to like them. However, she decided to play along with his plan for the time being.

"Sure, Gordon," she said. "You're in charge. I am just here to help."

She smiled and looked around the room.

"Excellent," said Gordon. "So, Susannah, if you follow me; Henry, I will leave you to go through the detailed update from Peter and Tom."

"I suppose so, said Henry without enthusiasm, putting down his phone and gathering his thoughts. He had hoped to be a passive observer who could enjoy watching Peter being thrown to the lions, but it rather looked as if he was actually going to have to lead the session which would involve effort; all in all an extremely vexing turn of events.

Gordon left the boardroom and Susannah followed him out.

"Welcome to London," he said as he went towards his office. "You said it was an eventful trip? What happened?"

"Well, I won't bore you with the details but thanks to a couple who joined the mile-high club, I managed to get upgraded from my last-on-the-plane coach seat to First. But the hotel, Gordon! You've put me somewhere that reminds me of the Grand Budapest Hotel but without so much of the Grand."

"What do you mean?" he asked.

"Plumbing out of the ark and a manager who clearly regards visiting Americans as fair game," she said. "He was so aggravating."

"Sorry to hear that," said Gordon. "Do you want me to call them?"

"I can deal with it myself, thanks," she said, haughtily.

"Yes, of course, I didn't mean…" He tailed off as he showed her into his office and shut the door behind them.

"Don't worry. I know you are just being the British gentleman," she said. "I will sort them out but Jeez, they are annoying."

Gordon turned to her and took her in his arms.

"Oh Susannah," he sighed. "I've missed you. I can't stop thinking of that night in Las Vegas."

He leaned in to kiss her but she slightly turned her head so that he found her cheek rather than her lips and she gently pulled away from him.

"Now, Gordon," she said. "That evening was fun and we had a great time."

"I remember how much you said you enjoyed yourself," he smiled at her.

"Yes, yes. I know, but…"

He interrupted her. "You made me come like a bull elephant and I seem to recall a certain amount of screaming on your part as well. I remember the explicit instruction you gave me and I was only too glad to obey. The results were spectacular."

Susannah blushed and turned away.

"Yes, well, it was a good night and as I recall, we both said afterwards we needed it!" she said.

"And I for one need it again," said Gordon.

"Look," she said, moving slightly away from him as he approached her again. "It was great an' all, but I am here for business. You and I can't carry on. I mean, there are going to be far too many people around at the offsite for us even to think of anything like that and…"

She faltered as he attempted to take her into his arms once more. She stood there and held him back like a policeman controlling traffic.

"I would have taken you to dinner tonight to discuss the portfolio," he said, stopping in his tracks. "But my bloody wife is insisting on me going with her to see some pretentious French film instead."

"That is probably just as well," said Susannah. "I am not sure that we should be doing anything other than discussing the portfolio during my trip, Gordon, and over dinner is probably not the most efficient setting."

"Discussing my portfolio with you is definitely on the agenda." Tomorrow or Saturday I can make time to see you for sure. And at the offsite I am sure we can work something out."

"Mitch told me your wife was going to be there," she said. "Again, that is probably just as well. We are going to have to keep this strictly business from now on and just enjoy what we had."

"I enjoyed having you, for sure," he laughed. She smiled weakly back and turned away.

"Look," he persisted. "I am busy tonight as I said – nothing I can do about that – but why don't I take you to dinner on Friday night. I can easily tell Cressida that I have to work late with you preparing for the offsite. "

"I really don't think that is a good idea, Gordon."

Gordon decided that he was going to have to try to use his fundamental British charm as a more subtle way to convince Susannah. After all, that was how he had got inside her knickers in Vegas, he thought, so why would it not work again. Of course, he was more than aware that it was not only inappropriate but involved a high degree of risk to his reputation and undoubtedly his lucrative position at Aardvark. At the same time, he was only doing what any self-respecting man would typically do: think with his dick and worry about the consequences afterwards. As a wise man once said, "God gave man a brain and a penis but not enough blood to use both at the same time."

"I understand. Let's play it by ear and see if opportunity knocks," he said in a conciliatory tone.

Susannah looked at him with relief, "I really think that's best, Gordon." She wondered why he had backed off so easily; all she had to do now was make sure that opportunity did not knock at all during her visit.

"What is certainly true is that Riverjack Crypto is definitely a problem for us," he said, brushing her comment aside. "You heard what happened to the CEO?" he asked.

"Yes. Mitch told me that he wrote off his car, killing himself and his CFO in the process."

"But did he tell you what actually happened?" Gordon asked.

"Not exactly," said Susannah. "He said that you hadn't shared details with him."

"There's a reason for that," he said.

He gave her a blow by blow account, leaving out no detail and adding several lascivious scenes that he had created in his own mind (which were, unbeknown to him, a fairly accurate depiction of what had happened). Susannah gasped at the appropriate points and then could not help but giggle herself as Gordon finished off his narrative.

"I see," she said. "I suppose you could say that they are the UK's latest entrants for the Darwin Awards."

Gordon laughed. He wondered if the mood had been sufficiently changed for him to make another move. He looked at her and contemplated how he could turn the situation to his advantage. If only Cressida had not arranged to attend the fucking French Film festival he would have had time to work on Susannah and break her down.

At that moment, the 'phone on his desk rang.

"Don't tell me that's your wife again," said Susannah with a grin.

The phone continued to ring.

"Shouldn't you see who that is?" asked Susannah.

Gordon walked round to his desk.

"It's Mitch," he said and pressed a button on the phone to activate the speaker.

"Mitch," said Gordon. "Good morning. How are you?" He looked at his watch. Close to eight in the morning in San Francisco: a pretty civilised time to call given his recent track record.

"Gordon," Mitch's loud voice boomed over the speaker. "Good to hear your voice. Has Susie arrived safe and sound?"

"She's right here with me," replied Gordon.

"Hi Mitch," said Susannah, walking over to the phone to talk. "How are things?"

"Susie," said Mitch. Gordon smiled as he saw her flinch once more at the name. "You licking those Limeys into shape?"

Gordon reached over and hit the mute button.

"You can lick me into shape any time you like," he said.

Susannah made a dismissive gesture with her hand and pressed the mute button to make the speaker live again.

"We are just getting started," she said.

Gordon muted the phone and said, "Well, we would if you let me" to which she smiled and brushed him away again, unmuting the phone.

"That's great to hear," said Mitch at the same time. "I need you to sort them out, particularly with what's going on at Riverjack Crypto. I will pray for Jack's soul and poor Emma's in church this Sunday; I just hope he had time to repent before he met his maker."

Gordon leaned over and muted the phone again and said, "Repent? Well, I bet the last thing he said was 'Oh God I'm coming'".

Susannah mouth at him to be quiet, unmuted the phone and said, "It certainly is a less than ideal situation, Mitch. I am looking forward to hearing the details of what has gone on and then we will work on a rescue strategy. The key to success is to get the bottom of the problem."

"My biggest problem at the moment is getting to your bottom," Gordon said, leering suggestively over her.

Susannah pointed frantically at the phone; it was still live. Gordon mouthed, "Oh, shit" as Mitch said, "What? What did you say, Gordon?"

"I said my biggest problem is getting to the bottom line that Susannah has said is acceptable for Riverjack Crypto," he extemporised, breathing a sigh of relief.

"Oh, I see," said Mitch. "Good, Susie. You just make sure you are setting high standards for those Brits and don't hesitate to give Gordon a hard time."

Gordon leaned over to press the button but Susannah slapped his wrist, looked at him with a clear 'Don't you even dare' stare and said.

"You bet, Mitch. I have this."

"Sure you do," he said. "Keep me updated. Oh, and by the way, there's a couple of other things I want to talk through with you. Can we speak later when you are back at your hotel?"

"Absolutely, Mitch," she replied. "I will give you a call in a few hours."

"I look forward to it," Mitch said. "Catch you later, Gordon."

"Thanks, Mitch," said Gordon, and hung up.

"So you see," said Susannah, "We couldn't have dinner tonight. Mitch wants to speak to me and I for one need an early night."

"Tomorrow, then?" he said, hopefully, coming round from behind his desk and approaching her once more.

"Like I said, Gordon, I really don't think that is a good idea."

"It's not a good idea," he said, "It's a bloody great one."

She looked at him and silently shook her head. He returned her look for a moment and once more decided to back down gracefully. "Lose the battle but win the war", he thought.

At that moment there was a knock at his door. Susannah indicated with a gesture that he should respond and reluctantly he said, "Come in".

Peter walked through the door; he had the air of someone who had just been put through the mill.

"Yes, Peter," said Gordon curtly. "What can I do for you? You know I am busy with Susannah."

"We've finished, Gordon," Peter replied, "And I thought it would make sense to bring you up to speed. I wanted to discuss a couple of key points with you," he added as an afterthought.

Gordon thought for a moment, then said, "Susannah, I know Riverjack Crypto is the key priority. Why don't you and Peter focus on the business tomorrow with Tom? I will give my input to the rescue plan now so you have the full picture. I know you are tired after the trip and with your job you have a lot on your plate. As Mitch just said, you and he need to catch up later on. You and I can continue tomorrow pm as well and I will just spend time with Peter now."

Susannah looked at him with surprise. This was a change of approach and while she could not fathom Gordon's motives, nevertheless it was one she welcomed. It would make sense for her to absent herself from the office for what remained of the day, work on some other pressing portfolio matters, talk to Mitch and perhaps risk room service for dinner (if that goddam hotel offered such a thing) with an early night.

"Sure," she said. "I like that plan. Peter, I look forward to spending time with you tomorrow." She smiled encouragingly at him.

"Likewise," Peter replied with a slightly wan smile.

Susannah got up and left the room. She ran into Henry as she was leaving and spent ten minutes trying to extricate herself from offers of a coffee, a drink, dinner or for him to act as tour guide to the London sights by night. She felt she had probably already exceeded her quota of partners from the firm to have slept with and had no intention of repeating her… "well, it was not a mistake so much as perhaps an unfortunate lapse of judgment; yes, let's call it that", she thought. So she politely declined all such offers and walked back to her hotel.

In the meantime, Peter had been wondering how to approach the delicate challenges of Riverjack Crypto with Gordon and this discussion had given him a little bit of time to gather his thoughts. In preparing the presentation with Tom, through which he had just taken the rest of the Aardvark London team, they had agreed that it was best to focus on the current state of the product, feedback from the early customers and team morale. But he felt that he had to share with Gordon the detail of what he had ascertained over the last couple of days. It was not a conversation he was looking forward to.

It had become apparent very quickly on Peter's arrival in Oxford, as he reviewed the situation with the financial controller, Emma's deputy, that the Aston had indeed been purchased with company money. The car was officially deemed a write-off but the insurance company had already frozen the claim pending enquiries based on the police report; their attitude was that if they could prove gross negligence or at least careless driving on the part of Jack, they may well be able to wriggle out of paying. That was the first of several batches of bad news that came Peter's way during his visit.

Reviews of the product were encouraging in terms of the potential capability of the new platform but were once more disturbing when it came to the chances of a functioning product that could be installed for trials at customers. He had spent hours with the head of Engineering and they had at least constructed a plan to deliver the new platform in phases.

He had worked through a sales recovery plan with Ewan and had managed to speak to a couple of customers; they had accepted the timetable he proposed for product delivery and were generally sympathetic to the situation given what had happened to the CEO and CFO of Riverjack Crypto. However, one CIO of a company who had invested in the early version of the product was pretty forthright.

"Look," he said, "I appreciate you have some, how to put it, short term headwinds in the business. We are going to miss Jack at least for his personality and energy if not for his product. My boss demanded to know the status the other day and asked why I had agreed to buy a prototype based on a Powerpoint presentation. I told him that we had negotiated great terms and that we had been a very successful user of Jack's previous start-up's technology. In response he said that he was thinking his way of becoming a successful user of IT was to outsource the entire shambles to Uzbekistan – he said he knew they would be useless and incomprehensible but he had that already and at least it would be cheaper. So listen here, Peter, this is my bloody career on the line. I need you to deliver the platform without fail as you have just told me or I am, to use a technical term, fucked. And believe me, I won't go down alone."

Peter had had no doubt about the authenticity of his threat and gave him reassurances that sounded a lot more confident than he was feeling.

He had decided to call a company meeting to brief everyone on the situation and rally them to redouble their efforts. He did not want to scare anyone into resigning – he had already been told by the head of Engineering that a number of critical technical employees had questioned whether they should stay or take their highly marketable resumes out to recruiters who would salivate at the chance to place them with more stable companies – and he wanted to paint a positive picture about the future potential of the business without creating false hope. He needed everyone on board with a renewed effort to get the product out on time, to build a larger pipeline of potential future customers and to actually convert some of those to further sales.

He rehearsed what he wanted to say in his mind and was actually feeling quite confident of being able to pull it off. He had faced more difficult challenges in his life, for sure. He thought of all of those professional cricketers who had wanted to hurt him with a cricket ball when he walked out to bat, calling him a 'Fucking Educated Cunt'. He smiled at the memory: FEC had been the nickname for Michael Atherton, a man who had captained the England team with determination and distinction and was now an award-winning journalist. It was said to stand for 'Future England Captain' for the benefit of the Press but known to stand for the other phrase by all the game's insiders. That Peter had overcome similar challenges and disdain gave him confidence when faced with this adversity and he now he was standing up in front of about fifty expectant faces.

He had embarked on his opening remarks when he noticed that Ewan was not there. He broke off, caught the eye of Jennifer, the HR Manager, and asked her to find Ewan as his presence was critical. She nodded and headed out of the overcrowded meeting room to fetch him as quickly as possible. Peter just made a quip about Ewan's being engaged with a customer for once and carried on with his state of the union message. He was surprised when Jennifer came back about ten minutes later with a look of astonishment on her face and mouthing "We need to talk right now" at him.

He was just wrapping up what he hoped had been a Churchillian address and was answering a couple of questions about whether the company was going to go out of business. (His stock answer was that Aardvark would be supportive but he did not want to understate the seriousness of the situation) or how the company was going to win new deals (he had confidence in Ewan to drive sales and he would support him and his team in an executive capacity while they searched for a new CEO). It was at this point that Jennifer had come back in and, as he mentioned Ewan, she was shaking her head vigorously. He realised that there was something seriously wrong and so decided to bring the meeting to a close. There was a desultory round of applause and the employees of Riverjack Crypto filed out in silence. Peter looked at them and seriously doubted whether they were ready to "fight them on the beaches".

When everyone had left the room, Jennifer came up to him. He looked at her quizzically.

"Well, Jennifer," he said. "You do not look as though you are about to tell me something I am going to like very much."

"You could say that," she said and paused, wondering how to go on. "You know you sent me to find Ewan," she continued. "Well, you may or may not have noticed when you were speaking that Abigail was missing as well."

"Oh God," said Peter. "I'm afraid I may know where you are going with this but carry on."

"I am afraid what you are afraid of is right," said Jennifer. "I found them alright. In the Marketing cupboard. She was sitting on the photocopier as it was spewing out hundreds of copies of something."

"Oh no," said Peter. "Not like the proverbial washing-machine trick? Does that really work by the way, for a woman? I've always wondered."

"It depends," said Jennifer. "A bit like horse-riding for some people, you know. But I tell you what does usually work. It's if you are sitting on top of any mechanical device with your knickers round your ankles and a man with his head between your legs."

"Oh no, please tell me no."

"You had better believe it."

"Shit."

"That's what Abigail said when she saw me walk in," said Jennifer. "I won't repeat what Ewan said but let's just say it was not particularly polite."

"I can imagine," replied Peter. "What the hell did you do?"

"The only thing I could. I told Abigail to put her clothes back on and for both of them to leave the premises immediately and to consider themselves suspended pending further action."

"And what did they do?" asked Peter.

"Well, Abigail told me to fuck off and said that I was a sex-starved virgin who wouldn't know an orgasm if it hit me in the face," replied Jennifer.

Peter studied her appraisingly. "Well, I hardly think that's fair. I mean…" then he broke off as Jennifer raised an eyebrow. He started to stammer an apology but she smiled and said, "No problem, Peter. I appreciate your vote of confidence! Ewan just cackled and asked if I really was a virgin and whether I'd like him to do anything to help."

Peter looked at her in astonishment. He just managed to stop himself once from asking her if it was true.

"Really? He said that to you?" he spluttered instead.

"Indeed he did. I just repeated to both of them that they were suspended and they should leave the building immediately."

"Well, I am sorry you had to deal with this," said Peter, realising that he had finally better say something more appropriate than any of his thoughts and utterances to date. "I am not sure you could have handled it better. We are going to have to fire both of them, I suppose. Wonderful timing! I had of course just told the whole company how much confidence I had in Ewan to help us sell our way out of this mess; and now this. Just bloody brilliant!"

"Yes," said Jennifer. "I appreciate it is not a great situation for us. But still, I think you are right. We will have to fire both of them for gross misconduct. I will prepare the letters for you to sign."

"I agree," said Peter in a resigned tone. "No other choice, really. Still, now I really don't know what we are going to do with the business. Bugger on regardless, I suppose, and try to push the sales team to sell, even without Ewan to oversee them."

"The company certainly could do with a change of luck," said Jennifer. She turned away and left Peter to his own thoughts.

He was running through all this in his mind as Susannah left. He composed himself once more, thought of all of those aggressive fast bowlers and steeled himself.

"So the thing is, Gordon. We need to talk. Riverjack Crypto is…"

To his surprise, Gordon interrupted him.

"Riverjack Crypto is going through some challenges, for sure. But I am absolutely sure you have everything under control," he said.

This was not what Peter had been expecting at all. He stared at Gordon, trying to hide his bewilderment.

"Well," he stammered. "The situation is difficult for sure, but I have the outline of a plan for recovery. I just took the team through it and…"

He broke off as Gordon held up his hand to silence him.

"I am sure the plan is fine. You can go through it with Susannah in detail tomorrow. I will give you my full support. There's something more pressing I want to share with you," Gordon said.

"Right, Gordon," said Peter without a clue as to where this was leading. "Fire away. I'm all ears."

"What I have to say," said Gordon, "I am expecting you to treat in the strictest confidence."

"Of course," said Peter. "You can rely on me."

"Good," said Gordon. "It is just that if Mitch and Susannah found out you knew, it could jeopardise everything."

"Understood," replied Peter.

"It's like this. You do know why Susannah is here this week?"

"Well," said Peter, a little cautiously, "It's as you explained, right? She is here to review the portfolio and really drill into the problems at Riverjack Crypto at our offsite."

"Not exactly," said Gordon. "Mitch and I discussed that as an excuse for her to come over. Actually, we had agreed that you and I are more than capable of sorting out the short term issues at Riverjack Crypto. No, there's a very different reason."

"What's that?" asked Peter, now thoroughly intrigued.

"You know you have always said that you would be interested in moving to San Francisco?" asked Gordon.

"Yes, absolutely," said Peter, his eyes starting to sparkle with excitement.

"Well, it's like this. There's an opening for a new partner at Aardvark and we have decided that, with everything that is going on in the Bay Area, the role should be located over there. There's more work than that existing team can handle and we need another partner in the business."

"I see," said Peter, excited but still wondering where this was leading.

"And here's the thing," said Gordon with a smile, "Given our plans to demonstrate our global reach, Mitch wants someone with considerable international experience. So, all in all, we talked about you as a potential candidate, Peter."

"Really, Gordon?" said Peter, unable to hide his excitement. "That would be fantastic. I would leap at the chance, both for the promotion and to move to the US."

"Mitch likes the idea and I am very supportive," said Gordon. "Mitch is always saying that just our accent makes us sound thirty percent smarter over there. You are the obvious candidate and we like promoting from within, as you know."

"Right," said Peter. "This is really great news. But I am not sure where Susannah comes into this."

"That's just the point, Peter," explained Gordon. "She's over here to evaluate you on behalf of Mitch. He implicitly trusts her opinion, so whether Mitch finally approves your promotion or not is going to depend on her report."

"Got it," said Peter. "I guess it's my chance to shine. I will spend all day tomorrow and perhaps take her to dinner tomorrow night; maybe show her around London as well. Then I will spend all the time I can with her at the offsite and, by the time we are done, she will have had a chance to see everything I am capable of and we will have got to know each other pretty well as well."

"Stop right there, Peter," said Gordon firmly. "This is exactly what I mean about keeping things confidential. If you try to spend every second with Susannah, she will know something is up and that will definitely work against you. In fact, it could entirely scupper your chances. You need to behave as if you have no idea of the real reason she's here."

"I see," said Peter, reflecting more slowly. "Yes, that actually makes sense. I need to be a bit more subtle. So how do I play it?"

Gordon gave the impression that he had paused to think through the difficult problem and then said in a measured tone.

"I think the key thing is that you need an advocate to promote you to her and really push your cause. Someone who is going to just give you some cover whenever issues around Riverjack Crypto come up; and someone who knows Susannah pretty well."

Gordon paused again for dramatic effect and allowed the silence to develop between them to a suitably uncomfortable length.

"You see," he eventually went on, "If you get this job, it will reflect really well on the UK office and my ability to mentor people to career success, so I want to help as much as I can."

"Yes, of course", said Peter eagerly.

"I think the best thing to do, would be for me to play that role."

"You'd be willing to do that for me?" said Peter. "That would be incredible. Thank you!".

"Think nothing of it. Pure self-interest," said Gordon in a self-deprecating tone. "So, the plan must be you spend time with Susannah tomorrow as agreed taking her through the state of play at Riverjack Crypto and of course your rescue plan. I am sure it is in good shape already but make sure you respond positively to all her suggestions. Americans don't like to feel as though their input has been ignored and Susannah is very typical in that respect."

"Right, got it," said Peter.

"I will then take over from you tomorrow afternoon and if necessary, look after Susannah into the evening. That way she won't have any idea that you know what is going on and she won't feel smothered by your attention and smell the proverbial rat. And then during the offsite, I think you need to make sure I have a free hand to spend as much time with Susannah as possible, preferably uninterrupted. You know the issue that complicates everything is that my wife, Cressida, is going to be joining us."

"Sure," said Peter. "You'd mentioned that before. How does that impact me, though?"

"I need you to spend as much time as possible with Cressida to free me up to work on Susannah – entirely for your benefit, of course," replied Gordon.

"Are you sure that will be OK for both you and Cressida?" asked Peter. "I don't want to be a nuisance, however much I want the promotion."

"Not at all. You are my priority this weekend for all sorts of reasons," countered Gordon. "Leave Susannah with me and focus on Cressida. She will enjoy that a lot, so don't have any concern on that score. Of course, you know that her father was a founder of Aardvark with Mitch and as a result she has always said she wants to get to know the team better. The offsite is a good opportunity for that. What you may not know is that she does have a finance background – we qualified as Chartered Accountants together actually – so she is pretty knowledgeable."

"Really?" said Peter in surprise. "I honestly had no idea. That is amazing."

"Absolutely," continued Gordon. "You have a common background and she wants to get into the detail of our portfolio to understand some of the challenges we are facing. Riverjack Crypto will be right up her street. Your problem, once you start, will be keeping her out of it, I promise."

"Got it," said Peter. "I like the plan; and hopefully by the end of the offsite you will have worked Susannah sufficiently so that the job is mine."

"That's the idea," agreed Gordon. "You keep Cressida occupied while I work on Susannah."

"Outstanding," said Peter with unbridled enthusiasm. "Thanks so much, Gordon. I really, really appreciate it."

"No problem. Just doing my job. Your success will be mine," said Gordon with self-satisfaction.

He was momentarily surprised when Peter proffered his hand to shake and did so in an automatic reaction.

"Just make sure you keep this plan between us, though," he cautioned. "The slightest hint to anyone could spell disaster."

"You bet," affirmed Peter, turning to leave the office. "I am not going to shoot myself in the foot that way. I will just go and revisit the Riverjack Crypto plan to make sure I have incorporated some of the details suggested by Henry and Tom and then I will be ready for Susannah tomorrow. But mum's the word for sure!"

Peter left the office in a state of suppressed excitement. Gordon left in a state of overt irritation at the thought of the evening ahead and what might have been.

That Thursday evening was spent in very different ways. Gordon found the French film mystifying and fundamentally dull. He was uninspired by the question and answer session with the members of the cast and production team and positively loathed the detailed post mortem discussion he was forced to endure over moules frites with Cressida's book club friends. He noticed he was the only husband who had not managed to escape the ordeal and when he did venture an opinion, it was immediately dismissed as superficial or coming from the typically myopic male perspective. He chose to remain silent and pick morosely at his fries.

Peter spent the evening working on the Riverjack Crypto rescue plan and by the end of several hours' hard effort, felt he had a coherent approach.

Susannah found that her commitments after her call with Mitch meant that she was talking to various people in the USA until midnight her time. Her bathroom had been fixed, seemingly, and although the lack of shower was annoying, room service was surprisingly good and the Wi-Fi actually worked well. Moreover her tormentor of the afternoon behind reception had been replaced by a charming young man who clearly found her attractive and for whom nothing was too much trouble.

Henry had been thinking that the W could offer more entertainment, as a fresh set of Emirates crew would undoubtedly be in residence. However, he also realised that he was tired after the previous night's exertions and decided to conserve his energy; after all his new Brazilian friend had agreed to meet up again the night after the offsite ended and he felt that he could not afford any sort of 'Boeing Boeing' situation where he would have multiple lovers in residence at the same hotel, so in the end he had a quiet night at home.

Edwin had been invited to an alumni reception for his Business School and had gone there determined to be confident and, perhaps, to ask a female graduate out on a date. Unfortunately the glass of red wine he was offered on entering was knocked out of his hand by a wide gesticulation from a large man in a group who were guffawing with laughter. The wine cascaded dramatically over his white shirt and, despite the profuse apologies from his unwitting assailant, his resulting appearance destroyed his fragile self-confidence once more and he found himself talking to a couple of his former professors (who were evidently frustrated both that they had not managed to move on to more august academic institutions and that, more immediately, Edwin seemed to be determined to latch onto them all evening) before heading home alone once more.

Theresa spent the evening working on the portfolio valuation analysis for the offsite; she wanted to ensure it was absolutely up to date and moreover, as she thought to herself, she had nothing else to do to occupy her Thursday night; she was not unhappy at the thought.

Tom and Steve had met for a beer where the topic of conversation revolved around Lisa and Samantha and the best way to arrange a double date that would not terrify Lisa.

Lisa herself spent the entire night in her bedroom, hardly able to sleep as she worried about what could go wrong at the offsite.

Later Steve and Samantha hardly slept either that night but for very different reasons.

CHAPTER EIGHT

To: Susannah.Bierson@aardvarkvc.com
Cc: Peter.Williamson@aardvarkvc.com
From: Gordon.Fairbald@aardvarkvc.com
Subject: Today

Hi Susannah,
Sorry to report that I have had a terrible night thanks to a bad mussel I ate. I won't go into graphic details but I have barely time to send this between trips to the bathroom. Apparently no one else was affected so I am just unlucky, says Cressida. In all events I won't be in today. You and Peter should go ahead and meet on Riverjack Crypto and I will focus on getting myself ready for the offsite. I am guessing that I will not be fighting fit until Sunday. Will you be OK to make your own way to the offsite hotel? Lisa can sort you out, hopefully.
Looking forward to seeing you Sunday having flushed this right out of my system.
Peter – FYI.
Gordon

To: Gordon.Fairbald@aardvarkvc.com
Cc: Peter.Williamson@aardvarkvc.com
From: Susannah.Bierson@aardvarkvc.com
Subject: Re: Today

Hi Gordon,
Really sorry to hear you are not well. I hope you indeed get back on your feet for Sunday. Don't worry – I will spend the day with Peter and ask Lisa to help me get over to the offsite. Will figure it out.
Get well soon!!!
Susannah

Peter read Gordon's email it with mixed emotions. Given what he had been told about Susannah's real reason for being in the UK, it would have been useful to have Gordon attending the Riverjack Crypto review session, if only to provide some air cover when Susannah asked what would no doubt be difficult if perfectly reasonable questions. If he wanted someone else there for moral support, Henry would just be cantankerous and obstructive (and no doubt would be spending the time both undermining him and trying to impress Susannah) and Edwin just totally useless. By contrast, Tom was his friend, ally and involved with Riverjack Crypto almost as much as he was. He dropped Tom a quick email about Gordon's current state of health and asked him to be part of the session with Susannah which was due to start at 10am that morning. With that, he showered, dressed and headed into the office early in order to go through his presentation on Riverjack Crypto one more time and to be prepared for any angle that Susannah's interrogation might take.

In the meantime, Gordon had managed to send the email to Susannah and Peter between extremely unpleasant, frequent trips to the bathroom. At one point, having realised his suffering had lasted several hours, Cressida had chosen to show some sympathy and had inquired at the bathroom door whether he would like her to fetch a doctor. Gordon had just sworn at her and groaned.

"I think this is your own fault, Gordon Fairbald," she retorted, decidedly miffed that her attempt at being considerate had been rebuffed. "You overindulged in the mussels last night to such an extent that there were comments about how many you were eating. I have no sympathy; I told you to ease back but you would not listen," she added vindictively.

"How can this be my fucking fault," said Gordon in between bouts of retching. "The basics of hygiene were clearly not followed. I shall sue the Book Club for substantial damages. And they are too stupid to realise moules frites is Belgian, not French."

He groaned once more and turned his attention back to the business in hand.

"You will do nothing of the sort, Gordon." said Cressida. "No one else has suffered at all. I have checked this morning with several of the people we were with last night and everyone else is absolutely fine."

"I wouldn't trust anyone else who was there to sit the right way on the loo," shouted back Gordon.

"Well, just make sure you do or you are cleaning up the mess!" retorted Cressida. With that she left Gordon to his own devices and went downstairs to the kitchen. She had a tennis lesson that morning and wanted to get to the club early to practice; so to keep her strength up, a bite of breakfast before she left was vital.

Gordon's only response to Cressida's last comment was to retch violently again. Eventually he made it out of the bathroom, crawled back to bed and thankfully fell asleep. When he awoke five hours later he found that he no longer had need of the bathroom – although he was still feeling very weak. He reached for his mobile to check email but there was nothing about the Riverjack Crypto session and he did not have the strength to think about anything else.

He wondered about calling Lisa but decided against it; "No bloody point," he thought. "She's so preoccupied with the offsite that she wouldn't manage to do anything except blow up the new coffee machine in a panic." The effort of all of this had taken whatever energy he had and he flopped back onto his pillow feeling sorry for himself and vengeful against the world in general.

While Gordon had been asleep, Peter, Tom and Susannah had been talking through Riverjack Crypto in detail. Peter had decided that he would hold nothing back and was delighted to see that Susannah was not shocked by the revelations about Ewan and Abigail and that, having already learned of the cause of the fatal car crash, she was merely inspired to ask whether they had invested in a cryptocurrency payments platform company or the next Ashley Madison dating site. In fact the tone of the meeting was fairly supportive, much to Peter's relief. It was clear throughout that Susannah was extremely sharp, perceptive and experienced.

There were still major delays in the release of the product to manage despite the plan he had worked out to deliver a working prototype to customers. They would obviously need a new Chief Executive as well as Finance Director and Sales Director and attracting the right calibre of person was going to be no easy task given the company situation. There was still the issue of the money Jack had spent on the Aston and whether the insurance company would pay anything at all. Tom's legal opinion was not at all optimistic after he had scrutinised the company's policy. Finally there was the pending unfair dismissal claim that both Ewan and Abigail were bringing against the company, although Peter was more concerned about the unfortunate publicity the salacious details of the affair would engender, following on as it did so rapidly from Jack's and Emma's demise, rather than the merits of their case which he was sure any reasonable employment tribunal would dismiss.

All in all, Peter was relieved that he had not found himself in front of the proverbial firing squad, although he had no illusions about what he might face during the offsite and indeed what Mitch might say. The fundamental problem was that neither Susannah nor Tom, nor indeed Theresa, who had joined for part of the meeting, had been able to come up with any better ideas to rescue the business than he had. Edwin, of course, who had also attended, said practically nothing and as usual sat in intimidated silence. Despite Susannah's constructive comments as he outlined the situation and what he thought could be done to redress things, he was still faced with a potential disaster, with no guarantee the situation could be turned around and absolutely no certainty that Susannah was going to submit a positive report on him back to Mitch. It was overall extremely frustrating.

The meeting broke up around lunchtime and Peter took a few action items away to work on in the afternoon; Tom had agreed to join him to help while Susannah had been forced to endure a couple of hours with Henry, listening to him pontificate on investing in Europe, grill her on what Mitch thought of Aardvark's UK performance and find ways to get her to accept a dinner invitation that evening. She drew on her extensive experience in dealing with unsuitable suitors to refuse politely while in no way implying that Henry had anything untoward on his mind. Henry had eventually given up and returned to pondering whether another visit to the W that evening would in fact be a good plan after all.

All of this, however, had been nothing to the nightmare of a day that Lisa had suffered. Her sleepless night had turned into a day fraught with worry and confusion. Mary had left her all the relevant papers for dealing with the offsite and had sent Ms. Briggs, the hotel's business manager, an email to introduce Lisa as the new point of contact. Lisa had spoken to her and, although it appeared that everything had been properly organised, she had been asked to confirm all the names of the attendees and nationalities as well as make some pressing decisions about the menu for the dinners on Sunday and Monday night. She enlisted Edwin's help and they both realised that they had no idea about anyone's dietary requirements. Lisa decided the best thing she could do was to send an email to ask if anyone had any dietary restrictions and promised to call the hotel back.

Lisa's day was not made easier by Henry interrupting her on a regular basis on the pretext that he wanted to know some detail about the hotel – was there ample car parking and then did the fitness centre have a jacuzzi and sauna and was it mixed or single sex? When Lisa called Ms. Briggs for the fourth time in an hour, the woman was quite rude to her and suggested that she send any further queries by email. Henry enjoyed teasing her and insisted on going on to ask whether fresh flowers would be placed in his bedroom on a daily basis and whether she could guarantee that the décor would not be pink as the colour upset him (Lisa was so flustered at this stage that she did not even notice that he was wearing a pink shirt). Even Henry, however, realised he may have been pushing things too far as Lisa, on being asked whether she had organised a seating plan for dinner on Sunday night and made sure that there was an ample supply of working marker pens for the flipcharts in the meeting room started to well up. He could see the telltale wetness in her eyes, so made some reassuring remark and left abruptly; he was indubitably afraid of Mary's reaction if she learned he had upset Lisa.

Edwin witnessed these interchanges and did his best to reassure Lisa and at one point to intervene in what he thought was a protective way, but Henry just ignored him. He felt tongue-tied in Lisa's presence although she was so nervous and distracted she did not seem to notice; she was just grateful for his assistance and such reassurance as he was able to give.

By about six o'clock Lisa felt that she had everything sorted out as best she could. She and Edwin emailed out final directions to the hotel, which was close to Horsham in Sussex, south of London. She planned to get down there early on Sunday by train to make sure everything was in order and Edwin (who could not quite believe he had had the courage to speak up) offered to go with her which she appreciated very much. They agreed to meet at Victoria station on Sunday morning. They worked together to put all of the papers for the offsite – hotel room confirmations; meeting room reservations; food and beverage orders and the like – into some sort of order in a file. When they had finished, they both looked at it suspiciously and wondered what had been forgotten, both unable to speak and utterly terrified at the prospect of what could go wrong.

At that point Peter and Tom emerged from Peter's office having concluded as best they could the action plan to set Riverjack Crypto back on its feet. Peter had no idea whether what they had to propose to the rest of the team would be sufficient to carry the day but he did know that at that point, he needed a drink. He proposed the same to Tom who agreed immediately and turned to Lisa.

"What about you, Lisa?" he asked. "I know how hard you have been working to get everything ready for Sunday. I bet you could do with a drink as well. You look like it for sure and you deserve it, being responsible for keeping the rest of us under control!"

Before Lisa could reply, Susannah came in. She had finally extricated herself from Henry's clutches and wanted to see how Peter and Tom had got on. She had had a brief call with Mitch to report on progress, such as there had been, and was wondering what to do with her evening. One of her former classmates at Harvard had had to cancel a dinner date they had arranged only that morning over email so she found herself a little at a loose end.

Peter, of course, did not want to appear too forward with her. He remembered Gordon's advice and although he did not want to be antisocial, thought it best that they did not spend any more time together before Sunday. Much as he had already started to enjoy her company, he certainly did not want to give the impression that he was ingratiating himself in any way to her. However, before he had any time even to think about how to avoid inviting Susannah to join them, Tom said:

"Hi, Susannah. How was your afternoon?"

"Good, thanks. Just had a long catch up with Henry," she replied somewhat neutrally.

"How lucky for you," smiled Tom. "Now, we were just contemplating a drink and perhaps dinner. If you have no other better offer, would you care to join us? We can promise you the best of British fare: boiled vegetables, greasy fish and warm beer."

"Put like that, how can I refuse?" countered Susannah with a laugh.

"Great," said Tom. "Peter, Lisa, I suggest we head to the Bunch of Grapes and then if you have nothing else to do, there is the Burger and Lobster around the corner which should cater to all appetites.

"Really? I mean, are you sure you want me to come along?" stammered Lisa. "You three must have really important things to discuss and I don't want to be any trouble."

"Nonsense," said Tom. "You are going to be the most important person at the offsite because without you, nothing will work and we will all be running around like headless chickens. We are counting on you!"

"I hope not," whispered Lisa meekly.

"You bet we are," smiled Susannah. "None of us could run a bath so it's all on you, girl."

"No, please, don't say that," wailed Lisa.

"I am kidding," said Susannah, laughing. "We girls must stick together. Don't you agree, boys?" she added turning to Peter and Tom.

"Absolutely," said Tom. "Girl power it is. You ready, Peter? You're buying. After all, it's because of your fiasco that Susannah's been dragged halfway around the world."

"That's not entirely the reason," said Susannah with a slight smile. She turned to Edwin and said, "You've made sure Lisa has everything under control?"

Edwin looked at her, blinked and stammered, "Er, yes, I mean, that is, I have done my best."

"You see," continued Susannah. "At least Edwin has done something useful this afternoon. Good for you!"

"And I hardly think fiasco is the right word to describe what remains an excellent investment opportunity," said Peter, finally intervening and feeling as though he should say something to defend the situation.

"Nothing that beer won't put right," said Tom. "Let's go. Oh and Lisa, you bring up the rear and turn the lights off, will you?"

"Um, yes, but, er, I don't know how," flailed Lisa.

"We will leave you to figure it out," said Tom with a laugh.

"Behave, Tom," said Peter. "Lisa, don't listen to a word he says. They are automatic and turn off by themselves."

"Damn you, Peter," said Tom with mock aggression. "I wanted to leave Lisa struggling here for ten minutes and then come back as the knight in shining armour to rescue her. The best laid plans..." he added.

"Don't listen to them, Lisa," interjected Susannah. "Men! They are only young once but immature forever. You know where this pub is?" she asked her.

Lisa nodded.

"Then show me," Susannah went on, "And we will leave these clowns to follow in our footsteps."

She paused and looked around. "Is this your file for the offsite?" she asked, picking up the folder Lisa had been preparing. Lisa nodded silently once more, totally overwhelmed.

"Great," said Susannah and handed it to Tom. "You are in charge, Mr Attorney. You can carry it and finally prove that lawyers do have a use."

With that she took Lisa's arm, guided her up out of her chair and out of the door, leaving Peter and Tom looking slightly nonplussed.

"You heard her," said Peter, finally. "Do something useful and bring the file. I'll stay here and turn out the lights."

They looked at each other, both breaking into a laugh at the same time.

Edwin stood up somewhat tentatively. Peter looked at him and said, "Are you coming too, Edwin?"

"Oh, can I?" said Edwin, gratefully. "I don't have any other plans. That would be great."

Peter wasn't just being benevolent; he also felt that Edwin's presence could be a very useful distraction from any further discussion about Riverjack Crypto.

They found Susannah and Lisa in the pub where Susannah had expertly negotiated the Friday evening rush to procure drinks while Lisa had managed to find a free table in the far corner. Tom and Edwin joined them while Peter went off to do battle with about twenty other people crowding up to the bar and demanding to be served.

"So, Lisa," said Susannah kindly. "How are you enjoying Aardvark? You haven't been with us long, have you? Have we treated you well?"

"Oh yes, everyone's been really kind. Mary in particularly has really taken trouble to look after me and Peter is so considerate as a boss."

"Are you kidding?" laughed Tom. "You haven't seen his mean, macho side yet. He hides it well but he has an evil temper and can rant and rave with best of them."

"Don't pay attention to anything Tom says," said Peter, as he returned with the drinks balanced on a tray. "I am benign through and through."

"Like hell," snorted Tom, taking a long draft of beer. "But don't worry, Lisa. If he ever gets out of control, I will be there to rescue you."

"You and your Sir Galahad act," Peter said.

"Well, I already rescued Lisa from the evil clutches of the coffee machine," said Tom. "That was just after she had used my ear as a handle to stop herself falling over on the Tube."

"Oh, I am still so sorry about that," sighed Lisa. "I really didn't mean to."

"No worries," said Tom, "My ears are there whenever you need them."

"What happened?" asked Edwin, wanting to be part of the conversation.

"Lisa has a particular way of introducing herself to her new colleagues," laughed Tom. "It involves grabbing parts of their anatomy and holding on for dear life. Traveling with Lisa can be a dangerous occupation."

"Oh," said Edwin, still not understanding. "We are going down by train together on Sunday."

"Really?" said Tom, looking at them both.

Suddenly there was a slightly awkward silence around the table. Susannah looked between Lisa, Edwin and Tom with some amusement. She noticed Peter taking a pull of his beer and suddenly looking pensive, as if the reality of the offsite and the potential consequences had broken through to dominate his thoughts.

Susannah decided that she should be the one to put everyone at his or her ease, given that no one knew her well and perhaps expected the conversation with her to revolve around work, so she turned to Peter and asked a question that American often like to ask when drinking with anyone who is British.

"Peter, I have to know something," she said. He turned to her with an inquiring look on his face, "You have to explain the rules of cricket to me. How can a game last five days and end in a tie?"

Peter said, "It's a draw, actually. A tie means something very specific in cricket."

Tom added, "And it's laws, by the way."

"Excuse me?" asked Susannah.

"He means," explained Lisa, surprising herself, "That cricket has laws of the game, not rules."

All of them turned to Lisa, astonished both at her speaking without being prompted but also at her specific knowledge.

"Wow!" said Tom. "Forgive me for sounding like a condescending mansplainer but how do you know that? You are right, of course, but I would never have guessed you knew. Not many people have any clue about the game. Are you a fan?"

"No, not really at all," said Lisa, turning red as she had become the centre of attention. "It's just my Dad took me to watch Nottinghamshire play once and he tried to explain what was going on to me. I couldn't really follow but I do remember when I asked him to explain the rules, he told me that cricket doesn't have rules but laws. I suppose it has just stuck with me." Her voice petered out sheepishly.

"That's brilliant," said Tom.

"Did you go to Trent Bridge?" asked Peter. "The main ground in Nottingham."

"Yes, I think so," replied Lisa. "I remember the name because we studied rivers a lot for my degree and the Trent runs through Nottingham."

"Great ground," said Peter. "I've played there a couple of times."

"What?" said Tom, suitably impressed. "You've played at Trent Bridge?".

"Yes," said Peter. "I've played at a lot of the grounds around the UK, mostly against the county sides for the Combined Universities team."

"That's impressive," said Tom. "I had no idea you were that good. I need to get you into my club side as a ringer."

"Oh, I haven't played for quite a few years so I am totally rusty." said Peter modestly.

"I was hopeless at cricket," said Edwin. "I couldn't see anything without my glasses and I was always the last one picked."

"Have you played at Lord's?" asked Susannah.

It was her turn to be stared at in astonishment.

"Yes, I am not just some dumb American who hasn't traveled outside Texas," she rebuked them, laughing. "I've actually been to Lord's to watch a game. Although," she added, turning to Lisa, "Like you, I had absolutely no idea what was going on. It seemed to me that most of the time people weren't the game at all and spent the whole day getting completely blasted instead."

"Sounds about right," said Tom. He turned to Peter and asked, "So have you played at Lord's? You're a Blue, right?"

"I have played at Lord's but unfortunately I'm not a Blue," said Peter. "I was injured or ill during the Varsity match all three years and so I was never awarded it. Another unfulfilled ambition!" he added, in a slightly wistful tone.

"You're a what?" asked Susannah.

"It means you played sport for Oxford or Cambridge against the other," explained Peter. "I was in the Oxford cricket team for my three years but was just unfortunate with timing. You only are awarded a Blue if you play in the actual game against Cambridge and I never did."

"Bad luck," said Tom.

"Yes, wasn't it?" said Peter in a tone that hinted at deep regret.

A brief silence ensued before Peter took up the gauntlet of trying to explain to Susannah and Lisa how cricket is played. However, despite enlisting both the help of Tom and using their glasses and beer mats to represent the pitch, the wickets and the ball, he felt as though it was something of an uphill struggle and ended rather tamely by offering to take them to a game himself so he could explain it better.

"The other crazy sport that you guys play over here is rugby," said Susannah. "What is that all about?"

"Ah," said Tom. "Now you are talking. That is real man's game. None of the protective gear you have playing cricket – or even American Football.

Just real men slogging it out in the mud – although," he added with a brief pause, "Women play it a lot now, too."

"The best thing about rugby," said Peter, "Is that as spectators we usually have a pretty good idea of what is going on when it comes to the big picture, but more often than not have absolutely no clue about the detail of why the referee made a decision against one team or the other. It means everyone has an opinion and you can argue about it in the pub for hours afterwards."

"I reckon the players are pretty clueless as well," said Tom. "The look of shocked innocence on their faces when the referee blows for a penalty always makes me laugh. Most of the time the referee just seems to be guessing, anyway. It can be pretty technical as well as vicious and it's anyone's guess what really happens when there are ten guys all lying on the ball, doing whatever they can get away with as long as they are not caught on TV."

"I'd love to go to a live game one day," said Susannah.

"Well, you know there's a big game tomorrow," said Tom. "Harlequins against Wasps. Two London clubs so it's a local derby and the game has been moved to Twickenham because of the demand for tickets. Steve Miller and I are season ticket holders at Harlequins so we are going. I could see if I can get tickets for you – there may be some left because Twickenham holds about 80,000 people."

"Twickenham is where the England national team usually play," explained Peter. "It's quite unusual for a normal domestic league game to be played there."

"If it's not too much trouble, Tom, I would love the experience," said Susannah. "I'd need an escort, though." She turned to Lisa, "Would you come with me?"

"Oh, what, me?" stammered Lisa, once again totally taken aback by being included. "Really?"

"Absolutely," said Susannah. "I need someone to look after me as I have no idea how to get there."

"Nor do I," wailed Lisa.

"Then we had better have Edwin look after both of us," said Susannah with a smile, turning to him.

Edwin gulped slightly but said he would be glad to go if that was the plan.

"You like rugby, Edwin?" asked Tom.

"Actually I was as hopeless at rugby as I was at cricket," admitted Edwin. "But I love it as a spectator. I've been to Twickenham internationals quite a few times."

"You're kidding," said Tom. "I didn't think you had it in you."

Edwin went slightly red and said nothing.

"That's settled, then," said Susannah. "Edwin knows the way and can take Lisa and me."

"You'll come too, Peter?" asked Tom.

Peter was immediately torn. Going to the rugby with everyone would undoubtedly be entertaining and might also give him the chance to build a closer relationship with Susannah, in spite of Gordon's warning. On balance he decided it would be overall manageable with care.

"Yes, absolutely," he said decisively.

"Right," he said. "That's settled. Leave it with me. I will go and see if I can get more tickets. Give me five minutes to check with Steve and then we will see what can be done." He turned to Edwin and said in a slightly brusque tone, "In the meantime, Edwin, make yourself useful and get another round in."

Edwin nodded and got up. Tom headed outside the pub, dialing Steve as he went.

Lisa turned to Peter and asked tentatively, "Were you really that good at cricket?"

"I don't want to boast but I was, actually," he said. "I really thought about playing it professionally but decided that I could not deprive the venture capital industry of my talents and so didn't in the end."

Susannah laughed and Lisa added, "That's amazing. I've never met anyone who was that good at anything."

Peter just smiled as Tom came back to the table sooner than expected.

"All done," he said,. "We have tickets for tomorrow's game. Steve's organising them and says Samantha is up for it as well."

"Who's Samantha?" asked Susannah.

"Steve's girlfriend and actually Lisa's flatmate," said Tom.

"Really?" said Susannah.

"Yes," said Lisa, "She's my cousin."

"I didn't know that," said Tom. "Keeping it in the family, huh?"

"She's very kind," said Lisa. "She's the one who introduced me to London and Steve helped me get the job at Aardvark."

"Then we should buy both of them a drink," said Tom. "Talking of which, where is that idiot Edwin with the next round?"

"He's trying to figure out how to get five drinks back over here without spilling them over everyone by the look of it," said Peter. "I will give him a hand."

Peter went up to where Edwin was struggling to manage the drinks, picked up three beers with rapid dexterity and turned back, leaving a grateful Edwin following behind.

They discussed the logistics of the next day and agreed a rendezvous at Waterloo station around midday in order to get down to Twickenham in good time for the game.

After a while, they moved on from the pub to the Burger and Lobster restaurant. It was Lisa's first experience of lobster and she rather liked it. Tom was the only one of them to take the burger option. He complained that, as he put it, "he had once lost a fight with a lobster in Boston and as a result was confined to bed for 48 hours." Lisa was on the point of asking how big the lobster had been when Susannah expressed surprise because of Boston's enviable reputation for seafood restaurants.

The conversation drifted to travel, diverse experiences around the world and inevitably to relationships. Lisa, whose time abroad had been limited to family holidays on the Spanish Costa del Sol said little but listened intently as the others related various stories of their respective globetrotting. She looked at them with a sense of admiration and faint jealousy that their lives had been so much more glamorous than hers.

With the second bottle of wine that Tom ordered, the conversation inexorably became more risqué. Peter started talking about his experiences in Bangkok.

"It's an amazing place," he said. "I was there with a friend on holiday. We went to celebrate having just passed our final accountancy exams. We were single, newly qualified, feeling pretty well-off and," he paused, took another swig of wine and went on, "I have to admit it, extremely horny."

Edwin looked at him with admiration and Lisa stared in amazement.

"It sounds like a perfect combination for a great holiday," said Tom.

Susannah was perfectly relaxed with the flow of the conversation and thought that it would be entertaining to learn a different side of Peter, so long as no one mentioned Las Vegas – no way was that going to be a topic over dinner.

"It was," continued Peter. "We massively enjoyed ourselves. We spent pretty much every night on Soi Cowboy which is one of the red light districts in the city. Mostly it was just drinking beer, buying the girls drinks and talking to them."

"Talking to them?" laughed Susannah. "You were in Bangkok young, single and by your own admission, horny, and you want us to believe that's all you did."

"Er, well," said Peter, "Perhaps not quite all. But before I say any more I want to make it perfectly clear that whatever I may say does not constitute in any shape or form the creation of a hostile environment for my female colleagues. I ask my legal counsel," he added, turning to Tom, "to bear witness to the verbal indemnification to be made by both Susannah and Lisa for any subsequent content not be taken as offensive."

"A wise precaution by my client," said Tom. "Susannah?"

"I am a Californian girl. Believe me, I have seen (and perhaps done) way more than you would ever expect. You'll get no lawsuit from me. So yes, granted."

"Very good," said Tom. "Lisa?"

"I don't understand," said Lisa, bewildered. "What am I am meant to do?"

"Just say yes and trust Tom," said Susannah.

Lisa looked at her wide-eyed but turned to Tom and said, "Er, OK, yes, I suppose so."

"So, there are these bars which are called," said Peter, pausing and turning to Tom, "You are quite sure I am fully covered and indemnified?"

"Quite sure; pray continue," said Tom.

"Well, they are called Blowjob Bars," said Peter, looking at Susannah and Lisa for their reaction. However, Edwin was the one who spluttered into his beer.

"What goes on there?" asked Susannah in mock innocence.

"The girls don't give you a blow-job in public?" exclaimed Lisa, turning red at what she had said.

"Well, that's exactly what they do, actually," said Peter. "You and your friends."

"You know the Finns build saunas wherever they are in the world, get naked and get drunk; and it's men only" said Tom. "I guess this is just another way of entertaining yourself when abroad," he added with a laugh.

"You can go upstairs in a booth if you like," said Peter, "Or you can just sit at the bar and have your dick sucked while you have a beer."

"And talk to your friend about the weather at the same time?" laughed Susannah.

"Yes, for a while and then, well, you sort of get distracted, if you get my drift," replied Peter.

"Like Jack driving the Aston, I suppose," mused Susannah. "It does sound entertaining indeed. Do they offer a similar service for women? Maybe Ewan could go out there and get a job as a professional pussy-licker."

Tom and Peter both roared with laughter and Susannah chuckled; Lisa went red again and Edwin continued to stare at all of them in astonishment.

"The only downside," added Peter, "Is that you are getting a blow-job but you are wearing a condom."

"Oh God," said Susannah. "The girls must get used to the taste of rubber. But it must have something of a dulling effect. Does it work?"

Peter paused and said, "Eventually!".

He and Tom looked at each other and laughed loudly again.

Edwin suddenly asked, "So Peter, did you sleep with hookers there?"

"Really, Edwin," said Peter. "That's a question no gentleman could ever answer."

"Venture capital is no job for gentlemen," said Susannah. "My colleague asked a very reasonable question," she added. "I think we would all like to know the answer to that."

Peter turned to Tom. "Am I still covered?"

Tom said, "I would plead the fifth amendment if I were you," and chuckled.

"That does not apply to non-American citizens," Susannah fired back with a smile.

"We have all done things when drunk and excited that perhaps we wouldn't put on our CV," said Peter in response.

There was silence for a moment as they ran through their own personal histories. Susannah's mind was of course dragged immediately back to Vegas. The silence across the table lingered for a few more seconds.

Edwin was thinking morosely to himself that to be perfectly honest, he had not had enough experiences he was ashamed of. Lisa wondered if she would be forced to talk about her first lover and hoped that the topic could be avoided.

"Shall I get the bill?" interjected Tom to break into everyone's thoughts and to take a step away from any dangerous confessions that might be regretted in the morning. They all willingly and rapidly agreed this was a good idea. Lisa's offers to pay were brushed aside by the others and in the end Peter and Tom split the bill because the restaurant was uneasy about taking Susannah's credit card which did not use the Chip and PIN system.

"You Americans are so backward," teased Peter. "Maybe we should export some technology to you just so you can get dragged kicking and screaming into the 1990s."

Tom laughed and said to Lisa, "Come on, I will put you into an Uber." He turned the others and added, "See you at Waterloo tomorrow around 12? Let's meet in the pub there. It's called the Beer House and it is in the far corner of the station close to the Jubilee Line entrance. It's downstairs but easy to find."

"Sounds good," they said in unison.

"I will walk you back to your hotel," said Peter.

"There's no need," said Susannah. "I am a big girl and if I can survive in San Francisco, I can make it through the streets of London."

"It's no trouble," said Peter. It is sort of on my way anyway. I will just Uber from there."

They said their goodbyes to the others and headed towards Piccadilly.

"So what was it like?" asked Susannah.

"What?"

"Sleeping with a hooker."

"They don't really like to be called that, you know, in Thailand. They see themselves as providing an entertainment in the service industry. You know, in the main red light districts the girls are effectively self-employed. They earn a retainer from the bar but basically they can negotiate and choose who they sleep with."

"However it's dressed up, they are still hookers."

"Well yes, that's a fair point. Look, it was a while ago and as I say, I was drunk and young and pretty happy-go-lucky at the time."

"No reason to be ashamed," said Susannah, looking at him, smiling. "I mean, I've honestly had a couple of one night stands where the man has paid for dinner and while I can't say he was absolutely nailed on to get me in return and I didn't sleep with him just to be fed, I didn't really object. Girls can enjoy sex too, you know!"

"I get that!" said Peter, surprised at the look of amusement in Susannah's eyes. "That's what I learned in Thailand; or at least, it's what numbers 23 and 17 told me."

Susannah howled with laughter. "I've never been, actually. So really, you pick them out by their numbers. Is there a catalogue?"

"Not quite," chuckled Peter. "They are dancing in front of you and all have numbers pinned on them, so you can just take your time, decide which one you like the look of – maybe you catch her eye – and then you tell the bar staff which one you would like to meet and she comes down off the stage. First step is you buy her a drink and get to know her, as it were."

"And they speak English?"

"Oh yes," said Peter, "Really good English. Often they might be students, you know, so pretty clever. They are usually just girls who want to enjoy themselves and at least in those parts of Bangkok, as I say, they are all self-employed and not, er, managed."

"OK," said Susannah. "And then?"

Peter went on, "Well, basically you ask her if she would like to come away from the bar with you. She invariably says yes and you agree whether it's for a "short time" – that means an hour or so in a local cheap hotel that she knows – or "long time" which means she'll spend the night with you or stay until you throw her out. She does expect you to buy her breakfast, though! Then you agree a price and pay the bar fine,"

"The what?" interrupted Susannah.

"Oh, it's what you have to pay the bar for the privilege of taking one of their girls out. And then that's it."

"And how much, in total?"

"For the night, it is about a hundred, hundred and twenty pounds, something like that."

"Pretty reasonable."

"Totally, when you are young and just wanting to get laid. The girls are really attractive and they want to please. For the night you have a lot of fun and nothing is off limits; but you make sure you are wearing a condom at pretty much every juncture. No protection is really not a good idea however clean and wholesome the girls look."

"A wise man always takes precautions," said Susannah, with a grin.

They turned into St James's Street and came to the hotel entrance.

"Can I invite you in for one last nightcap?" said Susannah. "We haven't talked about Riverjack Crypto all evening."

"I think we have covered pretty much every other subject," said Peter with a smile.

"True, that," said Susannah.

"We'd better call it a night. I will see you tomorrow," hesitated Peter. "Thanks for a great evening. I have really enjoyed getting to know you better."

"Likewise," said Susannah. "I had a lot of fun."

They stared at each for a moment, then Peter lent in, gave her a valedictory peck on the cheek and got his mobile out to order an Uber. Susannah turned into the hotel entrance, waved and said, "Goodnight. See you tomorrow at Waterloo."

"You know where you are going?" asked Peter.

"I will figure it out," she said. "I told you I am a big girl."

Peter laughed again as she walked into the hotel. His Uber arrived and he headed back home, thinking how he had directly contradicted Gordon's advice but how he was glad he did.

Susannah went into the hotel and surprised herself as she went upstairs by thinking about the evening and how much she had enjoyed it. She went to bed without another thought; in particular, she had not thought about Gordon all night.

This was unfortunate from Gordon's point of view as he had spent the evening thinking about her and getting decidedly frustrated that he was still housebound. He had not stirred from bed all day. Cressida had looked in occasionally on him and commented that he seemed better. She was sufficiently conciliatory to bring him some light beef broth which he sipped suspiciously.

As he was not able really to do anything, she had arranged to go out for a drink with a girlfriend and left him to his own devices. He was grateful as it allowed him to think of Susannah without interruption. However, he was still not fully recovered for sure and decided that he would spend that night in one of the spare rooms to allow both Cressida and himself the best chance of a good night's sleep.

He wondered if his removing himself from the marital bed portended the future; perhaps he could contemplate divorce after all. It would be expensive but not insurmountable and he was sure he could find a way to navigate Mitch's wrath. He tossed and turned with his jumbled thoughts all night so that when he awoke late on Saturday morning, he found himself still quite weak. He resolved to do not very much that day and make sure he was in the best possible shape for the offsite. He would relax in front of Saturday afternoon TV and watch the rugby.

Meanwhile, Tom, Lisa and Edwin had stood together for a minute or two before Tom said,

"Right, Edwin. You head off and I will see Lisa home."

Edwin had the courage of beer and wine flowing in his veins and said, "But Tom, you live over in Canary Wharf somewhere, don't you? Actually I am in Chiswick so it's easier for Lisa and me to share an Uber."

"It's no trouble, Edwin," said Tom. "You look after yourself and I will see Lisa home."

"But that makes no sense," said Edwin, still emboldened. "What do you think, Lisa?"

"Yes, I agree," she said. "I will get the Uber, as you paid for dinner, Tom. Thank you so much."

"My pleasure," said Tom, somewhat irritated. "Well, I will see you tomorrow then, if you are sure you can manage to get Lisa home, Edwin. If I hurry I can still get the Tube back east so I'll be off. Goodnight."

He abruptly turned and walked off chuntering to himself.

Lisa called an Uber without trouble and they both headed west; she turned to Edwin and asked, "So, has Peter really slept with Thai prostitutes?"

Edwin looked at her and said, "I should think so, wouldn't you?"

"I didn't understand what he said when he said he would plead the fifth amendment"

"He was referring to the idea that he wouldn't say anything that would incriminate himself. It comes from the US constitution."

"Oh right," said Lisa, vaguely aware of what Edwin meant. "Have you ever done it?" she asked him after a pause.

"No, I never dared. I was always afraid I would ask the wrong girl at the wrong time and get murdered or something. When I was in Kenya there were so many stories of women picking up men in hotels and having anesthetics spread on their," he paused and looked at her a little sheepishly; however, the wine took control and he went on, "Well, you know, on their boobs."

Lisa giggled in slightly drunken fashion.

"And so when you lick them," said Edwin, to which Lisa gave a little gasp and another giggle, "Apparently you pass out and you wake up with a kidney removed or something like that."

"No," said Lisa. "Really?"

"I never knew whether it was an urban myth or true. But I was worried about AIDS as well so I never had sex while I was there," he said. "To be honest," he went on, "I really didn't dare to ask."

"You are sweet," said Lisa, patting his leg.

Edwin looked at her and said, "If I can be honest, I hate being sweet! I would far rather be confident and good-looking like Tom and Peter."

By this stage, they were pulling up outside Lisa's flat. She turned to him, "Sweet can be nice, you know."

Edwin looked at her and suddenly felt short of breath.

"Thanks for seeing me home. Will you be OK getting back yourself?" she asked with what seemed like genuine concern.

Oh, yes, it's not far," he replied.

"Oh, I see," said Lisa. "That's good. See you tomorrow then," she said and looked at him.

He stared back at her as she moved to get out of the car.

"Wait, Lisa," said Edwin.

"Yes?"

"Er, no, I mean, I just wanted to say, I enjoyed tonight and…" he faltered.

"I did too," she said and smiled at him. She got out of the car, closed the door and waved.

He waved back as the car drove off and he sat there wishing he was not who he was.

CHAPTER NINE

The next day, over coffee in the flat before setting out for Waterloo, Samantha and Steve interrogated Lisa about the night before.

"So, darling, did you have a good time? How was Tom?" asked Samantha with something of a sly smile.

"He was very nice," said Lisa coyly. "I came home with Edwin." she added.

"Edwin?" exclaimed Steve. "He didn't sleep here? Don't tell me you fancy Edwin over Tom?"

"I don't know what you mean," said Lisa, sounding confused.

"Look, darling," said Samantha. "You really need to get with the plot. They both clearly want to sleep with you."

"No!" said Lisa. "Me? Tom? Edwin?"

"Well, Tom for sure," laughed Steve. "He'd already suggested going to the rugby game as some kind of double date and now there are at least two chaperones for you."

"Sleep with both of them, darling, and see who you prefer," suggested Samantha.

"What, at the same time?" cried Lisa. "I couldn't do that."

"Oh you should try it," giggled Samantha. "I did once. It was fun."

"Is there nothing you haven't done?" laughed Steve.

"That's for me to know and for you to find out," replied Samantha pertly and glanced at the clock on the wall. She got up from the table and Steve took a swipe to spank her but she neatly dodged him.

"Enough of this pillow talk," she said. "We had better get going. Look at the time"

Lisa was in a state of real perturbation as they headed for the Tube. When they made it to Waterloo and headed downstairs to the pub they found Tom and Peter already waiting for them, a couple of pints in front of them. Steve headed to the bar and Lisa and Samantha sat down.

"Hi Tom," said Samantha. "How's tricks?"

"All good. Great to see you again." Tom paused and went on, "Lisa, did you get home OK? Edwin didn't get you lost?" Tom said.

"No, he was very sweet," said Lisa. She thought of Edwin and the pause between them in the Uber. She looked at Tom and noticed again how very good-looking he was. She then saw that he was looking at her intently and blushed.

"Hi, I'm Peter," said Peter, leaning over to shake Samantha's hand. "We haven't met but Steve has told us all about you."

"Not all, I hope" said Samantha, smiling.

Steve came back from the bar just at that moment and said, "Now then, Sam, are you flirting with my colleagues already?"

He turned to Peter and added, "She's an alley cat, you know. So just warning you!"

"Oh, Peter's clearly met a few of those judging by what he was telling us last night," laughed Tom.

"Really?" said Samantha. "Do go on."

"Not before the nine pm watershed," said Peter with a smile. "Besides, I think Lisa is still getting over the shock."

"I told you he was not all sweetness and light," said Tom to Lisa.

At that moment they saw Susannah and Edwin come into the pub and waved them over.

"You found it OK?" asked Peter.

"Well actually," said Susannah, "I was wandering around the station hopelessly lost when I bumped into Edwin and he brought me here."

"Edwin," exclaimed Tom. "I didn't know you had it in you!"

"My brother and I have met here before for a drink," said Edwin sheepishly. "So I did know where to come."

"Your brother?" exclaimed Steve. "Don't tell me there are two of you. I don't think the world is ready for that."

"He's, er, a bit different from me," said Edwin in a meek voice. "He's a captain in the army."

"Bloody hell," said Tom. "Edwin's brother is our last line of defence. If Putin hears about that then we can all rest easy in our beds as the Russians will never invade."

Everyone laughed and Edwin blushed. He looked up and saw that Lisa was the only one not joining in; she was looking at him with sympathetic eyes and he smiled sheepishly back.

Steve glanced at his watch and suggested that they all drink up to arrive at the game in good time. They duly left the pub, caught the painfully slow train down to Twickenham station and emerged into the growing throng of people heading to the stadium.

"The great thing about rugby crowds," Peter said to Susannah as they walked up, "Is that you get rival supporters getting happily drunk together and there is never any trouble. Now if we were going to a football match, I would struggle to guarantee your safety without a squad of Marines."

Susannah laughed and they carried on talking about the respective behaviour of sports fans around the world.

Tom went to collect their tickets and rejoined the group.

"Right," he said. "Now let's sort this out. Steve and Samantha are obviously together. Here are two in the East Stand for you and Susannah, Peter. The quickest way there is just to carry on up there. Lisa and I will come with you because our seats are pretty close to yours in the upper tier."

He turned to Edwin and said, "Sorry, Edwin, but the only seat I could get you is in the West Stand. You're on your own, I'm afraid."

"Oh, that's a shame," said Lisa, as Edwin blinked at Tom. "Will you be alright?"

"He'll be fine," said Tom. "He's been here before so don't give it another thought. Now, Steve, shall we all meet in the Cabbage Patch after the game?"

"Good plan," said Steve. "Come on, Sam, we're in just here in the South Stand. See you later, guys," and he walked off, taking Sam's hand and saying something to her which made her roar with laughter.

Edwin looked about morosely, gaping in a confused fashion as the others left him. Going to the rugby had suddenly lost its allure. The stadium always seemed massive to him and it took him an age to walk around to find the right entrance, climb up to the top tier and find his seat which was in the middle of the second top row. He disturbed everyone as he made it to their seats and then, having sat down, realised that he wanted to pee before the game started and so disturbed everyone again. The comments he received when he came back from the loo, making everyone in his row stand up a third time were not very polite or friendly. He always found that the urge to pee was absurdly frequent and uncontrollable if it was inconvenient; on the other hand, if he was surrounded by bathrooms, then he never seemed to need to go. He resolved to cross his legs until half-time and turned to pay attention to the game, which was just starting.

In the interim Tom, Lisa, Peter and Susannah had made it to the stand where they were due to sit. Lisa asked timidly if she could go to the loo and before either Tom or Peter could say anything about missing kick-off, Susannah leapt in to say that she needed to as well.

Tom looked at his watch and said, "It's OK. We still have time. Twickenham is the only place on the planet where the queue for the Gents takes three times as long as the Ladies. We'll wait for you here."

As predicted, Susannah and Lisa were gone a relatively short time and they sat down in their respective pairs of seats just as the players ran out on the pitch and the volume of noise from 80,000 people grew to a crescendo, with cheers reverberating around the stadium.

"It always gives me goose bumps when I come here," said Tom to Lisa. "It's an incredible stadium."

"I'm a bit chilly too," said Lisa.

Tom looked at her with a bemused expression. "No," he explained, "I mean the atmosphere sends shivers down my spine."

"Oh, I see," said Lisa. "I thought you meant…" and she petered out.

"Never mind," said Tom. "If you are cold, would you like my jacket?"

"Oh, I couldn't, I mean, won't you be cold?" she stammered.

"Soon warm up with the game on," he said, and slipped off his jacket and put it over Lisa's shoulders.

"Thank you," she said. "That's very kind."

"No problem," said Tom, trying to ignore the shivers of cold that had just gone down his back. "Chivalry is my middle name."

"I thought your initial was…" and again Lisa faltered, paused and giggled. "Silly me! I see what you mean."

Tom smiled at her and turned to pay attention to the game which had started at breakneck pace.

Meanwhile Susannah was asking Peter questions about the game which he did his best to answer.

"All you have to know," he said, "Is that you have to pass the ball backwards. The objective is to score a try, which means touching the ball down in the goal area behind the posts."

"A touchdown?" laughed Susannah. "How many points is that worth?"

"Well, if the try is converted – that means the extra points gained by a kick through the posts – it is seven."

"Just like in proper football," she said. "You guys stole all the best ideas from us."

The game went on at the same level of adrenalin-pumping drama and at half-time they met up with Tom and Lisa. This time it was Lisa's and Susannah's turn to wait as the men joined the interminable queue for the Gents.

Lisa stood there nervously until Susannah asked her, "So how are you enjoying the game?"

"Yes, a lot. You?"

"Amazing!" she replied. "Not sure of what is going on most of the time but who cares? We've got thirty hot men beating the crap out of each other. What's not to like about watching that?"

Lisa giggled and nodded in agreement.

The second half came and went in something of a rapid blur and the game ended in a single point win after a try had thrillingly been scored in the last minute. They joined up with Samantha and Steve in the famous Cabbage Patch pub on the High Street and the men replayed the game in their conversation, dissecting the key points.

"What amazes me," said Susannah to Samantha and Lisa, "Is how men can retain the useless detail of every sporting occasion they have ever been to or read about."

"Well," laughed Samantha. "The point is that they use their entire brain capacity to do that so there is no room for anything else."

Susannah laughed too and turned to look at Steve, Tom and Peter who were still engaged in a vigorous debate about the technicalities of the scrum.

"Do they really stick their heads between the butts of the players in front of them?" asked Susannah.

"It's better than that," said Steve, looking up as he overheard the question. "They've got their hands through their crotches as well to grab hold of their shorts."

"Jeez," said Susannah. "That's unbelievable. And you actually play this for fun?"

"Nothing wrong with having your crotch grabbed," said Steve.

"It depends who's doing it, darling," said Samantha, to general laughter.

"And here's Edwin finally, he can give you a demonstration," said Tom, as Edwin came tentatively over to the table where they were sitting. Lisa squeezed up next to Samantha and Edwin sat down. He had had some trouble getting out of the stadium and had not found it easy to navigate the massive crowds.

"Don't sit down, Edwin," said Tom. "Make yourself useful and buy another round."

"Right, yes, of course," said Edwin. "What will you have, everyone?"

They all shouted their drinks at him at once which made them all laugh as he struggled to keep up. Eventually, however, Peter felt sorry for him and got up to give him a hand.

"No, Peter, let him struggle," said Tom. "It's more fun that way."

The conversation drifted and they had another round of drinks. Then Steve turned to Samantha and said, "I am sorry to say we need to get going."

"Oh why?" asked Tom.

"We have tickets to 'Hamilton'. We booked them months ago"

"Oh, it's wonderful," said Susannah. "I saw it on Broadway last year. Just incredible."

"Have a good time," said Tom.

Steve and Samantha got up, said their goodbyes and headed out of the pub back to the train station.

The others were silent for a moment and then Tom asked, "So, does anyone have plans to eat? I for one am getting hungry."

"Definitely," said Susannah. "What do you have in mind?"

"Well," replied Tom, "There's a new place I have been wanting to try for the last couple of months. It's called Nox Cena. Apparently you eat in total darkness served by visually impaired or blind people. You have no idea what you are eating and are meant to rely on your other senses."

"That sounds incredible," said Susannah. "I'm up for that. There's a similar place that opened in San Francisco but I haven't tried it yet."

"Excellent," said Tom. "Lisa, you game?"

"Oh, it sounds scary. How do you see anything?"

"You don't! That's the whole point," said Tom. "It will be fun. Peter?"

Peter hesitated. He did not want to miss out on what would be a fun evening but he was still somewhat conscious of Gordon's advice. Equally he was very much enjoying Susannah's company and suspected the feeling was mutual. He hesitated and said, "I am not sure. It's going to be a long couple of days. I may just call it a night."

"Come on, Peter," said Susannah. "You must come along. Maybe the dark will help the creative juices flow to come up with some magic solution for Riverjack Crypto."

Peter laughed and replied, "Ok, well, if you are all up for it."

"The only trouble is that I may not be able to get a table. It's incredibly popular. Let me give them a call and see," said Tom, getting up to step outside and avoid the noise of the pub.

There was a pause and they all took the opportunity to check their emails. Peter opened his and as he read, the expression on his face changed to one of real concern.

To: Peter.Williamson@aardvarkvc.com
From: Gordon.Fairbald@aardvarkvc.com
Subject: WTF???

Peter,
What the fuck is going on??? I was sitting at home convalescing watching the rugby and I just saw you on TV sitting there next to Susannah? What the hell are you thinking????!!! I told you explicitly that spending any time with her could be a fatal blow to your chances of the SFO job. Which fucking part of that was hard to understand? I just hope you haven't blown it. Call me!!!
Gordon

"What's the matter, Peter?" asked Susannah. "You look like you've just seen a ghost."

"Um, no nothing really," said Peter. "Just a message from Gordon with something I need to figure out."

"Can I help?" she asked.

"Ah no, it is OK," he said, looking up. "I will work through it with him tomorrow. But it does mean I really shouldn't go to dinner. I must get back."

"If it is that serious, I must be able to help," insisted Susannah. "Otherwise I know it's going to be a big couple of days so you should relax tonight."

Peter hesitated and thought about the consequences. Gordon would be madder than hell but he could always say that Susannah had insisted and he thought it would be less suspicious than to keep on declining. He wondered if he should call Gordon but before he could decide to do anything, Tom came back into the pub.

"Good news," he said. "They've had a last minute cancellation. It's a table for five at nine o'clock. I told them we're four but they are OK with that. Probably happy just to sell the table at all at such short notice." He glanced at his watch. "We had better get going if we are going to make it. Good news is that it is just a quick hop from Waterloo so if we catch the fast train, we can just be in time. The crowds should mostly have dispersed by now."

It was true; the pub was a lot emptier than it had been about an hour earlier.

"But we are five," said Susannah, smiling at Edwin encouragingly. "You've forgotten Edwin."

"Oh yes, Edwin. Of course. How could I forget?" said Tom without enthusiasm. "Well, five it is. Come on then, let's get going."

On the train Peter decided that to ignore Gordon completely would be a mistake, particularly when he received a text from him demanding to know where he was. He dropped him a quick email to explain that Susannah had insisted on spending the day together and now was demanding dinner with Tom, Edwin and Lisa and he could not get away. He hoped that would be good enough and resolved to worry about Gordon in the morning. He would just make sure he avoided showing too much enthusiasm for being with Susannah; he would be polite but not too intimate and hope that she would not suspect anything. He would need to be careful, though.

When they arrived at the restaurant, they found themselves in a dimly lit cocktail lounge. The hostess came up, took their drinks order and then explained the way the dinner would work.

"First, I need your mobiles, watches or anything that emits a light at all. We want it to be completely dark up there."

"Completely dark?" said Lisa nervously.

"Pitch black, madam" said the hostess.

They all placed various items into a large container the hostess had put on the table.

"Thanks," she said. "I will take care of these. Now, in a moment I will introduce you to your waiter. His name is Chris. He is blind but, upstairs in the restaurant, he is in his natural element. He will look after you and if you need anything, just call his name. We are serving a starter; a main course and a dessert. Does anyone have any food allergies?"

They all shook their heads.

"Great," she went on. "Each course consists of four small plates. You want to eat each plate in order from six o'clock, to nine, to twelve, to three. Does that make sense?"

"I don't understand," wailed Lisa. "How will we see what we are eating?"

"You won't," said the hostess. "We will bring you back down afterwards and show you what you had. You will have to guess. It is part of the fun"

"Oh, I don't like the sound of this at all," said Lisa.

"It's going to be fine," said Tom. "I will look after you."

"And we offer a wine pairing option with each course," said the hostess. "That's usually the best way to enjoy the meal."

"Sounds good," said Tom and Peter together.

"Right," said the hostess, looking over her shoulder. "Here's Chris. You are in safe hands. All yours, Chris."

Chris introduced himself and they all did likewise.

"Now then," he said, "We are heading upstairs and it is totally dark. But I am your eyes so follow me and trust me. What I need you to do is to line up behind me and put your hands on your friend's shoulders in front of you. Whoever is behind me do the same to me. That way I can guide you."

"Got it," said Tom. "If you like I will go first; then Lisa, come behind me; then Peter. That way, Lisa, you are between the two of us and can't get lost. Then Susannah and finally Edwin."

They lined up and Lisa reached up to Tom's shoulders; given the height discrepancy this was a bit awkward.

"Remember it's shoulders not ears, Lisa," said Tom, laughing.

"It's a bit of a stretch; you're too tall," said Lisa.

"Grab my waist; fine by me," replied Tom.

"I think that sounds safer all round," said Susannah, doing the same to Peter. Peter himself felt slightly embarrassed and kept his hands resolutely on Lisa's shoulders. Edwin got confused between the two and was nearly left behind.

"Lead on, Macduff," said Tom, as Chris called out to check everyone was ready and moved off.

They turned through an arch with a curtain hanging down; once they passed through that and started to climb the stairs to the main restaurant, the light faded so that after only a few steps up they were in complete darkness.

"Oh no," cried Lisa. "I don't like this at all. How does Chris see where he's going?"

"I don't," said Chris. "I told you, you just have to trust me."

"It is certainly a very strange feeling," said Peter.

"You are not wrong, buster," said Susannah. "I sure hope our friend knows his way around here."

"Don't worry, madam," said Chris as he turned into what was evidently the restaurant and started to make a noise like a series of sonar beeps. They found they could sense other people in the darkness and hear some subdued conversations from the different tables around them, but other than that they were in pitch black and could see absolutely nothing.

"Why are you making that noise?" asked Tom. "Is it your call sign so no one else runs into you?"

"Exactly," explained Chris. "If I hear other waiters making their noise coming our way, I can take evasive action."

Chris guided them to their table and sat each of them down. They were not actually sure who was sitting next to whom; the table seemed round and relatively small so there was a sense of intimacy in the darkness.

"Oh," said Lisa, "I still am not sure I like this."

"It is OK," said Tom, putting a reassuring hand on her knee. "I will look after you" and he squeezed her knee in an affectionate way.

"Who's squeezing my knee?" said Susannah with a giggle.

"I think you could squeeze all sorts of things in here and no one would notice," laughed Tom to hide his confusion. If Susannah was there, where was Lisa sitting? He was pretty sure Edwin was next to him on the other side.

"I am not so sure, actually," said Peter. "Look over in the corner at that red light. I think that's an infrared camera to stop temptation in its tracks."

At that moment their attempts to hold their hands up to the red light to see them – fruitless, as it happens – were interrupted by Chris who returned with their first course and the wine. With amazing dexterity he placed the dishes and the wine glasses in front of them. Then he placed a bottle of sparkling water which they had requested on the table.

"Now, the water is your problem," he said with an evident smile. "My advice is to have one of you pour it with each of you handing him or her your glass. Whoever's pouring will find your middle finger is your best friend."

"I've always found that, wouldn't you say, Lisa?" said Susannah, giggling again. Peter spluttered the wine he had just managed to start to drink. Tom howled with laughter, as did Chris.

"Indeed, madam? The idea, however, in here is that you measure the water level in the glass as you are pouring."

"I get it," said Susannah. "And no way we can trust the men with something so delicate. I will take charge."

Each of them groped in the dark for a glass, passed it gingerly to Susannah and she filled each in turn. It was a very strange experience to do everything by feel. By this stage they had started eating and were trying to guess what each small dish was.

"I think that is a scallop," said Peter. "The second dish at nine o'clock, at least."

"Was that third one chicken?" ventured Edwin, tentatively.

"Chicken?" scoffed Tom. "More like tofu."

"Whatever it was I think I just dropped it down my cleavage," said Lisa in a tipsy voice. "It's terribly slippery."

"Can I help?" laughed Tom.

"Remember the infrared cameras, Romeo," laughed Susannah.

Peter was replaying the day in his head and realised that they had actually drunk far more than any of them had anticipated; he was trying to keep a clear head and stay collected but it was proving more and more difficult.

The main course came and went with similarly failed attempts at guessing the menu. They all concluded that the food was exceptional even if they had no idea what they were eating.

As they were eating dessert, there was a sudden sound of a glass falling over and Tom felt wine pouring over his trousers.

"Bloody hell," he said. "Who just knocked over the wine? My trousers are soaked."

Edwin hesitated and then confessed, "Sorry, Tom. I couldn't see a thing. I tried to put the glass down on the table but it overbalanced."

Before Tom could react, Susannah intervened, "The only surprising thing is that we haven't all done that before now," she said. "Just your bad luck to be the victim, Tom".

Edwin was grateful for being spared insults from Tom, who decided that the best course of action was to laugh it off, disgruntled though he was. He dabbed ineffectually at his trousers.

Once they had finished their meal, avoiding any more hazards, Chris came and guided them downstairs where they thanked him profusely for an amazing experience. The hostess took them to a table in the cocktail lounge, offered them coffee and then asked them to guess what they had eaten for each course. She then took them through the menu with pictures on an iPad of every dish. The quality of the food had been exceptional but they had managed to identify correctly no more than half the dishes they had eaten. They chattered eagerly about the experience as they gathered themselves into their coats and left the restaurant.

"That was an incredible evening," said Susannah. "A great end to a fantastic day. Back to reality and work tomorrow but thanks everyone. Now, where are we exactly?"

"Pretty close to your hotel, actually," said Peter. "If you like we can have a repeat of last night and I will walk you back."

"I told you," said Susannah, "I am a big girl and…"

"No doubt at all," said Peter. "But still, a gentleman is a gentleman."

"And we've already established that you can't qualify on that score given the job you do," laughed Susannah. "But I accept the offer gratefully." She looked around, "I guess these could be mean streets for an unsuspecting all-American girl."

"Are you going to take Lisa back, Edwin?" asked Tom slightly reluctantly.

"Actually, I was going to stay at my parents' place tonight in Eaton Square. I thought it would be easier for getting to the offsite tomorrow so I took my bag there earlier today."

"Your parents live in Eaton Square?" said Tom, slightly incredulously.

"Yes, they have a flat there."

"Wow," said Peter. "I didn't know."

"What's so surprising?" asked Susannah.

"That's like owning a place on Central Park South in New York," said Peter. "Pretty fancy."

"Nice one, Edwin," said Susannah.

"Well, that's settled then," said Tom. "Lisa, I will escort you home."

"There's really no need," said Lisa. "I can manage myself." Just as she said that, she stumbled and nearly fell over.

"Really?" said Tom, "Just like you managed the coffee machine?"

"Now, that's not fair," said Lisa.

"Still," said Peter, surveying the situation, "Uber or not, I think that is an offer you should not refuse."

"Excellent," said Tom, reaching for his 'phone and ordering a ride.

"Are you going to walk, Edwin?" asked Peter.

"I think so," said Edwin. "It's only a mile or so and I need to clear my head!"

"I think we all do," said Susannah. "Onward, Sir Galahad," she added, turning to Peter. "Goodnight, all. See you tomorrow."

"I will meet you at eleven tomorrow morning at Victoria, Lisa," said Edwin as the Uber arrived.

"OK," said Lisa with something of a drunken slur and got in the car. Tom followed suit and Peter looked at him, winked and said, "Have fun you two" as the car door closed and they drove off.

Edwin blinked at the departing rear lights and somewhat slumped, before settting off up the road.

"This way," said Peter to Susannah. "'Night, Edwin," he called. Edwin waved a desultory hand without turning around. As Peter and Susannah headed off, she slipped her arm through his.

In the Uber, Tom was examining his trousers. "Bloody Edwin," he said. "My trousers are soaked."

"It wasn't his fault," said Lisa in a slightly indistinct voice. "You really couldn't see anything in there."

"It was amazing, though, wasn't it?" said Tom. "And I guess I would rather have my trousers covered in wine than have someone slip and grab another part of my anatomy."

They both laughed and discussed how incredibly skilled Chris the waiter had been; they agreed their other senses had been enhanced in the darkness.

By this stage, they were pulling up outside Lisa's flat. She turned to Tom, "Thanks for seeing me home. Will you be OK getting back yourself? You live so far away. And your trousers are still soaking."

He looked at her with some intensity and then with his mind made up, he leaned across, put his hands on her shoulders and kissed her. Lisa was so surprised that for a moment she did not realise what had happened. She felt his lips on hers and did not respond out of shock.

Tom pulled back and looked at her, "Sorry," he said. "I didn't mean to be too forward but I've wanted to do that ever since you nearly pulled my ear off on the Tube. I guess you didn't want me to and I apologise."

She looked at him, wide-eyed and still not quite believing what had happened. "No, no, it's alright, I mean, I liked it, I just, er, I didn't expect it, it was so sudden, and after all, you are so clever, and good-looking, and I am just Peter's secretary, and so what…"

She was interrupted by Tom coming towards her and kissing her again. This time she responded with much less surprise and much more enthusiasm.

"Sorry to interrupt you two lovebirds," said the Uber driver. "But we arrived hours ago and I need to pick up my next ride."

"Oh yes, of course, sorry," said Tom. "I'll add a tip and give you a five star rating, is that OK?"

"Sounds good to me," said the driver.

"Have you got another fare?" said Tom, "Because if not I was going to book you to take me back."

"Oh," said Lisa. "I mean, you could, if you wanted to, you know, not go back just yet. That is, actually, well, I am not sure I can take you up with Steve and Sam there, I think I'd be too embarrassed but, well, maybe we could just talk a bit more out here?"

"Actually, Steve told me they were planning to stay at his place tonight after the theatre," said Tom with a glint in his eye. He rather hoped that Lisa would not discover that he had acted as the gentlemanly escort home while knowing this vital piece of information.

"Oh, I see," said Lisa. "In that case, then would you like to come up?"

"I think you're on a promise, mate" interrupted the driver with a cackle. He tapped on his mobile app a couple of times and said, "Anyway, I have another passenger confirmed about a quarter of a mile away so I'm off. You go and have fun."

Tom made a decisive move to open the door and got out. Before Lisa could do the same he ran round and opened her door.

"Oh thank you," she said. "I'm not sure anyone's ever opened the door for me before."

She giggled and got out of the car, taking Tom's arm as he shut the door behind her and the car sped off. They walked over to the entrance to the building. Lisa fumbled for her keys and eventually succeeded in opening the door. They staggered upstairs and into the flat after a couple of abortive attempts on Lisa's part to fit the key into the lock.

"I think I am drunk," she said. "You wouldn't take advantage of a drunken girl, would you?" she said, looking at Tom with a smile.

"Only with a signed indemnity" he said, looking at her back.

"Come on in and I will sign anything you like in the morning," she said.

Happily accepting the invitation, Tom walked through the flat and followed her into her bedroom. She turned to him and they kissed again. She tasted sweet and he could feel the warmth of her breasts pressed against him, her arousal now clear. He pulled away from her and said, "I hate to break the mood but before anything else happens, I have to pee! Where's your bathroom?"

She giggled and pointed him to the en suite door. As he went through it, she lay down on the bed, sighing contentedly and waiting for him to come back. In the meantime Tom managed to extricate his burgeoning erection from his flies and splashed water on his face to control himself. It took him a couple of minutes to calm down enough to perform the necessary physiological function and during that time he removed any thought of Lisa from his mind. He found that focusing on the rugby technique of the lock forward was a very satisfactory way of achieving the desired result. He decided that walking back into the bedroom with his flies down would be too forward and so, zipped up and modestly attired, he turned off the light and stepped through the door. Lisa was breathing quietly, lying on the bed.

"Lisa," whispered Tom. "I'm back." There was no reply. "Are you awake?" he added after a moment.

There was no sound except a faint sigh and a rustle of duvet as she turned on her side. Tom looked at her. She was beautiful and looked so innocent. He consciously banished all thoughts from his mind other than a desire to make sure she was comfortable. He gently took off her shoes and placed them on the floor. Then he slowly pulled the duvet from under her, being careful not to make any sudden movements. Lisa sighed again but did not stir as he placed the duvet over her, bent down to kiss her forehead and went back into the main living room, quietly closing the door. Then he paused, returned to her room and found the digital alarm clock on her bedside table. He set the alarm for nine in the morning then turned and went out of the bedroom again.

The last thing he did before leaving the flat was to write her a brief note:

Hi Lisa, I went to the bathroom and you went to sleep! It was a fun evening but maybe given we have the offsite coming up, it has ended for the best! I will see you tomorrow at the hotel. Tom.

He looked at his 'phone. There was a text from Steve. 'Good luck tonight, Mr Gorsky.' He laughed and replied, 'The eagle has not landed.'

Meanwhile Susannah and Peter had walked back to her hotel. They too had discussed the evening dining experience in detail and had found that they both not only had really enjoyed it but shared a penchant for new, different experiences.

"I must admit," said Peter, "That is where I spend my money – on experiences, I mean. You know, travel and other things. I am learning to fly at the moment, actually. Something I have always wanted to do."

"I know about you and your experiences, Sir Galahad," laughed Susannah. "You over-shared with me last night, if you recall."

"You did ask!"

"True. I can only blame myself. So, you are becoming a private pilot? That's pretty cool. You can take me up one day."

"I need to qualify first, but it's a date."

They arrived back at the hotel. She looked at him intently. "For God's sake, Susannah," she thought to herself. "I know you haven't been laid since Gordon but you can't sleep with every single one of your colleagues, even if you want to."

"Well, this is where I will leave you," he said. "You will be OK to get to Victoria tomorrow? Remember it's Victoria not Waterloo."

She laughed, "What I love about London is the history. Everything in the US seems to have started in the 1930s."

"Downside of that," said Peter, "Is that everything here is still from the Victorian era. You are much better off being a modern country. Our infrastructure is falling apart."

"Oh, ours is too," replied Susannah. "It's just we don't have the consolation of any historical value to it."

A brief silence descended and they looked at each other once more. Susannah went through the same calculations she had made in the bar in Las Vegas and found unsurprisingly that the answer was the same.

"Would you like to come in for a final nightcap?" she asked.

"I shouldn't, you know," said Peter, as conflicting thoughts played out in his mind.

"That is not what I asked you," said Susannah with a smile. "I asked you if you wanted to."

"Very much," said Peter, grinning.

"Done," said Susannah. "Follow me, Sir Galahad."

They walked into the hotel where Susannah was not surprised to see her nemesis on duty.

"Good evening, madam," he said. "I trust you have had a pleasant evening."

"Very pleasant, thank you," said Susannah. "How's the plumbing?"

"Functioning as well as ever, thank you madam."

"That's hardly reassuring,' said Susannah primly and guided Peter through the reception area.

"Trouble with the taps?" asked Peter.

"Taps?"

"Oh… faucets."

"Oh, got it. Yes, indeed, positively Victorian," and she told him the story of her arrival. They went into the bar and found that they were the only ones there. The barman was exhibiting all the signs of wanting to close up and sighed audibly as they sat down.

"What'll you have?" asked Susannah.

"This time of night it has to be JD and Coke, thanks," replied Peter.

"Good call," said Susannah. "Make that two JD and Cokes, please" she called out to the barman who nodded in a nondescript fashion.

"So," she went on. "Tom is escorting Lisa home. Where will that end, I wonder?" and she smiled in a knowing fashion.

"He has liked her from the first time he saw her," said Peter. "If I am honest, I am not sure that it is a match made in heaven; having said that I do know him pretty well and however talented a lawyer he is, I know that off duty he doesn't necessarily need to be discussing Greek philosophy with his partner."

"Probably just as well if he is going to date Lisa," said Susannah, not unkindly.

"Indeed," said Peter.

"She's very sweet," said Susannah, "But do you think she can really handle the pace of our office life?"

"It's early days. She's doing OK so far. We are not an easy team to cope with, for sure."

"You can say that again," said Susannah reflectively. "So, what did Gordon want earlier, anyway?"

The barman arrived with the drinks which gave Peter a convenient excuse to raise his glass, say "Cheers" and dodge the subject.

"The only thing is," he said, "Is that if Lisa and Tom do start dating, is it going to be OK for Lisa to keep working for us? That could be a bit tricky. I am not sure how Gordon would view that."

Susannah had a very clear view as to how both Gordon and Mitch would react.

Peter was speaking, as if to himself, "It's not as if I would object, actually. I don't have any professional secrets from Tom so even if Lisa as my EA is aware of everything, it won't matter. I like Tom a lot and as I say, I think Lisa is just his type. It could actually work out fine. I am just worried about how the others will react. And whether Mary will cut Tom's balls off with a rusty knife."

His monologue was interrupted by Susannah's laughter. "Would she do that?" she asked.

"You bet if Tom puts a foot wrong," explained Peter. "Mary has quickly become very protective of Lisa. She is the maternal figure around the office. And she already has Henry running scared of giving Lisa a hard time; and that takes some doing, I can tell you."

"I see," said Susannah.

They both took a sip of their drinks. The silence grew between them until Susannah asked, "So, Peter, is there a Mrs Williamson?"

"Good Lord, no," said Peter. "I'm not married. I wouldn't inflict my lifestyle on somebody else; my inability to handle commitment makes that unlikely to happen, anyhow."

"You sound like my mother talking to me."

"I take it you are in the same position? No one else to share the drudgery?" he asked.

"Just Ginger."

"And Ginger is?"

"My cat, yes." Susannah added. "I am such a cliché. Career-oriented female making it in a male world, not letting anyone else into her life as a companion except her cat."

"Sounds perfect to me. Maybe I will get a cat although I always wanted a parrot that would sit in the kitchen and squawk 'Fuck off' at everyone who came in."

"I like it," said Susannah. "A second line of defence ." She paused and went on, "If you don't mind my asking, why so averse to commitment?"

It was that time of evening when in vino veritas would no doubt come back to haunt Peter in the morning, but by implication there were no restraints so he told Susannah the story of his experience with Katherine at Oxford. Whatever he expected her reaction to be, it probably was not her complete mirth at the story.

"You are telling me, you found her in bed with her best friend which she said was an experiment to test everyone's reactions? Wow, that is one mighty screwed up chick. I think whatever she has done to your ability to form relationships, you would clearly be paying even more to your therapist if you had stayed with her longer."

"It's a fair point and one I can only agree with," said Peter. "I am over it now, of course, but her legacy lives on. Frankly, sharing my place with my own Ginger is looking like my destiny."

"Until you find a girl who is as screwed up as you then you can tell each other that you are not committed and spend the rest of your life with her."

"Not sure where one of those is going to come from," said Peter with a faint grin.

"She could pop up anywhere," said Susannah. "Maybe in the bar of a quaint hotel in London at midnight when you are drunk and not able to see it," she went on.

Peter listened for a moment to what she said and then thought to himself that he was indeed quite drunk – he once more calculated how much they must have consumed over the course of the day and wondered how he was still functioning – as a result could not be absolutely certain of the implications of what Susannah had just said. Suddenly he was massively excited but simultaneously terribly cautious; it was a cocktail of emotions that he hoped would not explode in his face.

"And if I couldn't see it, what would happen?" he ventured.

"Oh, the girl would have two options. Either to stick up a very large neon sign pointing the way or be resigned to going back to her feline fetish and reflect on what might have been."

"And," Peter countered, trying to pick his words very carefully, "How bright is that neon sign right now?"

"Pretty glaring, actually."

"I see," said Peter. He suddenly switched tack and went on, "It's just like that brilliant Steve Martin movie, 'L.A. Story', where he gets advice from the roadside sign."

"Oh, I love that movie," said Susannah, "One of my favourites, actually. He's so engaging in it and the scene at the end is just perfect."

"You mean, when the sign says, 'Kiss her, you fool'?"

"That's it."

He paused and looked at her intently.

"That was another Anglo-American consortium, if I remember correctly; and I can see that sign above your head, Susannah."

"Well, you fool, what are you going to do about it?"

He hesitated no more and lent towards her. He saw her close her eyes as he kissed her. Their mouths melded together and he felt a fluttering in his chest which he had not experienced for an extremely long time. He pulled back slightly and brushed her cheek with his lips. She sighed very slightly.

"I hope that was what I was meant to do," he breathed.

"You can read the sign after all," she smiled.

They looked at each other for a moment, said nothing and then simultaneously burst out laughing.

"If I had a cat already," said Peter, "It would be a perfect opportunity for us to test out the Mixandmatchbypet platform."

"The what?"

"Oh, it's the investment we are going to be talking about other than Riverjack Crypto at the offsite. It is a new platform that combines social media with pet ownership and dating, I think. Steve is representing them and Henry is keen on doing the deal. Edwin was telling me that it actually could make a lot of sense; although anything Edwin thinks makes a lot of sense we probably shouldn't touch with a barge pole."

"Actually I like the play," said Susannah. "Almost as much as that one you just made."

"It worked so well the first time, I think I should repeat it," he said softly.

"The sign says so," she whispered back.

He lent forward and kissed her again. He put his hands gently on her waist and drew her towards him. She moved willingly closer to him and sighed deeply.

"I am not sure what you have done to me, Sir Galahad, but I like it," she said to him, pulling back, opening her eyes and smiling at him.

"Can I say something that I really don't want to?" he said in a slightly serious tone.

"You can do anything you like," she replied.

"What I want to do right now is to take your hand, lead you up to your room and make passionate love to you.".

"I would have no objection to the plan but there is an obvious 'but' you have missed out," she said in a slightly disappointed voice.

"You are right. I really am going to be Sir Galahad and leave you now. Not," he added very quickly, looking at the expression of incredulity in her eyes, "for any other reason than I am tired, I am drunk and I am not sure I would be capable of doing either of us justice if I put my plan into action. How much would you hate me if I told you I really need to sleep?"

"Not at all," she said. "Perhaps, given the next two days, it is just as well."

"And then we see?" asked Peter.

"And then we see," she replied, smiling. "You can come back and see what the sign says."

She was the one to take the initiative this time as she lent forward, kissed him and slowly intertwined her fingers with his.

"I think we should have my lack of commitment meet your lack of commitment for lunch and see what happens, Sir Galahad," she said with a smile.

"It's a date," Peter said, reluctantly getting up.

"So, Victoria tomorrow?" she asked.

"Yes," he said. "But I will drive down. I would offer to pick you up but I only have a two-seater and I am giving Tom a lift down as he lives near me."

"I have told you, I am an all-American girl who can look after herself," she replied with a slight laugh. "I shall see you tomorrow, Sir Galahad, and will expect the plan to end all plans to come to fruition." Her eyes twinkled as she went on, "And I am talking about the Riverjack Crypto rescue plan and nothing else!"

"I could not even begin to imagine you meant anything else," he responded. Although he tried to maintain the jocular tone of levity, the mention of Riverjack Crypto made him think of Gordon, how complicated his situation was, and how terribly he wanted to take Susannah to bed. He made one final effort at light-heartedness: "I shall buy a cat first thing on Tuesday when we are back from the offsite. That way I know you will want to see me again."

"That might just do it," she said, laughing.

She sprung up, gave him a brief peck on the cheek, turned and tripped lightly up the stairs to her room. Peter stood there watching, still unable to sort his thoughts out. He went back out through reception, where the manager looked at him with unfiltered disdain.

CHAPTER TEN

When the alarm went off in Lisa's bedroom, it sounded as if a fire engine had crashed into her bedroom with its sirens blaring. She opened her eyes and groaned; the room seemed to be revolving around her. She tried to sit up and found the effort almost too much for her. Glancing at her clock-radio she realised she had better force herself out of bed otherwise she would miss the train.

She pushed the duvet back and saw that she was still dressed. She desperately tried to recall what had happened the previous night but found she could remember very little. All she knew was that she had a terrible hangover and she needed to swallow two aspirin for breakfast. She went into the kitchen, turned the kettle on, raided Samantha's aspirin bottle and groaned to herself again. Deciding she could not face tea after all, she headed back to her bedroom. That was when she saw the note Tom had left on the table. She picked it up, read it twice and tried once more to think what had happened.

She could recall dining in the dark and getting an Uber back here with Tom — that was it, he had helped her home after she had tripped up on the pavement. What on earth had happened after that? If she read the note correctly, it sounded as if Tom had come into her bedroom and that they had been about to… really, could that be possible? She gasped at the thought as she remembered kissing him in the back of the taxi. It had been very pleasant, she recalled. That meant she had evidently invited him up; but if the note was to be believed, nothing else had happened because she had fallen asleep. But who set the alarm? It must have been Tom.

She smiled at the idea of what a kind thing it had been to do. In fact, he must have behaved like a proper gentleman because clearly she had been there to be taken advantage of and judging by the fact she had woken up with all her clothes intact, he had not done so.

Suddenly, a wave of nausea hit her as the memory made her head swim again and caused her to groan once more. She rushed to the bathroom and spent a decidedly unpleasant thirty minutes or so fluctuating between sluicing from both ends, splashing water in her face, rinsing her mouth out and feverishly trying to stop the room from going round and round under the shower.

Eventually she emerged, a cold shower having been a surprisingly effective remedy, and pulled her small traveling valise from under her bed. She made a supreme effort to concentrate on her packing and looked at her watch. She was clearly late but it could not be helped. She texted Edwin to tell him that she would not get there on time but was being as quick as she could be and decided to walk to the Tube rather than take an Uber because she wanted to clear her head. As she emerged from her apartment building she found it was an extremely bright autumnal day; the sun seemed to be glaring straight into her eyes from every available reflective surface. She immediately turned back to fetch her sunglasses; wearing them at least stopped her head throbbing quite so badly. She staggered off down the road and made it to the Tube without any further mishap.

In the meantime, Edwin had woken up surprisingly clear-headed. He thought longingly about Lisa and wondered what had happened when Tom took her home. He had wanted to find a way to invite her back to Eaton Square; that would have impressed her, for sure, but he had not dared to ask her in front of the others. He was not sure what would have happened if she had accepted – actually, he was pretty sure nothing at all, given his track record – but he still felt a pang of jealousy flow through him. He could not compete with Tom at all on looks, brains or success but perhaps Lisa would not be impressed with those things.

"After all," he said to himself, "It's not as if she can match Tom intellectually, so he would get bored with her sooner rather than later. She might not see that; but he would certainly figure out there was no long-term future for them, so he really is only after one thing. I can't blame him for that but with me she would get undying loyalty and gratitude. Yes, that's it, loyalty and gratitude. I really am a much better bet."

However, he could see that loyalty and gratitude were not characteristics that would sweep her off her feet and into his bed. He stomped around the flat morosely, cursing life, the universe and everything and wishing he could at least have inherited some of his brother's looks, physical attributes and courage. "Bugger! Bugger! Bugger!" he thought and slumped into the shower.

He got dressed, packed for the offsite in a desultory fashion and came out into the sunlight. He hailed a cab and headed for Victoria. He did at least want to be on time to show Lisa he was reliable. As the cab pulled into the station he received Lisa's text. That dampened any enthusiasm he might have been feeling about seeing her because it seemed to him there could be only one explanation for Lisa's being late: she had had other distractions that morning to keep her from getting out of bed. He went into a convenient Starbucks to buy himself a consoling cappuccino and absent-mindedly kicked the counter a couple of times in frustration.

The manager who took his order looked at him in a stern fashion. "If you vandalise our store again, sir, I will call the police."

Edwin quickly apologised and took his drink into the corner. He checked the time of the next train to Horsham and found that even on a Sunday they were relatively frequent. He texted Lisa back to tell her where to meet him and lay back in his seat, once more frustrated and angry at himself and the world in equal measure.

Susannah had given herself the luxury of a lie-in, which was a real rarity in her life. She had decided that, for once, particularly as she had no Ginger to jump up onto her bed early on a Sunday morning to lick her face until she got up to provide breakfast, that she would not force herself into the gym. She did not need to leave for another couple of hours so she lay in bed, amusing herself on her mobile 'phone by re-reading the synopsis of *LA Story* on IMDB and downloading it on her iPad to watch as she got dressed and on the train journey down. She thought back to the evening before with Peter and smiled. They had connected in an entirely unexpected way and she was excited.

She wondered whether he would ever contemplate moving to the US. She would not mind relocating to London, but at that stage in her career, she was building such a strong reputation in Silicon Valley that she did not feel it was the right time to move. She had her own ambitions to fulfil. For once it would have to be the man who did the chasing. She wondered whether Peter would consider it worth it.

Then she shook herself out of it, telling herself that one kiss – well, two or three perhaps – did not mean a lifetime together. This was not a Hollywood romance and life did not work like that. Still, as she got up to run her bath, she started to watch *LA Story* and decided that even if real life could not turn out like a movie, there was no harm in a little escapism. Though that in turn reminded her of what Gordon would be contemplating at the offsite. "Oh fuck," she said out loud, "How the hell am I going to manage this one?" At that point Steve Martin had his first encounter with the road sign. "Now that," she added, "would be an extremely helpful thing to have handy. I sure could use some good advice right now."

Peter had taken an Uber home in something of a daze. It was not just the alcohol, he thought; he was intoxicated in a way that stirred memories of his first summer at Oxford and aroused feelings of excitement which he had not really experienced since then. When he woke up, he found that the effect of the significant quantity of alcohol consumed the previous day had more or less worn off but that the sense of excitement had not.

"How the fuck is that possible?" he said to himself. "I have known her three days and yet… no, don't be absurd, Williamson. It's not as if you have known her forever but it certainly is different from anyone else since her."

He knew it was a bizarre habit, but whenever he thought about Katherine, and it was not often, he did not refer to her by name. It was salutary that, when unusually for him he had found himself telling Susannah about her, all she had done was laugh. Suddenly and to his surprise, he laughed too; first quietly and then with increasing volume.

"I must be losing my sodding mind," he thought as his laughter subsided. "But I think that means Katherine no longer has the spell on me that she did. And Hell's teeth, I just said her name!"

Suddenly, the feeling of Susannah's lips on his; the sweet smell of her hair; the softness of the sweater she had been wearing the previous day; her smile; her accent; her final whispered words to him last night; and the sign yes, the bloody road sign in the movie they had talked about… this jumble of thoughts, memories and feelings overwhelmed him and he let out a whoop of joy. He practically danced into the shower singing "Simply The Best" at the top of his voice and felt as though he was invincible and the offsite no longer held any terrors for him.

As he got dressed, however, he saw he had a missed call and a text from Gordon. That rather set a dampener on his mood and he felt duty-bound to return the call.

The conversation was brief but not pleasant. Gordon lambasted him with practically every other word being an expletive. Peter explained how he had really been constrained by Susannah's insistence on his being part of the party for the rugby and dinner afterwards.

"And I suppose you went back to her bloody hotel for a nightcap," Gordon shouted.

"Well, I admit, a quick one," replied Peter. "But we were just discussing the day; nothing else happened."

"What do you mean, nothing else happened?" roared Gordon. "Of course nothing else fucking happened. But you realise you have made a 5,000 candlepower arse of yourself by spending so much time with her and she is going to think that pretty strange behavior and judge you accordingly, Peter. I thought you had more sodding brains than that but clearly you totally ignored my advice and I don't take kindly to that."

"Sorry, Gordon," said Peter. "But no harm done, I'm sure."

"Well, we will bloody well see about that," said Gordon, sounding slightly calmer. "Remember, you leave Susannah to me this weekend and make sure you focus on Cressida."

"Yes, Gordon," said Peter, "I will be sure to do that."

"Right," said Gordon. "Let's just leave it at that. I will see you this pm."

"I look forward to it," said Peter, glad Gordon had seemingly been appeased for the time being at least. "See you later on," he added, but Gordon had already hung up.

Peter shrugged his shoulders, finished packing and texted Tom that he was on his way.

Lisa had eventually shown up at Victoria and she and Edwin had made it onto the train. Edwin wondered how to broach the subject of the previous night.

"Did you get back OK?" asked Edwin.

"Yes I think so," said Lisa. "I don't remember much and my head still hurts from what we had to drink. That's why I was late. I, er, had trouble getting out of bed this morning."

"I see," said Edwin neutrally and pointedly turned to look out of the window.

Lisa looked at him, not sure what to say next. On the one hand, she remembered what Samantha had said about Edwin fancying her; she was struggling to believe it was true but at the same time, she realised that if he thought she was with Tom last night, he might be upset. On the other hand, she could not decide if she liked the idea of Edwin's being jealous or wondered whether she really just wanted to pretend she had not really understood any of what Edwin was feeling and focus on Tom. These thoughts swirled about for a while, ultimately confusing her rather than providing any sort of clarity.

She blurted out, "Tom didn't stay, you know. I went upstairs and, well, just fell asleep. I only just managed to wake up."

Edwin turned to look at her dolefully. "It would be none of my business who stayed with who, you know, Lisa." He turned back to stare out of the window.

"I just wanted you to know, that's all," she replied, deciding that to give any further details would probably be a mistake.

They both remained silent, lost in their respective thoughts.

Suddenly Lisa jumped up, "Oh no," she wailed. "I've left all the details of the arrangements back in the office. The file we prepared with the reservation details and dietary requirements and receipts for the deposits we've paid and everything. What am I going to do?"

"It's OK," said Edwin, turning to look at her. "Don't you remember? Susannah gave the file to Tom to look after,"

"Oh, thank goodness," said Lisa, sitting down again and becoming marginally less agitated. "I thought I was really in trouble."

"Besides," said Edwin. "I thought there might be a problem along those lines, so I prepared a duplicate set without telling you. I've got everything on email and this morning I also printed off a hard copy set of all the papers we need, so there's nothing to worry about, even if Tom forgets to bring the file."

"Really?" exclaimed Lisa. "You thought to print another set? That's amazing! You are an absolute darling, Edwin."

He blushed slightly but felt extremely pleased. He was even more pleased when Lisa lent over, gave him a hug with an exclaimed "Thank you so much" and kissed him on the cheek. She leant back in her seat and he put his hand to his cheek, touching the spot where she had kissed him. He blushed more deeply this time and looked at her. She smiled at him and reddened herself. He wondered what he could do to make the moment last, but as she turned away herself to look out of the window, he felt a frisson of disappointment as he realised once more that he could not find the right words. He was afraid that the kiss had been far too sisterly in nature and wondered how he could transform matters from a near-sibling relationship into something decidedly more exciting. He struggled with these thoughts as they sat in silence.

Eventually they felt the train's slowing and started to gather their things.

"We'll get a taxi from the station," said Edwin. "There are always cabs waiting for the London trains."

"I was wondering how we would get to the hotel," said Lisa. "I suppose Gordon won't think a taxi is too expensive? I was thinking we should walk."

"It's four miles," said Edwin. "I checked on Google Maps. Through country roads too, where anyone might be coming hurtling round the corner." He paused and then went on, "You know, in a company Aston and not looking where they were going!"

Lisa giggled and said, "Oh, yes, that's terrible. You wouldn't want to get in the way of that, would you?"

The ticket barrier was broken when they got out, but the inspector on duty just waved them through with a laconic gesture that implied a complete lack of interest. They found one taxi waiting outside, a rather dilapidated, uninspiring Ford Mondeo. The driver seemed equally uninspired by the prospect of actually driving his taxi anywhere but with a very obvious grunt of reluctance, agreed to take them to the Sussex Manor House hotel.

On the journey through the winding country lanes, the taxi driver gunned his engine down the rare straights and approached every turn as if he was a contestant in the Paris-Dakar rally. Lisa announced that she was going to be sick if he did not slow down and he reluctantly did so, at least enough for her to survive the journey. Eventually, they pulled up at a set of imposing iron gates that swung open automatically. There was a long drive with manicured lawns on either side which led up to the main hotel building which seemed very aptly named. It was a large, sprawling edifice that looked as if it had been the feudal lord's manor at some point. The drive ended in a wide circle around an impressive ornamental pond with a duck house in the middle. As they got out Edwin noticed large koi carp swimming in the water and a sign that said, 'Please do not feed our fish' in bold, unfriendly letters.

They paid off the taxi and having gathered their relatively modest luggage, headed into the main building. The taxi spun its wheels in the gravel and, with its engine gunned, seemed to burn rubber from its tyres as it roared off. They looked at it, both open-mouthed and stunned, not able to move, as if petrified and rendered immobile by what they had just witnessed and what they had to face.

Eventually Edwin shook himself out of his trance and on slightly unsteady legs, turned to walk through the imposing front door. Lisa looked after him for a moment as if uncertain whether to follow or simply turn and flee; but, finally emitting a deep sigh, carried on after him. They entered a capacious hall with a high ceiling, a deeply polished wooden floor which shone like a mirror and an imposing fireplace at the back, in front of which was a large hearth rug. Either side of the fireplace were two sets of wide, oak stairs leading away from each other and turning back on themselves at a landing, from which they presumably continued up to the bedrooms in opposite wings.

A stern-looking woman was working at a computer, sitting behind an impressive leather-topped desk which evidently served as reception. Lisa looked around, noticing how her reflection was visible in the gleaming floor and marveling at the impressive wood-paneling. Above the main entrance was a minstrel's gallery and along the walls were large oil paintings of severe looking gentlemen, many in military uniform. Just behind the reception desk was a heavy suit of armour complete with a long halberd. Lisa did not like the way the visor was down on the helmet so that it looked as though the eyes were black and vacant. The woman behind the reception desk looked up and said without a smile, "May I help you?"

Lisa replied in a tremulous voice, "Er, hello, yes, we are, I mean, we are from, er, Aardvark. We're here for, um, our meeting."

"Are you Miss Brown?" interrogated the woman.

"Er, yes, that is, yes I am."

"I see," said the woman. "And you are?" she added turning to Edwin.

"Ah, my name's Edwin," he said. "Edwin Snape," he added as an afterthought.

The woman gave him a hard stare for a moment and then turned back to Lisa and said, "I remember we spoke on a number of occasions about the arrangements for your meeting, Miss Brown. I think you will find everything in order."

She looked at Lisa over her pince-nez spectacles, as if challenging her to suggest that this would not be the case. Lisa looked at her for a moment and visibly shrank. She turned to Edwin for support but he was studiously studying his shoes.

"Welcome to the Sussex Manor Hotel," added the woman after a moment, seemingly begrudgingly. "My name is Briggs and I am the manager. I am here to ensure that you and your colleagues enjoy a perfect business meeting. Would you like me to show you to your rooms first or inspect the room where your meeting will take place? You have ordered dinner for seven-thirty tonight, I believe. Would you like to have cocktails served at six-thirty pm or seven pm before dinner? And would you prefer to take them in the library or the garden room? If you have come by car, please leave the keys with me and I will ensure that it is parked securely behind the main house in the stables. Do you need any help with your luggage?"

At this succession of questions, Lisa's remaining composure crumbled and she just gaped and said nothing. Edwin finally looked up and, seeing Lisa now incapable of speech, realised he would have to intervene. He summoned up as much courage as he could and said, "Thank you, Mrs Briggs."

"Ms.," she interrupted pointedly.

"Er, yes, quite," said Edwin. "I think we will do this. We will see our rooms first and then as it is a nice day we can use the garden room for cocktails. Seven o'clock should be fine."

"And your luggage?"

"Um, we should be OK thanks," said Edwin. He looked at Lisa who just stared at him in admiration and mouthed "Thank you" at him. Edwin smiled reassuringly, pulled himself taller and added to Ms. Briggs, "We came by train so no car to park, thank you."

Ms. Briggs looked at him for a moment and then nodded in agreement, looking slightly surprised by the way the rather anemic-looking Edwin had managed to assert himself.

Ms. Briggs tapped briefly on her keyboard and then turned behind her to open a small cupboard which contained a collection of keys, each individually labelled. She studied them closely for a moment and selected two. She stood up, came around from behind her desk and said curtly, "Follow me, please. You are both in the west wing."

They picked up their bags and followed her. She headed up the right-hand staircase.

"Mind your step," she said, as she turned back on herself on the landing and started up the second staircase. "You can see on the third step the carpet is a little frayed and has come away from the stair. I would not want you to slip so please step over it."

"Oh right," said Edwin, and stepped over the offending carpet. Lisa followed suit gingerly. They arrived without mishap on the first floor and Ms. Briggs turned down a long, dark corridor with several heavy-looking doors leading off it. After about passing four or five doors, she stopped and handed Edwin a key.

"This is your room," she said, turning the handle and pushing the door which creaked. "It is King Charles the First."

"It's what?" said Lisa.

"Each room in the Manor has an individual name. This one is called King Charles the First," said Ms. Briggs, with evident disdain.

"Oh, I see," said Lisa, shrinking back a little. "I have never stayed in a hotel with room names rather than numbers."

"You are next door, Miss Brown," said Ms. Briggs, "In King Charles the Second." She pointed to the door just before the one they were entering.

She invited Edwin with a brief gesture of her arm to follow her into the room. The centerpiece was a four poster bed with heavy gold drapes and large pillows. Edwin came into the room and looked at the bed with amazement.

"That's impressive," he said.

"Every room has one," said Ms. Briggs with evident pride.

The rest of the furniture in the bedroom also seemed to be antique and extremely valuable. There was a large chest of drawers; a stand-alone wardrobe and a table with a bronze lamp standing on it. Lisa had crept into the room and just stood and stared at the bed.

Edwin, who had considerably more experience of hotels than Lisa, looked around the room and asked, "I don't see a door to the bathroom. Where is it?"

"There are no en suite bathrooms in the hotel," said Ms. Briggs. "Each wing is equipped with communal bathrooms. We find our guests see the original layout and décor of the hotel as part of its charm."

"I am not sure Gordon is going to think that way at all," said Edwin, looking at Lisa in alarm. "Does he know that he is going to have to walk down the corridor to pee? He's going to go ballistic."

"I don't know," whimpered Lisa. "Mary booked everything."

"Well, I just hope she warned him," said Edwin, putting his bag on the bed. "Come on, let's get you installed and then go downstairs to look at the meeting room." He was starting to enjoy his new-found self-confidence. Lisa looked at him doubtfully but followed him and Ms. Briggs out of the room and into her own, which was very similar.

"The bathrooms are at the end of the corridor," said Ms. Briggs as they came out of Lisa's room. "You can see at the end it branches to the left and the right. There are more rooms down there and the bathrooms are at the end of the two branches – Gents on the right; Ladies on the left."

"Right," said Edwin.

"No, left," said Lisa.

"Right," said Edwin.

But before Lisa could say "no, left" again, she noticed Ms. Briggs giving her a look that made her fall quiet.

"You'll find your way, I am sure," said Edwin. "Shall we go downstairs?" he added, turning to Ms. Briggs.

Ms. Briggs turned away and walked down the corridor. Edwin followed with Lisa trailing hesitantly at the rear.

As Lisa went down the stairs, she forgot about Ms. Briggs' warning and her foot gave way on the loose carpet. She screamed as she flailed wildly in the air and careered into Edwin who was just on the landing in front of her. For a moment he managed to retain his balance as Lisa's full weight collapsed on him. However, the shock of the noise combined with the force of her impact proved too great for him to resist and he could not prevent himself tripping forward. Locked in a deadly embrace, they both tumbled down the stairs. Edwin yelled "Christ" in wild alarm as Ms. Briggs at the bottom of the stairs turned to understand what was wrong.

She had no time to react before they collided with her and their impact sent the three of them sprawling across the hearth rug. Under their combined weight and momentum, it careered violently across the polished wooden floor as though it was an ice rink. Time seemed to slow down as the rug continued unabated across the floor, transporting a howling, tangled mass of arms, legs and hair. Lisa screamed again as she saw their inexorable path towards the suit of armour.

It was Ms. Briggs' body that connected first with the metal and with a calamitous cacophony of collapsing chainmail, the suit fell in pieces on top of the three of them. Unfortunately, it was the right arm of the suit which had been holding the impressive halberd aloft; suddenly there was no restraining force to support it. Like a tree felled by a lumberjack, the halberd tottered for a moment and then tipped forward, the head of the axe slamming hard into the top of the reception desk, happily gouging something solid for the first time in several hundred years. Simultaneously the iron tip of the weapon skewered the computer with a perfect strike, shattering the flat screen and causing it to crash onto the floor, scratching the polished floor in all directions.

Ms. Briggs struggled to her feet, holding her right wrist, which appeared to be flopping at an unpleasantly unnatural angle. She looked at Lisa and Edwin who were also trying to get up – Lisa's blouse had ripped and had somehow ridden up to cover her face. Edwin was presented with the wonderful sight of her lace bra just inches from his eyes. Unfortunately he was in no position to enjoy the view as he was too busy trying to extricate himself from the helmet which had fallen on top of his head and wedged itself over his forehead.

"You crazy bastards," screamed Ms. Briggs, her professional decorum totally lost. "Look at the fucking damage you have caused. That suit of armour is five hundred years old and the desk is a priceless Queen Anne antique."

Edwin stood up and, having managed to extricate his head from the helmet, looked at the smashed top of the desk, the halberd impressively buried in the wood, the leather top indeed mortally wounded with a huge gash. He saw the remains of the computer scattered across the floor. He looked back at the halberd.

"That really is a fearsome weapon," he said, in a fruitless attempt to distract Ms. Briggs.

"I'll show you how fucking fearsome it can be, you lunatic," she screamed, tugging at the shaft as if she intended to swing it at Edwin.

"Now, hold on, calm down" said Edwin, backing away. "It wasn't my fault. Lisa tripped and I couldn't stop myself. I am sorry for the damage caused but it really couldn't be helped. I am sure your insurance will cover it."

"Insurance," shouted Ms. Briggs. "How do you think the fucking insurance company is going to repair that?". She pointed at the desk and continued her efforts to remove the halberd. She was hampered by only having the use of one hand.

"Oh, have you hurt yourself?" said Lisa, finally on her feet with her clothes more or less adjusted.

"Oh no," said Ms. Briggs, sarcastically. "My wrist always hangs at this angle."

"Oh, that's good," said Lisa.

"I'm fucking joking, you stupid bitch," said Ms. Briggs. "I think you have broken it."

"Sorry," said Lisa, not knowing what else to say.

"I'll make you fucking sorry," shouted Ms. Briggs. "I told you to look out for the step, but did you? Like Christ you did!"

"That is an interesting point," said Edwin, recovering his sang-froid and surprising himself with the return of his new-found confidence. "You really should have had that carpet fixed. It represents a hazard. You are lucky that Lisa and I are both unhurt or we could sue you for considerable damages. I am sorry about your wrist and your desk and," he looked around him, "Your suit of armour, but I think we really are blameless."

Lisa stared at him open-mouthed with admiration; Ms. Briggs stared at him with loathing.

At that point Tom and Peter walked in and took in the scene.

"Bloody hell, Lisa," said Tom. "Have you been up to your tricks again? Where's the coffee machine?"

"It wasn't Lisa's fault, Tom," interjected Edwin. "She tripped down the stairs on the loose carpet."

"She caused irreparable damage to priceless antiques," said Ms. Briggs, deciding it was time to assert herself. "Not to mention my wrist," she added.

"Yes, you have to be careful around her," said Tom. "My ear has not recovered yet from her attention on the Tube."

"I don't give a fuck about your ear," said Ms. Briggs. "I can tell you I will be pursuing legal action to recover costs to compensate for the carnage this stupid girl has caused."

"Was it your fault, Lisa?" said Tom, turning to her with a reassuring smile.

"I tripped," said Lisa.

"You see," said Ms. Briggs. "She tripped and you can see yourself what happened next. Totally her fault and she – or your company – are going to pay."

Tom ignored her. "Why did you trip?" he asked Lisa.

Lisa just stared at him, still shell-shocked. Edwin intervened on her behalf.

"It was very simple, Tom," he said in a confident tone. Tom looked at him in slight surprise. Edwin went on, "As we went up the stairs, Ms. Briggs warned us about the loose carpet on the third step, specifically saying that it was a hazard. When we came down we were both quite distracted because we had discovered that none of the bedrooms has en suite facilities and we were wondering what Gordon was going to say about that."

"No en suites," exclaimed Peter. "You have to be kidding! Communal bathrooms? That means you could run into anyone at three am when you get up to go to the loo."

"Just have to be careful to avoid you on my midnight prowl," said Tom, laughing. "But leaving that aside, you mean Lisa tripped on the loose carpet?."

"But I had explicitly warned her," said Ms. Briggs.

"On the way down as well?" asked Tom.

"Well, no," admitted Ms. Briggs. "But there was no need. She should have realised."

"Do you have a sign up displaying a prominent warning about the loose carpet?" asked Tom.

"No, not as such," Ms. Briggs was forced to concede again. "But how can we? There is nowhere suitable to put it on the landing. We can't hammer a nail into the paneling. It is irreplaceable."

"Unfortunately that does not provide a waiver under basic duty of care health and safety legislation," said Tom.

"And how the hell do you know that?" retorted Ms. Briggs angrily. "Who do you think you are? A bloody lawyer, or something?"

"Yes," replied Tom simply.

With the wind taken totally out of her sails, Ms. Briggs just stood there glaring.

"So, regretfully," continued Tom. "Any liability for damage is with you. Edwin, Lisa, are you hurt in any way? Do you need medical attention? Have you suffered any damage at all that we should ask the Manor Hotel to make good?"

"No, I don't believe so," said Edwin. Lisa shook her head and remained silent.

"Very good," said Tom. "Clearly no question of any liability on our side. We won't press for any compensation," he added, turning to Ms. Briggs. "We are sorry about the damage, of course, but you need to understand this has nothing to do with us."

She looked at him with a mixture of disgust and resignation and turned to examine her wrist.

"Can we help?" said Tom. "Would you like us to take you to the local hospital? Can you move your wrist?"

"It hurts when I do," admitted Ms. Briggs. "It may be just a sprain," she added hopefully. "There is a sling in the first aid kit in the office."

"Would you like me to help you into it?" asked Lisa, trying to make amends.

"Would I like you to do what?" Ms. Briggs spluttered in astonishment. "I think you have done quite enough already, don't you?" she added harshly.

"Sorry," said Lisa.

"I'll do it," said Peter. "I have my first aid qualification."

"Do you?" said Tom.

"Well, it's lapsed but it was the sort of thing I had to do when I played cricket," explained Peter.

"Oh right, that makes sense," acknowledged Tom.

"I will give your room keys, first," said Ms. Briggs, who had evidently calmed down and realised that it would be prudent not to pursue any discussion of legal action. She looked morosely at the smashed computer lying on the floor and, in a hopeless gesture tried to click the mouse (with her good hand) to see if that achieved anything.

"I will have to allocate rooms manually," she said.

She opened a drawer in the desk and brought out a piece of paper and a pen.

"Could you please write your names down?" she said. "Next to yours, Miss Brown, please put King Charles the First. To you," she said, turning to Edwin, "King Charles the Second."

Edwin and Lisa looked at each other and hesitated, but then did what they were told. Peter and Tom followed suit and then handed the paper back to Ms. Briggs.

She looked at the paper and said. "I will put you in the west wing as well. Mr Williamson, you are in Edward the First. And Mr Farrow, you are in Edward the Second next door."

"Wasn't he the chap who came to a rather unfortunate end with a red hot poker shoved up where the sun doesn't shine?" smirked Tom.

"He was lucky," said Peter. "It could have been that halberd instead."

They both started to laugh but were cut off by a look from Ms. Briggs. She reminded them in that moment of Theresa at her most ferocious. They took the piece of paper back and dutifully wrote down their rooms. Ms. Briggs handed them their keys.

"It's up the right-hand staircase," she said

"Thanks," said Tom and Peter in unison.

Ms. Briggs turned to Edwin and Lisa and struck a slightly conciliatory tone. She did not like the idea of the Health and Safety inspectorate paying a visit. "The Edward rooms are just down the corridor from the Charles rooms," she said. "Could I possibly trouble you to show your colleagues up there? My wrist is rather painful and I would be grateful for the help."

Tom said, "Give me your key, Peter. I will take your bag up while you play Dr Kildare. Then we can meet down here and check out the rest of the hotel before Lisa destroys the entire place." He turned to Edwin and Lisa: "Show me where to go, then, you two. And for God's sake, let's avoid the mantrap up there."

Lisa looked at him blankly.

"He means the loose carpet," explained Edwin.

They turned to climb the stairs. Ms. Briggs indicated to Peter that the office was through a door set in a recess behind the reception desk. Peter stepped carefully over the halberd and followed her in.

CHAPTER ELEVEN

Meanwhile, Gordon and Cressida had driven down to West Sussex, still arguing about Cressida's involvement in the offsite. Gordon had tried to persuade her even as they got into the car to set off that she should not come, but she had been adamant and wouldn't listen. The mere fact that he was so keen for her not to be involved made her wonder if he had some motive for trying to keep her away. She thought that the only possible reason could be to give himself a free hand with another woman and the only other possible woman was Susannah Bierson. She would have to watch them both extremely carefully.

In the frosty silence between the two of them, Gordon silently cursed and played out a number of scenarios in his mind to enable him to get Susannah where he wanted her – preferably alone with him in bed. It looked like it would have to be hers not his – not that he particularly minded. He had started to doubt her inclination in this regard but equally wanted to put her recent reticence only down to natural concern about exposing their relationship to their colleagues. He was going to have to be very prudent over the next couple of days; not only was it imperative that Cressida should have no inkling of what he was thinking, he would have to persuade Susannah to sleep with him, surrounded as they would be by the Aardvark team.

At least he could count on Peter to distract Cressida – the bloody fool had evidently fallen for the story about the potential promotion – and he would just have to wing the rest. He did wonder whether Peter's immediate denial that nothing had happened between him and Susannah the previous night actually might have been too quick. "Qui s'excuse, s'accuse" he thought to himself grimly.

He did consider that Peter was no doubt good looking and as he had already established that his own former athletic form had rather been replaced by excessive middle aged spread, perhaps a more obvious lover for

Susannah. "But he lacks my charm, sophistication or experience," he added to himself with a smile.

Cressida's voice broke through his reverie. "What will happen this afternoon? And then what is the plan for this evening?"

Reluctantly he dragged himself back from thoughts of Susannah and forced himself to adopt an amicable tone.

"Well, this afternoon, I am going to set the stage for the next two days. I will go through what we want to accomplish; what our challenges are; and how we should best deal with them. Peter will take us through his Riverjack Crypto rescue plan. I expect that will take most of the afternoon because it really is the problem child in the portfolio. Then we have drinks and dinner, I think. We will have a relatively early night because tomorrow we will be reviewing our overall investment strategy and look at a couple of new investment opportunities. But the main thrust of the next couple of days must be to have a viable plan to sort out Riverjack Crypto."

"Right," she responded. "I am looking forward to helping you with that."

Gordon glanced across at her with a distinctly unenthusiastic expression on his face but considered it advisable to say nothing more on the subject.

They continued in silence until they pulled up at the impressive gates of the hotel. They could see a taxi making its way up the long drive ahead of them and Gordon accelerated through the gates just as they started to close.

"That must be Henry and Theresa ahead," said Gordon absent-mindedly. "They said they would get here about now. I wonder if that silly girl Lisa has managed to sort things out."

He pulled up behind the taxi just as Henry and Theresa were getting their bags from the boot. Henry paid the driver and he sped off.

When Cressida got out, Henry walked over to her and gave a her a kiss on both cheeks by means of greeting.

"Cressida, darling," he said, "Gordon told us you were coming. It is so good to see you again."

"Hello Henry," said Cressida without undue warmth. She was more than aware of his exploits and felt his reputation was fully merited; she certainly did not want to give him any indication that she approved.

"Theresa, how are you?" she called over as Theresa picked up her bags.

"Fine, thanks Cressida," came the reply.

"Henry, help Theresa with her bags," said Cressida with the tone of command that was not easily disobeyed and they went into the quiet reception hall.

They surveyed the scene before them: smashed computer; damaged desk; broken armour.

"This looks like a scene from a Bruce Willis movie," said Henry. "What the hell has happened?"

"If I had to surmise, I would suggest Lisa got here before us," said Theresa.

"But not even she can have caused this much damage in such a short period of time," exclaimed Gordon.

"I don't know," said Henry. "Two minutes alone in the kitchen was enough for her to cause total carnage. Ten minutes here would have been quite sufficient. We can only be grateful the place is still standing. It has withstood battles and rebellions over the last five hundred years; but Lisa Brown has taken it down where armies failed before her."

He walked forward and examined the halberd buried in the desk. He reached out and tried to pull it out but it was solidly embedded.

"Like trying to get Excalibur out of the bloody stone," he muttered.

At that moment Ms. Briggs came back through with Peter. Despite her skepticism Ms. Briggs had let him bandage up her wrist and place it in a sling. But to her surprise he had shown considerable skill and, although she could not exactly describe herself as fighting fit, she did at least feel more in control.

"Peter, what the bloody hell happened here?" said Gordon.

"I didn't witness it myself," said Peter, "Tom and I just arrived ourselves. But I gather there was an accident; Lisa fell down the stairs."

"Ha!" exclaimed Henry. "I knew she would be behind this. Glad she did not let me down."

"Quiet, Henry," said Cressida. "Is she badly hurt?" she asked, turning to Peter.

"No. It appears the only casualty was Ms. Briggs here," said Peter. "I'm Peter, by the way. You must be Mrs Fairbanks."

"Call me Cressida, please" she replied with a smile.

Gordon cut in irritably, "Where are the others?"

"They have gone up to their rooms to unpack," said Peter. "I was going to follow suit."

"I suppose we should," said Gordon. "And then I want to get to work as quickly as possible. Can we start in thirty minutes?" He turned to Ms. Briggs and asked, "Is everything set up and ready?"

"Absolutely," said Ms. Briggs. "I will just sort out your rooms now."

She gingerly picked her way over the pieces of broken armour around to the desk and with only one hand, rather awkwardly retrieved the piece of paper on which she had written the rooms allocated to the others.

"The only problem with starting so soon, Gordon," said Peter, hesitantly, "Is that Susannah is not here yet."

"Well, where the hell is she?" said Gordon angrily. "I thought I made it quite clear that we were going to start on time. She can't just operate as a law unto herself. I will call her."

He walked away from the others and out through the main entrance, stabbing aggressively at his mobile.

"If I could just have your names then I will give you your room keys. Perhaps you could help me by writing them down for me?" said Ms. Briggs.

Cressida leant forward and wrote down "Mr and Mrs Fairbanks." Theresa and Henry followed suit.

"So," said Ms. Briggs. "I will put Mr and Mrs Fairbanks into Elizabeth the First; that is upstairs in the east wing. Left hand staircase." She handed Cressida a key and nodded towards the stairs. She went on, "And I will put the two of you just next door into Elizabeth the Second," she said to Theresa and Henry.

They looked at each other; Theresa in astonishment and Henry in amusement.

"There's been some mistake," said Theresa. "We are not going to share".

"Don't sound so shocked, Theresa," responded Henry. "I'm up for it if you are."

Theresa just gave him a cold stare.

"Oh, I do apologise," said Ms. Briggs. "I just naturally assumed, I mean..." She tailed off in embarrassment.

"Theresa can have Elizabeth the Second and I'll have Kate Middleton", said Henry lasciviously.

Ms. Briggs looked at him unamused and said, "Henry the Fourth, I think, will do very well. It's in the west wing at the far end of the corridor. Away from the others," she added, coldly.

"How very appropriate," said Theresa, as she wrote her name and room down. She handed Henry the pen without another word and gestured for him to do the same.

Meanwhile Gordon was talking to Susannah outside.

"Where are you?" he said in a quiet voice so as not to be overheard. "You know the meeting can't get on without you and frankly, neither can I".

Susannah judiciously ignored this. "Sorry, Gordon," she said. "The train is running slow on what they have just announced as the relief line, whatever that is. Apparently a goods train on the main track has broken down and everything is delayed."

"Bloody typical," said Gordon. "It would have been better if had driven down with me."

"But isn't your wife with you?"

"Yes, unfortunately, but either it would have been an excuse to get her to stay behind; or else there was plenty of room in my car anyhow. I just want to spend more time with you. Anyway," he went on, "We will have plenty of time later on."

"Now, Gordon," said Susannah in what she hoped was a decisive tone. "We really need to put what happened in Vegas…" but Gordon cut through her and asked, "What time do you think you will get here?"

"I guess about thirty minutes or so."

Gordon looked at his watch, "OK then," he said. "We will wait for you and aim to start at the top of the hour." He paused and then added, "As for me, I can't get Vegas out of my mind. I want you and must have you. You can't tell me your feelings have changed."

"Gordon," said Susannah. "There's nothing that can happen in the next couple of days with all your colleagues and your wife around. And then I am going back to the US. So let's just put Vegas down as a great memory and move on. OK?"

She spoke quickly and a little breathlessly, glad to have been so definitive and hoping that Gordon would be reasonable.

"And where have you moved on to, Susannah?"

He could hear her take a slight intake of breath followed by what seemed to him to be a guilty silence.

"I don't know what you mean," she eventually said in a slightly timid voice.

"Look," he said, thinking that pressing the point home would almost certainly be counterproductive. "I don't want to put any pressure on you. Let's just see what happens but I want you to know that I can't stop thinking about you."

"I am flattered, of course, Gordon," said Susannah in a more confident tone. She certainly had no desire to think about how she would explain to him that she felt as if Peter might be the one.

Cressida came out of the hotel and called, "Gordon? Where are you? What is the plan? When is Susannah coming?".

"So, we will just consider that option when you get here" he improvised in a much louder voice. "We'll get going as soon as you can get here. Travel safe."

He hung up and turned to Cressida. "We were just discussing options for Riverjack Crypto. She's been delayed but will be here soon. We'll start on the hour."

Meanwhile Susannah was left slightly bemused, staring at her mobile as it was disconnected, wondering what had caused Gordon to end the conversation so abruptly – not that she objected. In a few minutes she felt the train's slowing, looked up and saw that they were coming into a station. She heard the announcement that they were finally arriving in Horsham, gathered her bags and as the train came to a stop, stepped out onto the platform. When she finally made it to the hotel after a similarly perilous taxi ride, she almost bumped into Gordon who had stepped out to greet her.

He stood there arms outstretched, laughed and said quietly, "I said we would see later," as she stepped back.

In a louder voice he added "Great to have you here, Susannah. We are getting going in ten minutes. Just time to check in, go to your room and we will meet in the boardroom. Lisa has done her level best to destroy the hotel but some of it is still standing, at least. Get your room key and we will see you back downstairs shortly."

She went in, was greeted Ms. Briggs who handed her a room key – Queen Victoria in the east wing – and gave her directions upstairs.

A few hours later, Peter and Cressida were walking together in what was called the Chinese garden behind the hotel, deep in conversation.

The meeting earlier had not started well at all. Gordon had shouted at Lisa for the lack of en suite bathrooms and the fact that no coffee had been served in the meeting room. Lisa had just looked as if she was going to burst into tears at the criticism before Theresa intervened to point out that Mary had made the reservation and selected the hotel. Gordon was unmollified by the arrival of coffee – he merely complained that the biscuits were stale. He had therefore opened up the meeting in a bad mood and, as a result, for Peter, the meeting had been uncomfortable and intense.

After the introduction from Gordon and a review from Susannah of the broad investment strategy that was being contemplated in head office, they had dived straight into his presentation of the Riverjack Crypto recovery plan. He had barely started on his introduction before he was being lambasted for lack of judgement by Henry; for general incompetence by Gordon; for failure to do proper due diligence by Theresa. He was given some relief only from the intervention of Susannah, who had reasonably pointed out the collective responsibility for investment decisions, and then from Cressida, who had insisted that everyone – in particular Gordon – should focus on the future rather than the past.

He was grateful to Susannah – and encouraged by the surreptitious wink she gave him as she walked up to the flipchart next to where he was standing to illustrate a technical point on potential investment returns – but he was astounded by Cressida's contribution because of the evident expertise she had demonstrated throughout the meeting. However, the mood of the meeting had been far from constructive from his point of view and he had been extremely careful not to give any indication about his burgeoning feelings for Susannah; he could sense that Gordon was looking for any indication beyond a professional relationship. He had to manage the situation with supreme delicacy; he wanted the promotion badly and was not sure how things would transpire.

As they broke up an hour or so before dinner, Susannah had announced that she had to catch up on some work from the US; Henry had announced he was going to catch forty winks; Edwin and Tom had both headed for the gym to work out; Theresa had said she was going to the library to catch up with some background reading before the next day; and Lisa had said she would go and check that everything was in order for the evening ahead. Both Theresa and Cressida had reprimanded Henry fiercely when he suggested

Lisa might want to stay out of the kitchen because he had seen what she was capable of doing there and he for one did not want to miss dinner. As Henry protested that it was only a bit of fun, Lisa had started to blink back tears once more and as a result, Theresa and Cressida had given him no quarter. Taking advantage of this distraction, Gordon had taken Peter aside and under the pretext of talking to him about Riverjack Crypto had reminded him of his instruction to spend time with Cressida.

Hence a few minutes later, having suggested to Cressida a stroll in the gardens to discuss the plans for Riverjack Crypto in more detail, he found himself quite enthralled by her story.

"You see," she said as they walked through an opening in the yew hedge that surrounded the Chinese garden and found themselves going into what appeared to be a maze; they paused at the entrance and she went on, "My father was really the one who taught me everything. He was the first venture capital investor in London and founded Aardvark with Mitch. He took Gordon on about years ago, just after we were married."

"So may I ask, how did you and Gordon meet?"

"Actually, Gordon and I met at our first day at work. We were trainee accountants and joined the same firm in London. Don't tell him I told you this, but when we first met, I thought he was arrogant, bombastic and a bit of an arse, actually."

Peter laughed and turned to look at her. She was smiling and was clearly enjoying telling the story.

"There's another thing Gordon wouldn't thank me for telling you," she went on. "He failed his first set of exams, so that meant he was working for me at several client assignments."

"Really?" exclaimed Peter.

"Absolutely true," said Cressida. "He did eventually pass and, of course, given he was a man and supremely confident, as soon as he qualified he was promoted and was on the fast track."

"When did you actually get together?" asked Peter.

"At the party to celebrate the firm's centenary," replied Cressida. "There was a gala dinner at the Grosvenor Hotel with all the senior partners in the firm. Gordon and I found ourselves together towards the end of the evening. We were both quite drunk and totally euphoric. He had just qualified and been promoted; my career was seemingly heading for me to become the first female partner in the firm. It is incredible to think that, at that time, it was a completely male-dominated preserve. He made an indecent proposal and I thought 'Why not?'. We all had rooms in the hotel so it was very easy to meet upstairs.He was much better looking in those days and in good shape: actually, he was really handsome and had most of the girls hanging on his every word. I think he was probably chasing after me because I was the only one who hadn't thrown my knickers at him. I fancied him, of course, but really decided he could be obnoxious. You know the story of Paul McCartney and Jane Asher?"

"I don't think I do," said Peter.

"Well, rumour has it that Paul fell in love with her because she was the first girl he propositioned who said no. I think there was something of that with Gordon and me. Anyway, we met upstairs and you know what happened next."

"Love flourished from then on?"

"Not exactly. I actually had the worst sex of my life. It was terrible, as I recall."

Peter looked at her in astonishment.

She returned the look with amusement gleaming in her eyes: "Well, I always believe in telling the truth because it is easier to remember what you said," she said with a flourish.

Peter smiled. "That is very sound advice which I will definitely take on board." He paused and asked, "So what happened afterwards?".

"Well, it did get better, of course."

Peter looked at her quizzically. "Better?"

"The sex."

"Oh yes, right."

She laughed and went on. "Actually, as well as that, we did find we had a lot in common: ambition, drive, intelligence, acumen. However, if I am to be immodest for a moment, I was always better than Gordon at reading people and cutting to the quick of a problem. The challenge for me was that I fell pregnant and that was pretty much that."

"Oh, I see".

"In those days, it was still considered to be something of a scandal. And given we were both colleagues, I was the one who had to leave the firm. To be fair, Gordon and I were absolutely in love and were already secretly engaged. I remember when we went to tell my father. Gordon was terrified, actually, and I was not looking forward to the experience either. But to our amazement, instead of cutting me out of the will and casting Gordon into Hell, he said that he was really pleased; he had always thought highly of Gordon's ability and offered to bring him into Aardvark. And that was that. I brought up the children and Gordon built his career. When my father died, Mitch made Gordon Senior Partner in London." She paused and went on, "But I was always better!".

Peter laughed. "I can tell from the way you discussed Riverjack Crypto that you have a lot of experience. I was so impressed with the way you read the situation."

"Why, thank you, Peter. I really appreciate it. And now a question for you."

"Of course," he said.

She looked at him hard. "What is it with you and Susannah and what has my husband told you to do with me?"

Peter looked at her, wondering what on earth to say. She smiled back at him.

"Think what you just pointed out, Peter. I am good at reading people; and I bet that I am the only person in the room who saw Susannah wink at you when she got up to go through your figures on the whiteboard."

Peter was astonished at her perspicacity and still wondered what on earth he should say.

"Remember what I said, Peter", she went on calmly but insistently.

"Which part?"

"Tell the truth, it's easier to remember what you said."

Peter hesitated for a moment and then saw her encouraging smile. He felt as though he could trust her and decided to go ahead. He told her about Gordon indicating that Susannah was there to assess him for promotion to partner and a move to the US. He also told her that he and Susannah had definitely felt mutual electricity and he was wondering after many years whether she was the one. He decided, however, not to talk so openly about Gordon's instructions to occupy Cressida; he felt even though it was disingenuous not to discuss it, it would make the friendship he and Cressida were building seem inauthentic and he did not want to create that impression. He also omitted the details of his kissing Susannah in her hotel the previous night.

"So let me get this straight," said Cressida, after Peter had finished. "Gordon told you that Susannah has come over to assess you for a promotion. And I suppose he has told you to stay clear of Susannah while he works separately to persuade her of the merits of your case?"

"Er, that's pretty much it," Peter replied with some hesitation.

"I see," said Cressida. "How very interesting. How very interesting indeed." She stood there musing in silence. She seemed to come to a decision in her mind and said unexpectedly, "Shall we not go into the maze? We might not get out in time for dinner. I think we can follow this gravel path round and it should bring us back to the house."

"Sure," said Peter, wondering what she had really been thinking.

They carried along the path which led beyond the formal garden and gave onto a wide expanse of lawn; in turn this ran down to a small brook which trickled along, eventually feeding a pond at the far side of the grass. Beyond the brook lay a wooded hill which climbed away into the distance. The sun was just going down behind the trees and Peter stopped alongside Cressida and stared out over the tops of the trees which were swaying slightly in the breeze. It was, he thought, a beautiful and almost mesmerising view. The vista made him relaxed and calm with the feeling of serenity making him more at ease than he had been for months. He imagined taking Susannah by the hand and leading her down to the pond. He wondered if he would find a punt there and his mind wandered back years to that time at Oxford along the Cherwell. He could not help but smile inwardly at the thought of that most incredible early evening with Katherine; a real smile broke over his face as he considered that the girl he had considered the love of his life probably no longer was.

"It is indeed a romantic scene," interrupted Cressida. Peter looked at her in astonishment. Had she read his mind? What else might she know about what he was thinking?

"In my experience," Cressida continued, "There's only one thing that makes a man smile like that. I just wonder whether you were thinking of the past or the future. Perhaps both," she added with a cryptic twinkle in her eyes.

"Both," he said, realizing that honesty was the best policy with Cressida.

She turned and continued along the path which ran along the edge of the wide lawn, eventually turning back to the house. She looked back at him and gestured him to follow.

"I will tell you one thing, Peter. I know my husband extremely well and my advice is to be very careful indeed before trusting his motives."

Peter waited for her to expand on this statement but it had been delivered with a level of finality that seemed to allow for no further conversation and they went back into the main house in silence.

As they headed into the main hall and Cressida made to go upstairs, she halted briefly and smiled at Peter. "Thank you for the very illuminating discussion, Peter. I enjoyed getting to know you very much. I think you will find that it will all work out: Riverjack Crypto and anything else you are trying to resolve." She smiled at him again with a suitably inscrutable expression and climbed the stairs without a further word.

CHAPTER TWELVE

Meanwhile Gordon had decided to take the bull by the horns and confront Susannah. He was damned if he was going to let her just write Las Vegas off as an inadvertent mistake – he remembered that night with such vivid pleasure that he refused to countenance the idea that it could never be repeated.

After the meeting broke up, he waited for everyone to disperse before heading to the lounge for a drink. He decided he wanted to contemplate his next move over a whisky. He walked into the room to see a series of comfortable chairs set around low tables with copies of various society magazines and large, glossy books judiciously arranged to give the appearance of informality without any sense of untidiness.

Behind the bar there was a rather corpulent man in his fifties who was polishing glasses. He seemed to have squeezed himself into his green, velvet jacket. His bow tie was clearly prefabricated, much to Gordon's disgust – it was far too neatly tied to be anything else – and he had slight beads of perspiration on his forehead. It was an unedifying sight to say the least.

"Good evening, sir" the man said with a slight wheeze. "Can I help you?"

"A large whisky and soda," said Gordon curtly. "With ice."

"I can't manage the ice at the moment, unfortunately," replied the barman. "I'm afraid we had a rather unfortunate mishap with our freezer yesterday and, as it's the weekend, we can't get it looked at until tomorrow."

"Mishap?" asked Gordon acerbically.

"Er, yes sir," replied the barman slightly nervously. "Something jammed the compartment door open and the ice melted. The resulting water short-circuited the freezer itself."

"What the hell could jam the freezer compartment door in a fridge?" asked Gordon with astonishment.

"Well, actually, sir, I have to admit it looks as if it was a rodent of some kind, although as it was frozen stiff it was a bit difficult to identify."

"You had a fucking rat in the kitchen?" asked Gordon incredulously.

"No sir, based on its size, more likely a mouse, I would think," said the barman, who turned away to polish glasses with even more vigour.

"Jesus Christ," said Gordon. "No en suite bathrooms and a kitchen overrun with vermin. Some luxury hotel you are running here."

"Not overrun, sir," replied the barman, turning back to him having put the glass on the bar top and reaching for a bottle of whisky. "Glenmorangie suit you, sir?". He poured without waiting for a response.

"I would say if you have a mouse in the fridge, you can bet your bottom dollar that you've got dozens running amok in the kitchen," said Gordon. He nodded curtly at the barman who had stopped pouring and raised an eyebrow as a silent question as to whether Gordon wanted a double.

"Actually, sir, it was indeed rather unfortunate. It appears that the young daughter of one of the maids had brought her pet mouse with her when she accompanied her mother to work last week. The children of the staff often come up to the hotel to earn a bit of pocket money, changing sheets and that sort of thing. Apparently this girl was doing some washing-up in the kitchen when her mouse escaped. It used to live in her hair, it seemed; when she got home and was about to take a shower, she couldn't find it. The poor girl was distraught, by all reports; and unfortunately it was her mother who made the discovery. She had to go back home to break the sad news to her daughter."

"But what the hell was it doing in the fridge?" asked Gordon.

"We think it must have been after the cheese," said the barman without a hint of sarcasm. He reached for the soda siphon. "Say when, sir".

A large bead of sweat dropped down at that very moment onto the bar next to Gordon's drink. Gordon looked on with astonishment as the barman casually wiped it away with a cloth without a comment and pushed the drink towards him.

"There you are, sir. Shall I add it to the general account? Aardvark, isn't it, sir?"

"I can't imagine you have anyone else staying in this godforsaken establishment. Fawlty Towers doesn't begin to do it justice."

"There was that very amusing episode, 'Basil the Rat', wasn't there, sir?"

Gordon made no comment and turned away with disdain. He took a long draught of his drink and found his mood slightly improved. He gulped the whole thing down and turned back to the barman to order another.

"Been a bit of a rough day, has it, sir?"

"Just pour me another, will you?" said Gordon. "I haven't time for banter."

"I often find that whisky can help offset the worst of days," said the barman and reached for the bottle again. "Reaches the parts other drinks cannot reach, to paraphrase the saying."

"For God's sake," muttered Gordon. He took his drink abruptly before the barman could engage him in any more conversation then decided to head upstairs to find Susannah. He needed to talk things through with her and get her to see matters from his point of view. "After all," he thought as he walked through the deserted main entrance hall to the reception desk, "I distinctly remember her saying she hadn't been laid in a while and I certainly gave her what she needed."

He went over to the desk and checked the piece of paper which had served Ms. Briggs as a guest register.

"Queen Victoria," he muttered, as he read Susannah's name against a room. "I think that is further down from our room. east wing, then." He turned and went up the stairs, turning onto the landing out of sight just as Lisa came hurrying into the main hall from the office and Edwin, still in his gym kit and sweating from his workout, entered the hall from a door on the other side.

Lisa looked at him in panic." Oh my God, Edwin," she moaned. "You have to help me. Gordon's going to go berserk and I have no idea what to do."

"What's the matter?" said Edwin with genuine concern. "Tell me the problem. Of course I will help".

"It's dinner," said Lisa. "Ms. Briggs just told me that the foie gras is off and so is the chicken; and that's what Gordon chose. So he's going to have to have the smoked salmon and the steak. And he's going to be so angry with me. It's not my fault. Mary should have made sure everything was in order. Oh, why did she have to have this weekend away? Couldn't she have just told her stupid husband she had to be here?"

"That," said Edwin pensively, "is not good news. Not good news at all."

"What am I going to do? I can't tell Gordon; I just can't."

"I tell you what," said Edwin, full of that newly-found self-confidence once more. "I will tell him for you." He suddenly realised what he had offered to do and immediately regretted his impetuosity. It was not as if Gordon thought of him in any better light than Lisa. But before he could even start to think of a way of backing out, Lisa had flung her arms around his neck and kissed him on the cheek.

"Oh, would you? That's so kind. I am so grateful, Edwin. Thank you so much. That's such a relief. He won't be nearly so angry with me if you tell him. You are an angel. How can I ever make it up to you?"

Edwin was surprised by the indecent proposal that came to mind when she said this but merely smiled and said, "My pleasure, Lisa. Of course I will do it."

He paused and went over to the desk.

"He must be in his room," he said, "Getting ready for dinner. No time like the present. Best get it over with before everyone meets for cocktails."

He checked the register and added, "east wing. Elizabeth the First. Right. Leave everything to me."

As he turned to go up the stairs, Lisa waved at him and said, "Good luck! And thank you!". He smiled weakly at her and, in spite of his sense of foreboding, hurried up the stairs.

As he got to the main corridor, he saw Gordon at the far end stop at a door and without hesitation, open it and go into the room. He braced himself once more and hurried after Gordon.

In the meantime Susannah had finished catching up on email and decided to try to find the bathroom to take a shower before dinner. She undressed to just her underwear and pulled on a short silk dressing-gown. What was it about the plumbing in these English hotels? There had been the farce in London with the bath and now she had to wander down the corridor practically naked to find the communal washrooms. She felt as if she was back at the very expensive if spartan girls' boarding school near Boston her parents had sent her to. She shivered at the memory of the freezing New England winters and the brutally cold wind whistling through the windows which were kept open all year round.

"A cold body makes a hot mind," the headmistress had always said although in retrospect Susannah thought it was more likely she had wanted to see her pupils' nipples erect with cold even under their bras. Academically it had enabled her to excel but the facilities were positively Victorian and the sexual inclination of most of the female staff not in doubt.

She tightened the dressing-gown around her in an instinctive movement just as Gordon came into her room.

"Gordon, what the hell are you doing here? Don't you know about knocking, first? I might have been completely naked," she said angrily. "Will you get out, please?".

"Nothing I haven't seen before," said Gordon with a wry laugh. "And don't feel obliged to get dressed on my account. Naked sounds much better to me."

"For God's sake," she said. "You can't be in here. Supposing one of the others saw you. Or even your wife," she added vehemently. "What the hell would you do then?"

"They are all busy scattered around the hotel. It's why I took my chance to come and see you." He paused and added, "Drink?" gesturing to her with his glass.

"No!" she exclaimed. "I do not want a drink. You need to get out now."

"But I don't want to," he countered. "I want to talk to you."

"Talk?"

"Well, that is unless you have a better suggestion," he laughed.

She flushed with anger and looked away.

"You know, Susannah," he said, suddenly coming towards her and putting his arms around her waist. "I told you on Friday. I want you and I need you. I'd do anything for you. I would even leave Cressida for you."

"Now you are just being ridiculous," she said and struggled out of his grasp. "I told you," she added, reddening again. "I had a great time in Vegas and...", she paused, embarrassed and lost for words for a moment. "I mean; well, you know what I mean," she stammered, turning away from him.

"And we can have the same time again," insisted Gordon.

"No way," countered Susannah. "I've told you, it's over. I don't want to say I regret it but come on, Gordon, just look back on it as a bit of madness and treat it for what it was. A bit of fun and that's all."

He reached for her again but only managed to grab the silk belt around her waist. As she jumped backwards, he tugged on the silk and the dressing-gown fell apart, revealing most of her body to Gordon.

He exclaimed in pleasure. "Now, that's what I wanted to see. I think you are getting the message."

"For Christ's sake," she shouted, "Are you planning on raping me or something? Give me my fucking belt back."

"Look, Susannah," he said, still holding the cord. "I want you so badly and I am not going to give up." He came towards her with a glint in his eye and a smile. For a moment she wondered whether he really did plan to try to force her and whether mentioning rape had perhaps not been so smart. She thought about slapping Gordon but decided that a knee to the groin would be a better deterrence and was bracing herself when there was a knock at the door.

"Who the hell is that?" said Gordon.

"How do I know?" replied Susannah. "But I told you that by coming in here you could get in trouble."

"Gordon," came a voice. "Gordon, are you in there? I urgently need to talk to you.

"That's Edwin," said Gordon. "What the Nigel Christ does he want?"

"You'd better go and see," said Susannah, grabbing the belt from Gordon's now loose grasp and fastening her dressing-gown.

Edwin had seen Gordon go in through what he assumed was his bedroom door at the far end of the corridor. But before he reached it he had seen a carved wooden sign reading "Elizabeth the First" fastened onto another bedroom door. He knew that Gordon had not turned into that room and so, intrigued and confused, he walked to the end of the corridor until he came to the door marked "Queen Victoria."

He knocked at the door and called out. The door opened and Gordon was standing there, wide-eyed and evidently furious.

"Edwin, what the fuck is it?" snarled Gordon.

"Gordon," he stammered. Then he stopped before he could say another word; in the background he caught a glimpse of a Susannah in a flimsy dressing gown. Gordon turned round and saw what had caused Edwin's sudden silence. He turned back to Edwin and started to extemporise very rapidly indeed.

"Edwin," he exclaimed in a much quieter voice and in as gentle a tone as he could muster. "I'm sorry I lost my temper. I am completely on edge right now. I was just talking to Susannah. She was, er, yes, she was consoling me."

"Consoling?" asked Edwin. He heard what he thought was a faint snort coming from inside the room.

"Er, yes, consoling. I had to confide in someone and Susannah was kind enough to be a shoulder to cry on. Yes, that's it. A really kind shoulder to cry on."

Edwin could hardly believe what he was hearing. Gordon needing consoling was about as unlikely as a ravenous lion roaring, coming bounding up to you and then starting to purr. To his astonishment, it looked as if Gordon was wiping away a tear.

"Gordon, what on earth is wrong?" exclaimed Edwin.

"I've discovered," said Gordon, after a moment, "Yes, I've discovered that... Listen, Edwin, can you keep a secret? I need your help."

"Yes, of course," said Edwin, quite astonished and having completely forgotten about his original reason for needing to see Gordon.

"You see," Gordon continued in a conspiratorial tone, naturally drawing Edwin forward as he lowered his voice and pretended to gulp, "I am pretty sure that I have discovered my wife is having an affair."

"An affair?" exclaimed Edwin. "Who with?"

"Shush!" said Gordon in a forceful whisper. "Not so loud. Yes, an affair. And this is the astonishing part, I think she's having an affair with Peter."

"With Pet...," Edwin started to shout and then controlled himself. "With Peter," he whispered in complete bewilderment. "Peter Williamson?"

"Yes. I've had my suspicions for some time now. But I think they were confirmed when I saw them together in the garden after our meeting broke up. For some reason Peter suggested to Cressida that they take a stroll and she immediately accepted. It just didn't seem right and they have been gone so long. I want to believe that there's nothing to it; but the evidence just points to everything I'm afraid of."

"I can't believe it," said Edwin.

"Neither can I but I fear the worst," Gordon went on. "But what's killing me is the uncertainty. Is it happening before my eyes or is it just the green-eyed monster ravaging my soul?"

"Pardon?"

"Oh for God's sake," exclaimed Gordon, and then immediately calmed down again as Edwin eyed him fearfully. "I mean, am I just jealous for no reason?". He paused and went on. "So here's where I need your help, Edwin. I need you to follow Peter and Cressida and report on their every move. Don't let them think that they are being watched by you but watch them all the same. I need you to tell me if there is any sign of intimacy at all – do they flirt; touch each other; kiss or even…? No, I can't bring myself to think that the woman I have loved for more than twenty-five years…" He turned away as if overcome with emotion and caught Susannah's eye; she just gave him an infuriated glare.

"Of course, I will do that for you," said Edwin. "You can rely on me."

"Thank you, Edwin. I knew you would not let me down. You can be sure that I won't forget this as we are talking about the next round of promotions in the firm."

"Thanks, Gordon. I really appreciate that," said Edwin. "I am absolutely sure, given the chance…"

Gordon summarily interrupted him. "By the way," he said, "What was it that you wanted to see me about?"

"Oh, there's a problem with the menu tonight. The foie gras is off and you'll have to have smoked salmon."

For a moment Gordon looked as if he was going to explode into one of his famous bursts of anger and Edwin braced himself for the onslaught; but he collected himself and said in a quiet voice, "I don't think that dinner is my most pressing problem, Edwin. I am sure it will be fine."

Edwin looked relieved and hesitated for a moment.

"Well, get on with your mission, Edwin," commanded Gordon. "I need to know one way or another right away."

"Yes, you bet. I'm on it right now," replied Edwin. He turned and pretty much sprinted off down the corridor.

Gordon turned back to Susannah. She was applauding sarcastically.

"You have to admit," said Gordon, "As improvisation goes, that was pretty spectacular."

Despite herself, Susannah laughed. "I particularly liked the way you pretended to wipe a tear away," she said.

"Artistic verisimilitude," replied Gordon. "That idiot Edwin will be well and truly off on his wild goose chase."

"But what will happen when your wife and Peter notice him skulking about?"

"Not really my problem," said Gordon. "I have no idea if Edwin would make a good spy but I suspect a herd of elephants on your trail would be less noticeable. So I reckon they will see him and that is when the fun should start."

"Be that as it may, Gordon," continued Susannah. "All I need for you right now is to get the hell out of my room so I can take a shower."

"You sure I can't scrub your back for you?"

"Gordon! Get out of here or I will; I will; well, I don't know what I will do but we will both regret it for sure."

"Now, calm down," said Gordon. "I am indeed leaving. I will see you later." He looked her up and down and added, "Preferably wearing fewer clothes than you are now." And with that, he left.

Susannah shrugged and looked around for a towel. She decided to give Gordon another five minutes to remove any further temptation from his mind and then set off on her quest for the bathroom.

In the meantime, Lisa had been walking about the main entrance hall, fretting about what she should do. At one point she nearly followed Edwin up to the east wing. Then she wondered if she should go and wait in her room. She also thought perhaps she should go to the library and make sure that the cocktails were all set. It was in this state of mild panic that Tom found her as he in turn emerged from the gym, sweating but looking particularly handsome. Lisa stopped and stared at him for a moment. He certainly was a very attractive man and totally different from Edwin. She thought back to what Samantha had said about sleeping with both of them; then she saw Tom look at her with a smile and blushed.

"Hi," he said, approaching her. She started at the sound of his voice.

"You look preoccupied," he said. "What's up?"

"Oh, it's a problem with dinner and I am just thinking about what Gordon is going to say."

"What's the problem?"

"There was a muddle with the menus and it seems that pretty much everything is off except smoked salmon and steak."

"Doesn't sound too bad to me," contested Tom.

"Yes, but that's not what Gordon wanted. I know he's going to go ballistic. I didn't know how to tell him."

"If that's all it is," said Tom, taking a stride over to her, "Then no problem at all. I will tell him. He would probably find it a lot harder to shout at me than you."

"Oh, that's kind," said Lisa, "but Edwin's gone to do just that."

"Edwin offered to tell Gordon bad news?" questioned Tom. "Bloody hell! The worm has turned."

"It was very sweet of him," said Lisa.

At that moment Edwin came down the staircase, still in his gym kit, and paused in confusion as he heard them mention his name.

"What the hell are you doing, Edwin?" cried Tom.

Edwin gave a jump and looked around guiltily.

"I'm, er, I'm just, I mean, I was looking for Peter."

"You won't find him by sneaking around the place," said Tom with a wry smile. "Last I saw he was talking to Cressida somewhere in the grounds. But that was a while ago. What do you want with him?"

"I, er, I need to talk to him about something," said Edwin.

"How did Gordon take the news?" ask Lisa.

"What do you mean?" retorted Edwin. For a split second he thought the question meant she knew about Peter and Cressida as well.

"About dinner," said Lisa. "You did tell him, didn't you?"

"Oh that. He's fine. No problem at all."

"Really?" asked Lisa. I thought he would be madder than hell."

"No. He was, er, yes, he was just fine."

"What are you not telling us, Edwin?" asked Tom.

Edwin looked at him with wide eyes. "Nothing. Nothing at all. What do you mean?"

"It's hardly the sort of news that Gordon would take calmly," said Tom. "Lisa just told me that dinner is going to be a successful as your attempt to repair that desk over there with a halberd."

"He was fine," said Edwin more assertively. The last thing he wanted right now was to have to explain anything more to Lisa, let alone Tom. "He just needed me to, er, talk to Peter about something. I have to find him."

With that, he abruptly went through the door that led to the library and from there out through the French windows into the garden beyond.

"I wonder what he's up to," mused Tom.

"I have no idea and I don't really mind," said Lisa. "I am just grateful he sorted Gordon out."

"Good, but you mustn't let Gordon worry you," said Tom. "If he's causing you any problems, you can just call on me."

Lisa looked at him and smiled, "You'll look after me, you mean?"

"I think I have shown that already in the last twenty-four hours," said Tom.

Lisa wondered what he meant for a moment and then realised.

"Oh yes," she said. "I haven't thanked you for the alarm clock. Without that I would have overslept for sure." She hesitated for a moment. "And I guess for what you didn't do," she added with a slight blush.

"Do you remember the kiss?" he asked with a smile.

Lisa went from a slight blush to full scarlet.

"Yes," she said timorously. "I do."

"So do I," said Tom. "Sweeter than a sweet thing on planet sweet."

Lisa giggled. "I enjoyed it too."

"Shall we do it again?"

"Not here," she exclaimed. "Someone might see us."

"Later, I meant", said Tom. "After dinner. Tonight."

"If you like."

"Shall I come to your room?"

"But won't we get into trouble?"

"Not if we are careful. But only," he added, "If you want me to."

"Yes." She smiled sheepishly at him and he returned the look with a big grin on his face.

"So which is it?"

"Which what?"

"Your room!"

"Oh, King Charles the Second. Up that staircase."

Lisa pointed towards the west wing.

"Got it," said Tom. "Now, we don't know what time dinner will end but let's say an hour or two after everyone goes to bed. Ok?"

"Yes, OK" said Lisa timidly, wondering whether she was being sensible. Her mind went fleetingly back to their first encounter on the Tube. He was handsome and kind. Suddenly she was excited about the prospect of the night ahead.

"Right," said Tom. "I'm off to change for dinner. Goodness knows what the showers will be like here but I will manage, I'm sure. I will just do my best not to run into Edwin wearing no clothes." He winked at her, crossed the hall and went rapidly up the staircase.

On his return, Gordon found Cressida back in their room and they were having another blazing row, although years of experience of arguments in hotel rooms meant that they were whispering at each other. It did not, however, make the encounter any less vitriolic.

"What the bloody hell are you playing at, Gordon Fairbanks?" demanded Cressida. "What exactly have you told Peter is the reason for Susannah's being here? And what are you trying to achieve by spending so much time with her? I will castrate you with a rusty knife if I find any hanky-panky going on."

"Hanky-panky?" mocked Gordon. "Have you suddenly gone all Victorian on me? Who says 'hanky-panky' these days?"

"You know exactly what I mean," insisted Cressida, "And you had just better watch out. But don't try to change the subject. What have you told Peter?"

"The truth."

"The truth? You've forgotten what that ever meant."

Gordon tried a mollifying tone. "Now listen, darling, that's not fair. When have I ever lied to you?"

Cressida was having none of it. "When haven't you, more like", she retorted angrily. "And tell me what the hell is going on. Peter seems to think

Susannah is over here to assess him for a promotion to the US. I can't begin to think that's true."

"And why not?"

This brought Cressida's flow to a sudden halt. She abruptly realised that this could indeed be the reason Susannah had come over. But what about all the candidates in Head Office? Wouldn't Mitch want to look at them as well? These thoughts were swimming round in her mind as she tried to gather herself and think through what Gordon was saying.

Gordon sensed her vacillation and pounced.

"It is absolutely why she is here and it is why I am spending so much time with her. I have to persuade her of Peter's merits. I am sick of Mitch telling me that all the talent in the firm is in the US. I want to show him that we can groom rising stars too. And so," he concluded as if wrapping up a Parliamentary debate in which he was clearly the winner, "That is all that is going on."

"I see," said Cressida, mollified but still suspicious. "And what about Riverjack Crypto?"

"That is definitely a problem," admitted Gordon. "We are going to have to find a way to resolve that situation to Susannah's satisfaction, otherwise we are all scuppered."

"True. I like Peter. I want to help."

"Well, the best way you can help is just to back off and let me get on with it."

"Don't be so bloody condescending, Gordon. You know I was always better than you."

"Well, at least understand that this is all that is going on."

"It you say so," said Cressida, dubiously.

"Right. Now, for Christ's sake, let's get down to cocktails."

CHAPTER THIRTEEN

Some time after dinner, Henry and Theresa were sitting together in the library. Henry was holding a large brandy up to the light and pontificating on the quality of the drink. He held it up to the light; swirled it with an almost loving caress around his glass and breathed in deeply its rich aroma. Theresa was looking at him with mild amusement as she sipped her espresso.

Ealier in the evening, the atmosphere initially during cocktails had been tense. Gordon and Cressida had clearly been in bad moods. Peter and Tom were distracting themselves by discussing the recent scandal involving the England football manager and three prostitutes who had apparently been procured as a incentive in return for information about an upcoming game. It had of course been a newspaper sting and they were scathing about yet another set up of a celebrity being successful.

Edwin had interrupted this conversation by rushing in from the garden, still unchanged, looking around desperately for Peter and Cressida and stopping suddenly in his tracks as he saw Peter with Tom and Cressida on Gordon's arm on the other side of the room. Henry, who had been sitting around a table with Susannah and Theresa sketching out a technical review of portfolio returns and debating the best sort of emergency cashflow injection measures available to companies in such a distressed state as Riverjack Crypto, looked up as Edwin stared around the room with a slightly wild expression on his face and said acerbically, "Edwin, I know we agreed that we would not dress for dinner, but don't you think you've taken the casual look just a little too far?"

Edwin gaped at Henry, not knowing quite what to say. Sensing the obvious tension and awkward silence as everyone stared at him, Lisa intervened to try to help.

"Gordon, I'm sorry about the restricted menu tonight but there was nothing we could do about it."

"What do you mean?" he turned and challenged Lisa abruptly, momentarily forgetting what Edwin had told him. She quailed in front of what she expected to be another onslaught.

"You know. We don't have foie gras or chicken tonight; just salmon and steak," she managed to blurt out in a nervous rush.

"First world problem," laughed Henry.

"It's completely unacceptable", roared Gordon with affronted anger. "Given how much we are paying for this place. It is beyond a joke. Why wasn't I told about this before?"

Lisa said in a timid whisper, "I thought Edwin told you."

"That's right, Gordon," piped up Edwin. "You remember. I came to find you when you were with…" and his voice trailed away as he realised he had already said too much.

"When you were with whom, Gordon?" demanded Cressida in the aggressive tone of a Gestapo interrogator.

"With, er…" he looked around desperately and tried to catch Susannah's eye, but she was studiously looking at the financial model Henry had sketched out, seemingly oblivious to the discussion.

"When I was with Susannah briefly this evening," he went on regaining his composure. "I had just called into her room to talk through an idea I had had on Riverjack Crypto and a possible refinancing option. I found her working and was just chatting it through when Edwin bursting in like a charging rhinoceros."

"Isn't that right, Susannah?"

She looked up and said rather non-committedly, "Oh yes, more or less."

"More or less?" asked Cressida scathingly.

Susannah saw the pleading look in Gordon's eye and went on, "Sorry. I was distracted by the discussion Henry, Theresa and I have been having. That's what happened. Edwin mentioned the change of menu and we went back to discussing Riverjack Crypto."

"Isn't that right, Edwin?" Gordon turned to Edwin and gave him a look which meant that he had no other option than to assent with a reluctant nod of his head.

"So, no problem about the change of menu, then Gordon?" said Cressida in a deeply sardonic tone. "It seemed the conversation just slipped your mind."

"Yes, it must have done," said Gordon. To distract the assembled company from his predicament, he turned again to Edwin and said assertively. "Edwin, like Henry said, I have no idea why you are still in your gym kit but for God's sake go and put some proper clothes on before dinner."

Edwin shuffled out of the door, slightly bewildered by the exchange but realising he should say nothing.

Gordon decided he needed to lighten the heavy atmosphere. He turned to the barman who was still squeezed into his green velvet jacket and sweating profusely.

"I think we should get this party going," he said. "Champagne, my good friend, if you please."

And so, as the corks popped and the bubbles flowed, everyone suddenly underwent a dramatic change of mood. Taking the lead from Gordon who seemed much more relaxed as they went in from pre-prandial cocktails to dinner, they all laughed uproariously as he told a story from a time when, as a trainee accountant, he had walked in on his senior partner rogering his secretary over the photocopier in the print room. He confessed that the sight of that flabby arse pounding away would be something he would have to live with for the rest of his life. He had studiously beaten a retreat on the grounds that he had no desire to be sent to the Shetland Islands to count sheep on a three month farm audit. Cressida chimed in about a time when she had audited a manufacturing company that specialised in sex toys and the adult toy industry in general.

"I had to count dildos for a week," she said to the general mirth of the company. "The first day I was with a female colleague who had been educated at a convent and had no idea what they were for. When I explained her eyes widened in astonishment. A week later we were having a drink together after work and she told me that she had bought one and it was the best investment she'd ever made."

Peter pondered telling the anecdote of Abigail and Ewan at Riverjack Crypto but decided that it would be unwise to bring everyone back round to the troubles at the company. He noticed Tom whisper something to Lisa who blushed and giggled. Next to him, Susannah was in deep conversation with Theresa; she had hardly said a word to him all evening. It was a real surprise when he suddenly felt a hand squeeze his knee. It was all he could do not to yelp and he only just managed to retain his composure. Meanwhile, Susannah had not broken stride once in her conversation with Theresa.

No one seemed to pay any attention to the changed menu – Gordon was even prompted to declare how delicious the steak was, receiving a snort of derision from Cressida. But the moment past and the general bonhomie, fueled by the additional bottles of wine Gordon ordered to be served, did not dissipate as the evening went on. Dinner eventually broke up with everyone in very good humour, drifting a little aimlessly in and out of rooms, talking quietly to one another and contemplating bed but not wanting the new-found spirit of fun at Aardvark to end.

Gordon had openly suggested to Susannah that they retire to the bar to discuss the plan they had started to consider earlier in the evening for Riverjack Crypto. Reluctantly and without any credible alternative, Susannah agreed. Cressida had suggested she join the conversation but Gordon had said he wanted to talk it through with Susannah alone – "For the reasons I explained earlier, darling," he added cryptically.

Cressida nodded and suggested to Peter that, as it was a fine night, another stroll in the garden could be a perfect aid to digestion. He accepted the idea and followed her out through the library into the garden, leaving Tom and Lisa still giggling together in the dining room. Edwin, however, had seen this exchange between the two of them and set off to trail them.

He was just heading to the French windows, which they had left ajar, when Henry called out, "Edwin, what the bloody hell are you looking so furtive for?". Edwin had not noticed Henry and Theresa sitting together in the shadows of a recess and jumped out of his skin.

"I, er, I just thought I would take a stroll as well. Lovely night for it."

"Yes, but sneaking out like George Smiley?"

"No, it's just that I was a bit preoccupied, that's all. The night air will clear my head."

"Good luck with that," said Henry unkindly and, as Edwin headed outside, he turned back to Theresa.

The wine, champagne and brandy had given him the desire to know more about Theresa and her private life. He realised that although they had worked together for a number of years, he really knew very little about her.

"No, I live alone. Just me and the two dogs," she replied politely but coldly in answer to his question.

"Dogs, eh? What breed?"

"Golden retrievers. I rescued both of them from Battersea Dogs Home."

"Or retrieved them, you might say," added Henry with a laugh.

"You might, I suppose," she conceded with a smile.

They fell silent and Henry looked somewhat morosely at his brandy. He started to contemplate the cost of his latest divorce and wondered if he had the stomach for the fight to rebuild his personal fortune for the fourth time.

"What do you think that was between Gordon and Edwin earlier?" asked Theresa, rather unexpectedly breaking into Henry's thoughts.

"It was somewhat awkward, whatever it was," pondered Henry. "I mean, clearly Edwin had met Gordon to tell him about the change of menu; and it looks as if he had met him in Susannah's room."

"But what actually happened there?" asked Theresa. "I mean, what should have been a very innocent explanation suddenly had layers of innuendo, particularly the way Susannah answered him at first."

"And what was it with Cressida's sudden interrogation?" added Henry. "That was strange. Not out of character, though, as she's always been suspicious of Gordon."

"Yes, but with Susannah? I mean, that hardly sounds likely. She for one could do much better." Theresa laughed and Henry considered her in a new light. He had never even heard Theresa say anything remotely derogatory about Gordon; indeed, he had rarely seen Theresa so much as chuckle. She had thrown her head back; the soft light of the standard lamp behind her had caught her eyes, causing them to sparkle. He had never noticed that they had a green tinge to them and that they turned bright when she laughed. It transformed her from a Gorgon to someone whose smile could light up a room. It was remarkable, in fact.

"That," he went on, "Is indubitably true. Gordon twenty-five years ago, perhaps, but not today. After all," he said after a brief hesitation, "He and Susannah don't really know each other at all."

"They were together at the Las Vegas conference," said Theresa. "And you know what they say about what happens in Vegas."

"'Go to the place where your accent is an aphrodisiac' or so the advert says on the Tube" said Henry.

"Exactly," said Theresa, with another astonishingly attractive cachinnation.

Henry took another swig of brandy. "Are you sure you won't have a drink to go with that coffee?" he asked.

"Well, after all, why not?" she said. "Everyone else seems to be letting their hair down. I reckon we can persuade Gordon to start an hour later tomorrow. I'll have a champagne cocktail, please."

Henry stood up and went through to bar. A few moments later he returned with the drink.

"You know, Theresa. Gordon was right. That barman is the most extraordinary specimen. He's in there still polishing glasses and sweating like a fat Finnish businessman in a sauna."

Theresa laughed and Henry was again surprised by how it changed her demeanour.

"Thanks for that image," she said. "Not one I will want to take to bed with me."

Henry decided to bring the conversation around to his favourite subject. He was starting to have surprising thoughts about how the evening could turn out.

"And what image would you want to take to bed with you, Theresa?". He rather blurted out the question and for a moment wondered if he had overstepped the mark. He could sense the Gorgon flash across her face for a moment; but then she relented and smiled.

"You know, Henry, no one has asked me that for a while. For too long, in fact," she said in a slightly wistful tone.

"I can't believe that," said Henry disingenuously.

She smiled and wagged her finger at him. She took a sip of her drink and mused "I have always liked champagne cocktails. They remind me of warm Mediterranean evenings in a beach bar, staring out to see and watching the sun go down." She paused and went on, "But to come back to your question, let me tell you that a fat Finnish businessman would not be it."

Again her smile lit up the corner of the library in which they sat.

"That's hardly surprising," said Henry, although there was something in her tone which suggested she had given him a trite answer to hide something more. He could not put his finger on it, however.

"And you?" asked Theresa in a playful tone which again seemed to take Henry by surprise. "You've had enough choices over the years but seemingly not found the right Mrs Farrell-Wedge?"

"Well," laughed Henry, "As you say, I've certainly cast my net far and wide. Trouble is, there was always a large hole in it. Or at least, a large hole left in my bank account as a result of each one. I think the only chance is to turn celibate."

"That would be a real waste," said Theresa with a new glint in her eye.

Henry looked at her askance. He wondered whether the alcohol was making him misinterpret what she was saying. There was a faint smile on her lips. She finished her drink, got up and smoothed her skirt down.

"Bedtime," she said. "I will leave it to you to negotiate the extension with Gordon. Make sure you do as we are all counting on you."

"Sweet dreams," said Henry.

"I will hope for something much better than a Finnish businessman to visit me," she said and, without another word, turned and walked out of the door.

Henry stared after her in amazement. For the first time in a long time, he found he had not had the last word in a conversation with a woman and had absolutely no idea what to think. He sat there musing for some minutes; then with sudden resolution he finished his brandy, stood up and walked to the door. He went down the corridor and into the main entrance hall. To his amazement he saw Ms. Briggs sitting at what was evidently a different desk, tapping at a new computer. He noticed that the sheet of paper with the manual room allocation was still on the desk in front of her and the impressive suit of armour had been reconstructed. All this had evidently been accomplished while they were at dinner. The desk itself looked as though it was the identical twin to the one which had suffered at the hands of the halberd; the polished wood gleamed under the desk lamp and the leather top looked as sumptuous as before.

"All fixed, I see," Henry said brightly to Ms. Briggs, who turned to look at him coldly.

"Yes. We sorted everything out when you were all at dinner. This desk is the second of a pair which we kept in a storeroom. We were able to rebuild the armour and bring the computer from the office out here. By the way, I hope everything was to your satisfaction."

"Very much," said Henry. He paused and added, "And here's hoping for no more accidents."

"Just keep that bloody secretary girl away from here, that's all" said Ms. Briggs acidly. She clicked on the mouse and reached over to turn off the computer, wincing slightly as she knocked her arm, which was still in the sling against the side of the desk.

"Indeed," said Henry. "Well, goodnight."

"I am calling it a day as well. I shall finish in the morning," said Ms. Briggs. After a moment she remembered to be marginally more polite and added, "Sleep well." She stood up from behind the desk and went back through the office door, opening and closing it without another word. Henry looked after her for a moment, shrugged his shoulders and headed upstairs.

CHAPTER FOURTEEN

A couple of hours later, Tom was lying on his bed, looking at his watch and wondering if everyone was asleep. He had passed a very pleasant evening, enjoying the reaction Lisa had to his asides and plying her with champagne – although not so much as to make her comatose. Indeed, he wondered if she would actually manage to stay awake as they had agreed. He somehow doubted it but at the same time, she had made it very clear that his visit would not be unwelcome. As a result he had spent the intervening time actually doing some work in order to distract his mind and help the hours pass.

In the end, however, the familiar tightening sensation in his groin had proven too much of an impediment to clear thinking on the Mixandmatchbypet potential investment papers he had been reviewing and he decided to pass the time just reading the book he had brought with him (a rather disappointingly predictable erotic novel about a naïve young girl who becomes besotted by a heartless billionaire – plagiarism at its worst). Even that proved not enough of an amusing distraction, so he just lay there, watching the minutes tick slowly by. In the end he could bear it no longer and he decided to risk venturing out.

He put on his shoes and tip-toed to the door. He remembered that the hinges were extremely prone to creaking and so with the gentlest of movements he turned the handle and eased the door open. The noise still seemed to reverberate around the corridor but, as he peered out, everything was silent and the big house gave the impression of being fast asleep. It was definitely an advantage that Lisa's room was in the same wing as his; however, as he went down the corridor, he halted in his tracks. Was she in King Charles the First or Second? It would not do at all to stumble in on Edwin instead. She had said Second, he was sure, but could she be trusted to have got it right? All in all, he was pretty certain she could not. Damn it! He would have to go down to reception and check. He just hoped that Ms. Briggs had not finished updating the register on the new computer she had had installed otherwise he was going to be in real trouble. If the handwritten register was still on the new desk, he would be able to check.

Very cautiously he crept along the corridor until he came to the top of the landing. It was only here that he dared use his mobile 'phone as a light to guide him. He would have been in real trouble without it as the faint moonlight hardly penetrated the darkness through the windows and for the most part, the house was as black as Nox Cena. Where was Chris when you needed him? He started down the stairs, remembering to avoid the loose carpet. He gingerly stepped over it and continued his passage. He paused briefly at the foot of the stairs before proceeding cautiously across the polished floor, taking care not to slip.

He reached the desk and was glad to see the piece of paper still lying there. He picked it up and read 'Lisa Brown: King Charles the First'. Just as well he had checked! Just then his eye caught a glimpse of a light from the Minstrels' Gallery above the hall. He froze; killed the light on his mobile and ducked down behind the desk. Above him, he could make out a shadowy figure, illuminated by the small torch beam of another mobile 'phone, crossing the gallery cautiously and leaving it through a door on the other side. Interesting that the Minstrels' Gallery seemingly provided a link between the two wings of the building. But who had discovered that and what was he – Tom was pretty certain it had been a he – up to? Probably best to stay put for a few more minutes, he thought, just to make sure everything remained quiet.

Meanwhile, Lisa had gone to her room quite soon after the dinner party broke up, with Tom's assignation still firmly on her mind. She was excited, nervous and slightly drunk but, having quickly undressed, she got into bed with the intention of staying awake to wait for him. Inevitably, she had promptly fallen asleep. She woke up quite abruptly with absolutely no idea what time it was nor, for a moment, where she was. Her mind floundered as she tried to make sense of the strange surroundings. Her room was quite dark with just a touch of moonlight coming through a chink in the heavy chintz curtains. She stared around her, recognised the shape of the four poster bed she was lying in and remembered where she was, and that she had been expecting the midnight visit from Tom. She started to smile in anticipation. But before that, she needed the loo! That could be quite an adventure in itself; she just hoped that she could make it there and back unscathed.

She pivoted out of bed and put her feet on the wooden floor. It was surprisingly cold against her feet. She shivered slightly and fumbled for the bedside light, before pulling a pair of pyjamas from her suitcase.

Feeling more at ease with something on, Lisa walked to the door and opened it, stepping into the fresh air of the corridor, which made her shiver once more. She tiptoed hesitantly down the corridor, groping her way as there was almost no light. She reached the end and was relieved to see that the pale moonlight coming through the window at that end of the corridor gave her a little more visibility. She crept through the shadows until she found what she thought was the bathroom door, felt around for the light switch and was relieved to see that she was indeed where she had been aiming for. Some minutes later she crept back out of the door, turning the light off and blinking as her eyes became accustomed to the darkness. She crept along the corridor until she came to the turn along the main passage. It was with some relief that she reached her bedroom door and opened it.

What surprised her was that the light she had left on was turned off. Tom must be in here already. In fact, she could hear a faint sound of breathing coming from the bed. He must have come in, found her gone, got into bed and fallen asleep waiting for her. How sweet! She would quietly get into bed next to him and surprise him. Suddenly she felt incredibly excited, aroused and daring, freed from any inhibitions.

She tiptoed across to the bed, climbed in next to the sleeping figure, shuffled across the large bed and curled her arm around Tom, snuggling up to spoon him.

Edwin had had a thoroughly unsatisfactory evening. First, there had been that extraordinary interchange with Gordon. He could not work out what was going on. Were he and Cressida really so distant in their relationship that she was having an affair? They seemed to be at least talking to each other. And with Peter? That seemed extraordinary. If his eyes had not been deceiving him, when he had found Gordon in Susannah's room it had really not looked as if she was consoling him. And yet Gordon's story had been totally credible. The situation was thoroughly confused and not made any clearer by Gordon's ordering the champagne and then excellent wine in a clear attempt to distract everyone. But distract everyone from what?

He had had to watch Tom's shameless flirting with Lisa with mounting jealously and the realisation that in the struggle between them for her affection, he was losing the battle. He was resigned to it; really, he had to admit that there had been no contest. He could not compete with Tom in any way. Accepting yet another disappointment in his life, he had been surprised to see Peter and Cressida disappear so quickly after dinner together. After being waylaid by Henry in the library, he had headed out into the garden and followed the couple at a distance.

There was a moon peeping through the clouds but it cast only a dim light and so he could not really see where he was going. He stumbled forward in the shadows and listened; he heard their voices more indistinctly now as if they were further away and so he hurried forward. There was a gap in the hedge that they must have gone through and he headed through it. He followed the grass path he was on as it twisted and turned two or three times.

He could now see very little and had to walk with his arms in front of his face; on a couple of occasions he had stumbled straight into a hedge which seemed to block his way. The first time it happened it caused him to howl in alarm. Putting a hand over his mouth, he froze, shocked at his carelessness. However, the night was silent all around him. He turned around to retrace his steps and suddenly realised that he could not remember which way he had come. He moved forward cautiously and his arms met another hedge blocking his route. It suddenly dawned on him that he must be in the maze and was consequently totally lost. He cursed under his breath and groped forward. It was hopeless; he could see very little in the scant moonlight and there seemed to be hedges blocking his way at every turn. He stopped for a moment and thought; then it struck him that he could at least use his mobile 'phone as a torch. He had shied away from doing so before as he had not wanted to give himself away in his pursuit of Peter and Cressida but that was of secondary importance to getting out of this bloody place. Wasn't there something about always turning left in a maze to get out of it? He would have to try it.

It took him another forty minutes, a lot of swearing, some painful scratches from the hedges and a dash of luck but he eventually emerged. He walked swiftly back to the house, feeling cold and damp with the night air and thoroughly depressed. He slipped through the French windows into the now deserted library and made his way to the entrance hall. There was no sign of anyone at all and, glancing at his watch and realising he had been struggling in the garden for nearly an hour, he climbed upstairs, got undressed to his shirt and underpants as was his habit and went to bed.

Now, deeply asleep, as if his subconscious was trying to make up for the disappointments of the evening, he was having a most pleasant dream. He was lying on a grassy bank on soft moss, half-asleep in the sunlight with a babbling brook next to him, when a beautiful, naked water-nymph rose up from the stream. She smiled and shook her long hair. Her nipples protruded towards him defiantly and, as she walked towards him, he could see the curve of her legs ending in a slight tuft of blonde hair.

She knelt down beside him and kissed him. He felt his penis stir in anticipation as her hands gently unbuttoned his shirt and pulled it open. She kissed him again, this time leaning over him so her lips brushed the back of his neck. He could feel her warm breath on his skin. Unhesitatingly her hands continued down his stomach, brushing lightly over his navel and reaching further down. She smiled at him again; kissed him once more and he gently moaned as he felt her hands free his erection from his underpants and gently caress his foreskin, teasing it over the now swollen head. He moaned again and he opened his eyes as the nymph's touch became more assertive. Suddenly he was wide awake, his heart banging like a base drum. He turned round, reached out his hand to touch the girl next to him and ran his hands through her hair.

"Lisa," he breathed. "You've come to me."

"Oh Tom," she said.

"Tom?" he yelped.

Edwin sat up in shock. Lisa suddenly let go of his erection with a yelp of her own.

"What do you mean, Tom?" said Edwin, with a mixture of anger and disappointment in the darkness.

"I mean," said Lisa. "I mean. Oh Edwin, it's you! I'm sorry!"

"Sorry doesn't quite cover it, you know," his excitement deflating as fast as his penis.

"But, I do really like you," continued Lisa. "It's just, you know, Tom…" She trailed off, not knowing how to explain.

"Yes, I get it," said Edwin now feeling thoroughly miserable and let down. "He's got everything I haven't. I know it and you don't have to remind me."

He paused as she said nothing. Then a thought occurred to him.

"Why did you think that Tom would be here, anyway?" he asked. "This is my room."

"Oh, I must have made a mistake when I came back from the bathroom. I thought Tom had come and got into my bed."

"Just as you two arranged, I suppose."

"Well… yes."

"I knew it. Tom is so fucking handsome, strong, clever. I'm just poor old Edwin. I am the one always in the bloody kitchen at parties."

"But, Edwin," said Lisa, trying to console him. "You are so kind and sweet."

"Yes, but kind and sweet doesn't get you laid," said Edwin.

A brief silence fell between them. Lisa suddenly thought about Samantha's advice. She wondered if she would prefer Edwin after all.

"Doesn't it?" she said softly in the darkness and reached over once more to touch his now soft penis. She immediately felt it jump in her hands. "We'll have to see about that."

She bent forward and to Edwin's surprise, he felt her hands gently finish removing his underpants and then stroke his once more rapidly hardening erection. His eyes closed and he was back on the grassy bank with the waternymph. He felt her lips close around him and gave a gasp of surprise. He had only ever fantasised about receiving a blow-job; he had never thought that it would happen to him. He felt her tongue flick the top of his head, probing the slit of his penis and pressing down on his stretched foreskin. He lay back on the pillow, unable to control the spasms of his body nor understand the sensational feeling of bliss he was experiencing. He emitted a soft groan that seemed to come from another person.

Lisa had been equally surprised by her bravado. She had very little experience of what she was doing but she could tell Edwin was similarly unversed in such things, so as a result she was not intimidated but excited. She discovered immediately that she liked the smooth feel of his erection; she felt her loins' glowing as she felt Edwin twitch and jerk at the touch of her tongue; she suddenly felt more in control than she ever had before. Perhaps sweet and kind was what she needed.

She slowly swirled her tongue around his head as she felt him quiver. Gently she withdrew her lips, enjoying the slightly salty taste of him as he became harder still. She moved up his body slowly, kissing his nipples and his neck. He closed his eyes as the image of the water-nymph came across his mind again. She lay on top of him and kissed him firmly; he felt her tongue find his and could sense his heat still inside her mouth. He moaned once more in pleasure.

She smiled, broke away for a moment, reached down to unbutton her pyjama top, then pulled her bottoms off. She leant forward again and kissed Edwin who lay there passively, unable to comprehend what was happening. She spread her legs and guided him into her. Edwin gasped as he felt her smooth skin embrace his. She leant down and kissed him again, their mutual passion enveloping them. Once more he could not quite comprehend the sensation he was feeling or understand what was happening; it was beyond all he could dream about – well, almost – as he felt the increasing urgency of her rhythm and his own approaching climax. They came together quickly and hard.

She withdrew from him and collapsed next to him, nuzzling up to his neck. He could say nothing; he was beyond speech. He had always convinced himself that he was not a virgin after an extremely drunken fumble at university with the younger sister of one of his friends who had come to stay with her brother for the weekend, but he could not really remember what had happened. In all events, he was certain that it had been nothing like that.

"You see," said Lisa with a gentle laugh, "Sweet and kind is not all bad."

"Oh my God, Lisa," said Edwin, eventually. "I can't believe it. That was the most incredible experience of my life."

She sighed and snuggled down further against him. He closed his eyes and felt her warm breath on his chest. He felt as though falling asleep would be a bad idea as neither of them had set an alarm. He resolved to stay awake; or at least to get up to set an alarm. But he was so comfortable, he thought he would do that in a few minutes' time. He closed his eyes briefly and promptly fell into a deep and very satisfied sleep.

Peter looked at his watch. It was close to 1 am. He picked up his mobile phone and read the text from Susannah again: "Sir Galahad. The sign says come to her room, you fool. You decide if and when." He smiled to himself and stood up from the surprisingly comfortable armchair in his room. His late night stroll with Cressida had once more been enlightening. They had talked of business; of life; of love and he had been absolutely transfixed by her stories. He had opened up to her once more in a way that he seldom felt comfortable doing and he had admitted to her that Susannah had totally captivated him and that they had kissed. She had been nothing but encouraging and had said that she absolutely understood.

At one point they had stopped, the flow of their conversation interrupted by what sounded like a howl in the darkness. Although the sound ended abruptly and was from some distance away, Peter could have sworn it was Edwin. He had said as much to Cressida who had laughed quietly and said that whoever it was, he was evidently not enjoying the night air as much as they were. They had subsequently wandered back into the hotel and found no one around; they had walked through the main reception hall, noticing the replacement reception desk and the rebuilt suit of armour, and parted company by the huge fireplace separating the staircases.

"Good night, Peter," Cressida had said with a glint in her eye. "Thank you for your company. Enjoy the rest of your evening, whatever it brings." She had smiled, leant forward and given him an affectionate peck on the cheek then, without another word, gone upstairs leaving Peter in an almost meditative state of tranquility. Somehow her endorsement of his potential relationship with Susannah had given him the conviction that if he did not take it further tonight, he would possibly be missing a pivotal moment in his life. He had bounded up the stairs with renewed energy and gone to his room.

Now, some time later, he yawned, stretched and pulled a dark sweater over his white shirt. "You can never take too many precautions," he thought, "and the last thing I want is to be seen clambering around the place at one o'clock in the morning. I'd better be careful."

He went across softly to his door, opened it noiselessly and looked around. There was not a sound to be heard and certainly nothing to be seen in the darkness of the passage. He closed his door silently behind him and set off, not in the direction of the staircase but the other way, towards the bathrooms.

When he had been helping Ms. Briggs and putting her arm in a sling, he had asked her about the history and architecture of the old manor house to distract her. He learned some fascinating information, not least was that there was a secret passage at either end of each wing. The door was under a portrait in the west wing of King Charles the First and in the east wing King Charles the Second. Peter was not sufficiently familiar with either monarch to be able to tell one from the other but he thought of large, flowing dark wigs and a haughty expression under a wide hat with a feather in it and reckoned he should be able to figure it out. Apparently each hidden door looked just like the rest of the carved wooden wall but a bird's head was actually a door handle and he would find a passage that led over the Minstrels' Gallery to the other side of the house.

He crept down the corridor and found that when he reached the turn to head to the right, there was just enough moonlight to be able to make out the vague shape of pictures hanging on the wall. At the same time, there was no chance of being able to see the subject of the portraits. He stopped and listened; the whole house seemed almost unnaturally quiet. He decided to risk the torch from his mobile and, carefully cupping the beam with his hand, he studied the paintings one by one as he cautiously advanced down the corridor. When he came across what looked like a cavalier with a long, dark wig and seemingly kind eyes – although the lips were pursed in an expression of clear determination – his heart gave a little leap. He stopped and studied the carved paneling beneath the picture. It was true that there seemed to be no break at all in the rather ornate pattern on the wood but there was indeed a bird – a robin, he thought – protruding slightly incongruously from the wall. He grasped it and turned it. Sure enough, he felt the mechanism engage and the door opened in front of him to reveal a long passage that stretched away into complete darkness.

He stepped through the opening, having to crouch a little in the confined space, and closed the door gently beside him. He crept along the corridor, holding his phone in front of him so that he could maximise the light from the torch. The passage he was in had evidently not been used for some time as there were cobwebs hanging from pretty much every beam of the ceiling, many of them with large spiders at the centre. As they sensed his passing, they scuttled quickly up onto the top of the ceiling and seemed to stare down at him angrily for disturbing their habitat. At one point he heard a rustling sound and looked down to see a large mouse disappear into a hole in the skirting-board.

"A right bloody menagerie," he thought. But he persevered and soon came to a turn in the passage. He continued and found that, at the end, there was another door with a similarly carved bird. He turned the disguised handle and stepped forward. He found himself in the Minstrels' Gallery, as expected. He paused and shone his light around, noticing on his right the balustrade that gave over the main hall. He looked over it as his eye was suddenly caught by a light down by the reception desk. He peered through the darkness but the light had been extinguished almost as quickly as he had seen it and he could make out nothing in the silence. He thought it must have been just a trick of the moonlight or something and so he carried on his way, noticing a door on his left hand side which evidently the main access to the gallery itself. Crossing to the other side he found the now familiar bird, turned the handle and carried on into a similar passage, closing the door once more behind him.

Susannah was dressed in her silk dressing-gown and her underwear once more. She was sitting cross-legged on the hard wooden floor – she wished she had brought a mat – in meditative pose after finishing a session of yoga. She had been practicing for some years now and found it a way of relaxing when she was tense – honestly, that was a state of mind that she found herself too frequently in with her job – and also when she was passing the time while waiting for something to happen. She was filled with a deep sense of tranquility from her routine and her meditation had allowed her mind to drift.

She opened her eyes and glanced at her mobile to check on the time. It was late. She read Peter's reply to her text once more: "My lady. I shall pay homage to you after eight bells. I trust you will not be la belle dame sans merci." She had to admit that she'd needed Google to figure out that he was going to come some time after midnight and that he was expecting to be on a promise. She smiled once more at the thought. She had found the image online of the road sign with the "Kiss her, you fool" writing and sent it as her reply. Somehow she felt this would become the motif in their lives going forward. It was extraordinary to be thinking this but in her semi-transcendental state, she had had this realisation and had felt a wave of reassured bliss wash over her. It was a strange, new experience for her.

She felt her heart flutter as there was a knock at her door and a voice said softly, "Susannah. Are you awake? It's past eight bells and there is a sign outside the door telling me not to be a fool."

She laughed quietly and opened the door. Peter stepped inside and looked at her in her short silk dressing-gown. He suddenly found it hard to breathe. She shut the door and looked at him, smiling, confident and sheepish at the same time.

"Do you always welcome your visitors so over-dressed?" said Peter, still breathless.

"Only the ones who call after eight bells," she quipped. "I had to look that up, you know. And la Belle Dame sans Merci. Keats, I gather. Are you really my knight-at-arms?"

"I am whatever you want me to be," he said. Without further hesitation he crossed over to her, put his arms around her and kissed her softly. She tasted sweet, almost innocent; he could feel the beating of her heart through the silk. He was tall enough for her head to rest against his chest and she broke the kiss and sighed deeply, resting her head against him as he kissed the top of her head, breathing in the delicious, intoxicating aroma of her hair.

"Oh Susannah, what have you done to me?" he whispered.

She looked up at him and smiled. "I was thinking the same thing," she said. "I think you are freeing me from my future with just a cat for company."

"And I think you are freeing me from my past with just a girl in a punt to think of."

She laughed again and stretched her head up to kiss him. Their bodies came together once more. He traced a light pattern down the back of her dressing-gown and rested his hand lightly at the bottom of her spine. He could feel her breath becoming excited and faster.

Again she broke the kiss and breathed into his ear, "I thought I was relaxed before; now I feel as though I am floating."

His hand moved down to the wonderful shape of her buttocks and he squeezed her slightly. "You are as light as a feather," he said. "I will promise to make you float forever but what was making you so relaxed before I showed up? I've been too excited to be relaxed!"

She looked at him deeply into his eyes. She felt this was another critical moment in their relationship.

"I was doing yoga and partially meditating."

"Really?" he asked, slightly pulling away from her and looking at her deeply. "You were doing yoga and meditating?"

"Yes," she said defiantly. "Is there anything wrong with that?" Somehow, she felt that, if this conversation did not go well, the magic between them would be broken.

"Wrong?" he whispered and pulled her close towards him. "Can you guess where I went on vacation last month?"

"Where?" she asked, hardly daring to breathe.

"Thailand."

"Thailand?" she said accusingly. "Back to, back to you know where?"

He laughed. "Not exactly. I was in Koh Samui for a yoga retreat," he said. "Just me. Alone basically for a week. Complete detox. Yoga and meditation."

She gasped with pleasure.

"The only thing missing," he said, "was you. I didn't know it at the time, but it's true nonetheless."

"Oh my God, Peter," she almost cried with passion. "You are bloody perfect. I think I am falling in love with you."

He smiled at her and kissed her. Gently he took her hand and led her to the bed. He was surprised to feel her resist.

"No, wait," she said. "Not here. Can we go to your room?"

"Er, yes, we can," said Peter in a surprised tone. "We can go back the way I came, I suppose. But why? I think everyone's in bed by now; although, as I was on my way, to be honest I thought I sensed at least one person on a similar midnight prowl to me. So we are probably better off staying here for a while."

He stepped forward to kiss her again but she turned away. He was at a loss to understand her reluctance.

"Susannah, what's the matter?"

She turned back to him, blinking back tears. He looked at her with deep concern. What had he done to upset her?

"I'm worried Gordon's going to come here," she blurted out suddenly.

"Gordon?" Peter almost shouted. "Why on earth would he come here at this time. Hardly to discuss Riverjack Crypto, I guess."

"Please don't hate me," she said, now actively crying and silently shaking.

He came across to her and took her shaking body in his arms.

"Darling," he said softly, "Whatever it is, let's not let it come between us. If we are going to spend the rest of our lives together, then there are going to be things we are both going to have to forgive and forget."

Then he paused, stepped back and looked at her, as a realisation slowly materialised in his mind.

"Oh God, no, Susannah, tell me you didn't sleep with him."

She blushed deeply and nodded slowly.

"Gordon?" said Peter. "Holy fuck!"

By this time Susannah's tears were flowing profusely. She had not known what would happen this evening but felt as though her happiness was draining away to be replaced by an empty void.

Peter continued to look at her in astonishment. He had said nothing would come between them, but had not quite expected the barrier to be quite so tall. He felt as though his own happiness was slipping through his fingers too.

"In Vegas?"

"Yes."

Peter paused again, and then he burst into a round smile.

"Well, that's alright then," he said. "We have all done bloody stupid things in Vegas. As long as they stay there, then that's Vegas for you. I will tell you one day when I know you better about my time with the three hookers and the priest."

"Three hookers and a priest?" she said, laughing slightly, blinking back her tears and reaching for him, suddenly realising it was going to work out. "I want to hear that story." She paused and looked once more deeply into his eyes. "You mean, you don't mind?"

"I think if either of us minds about the stupid things the other has done before we met, I had probably best turn around and walk through that door and never speak to you again."

"Don't do that."

"I have no intention of it. Just don't do it again."

"What?"

"Sleep with Gordon."

"Christ, no!" she laughed with pleasure, relief and incredible passion. He saw the life return to her face and said, "OK then, Bierson. My place it is. But may I recommend you put on something a little less revealing? Where we are going, looking like that, you might give the spiders a shock."

She looked at him quizzically and laughed again. Quickly she pulled on a dark sweater and jeans and followed him out into the silent corridor.

CHAPTER FIFTEEN

Henry lay in his bed, unable to sleep. He had to admit that his conversation with Theresa had left him intrigued and confused. He was not sure whether to interpret what she said as an invitation or whether actually it had just been the champagne, wine and brandy that had led him to place much deeper meaning on her words than she intended.

He had to admit that he now looked on Theresa in a completely different light. He had only ever known her as their Finance Director: austere; severe; disapproving; without a sense of humour and lacking any capacity at all, it seemed, for enjoying life. Certainly she had seemed totally sexless to him up until now. He was still amazed how her smile transformed her from someone who looked scathing all the time to what seemed to him a picture of Venus. Could a smile really have that effect? He thought back to all the women he had known and considered the problem from a number of angles.

Of course, those who were naturally endowed with more obviously attractive features than Theresa had not needed to smile to transform themselves into alluring goddesses; and he had to admit he had probably allowed himself to be allured too easily. At the same time, few had had Theresa's undoubted intelligence and business acumen. He wondered whether the constant disapproval of his antics he had sensed on her part had really been masking a subconscious desire to be part of them or at least to shake off the Miss Jean Brodie image that she seemed to cultivate so carefully. That must be right! Therefore she had been sending him a signal. If he knew women, and he usually prided himself that few could read them better, then a stronger 'come hither' message had seldom been sent! What was it she had said when he had suggested he might remain celibate? "That would be a shame!". Surely there was only one reasonable conclusion to be drawn about what she meant by that.

With sudden resolution he got out of bed. He stubbed his toe on the large foot of the bed as he leant across to turn on the bedside light but ignored the pain in his excitement. The only trouble was that he knew Gordon's and Cressida's bedroom was next to Theresa's. If he was right – and surely he was – that she was expecting him, he would have to be as quiet as a bloody church mouse and then, if what he was hoping for happened, they would have to be equally circumspect. However, that was definitely a challenge he was prepared to take on.

He pulled on his dressing-gown, opened the door and froze. He sensed someone had just surreptitiously crept past his room. He could not recognise who it was for certain but something told him it was Peter. He wondered what he was doing out of bed at this hour. Then it struck him that the lack of en suite facilities would dictate any number of nocturnal wanderings, particularly given the amount of drink they had all consumed. For a moment he wondered about following suit before he began his journey but decided there would have to be too many explanations and polite embarrassed exchanges. He pulled the door closed behind him and, without another sound, wrapped his dressing-gown tight about him and crept along the corridor, which seemed interminable. As he passed one room – a quick check of the name by the light of his mobile told him it was Charles the First – he could swear he heard faint sounds of gasping and what sounded like a bed's creaking. There was a very slight, high-pitched moan, but as he stopped to listen again, there was silence.

"Edwin or Lisa having a bad dream, I expect", he said to himself. "Wonder which of them it was, though. Still, nothing to do with me. Onwards and upwards!" He moved forward with surprising athleticism and went down the stairs.

It suddenly occurred to him that should he run into anyone, he would need a cover story, so he settled on the fact that he could not sleep, was terribly thirsty and had come downstairs to see if he could find a glass of water. It was pretty flimsy but it would have to do. He reassured himself with the fact that anyone else out at that hour was probably equally keen to escape detection. Just to be on the safe side, once he had navigated the loose carpet, he turned off the torch on his mobile phone as he went down the final flight of stairs.

He reached the bottom and was about to turn on the flashlight again when once more he sensed someone else in the entrance hall. He froze and listened hard. He could see nothing but was sure his impression was not misleading. Cautiously he hugged the wall, stepped past the fireplace and silently climbed the other set of stairs leading to the east wing. He could not be certain but it seemed to him that the other person had remained where he or she was, apparently as reluctant as Henry to be discovered prowling around. He wondered who it was; what he or she was doing there; and whether he had been detected himself. He decided it was not the occasion to wait to find out and rapidly climbed the stairs. As he turned on the landing he stopped, listened hard but could hear nothing. At least his mysterious companion was not evidently following him. He cautiously groped forward once more and swiftly ascended the staircase. He scanned the room names at the top of each door, found the one marked Elizabeth the Second and gently knocked on the door.

Gordon lay awake listening to Cressida's breathing next to him. He was thoroughly tempted to reach for his pillow and put a stop to it once and for all after the evening he had had. The ordering of champagne had temporarily deflected Cressida from further interrogation and she had been further distracted after Peter who, after a meaningful look he had cast in his direction, had come over to engage her in conversation.

Dinner had passed without further incident and he had been glad to see Peter taking Cressida out for a post-prandial evening stroll. That had left the coast clear for him to engage Susannah in what purported to be a discussion about Riverjack Crypto. She had declined his offer of a drink, and another whisky on his part – this time without the accompanying banter from the barman – had done did little to alleviate the tension between them. He had quietly tried to persuade her that he would indeed be willing to leave Cressida for her – not that it was true, of course, but he was not above trying anything to ensure a repeat of that night in Vegas – but she had unfortunately seen through him. She had done her very best to dissuade him from his suggestion that he should to come to her room later, telling him that it was both unwise in the circumstances and unwanted on her part. The furthest she had gone was to pat his knee affectionately and suggest once more that they let Vegas just be a secretive memory between them. He had reluctantly agreed and resolved to give up any notion of a late night assignation.

He had come upstairs to find that Cressida had not returned from her stroll with Peter. While waiting for her to return, he had resolved to try to reconcile his relationship with her. Clearly he was better off trying to rebuild their marriage and leaving any impossible fantasies as unfulfilled. He knew he had let himself go and wanted get back into shape. Twenty-five years ago he had charmed Cressida with his wit, his intelligence and his body! It was time to recapture that. Pleased with his new-found clarity, he waited for Cressida in anticipation.

As she came in through the door, he got up from the armchair, made to take her in his arms and tell her he loved her. But to his disappointment, surprise and then anger, she came in spoiling for a fight like a snarling lioness and once more they went ferociously for each other, whispered insults crossing the room like rapier jabs and creating a chasm between them. Eventually she had turned her back on him in disgust. She rapidly undressed and pulled on a nightie that she knew he found particularly unappealing, a symbol of their broken relationship, and climbed into bed. She glared at him with real animosity as he slowly started to undress as well. She reached over to the small cabinet beside the bed, opened the drawer and took out ear plugs and an eye patch.

It made him think back to many years before when they had eagerly gone to bed together in passionate anticipation and he would reach for whatever he had decided to surprise her with that evening, placed handily in the bedside cabinet. There had been a time when nothing was out of the question – handcuffs; vibrators; cock-rings. Earlier on in their lives they had driven each other wild in bed without inhibition.

He remembered her once reaching herself for the 'intimate lube' as it was so coyly described and offering herself to him. "Take me like *Last Tango In Paris*" she had said, her meaning unmistakable as she got onto her hands and knees. "Only use this, not butter". They had both laughed and then a few minutes later collapsed in newly discovered, blissful exhaustion as the intimacy and forbidden nature of anal sex had released unfound sexual energy in both of them.

Gordon lay there in the darkness, thinking of times past with real regret. He had made one further attempt at reconciliation by reaching for her when he got into bed but she had abruptly removed his hand from around her and shuffled away from him to the edge of the bed. Resentfully he made no further conciliatory gesture and continued to listen to her breathing. She was evidently deeply asleep. Well, for God's sake; if that was how she was going to behave, then he would damn well give her a reason to be upset (assuming she ever found out, of course, which he trusted she would not). He forgot his resolution to not try to repeat his Vegas experience. Susannah could surely not mean she could forget their experience so easily.

Gingerly he peeled back the covers and swung his legs over the side of the bed. He paused and listened. There had been no change in the rhythm of Cressida's breathing. He put his feet on the floor and put his feet in his slippers that were waiting for him by the bed. It was one of his habits never to allow his feet to touch other people's floors. Cressida found it an increasingly annoying habit but it was something that, because of some deep-rooted, subconscious obsession with hygiene, he could not shake off. It had become another source of tension between them in recent years. He stood up and crept tentatively across the room. If she awoke now, he would say he was going to the bathroom.

He crossed to the door, took his dressing gown off the hook on the back and put it on. Taking extreme care not to make any noise, he opened the bedroom door, stopped all movement and listened. Cressida's breathing was unchanged so he continued, slipping out through the narrowest possible opening of the door – still far too wide, he thought – and stepped into the corridor. Again with infinite pains not to let the door make the slightest noise, he closed it behind him and paused once more. If she was going to wake, it would be now. There was no sound from the room. He smiled to himself in satisfaction and padded softly down the corridor. He may have gained amount of weight over the years but he still retained an athletic gait; now, he allowed his feet to roll from heel to ball so that he minimised the sound he made with each stride. He knew which was Susannah's room from his previous exploits and reached it without mishap. He stopped, gathered himself for a moment and then tapped lightly on the door. There was no answer. He tapped again and softly called out her name. Still there was no reply. She must be asleep. He carefully turned the handle and opened the door, stepping over the threshold and closing the door quietly behind him.

"Susannah," he called out. "Susannah? Are you awake?"

He listened; then he listened more intensely; then he listened once more. There was no one in the room; he was sure of it. He crossed to the bed and felt the covers. It was still made! That meant she hadn't got into bed at all. And that could only mean one thing! She had planned another assignation all along. And he knew who it would be with. So, that was her plan! And that was why she had refused him. He had had his suspicions since he had seen Peter on TV with her at the rugby. And what had he said? "Nothing happened, Gordon" without prompting. Well now, he knew. Something bloody well had happened and Gordon did not appreciate it one little bit. He would have to show them the consequences of getting on the wrong side of Fairbald. They were in Peter's room; and he had a pretty good idea that they weren't there going over Peter's rescue plan for Riverjack Crypto.

He decided to go over to the other wing; claim he had seen her leaving her room as he came back from the bathroom and followed her as he was afraid she was sleepwalking. For that reason he hadn't called out because you should never wake someone who's sleepwalking, of course, but had followed her to ensure she came to no harm. But he had realised as she went into Peter's room that she was not sleepwalking at all but fulfilling an assignation.

He would expose both of them and, through the resulting furore, would be able to show Cressida that there had been nothing between him and Susannah. It was highly probable that he could dismiss Peter for gross misconduct and Mitch was almost certain to support him; and indeed he would probably dismiss Susannah too, which would just show her. If Susannah tried to turn the tables on him by talking about their Vegas affair, he would deny all knowledge and claim that she was just saying these things to deflect from her guilt. To his jealous mind, the plan seemed bloody perfect! He turned back to the bedroom door and hurried down the corridor.

Theresa had been sound asleep when she was woken by insistent tapping on her door. She opened her eyes and thought she must have been dreaming.

But no, there it was again and someone was softly calling her name. Then she heard the door handle turn but of course, having taken the precaution as she always did of locking her door, whoever was get into her bedroom was thwarted. She sat up, turned the beside light on, and stepped out of bed. She smoothed down her ankle-length nightie and went to the door.

"Who is it?" she said in an authoritative, distinctly annoyed tone of voice.

"It's me, Henry," came the voice. "Let me in."

"What do you want at this time?"

"Come on, Theresa, don't leave me standing out here. Let me in."

Theresa shrugged and opened the door. Better to have the idiot come in than continue there and wake the whole house. He stepped inside and shut the door behind him.

"What on earth do you want?" she asked.

"I came at your invitation," he said, and crossed over to her, attempting to put his arms around her and kiss her.

She put two hands up as a barrier and said, "What the hell do you think you are doing, Henry?"

He looked at her bewildered and slightly embarrassed.

"But I thought you invited me to your room?"

"Invited you here? When? Whatever for?"

"Earlier, of course, in the library, when we were talking and you smiled so brightly it lit up the room. You said it would be a shame for me to remain celibate."

Theresa started to laugh. "And you took that as an invitation? You are incorrigible! I was just saying that there was no way celibacy would suit a person like you. I wasn't inviting you to bed."

"You weren't?"

"No, you absolutely ridiculous man! Don't you know? I'm gay."

"You're what?"

"Gay, Henry, gay! I like girls. I haven't slept with a man since university. I haven't had a dick near me for more than thirty years. Ugly, smelly things! Ugh!"

"Not mine!" said Henry, defensively.

"Well, perhaps not," said Theresa with a smile, "But I for one am certainly not going to find out. Not tonight. Not ever! I am quite happy as I am, thank you very much."

"Oh, I see," said Henry. For the first time in his memory he was mortified with embarrassment.

"Does Gordon know?"

"I am not sure what that has to do with anything," said Theresa. "As a matter of fact, I have no idea and really don't care. All he knows is that I am the most competent Private Equity Finance Director he could ever hope to work with. And that is what I will remain to him; and to every other bloody man in the industry," she added with vehemence.

Before Henry could reply to this, there was a loud scream. In fact, there was a series of screams intermingled with shouts, the sound of running feet, more screams, shouts, a few cries of desperation and then an enormous crash. The events of the evening were evidently reaching a climax different from the one Henry had been anticipating five minutes earlier.

CHAPTER SIXTEEN

The journey back to Peter's room took him and Susannah much longer than it had taken him on the outbound leg. Their progress was slowed by his guiding her carefully; by his limited use of the flashlight to avoid detection; but most of all by their stopping to kiss very regularly. At one point, in a moment Peter thought could have come straight out of a 1970's sitcom, Susannah had screamed slightly and clung to him as the mouse took a return journey from its hole across the secret passage. He had taken advantage of the situation to stop and kiss her again.

They eventually reached his room without further adventure; he softly opened the door and pulled her towards him. They kissed again. He broke apart from her briefly, crossed to the window and opened the curtains. It would be an exaggeration to say that moonlight flooded the room but it was enough for him to see her, silhouetted and standing slightly nervously in front of him. He crossed back to her, cupped her face in his hands and kissed her slowly. He could feel her hands on his back, gradually sliding down to his waist.

He surprised her by letting go and bending at the knees. He kissed her neck just above her sweater and took hold of it by the hem, gently lifting it. Without hesitation she raised her arms to help him and he almost gasped as the shape of her breasts revealed themselves under a delicate lace bra. He kissed her neck again and his fingers danced patterns on her back. His lips moved slowly down her; he paused to brush the top of her breasts; he lightly caressed her nipples, now hard with desire and continued his downward journey. When he brushed her navel with his tongue, she gave an involuntary giggle and moved her hands to his hair, caressing it with her fingers.

He dropped to his knees, reaching for the button fastening the top of her jeans, and carefully opening it. The other buttons came apart easily and, still on his knees, he started to ease her jeans down her legs. Once more she came to his aid and wriggled out of them. She stood there, slightly trembling in the faint light, waiting for him to come back to kiss her.

Once more he surprised her by remaining on his knees and moving forward to kiss the inside of her thighs. Her skin felt warm and smooth; his lips brushed against her and she felt his tongue flick out and lick her thighs like a snake sensing its surroundings. Once more she gave an involuntary giggle and held his head. He turned and kissed the top of her panties, pressing his mouth to her and sensing rather than hearing her moan slightly. His hands reached behind her and gently felt the bottom of her spine; at their touch she bucked very slightly forward so that his mouth could feel the softness of her sex beneath the lace material. Her scent filled his nostrils as he eased his fingers into the elastic of her panties and pulled them smoothly down over her buttocks. Then he brought his fingers to the front, repeated the manoeuvre and dexterously pulled her panties down to her ankles. She stepped out of them and made to take his hand to lead him to the bed but he held her still and, remaining on his knees, returned his tongue to her skin.

This time she gasped audibly and he felt her open her legs for him. He kissed the top of her thighs and nibbled at her delicate tuft of hair. He felt his own hair being grasped as his tongue explored her, tasting her sweetness and once more filling his nostrils with the scent of her arousal. His tongue delved more deeply inside her and his fingers lightly danced on the firm shape of her buttocks. He moved his tongue slightly upwards and felt her shiver with pleasure as he lightly toyed with her clitoris. At the same time his fingers ran down the cleft at her rear and gently teased her.

He felt her legs opening wider for sensing her desire, his moved his fingers down until they were pressing lightly further inside her cleft. The grip on his head became more insistent, pulling him deeper inside her as his finger lightly touched her outer rim. She started to thrust herself forward and at the same time breathed his name in a way he had not heard for a long time. He could sense her growing passion as his finger lightly rested on her rosebud and his mouth embraced her. Her arousal was almost out of control but with insistence she abruptly said, "Peter, I want you. I want you now" and she almost dragged him to the bed. She lay back on the sheets, her climax close, and unclipped her bra to throw it aside.

He rapidly pulled off his jeans and she leant forward once more to free his erection. Without pausing to unbutton his shirt, she pulled him to her, kissed him hard, tasting her own juices on his tongue, and reached down to guide him into her. She felt him enter her and pulled him closer still, feeling him deeper inside her than she had ever felt before and ground her hips up to his, demanding him. His hands caressed her hair as she brought her own fingers to his back and gently ran her nails down his back. She felt him come as her own climax broke over her. As if in a trance she seemed to scream his name; he collapsed on her and cried out her own as if in response. From what appeared a great distance, she screamed again.

Slightly surprised and still inside her, he looked up and said, "Do you always scream when you come?"

She giggled. "Not for a long, long time. But that second scream, that wasn't me."

There was a third scream.

"Nor was that."

He abruptly pulled out of her and looked around.

There were shouts, screams and then after a brief pause, an almighty crash.

After he had seen the light above him in the Minstrels' Gallery, Tom had decided it would be prudent to wait a while before proceeding to Lisa's room. It would definitely thwart his intentions to be interrupted and he felt as though Lisa, who was already nervous about the potential for exposure, would need to be reassured and coaxed before succumbing to his seduction. He did not mind; he was sure it would be worth the wait.

Just as he thought it would be safe to move, he sensed rather than saw another person come down the stairs. He stopped dead still again and held his breath. Whoever it was seemed to stop as well; then he or she apparently crept along the fireplace and climbed the opposite staircase. He could see the slight movement of a shadow go upwards and turn the corner of the landing. What the bloody hell was going on? Half the household seemed to be awake! It was pretty amusing to think that his midnight assignation with Lisa was not the only one planned. He spent a few minutes contemplating who might be visiting who before deciding once more that the coast was clear and heading back across the hall to climb back up the stairs of the west wing.

Again, a little moonlight seeped through the window on the landing, giving him enough visibility to turn and climb up the second set of stairs. He came to the corridor, crept along it slowly, not wanting to make the slightest sound, and took out his mobile. He shone the light briefly above a door; it read King Charles the Second. "So that means", he thought to himself, "Edwin's room. Lisa's in King Charles the First; that must be next door."

He moved one door further down the corridor and stopped. His excitement was more than he had experienced in quite a while. Lisa was unbelievably intoxicating and to make love to her in the midst all their colleagues while who knows what other inappropriate behaviour was going on around them was causing a thousand butterflies to flutter in the pit of his stomach. He stopped to compose himself briefly; it was not like him at all to be this nervous. With renewed resolution, he tapped very softly on the door.

"Lisa," he whispered. "Lisa, are you there?"

There was no answer. He put his ear to the door and was almost sure he heard breathing. She must have fallen asleep. No surprise in that respect; but he knew just how to surprise her. He only hoped that she would wake up gently, remember where she was, who he was, what they had planned and turn eagerly towards him.

He opened the door very slowly and heard the faint creak of hinges; he paused, listened again and heard her soft breathing, clearly fast asleep. The hinges had evidently done their worst as they made no further sound as he slipped into the room. He did not risk any light but closed the door behind him, making sure once more that the hinges made as little noise as possible.

"Lisa," he breathed. "I know you are asleep but it's me, Tom."

There was a soft sigh from the bed. He took this as a positive sign and decided that the only course of action was the bold one.

In the darkness he slipped off his shoes and trousers and climbed into bed. He could feel the stirrings of his erection as he slipped under the covers and moved towards her.

She was on her side, away from him. He moved across and pressed himself to her, enjoying her warmth and the velvet feel of her skin. With one hand he caressed her hair lightly; with the other he reached over her and felt for her inner thigh.

Edwin's dream was not as pleasant as the one before. He was still on the riverbank, half-asleep on his side; but now it was not the water-nymph who was embracing him and reaching for his member but a mythical beast which had surged out of nowhere, hairy and with slavering jaws. He felt strong fingers grasp him.

"Jesus fucked," the beast said in a loud voice.

Edwin jumped up, "What the hell?" he shouted.

Lisa stirred, complaining at being disturbed with a few incoherent moans. Suddenly the light was on. She blinked at Edwin, who was staring beyond her in horror. She wondered who she could feel pressing into her back. She looked up into the very surprised face of Tom.

It took her a few seconds to realise what had happened. She screamed in panic and rolled over Tom, falling onto the floor in her haste to escape the unplanned and definitely unwanted threesome.

"What the fuck are you doing, Tom?" shouted Edwin.

"I can see what the fuck you've been doing, Edwin," shouted Tom back.

Lisa started to sob in hysterics. She had to get out of this nightmare. She jumped up, howling. Still naked, she ran to the door and without thinking, opened it and ran along the corridor with another scream. Edwin and Tom stared after her for a moment and, Edwin leapt out of bed, chasing after her and calling out.

"Lisa, for Heaven's sake, where do you think you are going? Calm down and come back. You'll wake the whole bloody hotel."

Without hesitation he chased after her down the corridor. Tom had the presence of mind to pull on his trousers before he rushed after both of them.

"Both of you stop," he shouted. "I'm sorry I interrupted you. I didn't realise. Come back. For Christ's sake come back otherwise everyone will hear."

Lisa was too hysterical to stop. She careered down the corridor and started down the staircase.

At this moment, Gordon was progressing at speed back up to the west wing on his mission to find Susannah in bed with Peter and expose both of them. He reached the top of the first staircase giving onto the landing as he heard the yells and shouts. He was then astonished when a naked Lisa ran straight into him. For a moment, time stood still as he fought for his balance at the top of the stairs while she clung onto him, by this stage completely unable to control herself. Gordon managed to grab onto the banister and steadied them both in some relief.

Edwin was not quite so lucky. Rushing down the stairs, he tripped on the loose carpet. The impact of a flying, naked Edwin crashing into Gordon and Lisa knocked all breath out of Gordon. He could not even scream. All he heard was a muffled cry from Lisa and an almighty shout of "Christ!" from Edwin as the three of them tumbled rapidly down the stairs. The rug by the hearth, which had only been replaced that evening, slightly cushioned their fall but as a result of their momentum, started its inexorable slide across the polished hall floor.

Gordon only had breath to mouth "Fucking hell!" as they careered towards the rebuilt suit of armour. Edwin closed his eyes in silent prayer as he could see the inevitable conclusion. Lisa's hysterical screams filled his ears and blocked out all other noise as they collided with the ancient metal, bringing their calamitous trajectory to an abrupt halt. For a moment he thought they would survive unscathed apart from a few bruises, but it was not to be. Tottering slowly, the suit of armour crashed about them. This time Lisa's breasts were in full view before the helmet once again came down crashing over his head, muffling his shouts.

Inexorably, as if drawn for a second time to its innate purpose, the halberd, released from the knight's grasp, came down like a felled tree. There was the wrenching sound of tearing leather; of rendering wood and of smashed glass and metal as the halberd fulfilled its destiny for the second time in twenty-four hours and felt the satisfaction of levying destruction and mayhem. It would not be denied.

Ms. Briggs came through the door leading to her office and, evidently, her bedroom in a long, Victorian-style nightie. She took in the scene of carnage before her, and the writhing, naked bodies of Edwin and Lisa on top of the groaning form of Gordon.

"Again?" she screamed. "You've fucking done it again? You stupid, stupid bitch," she yelled and aimed an enormous kick at Lisa's head. Fortunately or unfortunately she missed and her big toe collided with the solid metal of the helmet. Edwin's stifled yell could be heard as Ms. Briggs staggered backwards, desperately trying to hold her now broken toe. She collapsed in her own heap, frothing at the mouth, seemingly the victim of some sort of seizure.

This was the scene that greeted Mitch as he came through the door of the hotel. Gordon looked at him in disbelief and then, for the first and only time in his life, fainted.

CHAPTER SEVENTEEN

Six months later...

The water of San Francisco Bay lapped at the seafront of the picturesque town of Sausalito. The magnificent Golden Gate bridge, illuminated against the night sky, provided a stunning view to the right as Peter sat at an outside table in their favourite Italian restaurant on the waterfront. He finished reading an email which had evidently made him chuckle just as Toni, the proprietor, brought him a glass of Chianti – "A very special one, Mr Peter. Just arrived from back home. From the vineyard of my cousin. What do you think?"

He tasted it and it was indeed very good. He smiled to himself. Across the bay the lights of San Francisco smiled back at him.

"Miss Susannah not joining you tonight?"

"Absolutely she is, Toni. Tonight is a special celebration. She's just achieved the first close in her new fund."

"First close?" Although Toni had lived in the Bay Area for many years, he was unfamiliar with most of the aspects of the technology world. He preferred to focus on making La Dolce Vita restaurant the best Italian in the region. Few would disagree that he had achieved his ambition.

"Yes. It means she has raised enough capital to start investing. Others can come and join the party but it is quite an achievement for a first-time fund to raise money so quickly. It's all on the back of her track record at Aardvark and stellar reputation. And, in these times of #metoo, her fund's focus on female entrepreneurs who have had enough of male investor condescension has been a massive hit with the institutions who want to try to show they are doing their part for equality."

"Miss Susannah is a very special lady," said Toni.

"Yes, she certainly is," replied Peter.

"Who is what?" said Susannah, walking up to Peter's table through the restaurant.

He stood up to greet her, wrapping his arms briefly around her and kissing her.

"You are, very special", said Peter. "Toni was just telling me. I struggle to see it myself but he tells me I am wrong."

She smiled at him and punched his arm.

"Mean," she said. "You don't know quite how special. I just secured another five million. If I go on at this rate, we'll hit the second close target in a month. And I think I found my first investment."

"Not another payments company with a ridiculous name? asked Peter.

"Absolutely not," she said. "This is an Artificial Intelligence play to predict retail sales. Super-smart."

"Hasn't it been done already?"

"Not with this level of ROI. Initial trials are showing sales up by twenty percent at their early adopter customers and returns in the low single figures."

"That's impressive," admitted Peter. "But stop telling me how amazing you are as I know that already. Come here, have a glass of wine and look at the view."

She sat down next to him and looked at him with round, bright, sharp eyes that seemed to sparkle with the reflection of the lights themselves reflected in the water.

Toni poured her a glass of wine and she shipped it appreciatively.

"The new one, Toni?"

"Yes, Miss Susannah. Just in today. Splendid or what?"

She looked at Peter. "Splendid, indeed!" she said.

Splendid had not quite been Mitch's reaction as he surveyed the chaotic scene before him in the hotel. Gordon slowly came round from his faint, extricated himself from the writhing, naked mass that was Lisa and Edwin and stood up. Gordon stared at Mitch in astonishment, unable to comprehend who he was seeing. Mitch stared in equal astonishment but not at Gordon; he could not believe the sight of a naked Edwin – that was Edwin, wasn't it? – and a girl he did not recognise. There seemed to have been some debauched behaviour going on and he wanted to know who was responsible.

Tom came down the stairs and stared open-mouthed at the repeated carnage of the desk, suit of armour and computer. An irate Cressida appeared, who surveyed the scene with disgust.

"What the fuck do you think you are doing, Gordon?" she shouted.

Then she saw Mitch and mollified her tone. "Hello, Mitch," she said. "Nice to see you again."

"Good evening, Cressida," said Mitch. "Have you any idea what is going on here?"

"None at all," said Cressida haughtily.

By this time Ms. Briggs seemed to have recovered herself and was up again, shouting at Lisa and trying to get to her. Lisa, still naked, was cowering and sobbing by the fireplace. Edwin, who by this time had managed to remove the helmet, was standing between Lisa and Ms. Briggs. He, too, was still naked but like some parody of gallantry, was shouting at her to back off or he would not be responsible for his actions.

Mitch stared between the three of them, his mind just boggled.

Theresa and Henry came down the east wing stairs together. They were wondering what on earth had happened. Theresa took one look at Lisa and immediately slipped off her dressing-gown to cover her. Henry did the same for Edwin and they both stood there wearing only pyjamas.

Mitch gaped further.

At this point Susannah and Peter came down together. Gordon turned on them and shouted, "I knew you two were screwing. What the hell do you think you are playing at? Well, Peter, you can fucking well forget everything I have ever said about your future at Aardvark."

"Don't worry, Peter," said Cressida. "I don't think you're the one who has to worry about his future."

Gordon turned to her and started yelling. She yelled back. Ms. Briggs continued her vocal assault on Lisa and attempted once more to get past Edwin who grabbed hold of her sprained wrist in desperation. She howled in agony and staggered backwards.

Henry and Theresa took the whole scene in both started to laugh uncontrollably. Tom looked around him and did the same. Peter and Susannah just looked at each other, shrugged and embraced.

Only Mitch said nothing; he was still too stunned by the bedlam to make any contribution at all.

Mitch had flown in from San Francisco that evening. His plane had been due to land late afternoon but a fault had developed in one engine and they had been forced to put down in Toronto for several hours for repairs. They had been successful but, as a result of the delay, the plane had landed at Heathrow only just before the midnight curfew. There had been a single immigration officer on duty and the line had been interminable. He had eventually managed to procure a cab and had come directly from the airport to the offsite hotel – luckily he had received an email a couple of weeks earlier from Gordon outlining the planned event and giving details of the hotel, so finding the address had not been too problematic. The London cabbie had been pretty reluctant to drive all the way out to West Sussex but the promise of double the fare at the night time rate meant that he did not put up any further resistance.

The next morning, events moved at a pace. It transpired that Mitch had been in discussions with another venture capitalist from a rival firm who had expressed real interest in the Riverjack Crypto product, thinking that it would be very complementary to one of his portfolio companies, which was growing at a rapid rate. Mitch had been glad to seize the lifeline. They had talked things through and agreed a deal valuation that was far in excess of what they could have expected given the challenges with the company. The only condition was that the acquirer needed an executive from Riverjack Crypto to join the new combined company as Chief Operating Officer. Given the current state of the management team, Mitch had wondered if he could persuade Peter to step out of the firm and into the role and for this reason had decided to fly to the UK to discuss with him personally. After all, Peter had always made it clear he wanted to move to the US and this could be the perfect opportunity for him. Besides, he needed his signature on a lot of the paperwork as the acting Chief Executive so they could close the sale of the company immediately.

He had talked through Peter's profile with the purported new owner of Riverjack Crypto who liked the idea very much – he knew Peter was a financially savvy, investor-friendly operator who was smart, had significant experience and most of all would be able to charm his way through any situation he may find with the US thanks to his accent. It was an easy decision for Peter to agree to fly to the US as soon as possible to open negotiations for his future. It was certainly made even easier by Gordon reiterating that he had no future at Aardvark.

Despite his protestations, Cressida had openly declared to Gordon that she wanted a divorce and had summarily left the hotel, leaving at Gordon and Mitch open-mouthed, staring after her. In a private audience with Gordon, Mitch demanded he be told the reasons behind the collapse of their marriage. After all, he was Cressida's godfather and felt as though his late partner, her father, would have wanted him to continue to look after her. In his subsequent enquiries, the events of Las Vegas came to light, so it was not only Peter who had no future at Aardvark, as Mitch made absolutely clear to Gordon.

He spent some time talking to Susannah and questioned whether she could stay with the firm given her conduct. She made the conversation both very easy and extremely difficult for him. She told him that she would be leaving Aardvark herself to start her own investment firm. She hoped for his blessing and support but realised that her relationship with Gordon – which had been a drunken mistake, she fully acknowledged, and which had put Mitch into an impossible position – and her new relationship with Peter – which was absolutely not a mistake, drunken or otherwise – meant that it was best she offer Mitch her resignation. He tried to dissuade her, saying that with Gordon's leaving and Peter almost certainly taking a different career path, it was more than feasible for her to remain at Aardvark. However, it became very clear to him that she had made up her mind and he knew that it was essentially impossible for her to be persuaded to alter course once she had made a decision.

He was not so forgiving of Edwin and Lisa. They appeared before him, fully clothed but still thoroughly embarrassed at having been caught in flagrante delicto, as he put it. Lisa did not understand what he meant and Edwin had to explain, kindly and gently, that as they had both been naked in front of all their colleagues and had obviously been engaging in what Mitch called "extra-marital carnal knowledge" (another phrase that Edwin had to explain), they really were not long for the Aardvark world. Mitch knew enough about English employment law to ask Theresa to manage their exits. Theresa was as kind as she could be with Lisa and even found that her usual austere demeanour could not be maintained in the face of Edwin's gracious acceptance of his fate.

As they headed back to the railway station in a taxi, Lisa was utterly disconsolate.

"What am I going to do?" she said. "I have no job; very little money, and pretty much no chance of a new job given that everyone is bound to hear about what happened. I'm just going to have to go back home and hope my parents will take me back. Although when my Dad hears what's gone on, it will probably mean he never wants to see me again."

Edwin turned to her. "You don't think I'm going to let you go; not after last night. Lisa, you are mine now and I will look after you."

"But how?"

"Actually, you know, I have more money from my family than I ever let on. I'm not super-rich, or anything, but enough for us to survive on for a while. And besides, I have a new plan. I'm not cut out for the investment world. I've decided to train as a teacher. The world needs maths teachers and actually my maths is pretty good." He paused for a moment. "I'm also going to start seriously working out and maybe take up karate. I am not going to have a bunch of fifteen-year-olds kicking sand in my face."

"Oh Edwin," cried Lisa, and clutched his arm. Edwin put his arm protectively around her; for the first time in his life, he was truly at ease.

Before he flew back to the US, Mitch formally appointed Henry as senior partner for Aardvark in London and gave him the task of rebuilding the business.

"You'll need to recruit two new investment directors," he said, "And another secretary. Theresa and Tom have both agreed to stay on, of course, so you have some stability there. I will leave it in your more than capable hands."

Henry thought about this conversation as he too headed back to London. He remembered his date with the Emirates air hostess back at the W. It was going to be a fun evening telling her of his promotion. Champagne all round and then who could tell what might happen. Maybe the cabin crew would make great potential investment directors. He smiled to himself at the thought. He wasn't sure of their qualifications but he was certainly looking forward to the interviews.

And so, Peter and Susannah now sat by the waterside, drinking wine and contemplating how strangely life could turn out. He took her hand and gently stroked it; she looked at him and smiled deeply.

"Oh, I almost forgot," said Peter. "I was just finishing reading an email from Tom. Here, you should look at this. It's pretty funny!"

He handed her his mobile and she read it out loud.

To: Peter.Williamson@unitedpaymentsinc.com
From: Tom.Farrow@aardvarkvc.com
Subject: How are you?

Hi Peter
It's been a while, mate. I hope all is well and you are enjoying the Bay Area lifestyle. How's life with a real job? Managed to figure out what actually happens in a company rather than just investing in one? Has your sales director shagged the secretary yet?
Anyway, I thought I would drop you a note to say I am coming to SF in a couple of weeks so we must have dinner. It would be great to see you and Susannah again.
You may not have heard all the news from Aardvark. It's been an entertaining few months here. We did actually close that investment in Mixandmatchbypet.com and, would you believe it, it is looking good. Maybe Edwin's legacy is going to be something after all. Talking of Edwin, you know he and Lisa are together? There's major news there! Last week, Lisa won the lottery! Would you believe it? I met them for a drink a couple of days ago and they just could not stop talking about it. She cleaned up the UK jackpot and picked up about seven million quid. Just to think that she could have been mine! Still, I have to say, I am genuinely glad for them. They deserve a break. Edwin's started his teacher training. I asked him how he was going to deal with the 6th form when they start to tease him. Apparently he's started working out and is doing karate but I still worry for him. After all, we were pretty merciless on teachers like him when I was at school and I think things have only got worse. Mind you, being married and worth a few million quid should make a difference. Here's wishing Mr & Mrs Snape all the best – oh yes, I should have mentioned

they told me they were engaged and they want me, you and Susannah to come to the wedding!

As for me, I can tell you that all my attention is elsewhere! You remember Sam, Lisa's cousin and the girl who's shagging Steve – the Steve who brought us the Mixandmatchbypet deal? Well, it turns out she has a friend called Jenny who just moved to London and needed someone to show her around. Who else could do a better job than yours truly? She's working as a receptionist at a law firm I introduced her to and we've been together for three months. She's a lot of fun if you know what I mean – and about the only part of my anatomy she hasn't pulled hard are my ears, so she's already ahead of Lisa in my book!

I haven't heard anything from Gordon. Apparently Cressida is taking him to the cleaners for their divorce. Who knows where he'll surface but rumour has it he's back in the job market, applying for roles across all the PE houses in London. Good luck with that! No one liked him and I think a lot of people think he got what he deserved!

Henry is running the office with all the efficiency you would expect. But I have to say his recruitment policy of investment directors has been outstanding. Our deal flow has increased massively in the last three months. Everyone wants to meet them! Two girls who graduated from Cambridge and have MBAs from INSEAD. How shall I put it? It's not the academic qualifications which make them so appealing. I have no idea how Henry gets away with it but he does! Theresa and Mary do their best to control him but you know how easy that is! Apparently there's talk of another offsite but given the current circumstances, that really doesn't seem a great idea.

Anyway, that's all for now. Let me know if you are free for dinner. I arrive on the 24th so shall we say the 25th or 26th?

Love to S and give her a big hug from me – not that you two need any encouragement!

Tom

Susannah laughed as she finished reading.

"It sounds like not much has changed," she said. "Tom's right. I wonder how on earth Mitch let Henry get away with that recruitment."

"Women can be brilliant as well as stunning," said Peter.

She stuck her tongue out at him.

"Anyway, Sir Galahad, she said, "It sounds like you are well out of it. I always said that the world of private equity was no job for you."

"Oh yes?"

"Absolutely. You are far too much of a gentleman!"

EPILOGUE

To: Iloveedwin@yahoo.co.uk
From: Londonpartygirl@gmail.com
Subject: Congrats!

Lisa, darling
Congratulations from Steve and me on your engagement. We are so excited for you and Edwin, we must go out and celebrate. And we are both so thrilled for you to have got so lucky – and I don't just mean with the lottery although that is beyond bloody cool!
Looking forward to seeing you soon!
Sam x

To: Londonpartygirl@gmail.com
From: Iloveedwin@yahoo.co.uk
Subject: Re: Congrats!

OMG!!! OMG!!! OMG!!!
We still can't believe it. Seven million! We are dreaming. Edwin proposed the day before I found out we'd won so he can't be accused of chasing the money. I wouldn't care anyway because I love him so much. And you know he's quite well off himself although he's too much of a sweetheart to tell anyone about it. But OMG!!!!!
Yes, let's go out v v soon. Champagne on us!
Lis xx

To: Careers@Londoninvestmenthouse.com
From: Gordon.Fairbald2@gmail.com
Subject: Investment Director role

Dear Sir,

I am writing concerning your recently advertised position for an Investment Director. I was until a couple of months ago senior partner at Aardvark Venture Capital here in London where I led any number of investments resulting in successful exits. I was running the entire Aardvark business in London but have decided that my strong suit is investing and as a result, am seeking a new role where that will be my main focus.

I enclose my C.V. for your further attention and look forward to hearing from you soon.

Yours faithfully
Gordon Fairbald

To: Gordon.Fairbald2@gmail.com
From: Simon.Willis@Londoninvestmenthouse.com
Subject: Re: Investment Director role

Dear Gordon,

Thank you for your recent enquiry regarding the investment director role. As you can imagine, the quality of applicants for this role has been extremely high and on this occasion, unfortunately we will not be pursuing your candidacy further.

We will keep your details on file should any future suitable positions become available.

With best wishes for your future career search.
Yours
Simon Willis
Talent Acquisition Administrative Coordinator
London Investment House